THE WILD & ZANY GALACTIC ADVENTURES OF COMMANDER ZHANG & LIEUTENANT SIMON, SOUL MATES WHO INCARNATE ON EARTH AND SAVE THE WORLD

BY
VEGASTARCHILD584

Copyright 2022

Printed by Touch the Light Press

PRINTED IN THE UNITED STATES OF AMERICA
TOUCH THE LIGHT PRESS

DEDICATION

This book is dedicated to ALL starseeds of every age and
generation who have incarnated on earth with the desire to assist
Gaia and humanity to ascend!   We are at the final stages.   See you
soon at the way station near galactic center for the big
celebration! A special thank you to Glenn, Eric, Gaby, Marguerite
for her thoughtful suggestions and editing assistance, my parents -
early generation starseeds and, of course, to Zhang and Simon,
beautiful and brave starseed heroes for giving us so much lovable
fodder with which to work and love.

CHAPTER ONE

Rally Point 2.   Time to Wake Up!

"What the hell?"

The second he heard his front door lock disengaging Zhang jerked awake and blindly lunged for the door. He had no time to grab the bat he'd placed at the foot of the couch for protection in case of such a break in. By the time he made it to the door it was already swinging open.

Since being blacklisted 8 months before by the government, he'd been on edge, hiding behind closed doors like a criminal. He'd been threatened with death, suffered three attempted break-ins, his acting and singing career that he'd worked tirelessly to build over the last 10 years had tanked, and his name pretty much toast. He was also still being hounded by so-called truth seekers and the negative press. Never mind the internet crazies and nutjobs smearing him every chance they could get.

He used his foot to try to stop the door from opening further but was instead sent flying to the floor as the door swung toward him with some force.

"What the-"

"Ow!" A deep male voice protested from the other side.

Zhang scrambled to his feet but Simon was already inside, pouting and rubbing at his forehead. "That hurt—"

When their eyes met Simon stilled his hand, concerned. "Oh shit! Are you ok? I didn't think you were home-" He dropped rather casually looking like he had just come home from the gym. He wore a simple light bluish green teeshirt, a beige baseball cap to hide his tousled locks, white Adidas basketball shorts and gleaming white sneakers, his small black shoulder bag slung across his back. In his right hand he had a bag full of groceries.

"You bastard! What the hell are you doing here!" Zhang yelled. Simon was the last person he thought he'd see. After 8 months, he had the gall to show up unannounced, breaking into his apartment, never mind he had the nerve to use the key he'd given him when they'd still been dating. He cursed himself for forgetting to demand it back.

"Sorry! I didn't mean to startle you!" Simon said, a conflicted look on his face. But Zhang felt nothing but fury pulsing through his veins as they finally stood face to face. On the one hand he was glad it wasn't a stranger breaking in. But he had written the guy off after being dumped without a single word from him only weeks after his troubles began.

"Get out or I'm calling the police!" Zhang yelled pointing at the door.

Simon quickly set down the grocery bag and put both hands up and pouted. "Please! Just hear me out, babe. We need to talk."

"Don't 'babe' me! Get out!" When Simon made no effort to leave, Zhang went to the door and held it open, his breath starting to come in angry pants, his entire body pulsing with anger. It had taken him months to forget this asshole and the hole his sudden disappearance had left in his heart. He'd be damned if he was going to fall for that pout of his again.

"Don't make me beg because you know I'll do it!" Simon said

immediately dropping to his knees to prostrate before him. Now that they were finally face to face he wasn't leaving until he got what he wanted. "We need to talk!"

Zhang couldn't afford to make a scene and attract attention from the neighbors. Yet the last thing he wanted was to spend a single second arguing with the guy.

Simon blinked up at him without moving from his spot. The stubborn fuck. Zhang only reluctantly shut the door before he turned and glared down at him.

"You know you've got some nerve coming here!" Zhang huffed then moved past him to peer out the window to check if he'd been followed. Simon's shiny black SUV was parked across the street more than a foot off the curb on account of his crappy driving. "Did anybody see you?"

"No. Well maybe just the woman I followed in. I think she got off on the 2nd floor. And the mailman. I said hello as I passed him. Aside from that..." Simon said crawling to his feet. "I'm sorry. I didn't think you were home as you didn't answer the buzzer."

"So you just barge in here?" Zhang fumed.

"I used the key. I would've knocked first if I knew you were here," Simon explained nonchalantly.

"What the f—k is wrong with you? Where the hell were you when I needed you? Do you know the hell I've been through- -".

"You stopped taking my calls- -I was worried and -"

"What?! You were the one who stopped taking my calls and ignored my texts the minute all of this shit went down. Not the other way around!"

One thing Simon had was thick skin. He cut to the chase. "It was only because I was sticking to the plan and running around trying to get everything in place like we talked about."

"What running around? You mean chasing gigs while I was being roasted alive by the media and the internet crazies and threatened by people I don't even know? You've got the gall to even show up here after all this time," Zhang raged clenching and unclenching his fists.

It was bad enough he ignored his calls when he needed him but he'd also since learned from his attorneys that Simon might have something to do with setting him up in the first place not to mention the scandal dragging on for as long as it had. He'd always been a whiz at the SM stuff and buying links to drive traffic and boost his popularity. Zhang had no clue how any of it worked. But he knew the guy was driven. What he never suspected was that he would screw him over just to get ahead.

Whatever he was doing seemed to work. His popularity only skyrocketed while Zhang's crashed and burned overnight. His career was mud. To add insult to injury a billboard with Simon's latest endorsement for Boss fashions was practically outside his 12th story window. Everytime he walked to the corner store for toilet paper Simon stared down at him with that intolerably handsome mug of his. It was both infuriating and humiliating and he couldn't count the number of times he'd wanted to throw a raw egg at it.

Watching tv was even worse. Every few minutes an ad he had done peddling MoJosh shades, Elle fashions, Clorox soap, wipes, make up, skin cream and the like popped up. He stopped watching tv because of it.

Zhang couldn't remember the last time he walked around so casually outside. It got to the point where his safety was an issue. He'd since grown wary of going out and being recognized. Since when did his life become like this? Since he met this asshole who had just broken in.

"Give me back my key!" He demanded holding out his hand. Simon reached into his pocket as if he were about to oblige him then stopped.

"They warned me you were going way too deep and cleared me to just go in," Simon said in earnest. Despite the painful rumors, what the so-called "netizens" (who were a damn scary lot even to him) had said about either of them, none of it was true. The fact that things had gotten so out of control and the whole scandal took on a life of its own had been alarming. But Simon knew not to get too distracted and just stick to the plan they'd meticulously charted. But when Zhang cut him off completely based on rumors, ignoring his calls and texts, things went sideways quickly. Rally Point 2 went down the drain.

Then things went from bad to worse and just the month before, videos of Zhang bashing him and their joint fans from their hit drama series began surfacing. His studio contacts claimed they were deep fake AI. If they were, they were good. He had to see him for himself but Zhang had ignored him every time he reached out. That's when he realized they needed help.

He'd also heard from his own sources that forces were at work to drag him into the quagmire as well. People and fans both for and against them only muddied the waters further with all their speculation. And with only one of them awake it would've really set them back. He tried reaching him in his dreams, having him relive their most treasured times on the set, during the concerts, during that Happy Camp variety show. That incredible night in Shanghai. But it was hard to know if he was getting through to him as still Zhang never reached back out to him.

He'd already been told by a team leader that unless he and Zhang could salvage the situation, another team would be sent in. With so much at stake with the larger operation, there was little room for negotiation at this point. Refusing to give up on them and call it a wash, he decided to take matters into his own hands.

He cleared his booking calendar for the month and set all his SM accounts to auto post every few days, then drove the almost nine hours from Shanghai to Xinyu City in Jiangxi before stopping for groceries praying the whole way Zhang wouldn't lose his shit when he saw him. He decided to drive rather than fly to avoid the airport and the hassle of renting a car when he wanted to keep his head clear and maintain a low profile.

When Zhang didn't answer the buzzer downstairs, he waited for someone else to enter the building and walked in behind them like he belonged there, rode the elevator to the 12th floor and used his key to enter.

"You have to know I never, ever abandoned you, babe." Not my soulmate. Never. I missed you, missed you every day.

From the looks of things, Zhang was about to pop his gourd.

What the hell god damn nonsense was Simon spouting now? Zhang took a step toward him, fists clenched calculating that if he clocked the scumbag hard enough, catching him off guard, he just might have a chance to knock him out in one punch.

"I only did what I was told. What we agreed on-"

"What are you talking about?? Who told you?" Zhang demanded.

"You did," Simon responded calmly gauging his reaction.

"WHAT!???? When the hell did I ever tell you to drop me like I meant nothing to you but garbage?! Even after I let you- - aghhhhh!!!" Zhang seethed, about to tear his own hair out.

"Before we jumped...we agreed on everything. About how we would identify and then take down CAPA and the government — the ones behind all the corruption and greed. We said we'd reveal who was behind all the blacklisting that's been going on all these years and we'd do it as soul mates. Once you got in deep enough, we could call in backup if needed but then you got a little sideways and I decided to request assistance earlier just in case you screwed everything up and dragged me down too. The internet crazies tried that with me last year but—"

What bullshit was he spewing now? One thing was obvious, Simon knew how to cover his own ass and put everything all on him. Everytime they had -

He froze.

In that split second for some inexplicable reason his heart squeezed hard then hammered causing him to gasp despite himself; the thousands of words of rage and angst he'd been about to launch at him left in an instant. Instead Zhang took pause.

"Before we what?"

Simon was looking at him intently as was his habit, not only because he thought Zhang was the most delicately beautiful man that he had ever seen in his book, but because he was peering into his soul, willing his partner to wake up.

To his relief, Zhang seemed to pause, that handsome face mired in shock, that head of beautiful, freshly-dyed dark "auburn" hair now cocked to the side. Simon was about to take a step forward, hopeful that his "wife", as their fans had labeled Zhang, had come to his senses so they could finally get down to real business. But something told him to be patient. After all it was normal to forget when coming to this sector of the galaxy, and more importantly to Earth.

They'd been briefed on all this forgetting business countless times, executing and practicing numerous scenarios as a fail safe prior to incarnating. They'd trained and discussed the possibilities they'd likely encounter and only then did they feel prepared enough to begin the mission here.

Hell they even laughed about how easy the mission was going to be compared to every other crazy thing they'd done together, scoffing at the other candidates who looked more like frightened bunnies than seasoned masters. Besides, nobody who came to earth (what the SL-52 humans called their planet) for Mission Everlight (the mission) in the last 30 years or so was anything less than a Master in their own right. To say nothing in the last 10 years. At least that was what they'd been told. From what he'd experienced, though, Simon was still on the fence.

Whoever told him that had never met some of the so called "netizens".

Simon and Zhang's part of the mission was to get in deep enough with the influential organizations and individuals that preyed on those in the performing arts industry and expose their deep-seated corruption and ulterior motives. This included the government-linked China Association of Performing Arts (CAPA) and agency bigwigs, some of whom were also sexual predators, financially vested in the multi-trillion yuan industry which they skimmed to line their own pockets.

Zhang's role was as a popular actor, singer, and model who gets blacklisted by CAPA and railroaded, tanking his career. Simon's role was to provide him assistance while also uncovering some of the other players in the industry.

They recognized the scandal Zhang would be embroiled in was actually part of a larger effort to keep the masses distracted and postpone the mass awakening of earth humans on Gaia. As long as the humans were stuck in the lower vibrations of fear, sadness, uncertainty and despair, including their millions of fans, Gaia's ascension to the 5D could continue to be delayed.

The beings behind this dastardly plan originate off world and in interdimensional space. They feed off the lower vibrational emotional energies generated by Terra humans such as fear, grief and despair resulting in constant warfare, bloodshed, feelings of powerlessness and other atrocities. Worse, they cause humans to turn on each other. They use a number of tricks for this, including what earth humans call black magic or alchemy to influence humanity and it's world leaders into keeping the frequency here low. Earth was therefore a battleground between the Light and its counterpart, contrast.

Thus, Zhang and Simon had to come in as performing artists to reveal all this and set in motion events that would lead to the final takedown of these characters. They'd carefully chosen their earth forms together to play the part with precision. They'd agreed on their physical features, the clues they'd put in place to recognize one another, including several matching moles, their uncanny ability to mirror each other's actions much like twins, and a general sense of soul knowing.

Once they'd met, Simon had instantly recognized his soul mate. In Zhang's case he also saw they had a special connection but it was more along the lines of 'friends with benefits' or in a romantic sense. But in truth, they were two souls that had traveled the galaxy countless times together and connected in different spaces and places over many different lifetimes. But as Simon found out recognizing they were soul mates was one thing. Waking up to why one agreed to be born on earth was completely another. And Zhang hadn't woken up.

Most humans never did, never remembering their true earth mission, the real reason they agreed to incarnate much less find their soul mate. As a result there were so many unhappy people on earth, and Gaia needed help to ascend.

"Before we got here…" then, "You agree to assume and play a role at the soul level for the purpose of transmuting contrast back to light. To reveal and transform together with your soul mate the deep illness that exists in the minds and hearts of many in the country in which you will be born and around the world, for the purpose of aiding Gaia and by extension those who are mired in darkness and suffering to ascend." Simon recited from the soul agreements they signed hoping to jog his memory.

As Zhang gathered his wits about him Simon stood there silently, every now and then sneaking a look at his partner's inky dark eyes to see if he had finally come around. They'd both been well prepared to come in to help Earth and the earth humans finally get out of the long years of fear-induced darkness, overturn all the millennia old corrupted systems and help raise up the overall resonance of the planet. Afterall, Simon at his highest incarnation was an angelic being and Zhang, an Ascended Master.

What they hadn't anticipated was that the forgetting process would be so thorough. There was no guarantee both partners would wake up. Those who had come before who had woken up had to go through the forgetting process all over again in the next incarnation. And once incarnated if one got too overwhelmed with the drama of their human lives and never woke up, they often entangled themselves in karma ensuring they had to reincarnate again and again to deal with it.

Watching Zhang getting roped in like so many others had been excruciating until he decided enough was enough.

Meanwhile, Zhang stared at Simon in shock and slowly began to remember a little bit.

CHAPTER TWO

Zhang the Ascended Master

"Not afraid of failure...fall and rise up. No matter where I stand, I still have a direction to fly....be the sun in your own life." The words just flowed from his heart. Zhang wrote them down in his notebook and strummed a few chords on his guitar. He then sang the newly written words, his voice soft and warm, and adjusted it up a pitch until it sounded as well as felt good to his well-trained ears.

Whether wisdom or just his musings, he knew he had a gift. A kind soul, the sun always blazed in his heart no matter what. It powered his optimism and colored his views on everything.

"I will use my abilities to help those in need. This is my purpose. My heart is like sunshine," he wrote the day before.

There was a time he thought everyone felt like this. But soon quickly realized it wasn't the case. This optimism wasn't just simple or wishful thinking but something that burned within. But he also knew he was there to share what he knew and wrote with others. Whether to provide comfort or encouragement, he didn't know which. This drive burned within him. One could say it was a calling.

However, he now found himself in the surprising position of being alone and on the   defense.   And it was a bit unsettling even for him.

Navigate, Zhang. Just navigate...he told himself for the umpteenth time since everything had turned upside down for him. He had never expected such a thing to have happened to him, nor with the swiftness with which it had occurred. Nor that his world would be flipped as it had and that after so much goodwill he now would face such bitterness from others. He sighed, pushing past the urge to wallow in pity. It wasn't really his thing.

He'd always been what some call a deep thinker ever since he could remember. Thus it naturally reflected in the things he wrote and the songs he penned and sang. From the time he could remember, his thoughts were always filled with philosophical stuff and not the ordinary musings of a child or young adult his age. Yet, this was a side of him that few knew except when he shared his music or was asked to share his views about life.

Most others knew him as the high-spirited, zany, and fun loving guy who liked to joke with his friends and seemed to thrive on chaos, mostly of his own making. But when he was alone, in his own head, there was this other side of him that could find comfort in his own deep thoughts.

"Love is not two people gazing at each other in romantic bliss...it's us looking ahead in the same direction. I will always be there for you...to support you through every hardship...." He wrote the words that now seemed to pour from his soul. "No matter what the future holds, I will be by your side and support you. This is me saying 'I love you'."

It wasn't like he had a lot of examples in his young life to follow. His own parents divorced when he was quite young. But he knew deep inside that that was what love was. It was unconditional and he just knew that that kind of love powered the world. How he knew it, he couldn't say. Whether others were capable of grasping this....Images of Simon instantly came to mind and he quickly pushed them away. Don't go there, buddy. It's best not to go there. There was nothing there for him but deep pain and he knew to wallow in it served no great purpose.

His mind continued to whirl and he scribbled whatever flowed.

"There are those like me who walk the earth plane with the sun ever blazing in their hearts. Thus, no matter what trials or tribulations or stormy seas we face, we will rise...no need to suffer. We smile instead....Where others may despair, those with the heart like the sun continue to live with great, no, indomitable hope. We find our voice and touch the Light."

He felt life deeply. It meant the rising tide could never carry him away. And when he fell, he picked himself up and kept moving. If the way was blocked, he found another path. He couldn't help but feel with this human heart of his, and sometimes it hurt. But it didn't mean he would stay down.

Taking a break as he'd been at it all afternoon, he set his guitar aside on the couch and got up to look outside. There were a few reporters...die hard hold-outs since the scandal began four and a half months earlier, still camped outside his building waiting to ambush him and spin their stories. He knew now that no matter what he said, they'd twist it and get it all wrong. And that would only fan the flames and cause him and others even more grief. He just needed to bide his time. He'd been doing it alone now for nearly five months. He felt a tinge of sadness and heartache creep in and quickly pushed it away.

Heart like sunshine....navigate...just navigate.

When they saw him looking out, they pointed their cameras upwards and shouted questions at him. He waved then turned away. One day even they would understand.

Heart like sunshine...no matter what he always held hope, the light would blaze. That he would have his voice again. Everyone must find their voice.

He'd been writing all afternoon, his notebook full and as was sometimes the case, he felt a bit sleepy as if whatever stream of energy that was flowing through him had receded to allow him to rest. He went to the fridge, got out a bottle of water and took his time drinking it. If only he could get into the recording studio and lay down a few tracks. He had to wait just a bit longer…just a bit….he yawned, feeling the nagging draw to take a nap. He went back to the couch, picked up his guitar and held it tight across his chest and closed his eyes with a sigh. Just a little while longer….something had to give. It always did.

Zhang dreamed.

The sun overhead was a brilliant pulsing white. The sky painted in hues of green and blue streaked with purple. The air was tinged with the smell of the sea which pounded the rocks far below the cliffs. Their vibration could even be felt beneath his feet.

Zhang walked as he was often wont to do, deep in contemplation. His sandled feet moving softly and in unhurried fashion over the sandy planes as he made his way up the small hill behind his humble home. His simple cotton garments fluttering with the slight warm breeze against his small and thin body. In his right hand he carried a bone colored staff intricately carved of wood from a native tree.

The tiny bluish white grains tumbled and fell in little rivulets around his feet as he made his way. Zhang was well aware that each speck held a consciousness of its own. He gave gratitude to them each morning as he made his way steadily up the hill. No one paid his muttering any mind. Not the people who he passed in the marketplace minding their wares on long wooden tables that lined his path, nor the children who laughed and played noisily as they tossed around tiny sewn bags of sand in a game of catch and run and raced about dodging around him.

He found comfort in his simple routine, leaving his home to hike the short distance to where ocean meets sky. There he sat high up on the bare ground amongst the desert-like brush to meditate or contemplate.

The people were a peaceful lot. They lacked for nothing but knowledge which teachers like him sought to provide. He had no more riches than the next being, as all were of a sufficient enough state to call into existence whatever they needed through the power of imagination alone. They had long mastered the science of manifestation taught them by the angels who came to visit them, their ancestors and guides. If one sought to eat a piece of fruit, they would simply envision the fruit crystallizing in the palm of their hand. If they wished a new pair of sandals, they would imagine them already strapped on their feet. It was no mystery. It just was.

While others sought to entertain themselves through pleasant distractions, worried over or contemplated the mundane, his thoughts were thus…how can I utilize my life force and all the gifts of abundance that have been bestowed upon me and be of service?

He stared down at the marketplace below and observed. Even in a society of manifestors, some liked and excelled in manifesting fruit, others shoes, others clothing, others pieces of art, thus each being's creations were guided by their individual imaginations. A wellspring. The market place was the result of their collective creativity and desire to share with one another.   Thus in the town that he lived, one would still find bustling markets and places of exchange where people gathered much like anywhere else.

His thoughts were as they always were on this day, free to enjoy the visages of life as it played out below, oblivious to his presence observing from his perch above. He smiled up at the sun, squinting his eyes as they caught the bright glare.

What drove life? And the actions of society to advance? How could they evolve into something even more peaceful, beautiful and fulfilled? What was his role in making this happen?

He soon concluded as he had done every day since he had been coming to this spot, the rock upon which he settled against so familiar with the warmth of his body that it had conformed its surface to the small curve of his back —.

When one is capable of viewing life a certain way such as one of peaceful existence, one lives accordingly. This is merely a state of "being". From this space of "being", one of deep serenity and inner knowing, one is truly capable of impacting and influencing others and taking action. This is how masters influence the world.

From this thought which occupied practically his every waking moment, much as it had since he was birthed almost 1500 years before, he viewed life, and discerned all things, taking action where he could to fulfill this purpose.

In the shapes and colors of the landscape all around him, he found serenity. He found it in the laughter of the children, in the bustling exchanges from the marketplace, the sound of the pounding waves on the rocks far below the jagged sea cliffs. It was an ever-present flow. And there was a cohesiveness to it all. In the middle of this canvas, there he stood. Like a fulcrum and lever. Like every other being should they choose.

What does it mean to be self-aware? What does it mean to be of service?

To be self-aware is to have purpose. As one who has a purpose, one accordingly measures one's behavior, thoughts, words and interactions with all others. And for society to advance, one must also teach others. For a collective society learns from each other.

An ascended master is thus someone who has mastered themselves through self-awareness and behaves accordingly while teaching and learning from others from a space of unconditional love.

And so he thought thusly for some time as he watched the people in the marketplace below and the children playing, and the water in the distance as it met the sky above, as he stared at the shifting granules of blue and white sand beneath his sandals, in quiet contemplation while pondering his existence. His role in it all. And how he would go about being of service on this day.

And as the bright white sun began its descent in the distance, slowly sinking, heralding the coming of another inky night sky, he took to his feet and began to make his way down the small hill, retracing his steps as he made his way through the marketplace which had since gone quiet, the children all home with their families, the streets near empty….and he concluded as he did every day as he had since he'd been born into this existence, that the way to be of service to all, to contribute to the stream of consciousness of the people, to flow while teaching others, was to consciously have peace in his heart himself.

And so he did.

Zhang awoke from his slumber and gazed down at his socked feet. The last vestiges of blue and white sand beneath sandaled feet fading from his consciousness. His guitar still draped on his chest like a sweet old lover. He turned his head and gazed out the window. The sun had gone down, the room now brightly illuminated by the street lamp just outside. It was quiet. He sat up, turned on the lamp, then angled his guitar on his lap, reached for his notebook and once again began to write.

"The sun overhead is bright, so brilliant. It blazes in my own heart, nurturing my soul. Youth run and play, their tomorrow only limited by their imagination. No limits. My life, too, is boundless and free. I am at peace...."

Just then his cell phone buzzed. He reached for it and saw that it was Simon calling again as he did every day for the last few months. The urge to take the call was strong, so overwhelming, yet he'd been told by his lawyers not to have any contact with him and to steer clear until they could sort everything out. So he flipped his phone over, ignoring it and set his guitar down. He sighed, his heart squeezing painfully.

Navigate Zhang... just navigate. Heart like sunshine.

Heart like the sun.

He went to the window and gazed down. The reporters had since left, leaving the street below empty. He decided to take a shower then order food from around the corner all the while wondering what tomorrow would bring.

CHAPTER THREE

The Galactic Adventures of Commander Zhang & Lieutenant Simon

"Where are you, Commander?"

"Working out in the biosphere, track 4, level 8," Zhang answered. Simon sounded excited.

Simon found him in the massive domed room about to reset the program for their usual routine of 50 full-speed laps followed by 25 half-speed laps followed by 3 walking warm-down laps on the gleaming white treadmill belt. The workout room was located in the biosphere which was a 100-acre park like environment on the mothership equipped with lush mature green trees, large stretches of grass, gardens and serene park-like features.

As on the mothership perception was quantum, the park environment appeared to continue onto the ceiling and walls in a discoidal shape high above climbing back around in a continuous loop. Unlike a hologram, all the trees and greenery had been planted by the Science and Exploration team. The workout room was incorporated into the biosphere as well. Thus, when walking or running on the treadmill belts, the sensation was if one were actually enjoying the numerous walking paths in the biosphere's park. As the ship's atmosphere was controlled, one could move in any direction in the biosphere, even walk or run on the "ceiling" following a jogging path without falling. This was actually a common feature on motherships as space was at a premium to accommodate the large number of crew, families and visitors on any given day.

"Hi, Commander Zhang!" Two lovely Pleiadean females colleagues walked by and smiled flirtatiously at Zhang while waving.

"Hello Ladies! Beautiful day, isn't it" He waved back giving them an engaging smile. It was always a beautiful day in the biosphere having only one controlled setting of daylight. To experience an evening or sunset in a park or beach, one had to use the H-Deck or meditate.

As he worked out which he did whenever he could, the scene of female crew members walking to say hello was par for the course. He was pretty popular having distinguished himself and was one of the few captains with as many accolades for bravery on board aside from the Athena's own captain. All in a days work. He didn't notice that these same crew members only seemed to gravitate toward the biosphere whenever he worked out. He loved the attention though and always made sure to acknowledge them in return. It was probably on account of his handsome face, long blonde hair, and gleaming white skin-tight bio-suit as it accentuated his height and muscular build. When Simon walked up on him, Zhang had to agree with his assessment as they practically looked alike.

"There you are!" Simon caught up with him just as he sped the system up to a dead run. He turned it back down to a warmup walking pace so Simon could jump on without flying off and smashing headfirst into the ground.

"What's up, Lieutenant?" Simon jumped on and walked alongside him.

"Hi, Lieutenant! Commander!" More colleagues of the female persuasion walked by giggling and waving and smiling flirtatiously at them.

Simon smiled broadly "Hello!" Before turning back to his colleague.

"Captain asked if on our way to Lido in Fornacis1 if we could make a stop to Polaris to drop a package. He'd like to speak with you about it as soon as you're available."

"Why didn't he use the array or the broadcast?"

"It's kind of sensitive and I told him I was heading your way after having lunch with him."

"Alright. Let's go," Zhang said turning off the system and stepping off the belt. Simon followed suit. They walked to the control deck level and entered the bridge through a whisper quiet door where the captain and a crew of 12 commanded the ship. The room itself was fairly large with bay-like windows that jutted out and stretched from left to right. Before the windows were gleaming white control panels before which various beings and two little grays sat busy operating the mothership and ensuring they didn't go hurdling out of orbit and lose their prime parking and viewing spot. They were currently parked at 27 degrees Sagittarius jammed near about a million other ships on hand to support Gaia's ascension. Parking was a bit of a problem.

In the middle of the control room sat the captain's sleek white chair from which he directed all operations on the ship with the help of the crew and maneuvered the planet-sized craft through space. Captain Olin Alpha1, a Leonid being stood in the center of the room, hands clasped behind his back at attention as he stared out the large bay window dead ahead.

While it appeared he was peering into the blackness of space, they were actually bumped up window to window with another mothership that was cloaked and operated by the Pleiadeans. Had they not been cloaked, everyone would have a view of the goings-on inside and everyone knew the Pleiadeans liked to party. Zhang often moaned they'd been assigned to the wrong ship.

Commander Olin Alpha1 cut a handsome figure. Standing at 8-foot-tall, he had the head of a lion and the body of a human stuffed in a shiny light blue skintight uniform similar in color and design to the rest of the bridge crew save his sported the captain's insignia and numerous accolades and honors pinned across his chest. He was a Sirian officer of the Galactic Confederation and in charge of the incarnates for the Earth mission assigned to the Mothership Athena. That included working with their myriad guides and light beings in the higher dimensions including those in the angelic realm supporting the Sirian and other races incarnated as earth humans on their assigned life missions. He coordinated with the Pleiadean, Arcturian, Andromedan and even Orion motherships and their Commanders overseeing their incarnates as well. Thus, the success or failure of his team rested entirely on his shoulders as did those of the other incarnates upon their ship's captains.

Captain Alpha1 knew every one of the earth incarnates in his charge by heart. Knew their talents, strengths, their great capabilities, their weaknesses and even idiosyncrasies. All were fully capable for their assigned duties. He had absolute confidence they would all be successful in their earth missions no matter how long it took. He was especially confident with Captain Zhang and Lieutenant Simon, both extremely competent, well-trained officers under his command. Known for their bravery, wit, as well as quick thinking and action, he also knew they were willing to make sacrifices, putting others ahead of themselves. And with highly compatible personalities and spirits, they made an excellent team. The ship had in effect labeled them *The Dynamic Duo*.

He also knew Captain Zhang could be as serious when he needed to be. And when he was, everyone paid attention. But he also liked to play hard. He and his soul mate, the Lieutenant, both did, which sometimes led to minor complaints that reached his ears. But given the gravity of their missions around the galaxy and there was no certainty of return for many, he welcomed that playful streak and secretly rejoiced for them.

Zhang straightened out his suit and ran a hand through his hair and wondered if he should have taken a shower first. He had only been on the bridge a handful of times and so to be called in to meet with the captain and commander of the entire mothership, one of the largest in the Galactic Confederations' fleet, was a huge honor in his opinion.

Simon hearing his thoughts chuckled beside him. "You look fine. I told him you were probably working out."

The lights were muted giving the place a faint warm orange glow and the appearance it was evening. Standing on the deck beside the captain in profile was a beautiful woman, 8-feet-tall herself with jet black bluntly cut shoulder length hair decorated with gold tinsel threads and beads at her forehead and temples, dark eyes accentuated with charcoal black make up, and beautiful light copper colored skin. She wore a gold body accentuating gown that shimmered as she stood there motionless. She seemed to be surrounded by a light that separated her from the rest of the crew in the room, including the captain. Zhang wondered if she was a hologram.   Whether she was or not, she was still stunning.

"Captain! Commander ZhangZHXO511 reporting with Lieutenant SimonGJXO1129, sir!" He said as Simon elbowed him out of his revelry.

The captain turned upon their greeting and smiled.

"Ah! Commander! Lieutenant, it's good to see you. I'm glad you're here."

"Our pleasure, sir. How can we be of service?" His eyes went again to the mysterious woman standing at the captain's side.

"I have an important ask of you." The captain approached and then gestured to the woman.

"This is my wife Ariitzka."

Zhang could feel Simon grinning at his side. Zhang stepped forward and bowed his head, tapping his heart and 3rd eye chakra in greeting and trying not to feel like an idiot for checking out the captain's wife. Simon did the same in greeting, still grinning.

The jerk.

She smiled warmly at both of them. "Commander, Lieutenant. The captain speaks so highly of you. The honor is all mine."

"Boys, I would ask to trouble you to take my wife back to Polaris on your way to Fornacis if possible. In exchange I will give you extra time off and first pick on your next assignment and ensure you have eight additional merits for your service at your disposal."

She was the package.

Before Zhang could graciously accept the assignment and decline the perks as he didn't want to make it seem they would only shuttle the captain's old lady around, as lovely as she was, in exchange for payment, Simon blurted out, "Thank you, Captain! Your generosity is most appreciated."

"Wonderful!" The captain nodded back. Zhang wondered if the two had already made arrangements beforehand as the whole thing seemed a bit too contrived. He reminded himself to ask his partner later.

The captain turned to the gray at the console closest to them and nodded. The gray nodded back before sliding his digits in a zig zag pattern around the console.

"Your upgrades are now noted in the system. It should also reflect in your accounts and be visible on your smart pads."

"Great. We are scheduled to depart at ten bells Lady Master," Zhang said, bowing.

"I shall be ready."

CHAPTER FOUR

Gaia Needs Your Help

With that they left the bridge. Zhang gave Simon a side look as they returned to the dorm deck where most of the single crew rooms were.

"What?"

"That was a bit odd. Why do I get the feeling you and the captain discussed this beforehand?"

"Because I knew you'd say yes but wouldn't accept merits for it so I took the liberty to negotiate with the captain and his wife for us. Boy does she drive a hard bargain."

"What? What did you ask for?"

"Double the time off, first crack for the next 3 assignments which I felt was only fair, and 10 merits."

Zhang thought about it and nodded. "Then I think you did pretty damn good." He grinned.   Simon grinned back.

"Since when are you and the captain so chummy?"

"He's friends with my father. She's friends with my mother. Plus, they know you're the most accomplished captain next to him, you have an

8th dimensional lock, and she felt most comfortable with you. The
captain feels this way too," Simon said.

Zhang snorted. "That's obvious. He's entrusting me with his wife. What
an honor. And she's gorgeous," Zhang laughed. Simon chuckled. "That
she is."

They stopped in front of Simon's quarters. An 18x18 room equipped
with a hygiene room, a table, a desk and chair, four oversized lounge
chairs, a replicator, a bed, a hidden monitor and a small closet. Simon's
unit also had a window. Upon recognizing his energy signature the door
quietly slid open and the lights went on. "Good evening, Lieutenant."
Came the muted voice of the ship's computer.

As Simon was about to bid the commander good evening, as they had
an early start in the morning, Zhang pushed past him and went inside.

"Do you want to come in, Commander?" Simon joked instead following
behind him. Simon's unit was pristine. Not a thing in view to indicate it
was even occupied.

"How do you live like this?" Zhang asked jumping onto his bed, boots
still on and grimacing.

Simon shook his head.   "Uh, I sleep on that." He pointed to Zhang's
large, booted feet.

Zhang hung his legs over the bed and sighed. "I wonder what their kids
look like," he murmured thinking on the captain and his wife. Did all
the boys look like him and the little girls look like her?

Simon pressed a spot on the otherwise blank wall and filled the room
with ambient lighting and music. He disappeared into the hygiene room
and came out naked. His suit draped over his arm, he hung it in a special
silicon bag in his closet attached to a hydrolyzed ion unit for cleaning.
Zhang stared up at the pristine white ceiling and yawned.

Simon changed into a loose-fitting white top and wrap on pants before going to the replicator and conjuring up the equivalent of earth's beer. The clear liquid gave them a slight buzz that was heightened the more they imbibed. It tasted a bit like strawberry soda water. As it also made one violently ill if one imbibed too much as a failsafe, no one ever got drunk off of the stuff. He also conjured up cherry nuts, a favorite snack of his and put them on the table.

"Who's on our crew for Fornacis?" Simon asked knocking back a glass of the liquid.

"It's a new crew from Serpens. They'll rendezvous with us on FornacisBeta where we load up on equipment and supplies before heading out." He got up and stared out the window into blackness. Only a few faint stars were reflected. Simon pushed his drink to him and he only absently drank it down.

"What's on your mind, Commander?" Simon immediately picked up he was a bit distracted.

"I was thinking to go visit my grandfather in Sector 3."

"Is he not well?"

Zhang shrugged. "I heard him discussing with my mother he wished to transition permanently."

"Is it that moment for him?" Simon asked sensing a sadness around Zhang. Desiring to relieve it from him he moved to his side knowing all it took was a thought from him or a flick of his hand. But he decided against it instead allowing the feeling to move through his partner and dissipate of its own due course. There were some things not his to interfere with.

"He's already tens of thousands of now moments as far as I know," Zhang said thoughtfully. That was the equivalent of four thousand earth years. Simon supposed that was a heck of a long time to be walking around in the same physical form. He sorta' didn't blame him as things started to break down after a while. And while coming up with a new form was just a matter of simple technology and a few now moments in the med bay, some just chose to transition.

"Will you come with me when I do?" Zhang asked sounding as if his thoughts were faraway.

"If you wish. Of course. I'd be honored. We'll bring some of those little cakes he likes. He still has his teeth, doesn't he?"

Zhang laughed. "You asshole. Of course he does."

They both laughed, Simon happy his partner's aura was once again clear. "Well, since you're already in your sleep gear, I'll head out. If that isn't a hint, I don't know what is," Zhang snorted draining his drink and setting it aside. Simon walked him to the door and bid his partner and commander good evening.

The next day Ariitzka, carrying nothing more than a smart pad joined them at the shuttle bay. She was dressed in a long beige linen-like gown and a gold inverted crown, both forearms adorned with gold vambraces with turquoise and ruby gems. The captain was on hand to see them off. Zhang had even made sure to clean out the back of the shuttle craft where she'd be sitting as usually it was packed full of stuff to barter that they'd illicitly taken from the Athena's huge warehouse. He'd even sprayed a little air freshener in back to make sure she was comfortable and the place didn't smell like an old sock. He actually looked forward to chatting with her to find out more about her and the captain, how they met, and what life on Polaris was like, but was surprised to see she seemed to be encased in a weird atmosphere all of her own which he'd also seen on the bridge.

Simon explained she was protecting her auric field as it was necessary when away from her home planet. This would avoid her having to go through the arduous process of hygienic cleansing which could take time depending upon the length of exposure to any different energies. It was the equivalent of a spiritual healing or Turkish bath on earth. Some light beings and those of the higher dimensions were similarly encapsulated ensuring their own auric fields remained pure. So after settling her into her seat, making sure she was comfortable, they began their routine systems check. Lady Master Ariitzka meanwhile fired up her smart pad and appeared to begin to read.

After they were free of the mothership and hurdling through space toward Polaris, he noticed someone standing between them. Simon meanwhile was doing the calculations on his smart pad to make sure their coordinates matched up. Zhang practically jumped out of his seat out of fright when he saw movement out of the corner of his eye.

"Sorry, commander! It's just me," Lady Master Ariitzka apologized. She had unbuckled her safety harness sometime mid-flight.

"Is everything alright?" Zhang asked checking he didn't accidentally press the warp drive button and have them missing their target by a few hundred light years.

"Fine. I was wanting to see out the window. I rarely get to enjoy the view as I am usually chaperoned and accompanied by some of my brothers and sisters from Polaris."

"Why do you have to have someone accompany you?" Zhang asked.

"Because she's the equivalent of Sirian royalty on her planet," Simon answered still checking his calculations.

"Oh, well, you are welcome to stay and enjoy the view."

She settled in the little jump seat between them and strapped herself in.

"What were you reading back there?" He asked to make conversation.

"It's a book I wrote about two brilliant and brave galactic adventurers who are soul mates and who travel around the galaxy on various missions. They decide to incarnate on earth in a region known there as China after hearing Gaia's help to ascend. They decide to incarnate as two famous celebrities and performers-"

"Like clowns or mimes?" Zhang interrupted.

"More like multi-talented artists," she explained.

"Sounds like a soap drama," Zhang commented only half listening as he checked and rechecked the systems.

"They call it a soap opera on earth," Simon corrected.

"Well as things begin to go extremely well for them, one of the two gets swept up in a huge scandal and wrongly accused of impropriety by powerful organizations including the government which threatens his career and his livelihood. A scandal which has the power to end all corruption on earth, if he can only wake up and realize his role in that scandal is all part of his earth mission."

"Why is he sleeping?" Zhang asked. "Is he in stasis?"

"It's what happens when you incarnate there due to the veil and the lower frequencies," she responded.

"What about his soul mate?" Zhang asked. "Is he asleep, too?"

"No. He's wide awake as he holds the frequencies of the angelics and is there to protect his soul mate. He is in a battle with their guides to wake his partner up while carrying out his own mission to expose even more of the corrupt institutions and organizations that have existed since the fall of Atlantis on earth."

"Sounds like an ambitious story. How's it end?"

"You'll have to read it to find out," she grinned.

"Somehow I knew you'd say that," he grinned back. "Has the captain read it?"

"He has and he's also in it."

"Really? You wrote him into the book? Now that I have to read about," Zhang laughed. "What's it called?"

She leaned forward and whispered in his ear. Zhang's eyes went wide.

Just then Simon announced the calculations had lined up with the coordinates. They would be arriving in a few now moments. Up ahead Polaris was fast coming into view.

"Alright, Lady Master, I'm going to have to ask you to safely take your seat and strap yourself in back there. Next stop, Polaris."

What she whispered was, "The Wild and Zany Galactic Adventures of Commander Zhang and Lieutenant Simon, Soul Mates Who Incarnate on Earth and Save the World...." Then she added almost reverentially, "Don't forget to wake up, Commander. Gaia needs your help."

CHAPTER FIVE

Awakening - Time to Get Down to Business

"That's the mission."

Simon calmly and patiently waited to approach. Just moments before he swore Zhang was going to hit him. But it was now or never. He had just one shot to jog his memory and get him on the same page before things got way out of hand. If he failed, he didn't know when he would have this opportunity to try again.

Over the past year GJStudio, which he created to manage his career as part of the earth mission, had taken on a life of its own. His staff had him running from photo shoot to photo shoot and chasing down product endorsements all over the damn place. In a few weeks time, unless Zhang got his act together and woke up, Simon would have to leave again for Chang'an for a magazine shoot, then fly to Shuzhong for a 3 month shoot of a historical romance/comedy drama — *The Lies of JinLi* with him in the lead. All just to keep up appearances.

He thought about canceling those contracts but was advised by the guidance team to keep up appearances or risk running afoul of the mission. One thing was clear, he wasn't leaving his partner behind again.

Thankfully he had chosen to take a few weeks off to see Zhang, escaping Ming, his own assistant and her uncanny ghost agent-esque's clutches.

He'd wracked his brains on a way to get close to him since for the last more than half a year all his prior attempts to contact him had failed and met with the cold shoulder.

"How the hell could I have forgotten the mission??" Zhang bemoaned sitting his thin frame down heavily on his couch. The small space had also served of late as his *de facto* Instagram (IG) studio now that his career was in the dumps, the tell-tale abstract painting on the wall behind that served as backdrop shifting slightly with the jolt.

"I only woke up recently, too." Simon confessed (he lied). He'd always been awake but didn't feel it helpful to share that with his partner at the moment. He wondered if it was now safe to approach, that deep frown in his partner's handsome face still giving him pause.

Zhang looked up at him slowly, his expression pensive. "When did you remember?" He dared ask.

Simon heaved out a sigh thinking Zhang looked a bit too pale and had lost a lot of weight since he'd seen him last. He definitely needed to fatten him up a bit and get him cleaned up.

"The day we first met at the script reading with the director and producer Ma and we rehearsed a few scenes together."

"What?? That was two years ago!" Zhang said rapidly in his usual high spirited way. To Simon it sounded much like a staccato and usually meant he was excited. But this time, Zhang looked as if he was about to come unglued.

Back then production had just begun on their series and that had been their first meeting with all the other players and essential crew. To Zhang, Simon had pretty much been a no-name actor at that point although he had done a couple of cheesy dramas, none of which Zhang had heard of. As far as he knew his costar was nothing but a pretty boy model who cleaned up well and pushed mostly high-end women's make up, household cleaning products and fancy "gender ambiguous" clothing no one in their right mind would ever consider wearing.

He'd been prepared to meet some fluffed up white mochi-faced dough boy with an effeminate air. He never expected instead to meet the tall, extremely handsome, yet quietly introspective 27 year old with a seductively deep voice and wildly intense gaze that practically drilled right through him. While he himself was no slouch, Simon was…different.

On top of that he was blunt. He said exactly what he was thinking and did whatever drove him. So when Simon began to pursue him and Zhang felt himself feeling things he'd never ever felt before with a guy, he panicked immediately. But given the persona he'd been dishing out for years as "Crazy Zhang" the suave but daring, a bit loud, unrestrained and determined singer/actor/model/regular straight guy, he played it cool. Their relationship moved fast from being complete strangers to fast friends to something else entirely with Simon taking the lead. Zhang followed like a puppy. But he was definitely a willing partner.

He fell hard for Simon seeing within him something that made his heart thud and his blood rush. There had always been something very different about him than anyone else he'd thus far met. He was certain of it but couldn't quite put his finger on it. Simon was genuine.

Simon continued, "The second you grabbed my wrist as part of that scene we were demonstrating for the staff I became absolutely convinced of it. My heart slammed in my chest and then began to stutter like yours did just now. So…"

The frown on Zhang's face seemed to deepen. From the confusion reflected in his eyes, Simon could see Zhang was a man in the middle of something that he didn't really understand.

Seeing this would take a while, Simon dragged a chair from the kitchen and swung it around to sit backwards to face him. It was clear Zhang's career wasn't the only thing that had gone to the dumps. His usual tidy apartment was a complete mess. There were dirty clothes hanging on the remaining kitchen chairs and scattered on the living room floor.

Unwashed dishes were in the sink, a plastic bag with napkins and utensils from the corner "LiuNing Hotpot and Donuts" restaurant/coffee shop were left discarded on the little kitchen table along with three half empty take-out containers, a few discarded bottles of water not to mention the dried up food stains.

"What happened to your housekeeper?" He asked.

"She was afraid to come to work so I told her to just quit." Zhang rubbed at his face and groaned. Then, "Are you friggin' kidding me?"

Simon pouted at him. His poor baby had really suffered unnecessarily over this more than half a year. He wanted to touch him so badly, hold him even but decided to give him more time.

Zhang sat there trying to come to grips with the news. In just 2 short years he'd experienced the full range of emotions from heaven to hell. He'd been high as a kite for months while they shot the drama together. Throwing caution and apparently straight-hood to the wind, they had excellent chemistry together. Things escalated quickly and it wasn't long before they had slept together. But after the production ended, he was lost and sunk to deep, dark lows on account of missing Simon. Their booming popularity meant they were solidly booked, their schedules having them go in different directions. They rarely saw each other.

He also questioned himself and everything he was feeling, followed by his own internal struggle to understand who the hell he was. Just when he thought he had sorted it out, his manager gleefully announced the producers had scheduled two *Word of Honor* concerts forcing their reunion and additional bookings together including the Tom Ford party. Afraid of losing himself again he held back. But as soon as he saw Simon after months of being apart they quickly fell back into lock step as if no time had passed at all. He stopped trying to resist his feelings.

After that, he reached even more staggering highs, (being so lovestruck he even wrote a song about him) [Surround] only to crash and burn in flames just months later with that stupid scandal and feeling as if he'd been betrayed and abandoned by Simon and the world.   All on account

40

of a stupid selfie taken a few years back that mysteriously resurfaced on the web.   That single photo got him "cancelled" overnight in China just as things were taking off for him.   Once he was black-listed by the China Association of Performing Arts (CAPA) all his SM accounts were taken offline overnight.   Worse, he was branded a traitor to his country and considered unpatriotic by the media and netizens.   It threw him into a tailspin.   Despite his best efforts to stay positive, he'd been hit one after another with bad news until he felt boxed in. He was banned from the studio where he'd been working on a few new tracks. Then his agent stopped taking his calls as she tried to clear her own name from the mess. He watched in growing disbelief and panic as even those in his inner circle began to get dragged under after he'd been declared Public Enemy #1.

He'd always been a deep thinker. His views on life likened to those of a wise old soul. He shared some of his thoughts in interviews. He'd shared them out of a sense of love and his desire to help to bring the world and the people together. He lived with a sense that nothing was impossible and no matter how challenging life was, there was always light. And with determination, a desire to work hard, and try new things while one still could, life could be full and beautiful and full of light. One just had to reach for it and hold hope in their heart.

He'd once read a blog post that described how he always felt. "Those with a heart like sunshine know who they are and how few others like them exist within the masses, on this earth plane…in this sea of people… Thus where others despair, those with the heart like the sun continue to live with great hope for the future. This indescribable feeling is indelibly stamped into our souls…It is a lonely journey at times because those who walk this path with all this light in their hearts are few….We walk in the Light."

His heart always felt like sunshine. Even if the sun failed to shine, his heart remained sunny. He had thought everyone lived like this. He just didn't realize how much hatred and darkness people carried in their hearts until he'd been targeted by it. Nor how much he would be tested. But he also knew he wasn't alone. That somewhere out there, in the vast sea of people there were some who understood his heart and one day they would meet. Now he understood why he always felt the way he did. He'd incarnated here on earth for a reason. He just had to remember what it was.

Vibration on the earth is important. What vibration you are at determines your earthly experience.

Suddenly his heart squeezed and tears came hot and fast to his eyes. So all this bullshit was really just for the mission? How could he have forgotten something so important? The more that sunk in the more the heavy weight on his chest and shoulders began to slowly dissipate.

This intense relief was followed by a growing frustration. Up to now he'd been operating on the assumption this was the only reality there was. And it was a horrible one. But if it was really all just part of what they agreed to do when they incarnated, did he even dare believe it?

He put his head down for a moment before he steeled himself, took a deep breath and finally met Simon's eyes, a thousand words filling his heart.

Simon watched as a torrent of emotions washed over Zhang's face. Tears pooled in his eyes then spilled down those perfectly sculpted cheeks.

"Hey! D-d-d-d -don't cry!" Simon's eyes went wide. He leapt from his chair to rush and put his arm around him settling in on the tiny couch beside him.

"Are you friggin' kidding me?" Zhang repeated still trying to take it in, his emotions in upheaval.

Simon reached down to swipe at his back tenderly. "Hey, I'm just glad you're starting to remember. Everyone forgets…" he murmured, his own heart bursting with relief. Simon held him tightly in his arms, finally feeling that long bereft warm heart beating against his own. His entire being radiated his love. *Finally his soul mate was waking up! Zhang was back!*

Zhang rest his head in the crick of Simon's neck as the pressure in his chest slowly faded.

They'd become accustomed to being intimate after having fallen in love within weeks of shooting their tv drama together. He found comfort in Simon's arms which was why he fell apart when work had them going in different directions and then his life went to hell in a hand basket. He'd been adrift. Now he heaved out a breathy sigh of relief. With his perspective restored, their real earth mission could finally begin. He sat there trying to take everything in.

Meanwhile, Simon's skin prickled with the subtle heat of Zhang's breath and instantly went southward. He enfolded his arms around Zhang's trim waist to pull him closer. Angling his head he kissed his neck and chin ghosting his breathe there, taking his time.

CHAPTER SIX
Coming to Grips

"Uh, what are you doing?" Zhang asked.

Simon felt him shudder and he pulled Zhang in closer.

"Shhh. Comforting you. Besides, I missed you. Just let me..." he trailed off rubbing his back to quiet him. He savored the taste of his warm skin against his lips. Simon had felt his absence so acutely.

He fell hard and fast for Zhang from the moment they met, his feelings growing for him as the energy of being with him became even more intense and addictive. As he had anticipated their meeting on the set of *Word of Honor*, he began to pursue Zhang relentlessly in part for the mission and in part because they were soul mates.

Every emotion seemed to be heightened. He just ran with it. He became obsessed with doing everything for him, feeling the need to protect him and stay by his side. Zhang seemed to feel for him in much the same way as they fell in rank step together and more people began to notice. At first it was staff and fellow actors, then when the behind the scenes footage was released their couple or CP fans took to openly calling him *husband* and Zhang *wife*.

But it had been hard to watch as his partner was continually targeted and beaten down in rapid succession. Especially for someone whose heart was as kind and loving as Zhang. It was only his understanding of what they needed to do that kept him from losing in to grief and worry. When Zhang started showing signs of not waking up and falling deeper into despair, he grew especially concerned.

He asked to intervene sooner but was told to allow Zhang to self-correct on his own. That frustrated him to no end. He felt they couldn't afford to wait any longer and so he made a complete pest of himself seeking approval to go in and help Zhang. Knowing their guides overseeing things operated from the higher perspective he had to trust them and his partner.

Simon had worked on many occasions with other light beings on various missions and in one of his incarnations was one of them himself. Thus, he knew the importance of relying on their deep insight and ability to see the lives of earth humans and others in the now moment across the vast time/space continuum.

"We see you now, we see you twenty years from now and we see you twenty years in the previous moments—all in this now moment." Still it was hard to just sit around and watch while his partner slowly had a melt-down.

"Do you really think it's appropriate -"

"Come on. You should just let me. I haven't seen you since forever, babe," Simon said nibbling at his ear. Despite the verbal barb, Zhang wasn't fighting him. He took that as permission and dragged his tongue downward licking at the saltiness at his jugular. He heard Zhang's breath hitch then begin to deepen as the heat between them increased tenfold.

Simon ran a hand along the side of his face before he angled his head and kissed him gently at first, still testing the waters. Eager but yet not wanting to give the impression he just came to make up for lost time, he went back to planting unhurried kisses along his neck and chin. He was content to wait as long as he had to for the man who made his soul sing.

Zhang wasn't so patient. He reached a hand up and grabbed him by the hair, his fingers tightly gripping Simon's locks. "If you want to kiss me, then do it already," he growled then jerked Simon's head up and crushed their mouths together. Simon let him take the lead as his heart began slamming in his chest, thundering in his ears.

For the next several minutes they sparred with teeth and tongue, their mouths locked together. Things escalated quickly as their hands flew over each other, pulling and clawing at the other's clothes as they struggled to get even closer. Their knees colliding at the awkward position as they sat side by side.

Finally Simon pulled back, breathless, his pale skin flush. "Let's take this off." He began tugging at the bottom of Zhang's teeshirt. When he heard no protest he peeled it over his chest and flung it to the side and pushed him down against the couch. He crawled over him and discarded his own shirt.

"Are we doing this?" Zhang asked running his eyes over Simon's lily white torso before meeting his eyes. Simon only grinned down at him before lowering himself down to kiss his shoulders and neck again.

"Hell yeah." He whispered gunning for the especially sensitive spot just below Zhang's delicate looking jawline. Simon loved how they fit together, Zhang's slightly smaller frame complementing his own swimmer's build which was taller and slender. To stay in shape he worked out, paying particular attention to his abs but being mindful not to bulk up too much and distort his physique. Making his living on his appearance as he did, even the slightest change mattered. He gripped and twisted Zhang's nipple then lowered his head to gnaw at the nubby flesh, taking it between his lips before generously lapping at it until he felt Zhang begin to thrash beneath him uncontrollably with a loud hiss.

"Wait." Breathless, Zhang stopped him with a firm hand to his bare chest. Simon's heart squeezed. He sat up slowly and regarded him, his large hand near Zhang's heart. "If we are on a mission are we supposed to be doing this?"

Simon grinned down at him. "This is the mission."

"What?"

"We're soul mates...with very specific needs, I might add," Simon droned throwing in a pout. "It's part of our identities here. Besides don't you like it?"

Zhang had to admit he had no complaints. Simon was like a damn drug. He could never get enough of him. And he was happiest when they were together. But he had so many questions. There was a lot he still didn't quite understand.

"I do....But wait...Did you really betray me like my lawyers said?" Zhang's brow furrowed with angst.

Simon shook his head. "If they told you that then they flat out lied to you."

"Not even as part of the mission?"

"That was never part of the mission. Besides, I could never do that to you. I'm here to protect your ass behind the scenes...well and also to play hard with you when you let me," he smiled sweetly down at him. Zhang rolled his eyes at this.

"But they said you bought up those back links and encouraged all those CP fans to-"

"To what? Share what they already know? That I am madly in love with your crazy, stubborn ass? In case you're wondering, we're supposed to be together like this for the mission. That's why it feels right. As for those back links, here everything is still hardwired rather than telepathic so using the back links on their web system is the way to drive traffic to us here and reach more people."

Simon continued, "Once we reach them through social media and the web, we are able to connect with them on the energetic level. Of course since this is a free will zone, some will choose to connect in at the lower vibes. We don't have to concern ourselves with them so much. It's the others who can hold a high enough frequency that we need to connect with in the array. We use it to communicate telepathically and garner their support when we or they need it."

Zhang thought a while. He was crazy for Simon in ways he never thought possible. The energy the two of them gave off together as soul mates alone could power the world it seemed. It was that huge. He'd never fallen so hard and deep for anyone as he had and thought he was losing himself. Now he realized it was supposed to be.

It started within the first few weeks of filming the series together, allowing him to easily get into character. He'd never laughed or played so hard before with anyone in his life. He knew he found someone he wanted to be with forever but didn't know how it was possible. For two guys to be together that way despite the popularity of boys love among the largely female audience of their series.

Not that he thought anything was wrong with it. He'd just never fallen for another guy before and was afraid of how his family and friends who knew him best would perceive him.   After all he was crazy Zhang, the athletic, daring and fun loving dude with a string of girlfriends. There was never any question he was straight. And Simon, while extremely handsome, was much more reserved and quiet, his tall, statuesque physique elegant yet disarming. Beautiful as he was, he was still another dude.

"What's the array?" He asked.

"It's a frequency band…We use it to communicate with like-minded souls. Each planet or sector has its own array that the beings living there are connected to. All the arrays are further connected to the larger array or web that connects back to Source. We can talk to each other in the array at the frequency we broadcast or hold. We use the 5th through 9th frequency bands to communicate telepathically with others also at the 5th through 9th dimensions. It's how we can hear our guides and colleagues but others can't." Simon explained.

Zhang tried to absorb it all. He had no recollection of what Simon was talking about though it made sense...somewhat.

Simon ducked his head again to ruthlessly torment his nipples with that expert mouth of his. To keep from losing his train of thought he stilled Simon's head.

"Babe, they said you were behind my being blacklisted in the first place. That you're neck deep with CAPA which is why you've been getting all those gigs. Is that true? Is that part of the mission too?"

Simon lifted his head slightly to gaze back at him as he lapped his tongue across Zhang's other nipple causing goosebumps to rise all over him. When he saw the pointed worried look on Zhang's face he stopped his ministrations and sighed.

"That's just bullshit spun on the web. If I was in with those assholes, we wouldn't need you to go through all of this trouble with them in the first place. But we needed someone to get embroiled in a scandal that would catch their attention so we could fight them from the inside and blow everything wide open. To show the whole damned world how corrupt they are and how they've been taking advantage of hard working artists for a long time. That's your role, baby. I'm just here to support you behind the scenes. That's the mission and the reason we came here," Simon said growing serious, straightening slightly over him to cup his cheek. "I'm just sorry you had to suffer behind it all and all the lies needlessly."

"Well, if I had woken up earlier like you did, I wouldn't have been suffering," Zhang said.

"You've always been the more grounded of the two of us and best suited for all this.   Besides, you're the deep-thinking philosophical type whose far more connected with the earth masses than I can ever hope to be. I'm just the pragmatist with orders to connect with those working on this mission in other spaces and places. But my deepest connection on this earth plane...no, everywhere, has always been you."

Zhang listened intently. He had to agree. Simon sort of floated through life where others struggled. Not that he didn't struggle too. He just made it look easy while seeming like he was just a regular guy. Nothing seemed to really bother him much. It was quite interesting to watch. And what he felt with Simon was difficult to explain. It seemed to transcend logic.

"Like who? I still don't get how we're supposed to know who the hell is who. How do I know who is here to support and who's just corrupt? Hell, I thought you were responsible for bringing me down," Zhang confessed. He had to admit, what Simon said made a lot of sense and went a long way to explain all the crap that had gone down that he was still dealing with that led him to temporarily lose his mind and publicly deny his relationship and feelings for Simon....

Although he was remembering slowly, it seemed there was still a lot he didn't know. He had to trust his partner to fill him in until everything became clear and all the pieces were revealed.

Simon shook his head. "That's just because you were still asleep. But still, it's like a game. I don't know exactly who, but it will all reveal itself." He tapped his fingers near Zhang's upper chest and heart above where he'd been voraciously toying with him with his mouth just moments earlier. "We have to just use this to intuit all that in the meantime. But you already know how to do that. You're so damn level-headed and grounded you make me sound like an idiot at times." Simon chuckled.

"Just sometimes?" Zhang teased.

CHAPTER SEVEN

Zhang Gets Answers

Zhang knew one thing Simon wasn't was an idiot. On the surface people thought he was a bit dim. But that was misleading. Simon was different. An enigma. He could go from innocent and naive to sophisticatedly accomplished in zero seconds flat. In order to know with whom you were dealing with, you had to pay attention.

He'd started his own entertainment studio when he got out of college and had been successfully managing his own career and business with just a small staff. Having his own studio had enabled him to cut out the middleman, keep more of the profits and make valuable connections in the industry which was a genius move giving the cutthroat nature of the business. Thus he called all the shots related to his career where Zhang had to rely on others to make a lot of decisions including which dramas and shows he would do, how much he'd be paid and for how long.

It allowed him to go with the flow but also gave him blinders which in hindsight might have led to the predicament Zhang found himself in. But he supposed at this point there was no sense moaning about it given he chose that role for the mission. Now he just had to sort everything out.

Just because he was remembering didn't mean he had all the answers yet. But remembering helped to go a long way to putting everything in its proper perspective.

Simon laughed.

"I just had to make sure that I didn't step on any landmines along the way and get caught up in the net myself. I still might but we will deal with that if it arises. Those fans can be fickle and brutal, never mind CAPA..." he stopped short of mentioning the government's involvement. He knew the fans were just expressing their pent up frustrations, deep seated unhappiness and helplessness as citizens. He couldn't really blame them but knew not to relax around them especially when they weren't yet awake and vibing high. If anyone had any doubts all they needed to do was look at the comments they spewed.

"How the hell did you manage that?"

"Lady Nada is here and working on the inside at that big Labor Law office in Hunan.   She's been really helpful."

"Lady Nada?" Zhang asked.

"She's an officer on the Athena on assignment here." The captain trusted her to assist and be at the ready for he and Zhang knowing things could get complicated.

  Zhang rolled his eyes. "So she's not from here? Like she's from space, too?"

"Yes."

"And how did you find her?"

"She contacted the studio and introduced herself. Our guides have also been working with your Mr. Li to give you a voice with the public."

Li Zhan was the Vice Chairman of the China TV Artist Association and a director who had taken an interest in Zhang's case and had been advocating for him and helping him explain his side of the story to the public since he had been banned from all public appearances until the matter was sorted. Thus, he'd made both tv appearances and took to social media to help raise awareness of all the railroading that had been going on against Zhang. He questioned CAPA's authority to blacklist artists, and whether CAPA had the legal authority to impose sanctions against SM influencers and performers. Well, until he got blacklisted himself.

By challenging their authority as a branch of the Ministry of Culture and Tourism, he was attempting to expose one area of corruption within the industry. He'd heard others were doing the same but Li had been his voice all this time since he'd lost his. Then he remembered something.

"But it was Li who got the two attorneys on board that said you were working against me in the first place."

"I don't know much about them yet but I was told to keep a low profile with you once it all started, to stay busy and keep making money. That we would need it at some point. The rest they would look into. Li might just be a loyal human for all I know. For a long time they said you were handling it from the inside and wouldn't let me intervene. It was only when my studio picked up chatter you were dragging me in that I had to ask for more direction."

Zhang turned a shade darker and darted his eyes away. He was obviously referring to his IG posts where he'd hand wrote out some of his frustrations then later went nuts and decided to just post a video on it bashing Simon for abandoning him although he hadn't exactly named names. "Uh yeah…about that…sorry about that…I was a little out of my mind."

Simon frowned. "You scared the crap out of me…though when I thought about it, I realized you still loved me because you seemed to hate me so much. But you did cause a few heads to roll blaming the CP fans like you did."

"Yeah…I guess I didn't know what I was thinking," Zhang said looking sheepish.

"Most didn't believe a damn thing you said anyway," Simon smirked then grabbed Zhang's hand and pressed it to his heart.

"But you did scare me so I consulted with Mencius who after connecting with a few others suggested that I use the array and do a broadcast to reach some of the light workers on the ground already anchoring energy here to send light directly to you."

"Whose Mencius?"

"Our master guide. We have a whole team of guides, galactics and light beings and angels lending support. It's a little complicated. It'll all come back to you."

"Huh…"

"As soon as this blows over and all is done, we get to do some real healing then. We'll be able to leave here and travel the world together and play as hard as we want."

Zhang's face lit up. "How long more?"

"I don't know exactly but I'm being told now that we are back on track ETA is about 2 earth years before the system is completely defunct."

"Two more years?" Zhang looked exasperated.

"Maybe sooner. But you just have to expose the corruption. Others will take over from there." Zhang looked relieved. He didn't know how much more of the pressure he could take although knowing now it was all part of the mission did eliminate some of his anxiety over it.

He thought of all the information Simon had just unpacked and decided to tackle it one by one as he got more up to speed. Simon massaging his chest and occasionally plucking at his nipples as he was was a certain distraction, those godlike hands warm. He decided against stopping him and to instead just enjoy it.

"What else did this Mencius guy say?"

"Just that the higher ups and guides finally gave me the go ahead to come over here to try to talk sense into you. You going dark on account of being SM offline was the second rally point when you and I were supposed to meet up. But you disappeared on me instead. They know how sensitive things are for you and didn't want me to just go barging in and told me to give you some more time…well, until you did those IG posts. Then they said to just go on in and try. If I didn't succeed they said they would go to Plan B."

"What's Plan B?"

Simon shrugged. "In a nutshell, replace me, wash us both, take your IG accounts offline."

"Wait what? Replace you? Wash us? Like scrub the whole mission? So they were the ones who took my accounts offline?"

"No that was CAPA and the government. But we needed that to happen so we knew the mission was on track. We needed them to go hard on you so you could shed light on all the crap they've gotten away with in the past. Because of you, what has quietly been happening to a lot of others is finally coming to light. If you couldn't wake up they were preparing to call it a wash and just let things proceed according to free will," Simon said, his voice deep and thoughtful. "But when you started to show signs of caving with the pressure, I asked those that could hear me to send you Love to help with the mission."

"How did you do that?"

"I used the 5th through 9th density array. What the earth humans call the unified field."

"What? Earth humans? Aren't we earth humans?" Zhang didn't mask his confusion.

"We are galactic humans ensouled in human bodies. Sirian human souls to be exact. We were born to earth parents just like every other human but we are here to help humanity and thus Gaia ascend."

To his credit, Zhang's eyes didn't glaze over. So Simon continued. "I've been plugged into the array for awhile and just put out the SOS that we needed help. Some in the array responded by sending Light directly to you, others to the situation." He didn't tell Zhang he'd always been plugged in, feeling it would unnecessarily overwhelm him.

Zhang grew flush. Sheesh! All this trouble on account of his not remembering anything. He had to admit while he had lost it a few times he had quickly rebounded and had more clear days of late than bad. He just hadn't realized it had been because of all the good energy people had been beaming at him. Geez, was that really even a thing?

"This array…how many people on earth can hear it or are in it?"

"150 million. Not many now but more of the masses are slowly moving up in octave.   Most are still at the high threes to low fours but there are more in the low fours reaching into the high fours and low fives than before with all the ultra-high resonance energy and other support pouring in from the confederation. Not everybody needs to be at that level. Just enough of them to keep us on the trajectory we are on."

Zhang shook his head as he struggled to understand all that was being said and make sense of it. Simon smiled back goofily.

"Where do we go for the healing?" He suddenly asked lifting a hand to caress Simon's protruding collarbones. For some reason his big hands and collarbone always held a certain appeal to him.

"How about Hawaii?" Simon grinned. Hawaii was all that remained of the Lemurian continent. It was still a powerful healing vortex. He'd heard it was incredible though he'd never been.

Zhang's heart thudded. "Can I even go there? I think my passport's been cancelled."

"Doesn't matter. That'll all be taken care of."

"Then let's leave now!" Zhang said excitedly.

Simon looked sympathetic, "Soon. I promise."

"Ugh! Who else have you been in contact with?"

"Lady Master Ma'at. She's one of the ones who answered the call and has been sending you healing and clearing for the last few months. Oh and I promised her you'd sing with her when we got to Hawaii where we will meet."

Zhang laughed and thought about how much of an idiot this Lady Master Ma'at and all the other mission workers must think he was given the crazy state of mind he was in.

"So if you didn't succeed in convincing me to take your ass back or went off track yourself who would have been your backup?"

"So you are taking me back then, right, although I never left. I'll be sure to make a note of that."

Zhang smirked. "Ha! Ha! Jerk. Tell me who's the backup."

"Some guys you or I worked with before. Gunner from Sector 5, Zeeter from Unit ZR and Alpha6 from Polaris." They'd worked with Gunner and Alpha6 pretty closely on different missions before although they were a bit stiff in his opinion.

Zhang seemed thoughtful as he named them.

"Zeeter? Who'd name their kid Zeeter?"

"What can I say? He's Reptilian."

"Huh…" Zhang shrugged. "And you say I worked with him."

"No, just me after you jumped. Sort of a weirdo. Anyway, the hell if I'd let any one of those morons jump down here and replace us for this mission." He made a disparaging face for fuller effect. Zhang snorted. Simon reached beneath him and grasped Zhang firmly on his privates giving him a squeeze to drive his point home immediately garnering Zhang's attention.

"If they look like you who cares?" Zhang said nonchalantly. Simon gave him a lopsided grin.

Simon knew had he not succeeded in waking Zhang up, it would have prolonged Zhang's earthly sufferings unnecessarily. When one isn't awake they continue with their earth lives without realizing it's a mission they have agreed upon. Instead as Zhang experienced, it seems as if it's the only "reality" in play. With only one of them awake, and knowing how much Zhang was needlessly suffering had been agonizing for him as well. Still, even now he could see questions and a bit of doubt in his eyes that would take time to overcome. The important thing was that Zhang had opened up and allowed him back in. Simon kissed him on the forehead, grateful.

CHAPTER EIGHT

Are We Doing This?

"So are we doing this now or do you have more questions?" Simon asked cocking an eyebrow at him.

"What about the mission?" Zhang asked tentatively, his body tingling with the pointed attention.

"Didn't I already tell you this is the mission?" Simon being direct in all things snorted. He leaned down and brushed his lips against Zhang's before angling his head to kiss him more fully.

Zhang sighed as he met the warmth of Simon's mouth against his own while those godlike hands continued to massage him below. Unable to lay there without reciprocating, he wrapped his hands around the back of Simon's head and pulled him closer, crushing their lips together and ramming his tongue between Simon's lips again. He'd missed him so damn much.

Simon collapsed his elbows until he was laying flat on him, his own root an unyielding mass pressed against Zhang's thigh. Zhang groaned against his mouth, his hips jackknifing upward with the contact. Simon always had that effect on him. If he wasn't so damn horny like he was he'd lay there like putty in his hands. He slid a hand between them and ran his palm along the full length of Simon's member before squeezing him there possessively their hands and wrists bumping up against each other's.

"I really missed you, baby," Simon whispered against his mouth. That went without saying. "I really missed you, too." Zhang responded without relinquishing those soft lips. Then he thought of something.

"Did you screw around on me all this time?" He asked prompting Simon to lift his head to look at him. It'd been forever since he'd actually seen him and Simon was a hot piece of ass.

"Every chance I could," Simon said then chuckled when he saw Zhang's expression deaden.

"I'm kidding. I didn't," Simon said in all seriousness. Zhang's expression didn't change. Simon laughed at this. "I swear! I've been a good boy!" He followed up. Zhang peered at him deeply and only when he was satisfied Simon wasn't lying did he relax. "You better not have or you're dead," he said levelly.

"And what about you?" Simon countered gazing back at him so intently Zhang almost averted his eyes. But he held out knowing Simon likely would have thought he was lying when he answered had he done so.

"Who the hell would be crazy enough to do it with me? My name is toast, remember!"

"I would do you. But you still didn't answer my question," Simon pointed out bluntly. "What about that dumb make-up artist you kept mentioning on the set and in those interviews?"

"She's not dumb," Zhang retorted then laughed when Simon cocked a testy eyebrow at him and grabbed him by the hair. A jealous Simon was a dangerous Simon. "Ow! Of course not."

Simon studied his face before pronouncing him sincere releasing the grip he had on his locks. Zhang recalled the first time Simon looked him in the eyes when they met after casting. It made his heart stammer in his chest. He hadn't understood the reaction he was having so he pretended to be totally disinterested in him. Not much longer though after filming everything totally changed. There were times on the set where Simon had gotten him so aroused just by being near him Zhang often walked around with a woody in his trousers. The one time Simon discovered it, Zhang froze. It caused Simon to forget his lines. They laughed about it later.

The script itself encouraged their open affection so they went for it. In fact, they'd grown so comfortable around each other the directors constantly chastised them to control themselves. For Zhang always being a guy's guy sort of dude, all this was new to him. His very identity became a blur and he hardly recognized himself.

Simon now shimmied out of his shorts revealing he shamelessly wore no undergarment underneath. Then with one fluid motion he pulled off Zhang's shorts as well until they were both naked. Simon looked proud of himself as he regarded their nakedness from above. Zhang only rolled his eyes.

"Move off so I can do you," Zhang said shifting beneath him, his root a hard mass against his belly.

"What? Fat chance! I'm the one who had to wait until your dumb ass woke up. The honor should be mine," Simon protested. Before Zhang could say anything, Simon spit on his hand and wet the tip of his already greedily dripping member. Knocking Zhang's knees apart, he positioned himself.

"Hey! No more foreplay?" Zhang teased.

Simon snorted. "The foreplay was that long winded explanation I gave you to get you and everyone up to speed. Now it's time to get down to business." At this last bit he pushed his way into Zhang's wet heat with the thrust of his hips. Zhang's breath hitched and he stiffened at the sudden intrusion. But any discomfort was quickly dissipated by the loosening of his muscles as he swallowed him in one fluid motion. They both let out a long, protracted groan.

Simon steadied himself over him with his arms outstretched on either side of Zhang's head and threw his head back. Zhang wrapped his legs around his hips and groaned louder as Simon stretched out his innards. Whatever thoughts were in his head quickly left him and his mind went completely blank. Before he could catch his breath, Simon was already thrusting inside him.

As Simon steadily moved his hips he lowered his head and kissed Zhang whose eyes were closed, his lips slightly parted. Simon thought he looked so beautiful and gently began a slow perusal of his mouth as he worked out his pent up frustrations on Zhang's nether region. While he had been desiring this for so long he wanted to take his time for Zhang's sake. He had a rough last 8 months and deserved this small measure of peace. There was still a lot to do and the job ahead challenging. But for now, he wanted to give Zhang this one thing. From the sound of his lover lowing in heat against his mouth, he was doing a pretty good job. When Zhang squeezed his muscles tight Simon just about lost it.

"Oh f—k -" he wheezed, his balls tensing. Zhang kissed him in earnest, grabbing him by the head and holding him in place as if afraid he'd run off. Simon thrust harder, his breath growing more labored as he picked up his pace, sweat dripping from his forehead.

"Ohhhh…" Zhang cried, his hands moving steadily over Simon's chest, his shoulders, his back, gripping his buttocks with greater urgency. Meanwhile his member dripped liberally onto his belly.

Simon reached between him and grasped Zhang's member to fist it, his grip tight as Zhang grew flush. When Simon swiped at the precome glistening on Zhang's cock then lapped it up with his tongue, Zhang totally lost it, his hips shooting forward, legs wrapping around Simon to lock him in place.

In the next moment he gave a shout as he was flying and convulsing wildly beneath him. He lost all sense of time and direction as he exploded, his release violently splattering both their stomachs and chests, and the intensely exhilarating sensations coursing through him robbed him completely of his senses.

At some point he heard Simon gasp and then cry out above him and then his sphincter was filled with wet heat as Simon came. He reached up to pull Simon's mouth to his own and kissed him deeply as he received Simon's seed inside of him. He felt Simon's entire body pulsing above and within him as if they were one until they were both spent. With a shuddering groan, Simon collapsed on top of him, his body warm, flush and slick with sweat and Zhang's seed. Zhang reveled in the moment, licking at the saltiness at Simon's neck and throat as his lover's breath grew more steady. Only then did he drop his legs and sprawl out beneath him.

"Next time I get to do you," Zhang whispered against his neck.

"You can try." Simon smirked.

"What do you mean try? That's not what you said last time as you begged for it," Zhang retorted as Simon began to laugh.

Zhang suddenly grew serious and cupped Simon's cheek, his eyes growing sad. "You left me for such a long time," he whispered. In the silence that followed, tears slowly pooled in his eyes. Simon's heart gave a leap in his chest as he felt the weight of Zhang's sadness fully. It brought tears to his own eyes.

"I never wanted to be apart from you for even one second. And there was never a single moment that I wasn't thinking of you and wanting you by my side. I swear. Not a single moment," he said slowly, his every word imbued with all the love that filled his whole being for him. Zhang sobbed out and closed his eyes.

"Look at me," Simon said with conviction and waited until Zhang opened his eyes and gazed back at him. "You are my heart and my soul. And I am so sorry I couldn't get back here sooner. There isn't a day that went by that I asked myself if we should have even come here and if I should have convinced you so hard to do this mission. I love you so, so much," Simon said softly, his own voice breaking as he wiped the tears

63

from Zhang's cheek with the pad of his thumb as his own fell. Zhang gave out another sob and closed his eyes again.

"Is this real? Are you really here? Because if not...I don't think..."

Simon immediately dropped his head and kissed him deeply, cutting off his words. Zhang cried against his lips but Simon continued to kiss him gently, pouring his whole life into the heart-felt contact until he stilled. "We're partners forever, remember?" He said with a hint of a smile.

"I love you so, so much, asshole. You can't ever leave me again. You hear?" Zhang said reaching up to wipe Simon's tears away, a frown marring his face.

"You don't ever have to worry, baby. We're together to see this mission through to the end and then we get to go home, I promise." Simon sent a wave of calming energy over them both and felt Zhang instantly relax beneath him. He kissed him again, this time suckling his tongue and swiping his slowly over Zhang's own until he felt Zhang stirring again, the ever so subtle scent of his lover's pheromones tickling his ultra-heightened senses. He caressed his hand slowly down Zhang's side before coming to rest at his hip as he once again explored and savored Zhang's mouth in slow, deep measure. At some point they migrated to the bedroom where they began again in earnest.

They spent the next three days in bed not bothering to shower, only getting up to piss or to forage for whatever they could find in the refrigerator to snack on after they demolished the chips and other snacks Simon had bought as they made up for lost time. When they grew too exhausted to do anything they fell asleep, a tangle of arms and legs, dead to the world.

Inevitably one or the other would wake a few hours later to find themselves fully impaled and the other desperately thrusting away with abandon. They were covered in spent seed, using whatever was in their grasp to clean themselves and then, completely drained of all vigor and their senses, fell asleep practically comatose before repeating the whole cycle all over again.

Simon wondered why the Pleiadeans had lied during the sexual training
class they both took prior to incarnating, telling them sex in a bonded,
loving relationship could revitalize one's body. While he had to admit
it did take you to different worlds, and made them see stars, they'd both
always felt completely drained in the aftermath to say nothing of now.

While they were both slumbering barely able to move, Simon's phone
vibrated on the bedside table. He groggily picked it up and saw it was
Ming calling him and groaned. Still half asleep he grunted out a hello
and then only half-listened as she began yelling at him for not
responding to her texts from earlier.

"Where have you been? Elle Magazine wants to do another shoot with
you on Thursday in Beijing."

"I'm busy," he muttered still half asleep.

"I already told them you'd do it and got them to push it back three
days."

At this Zhang woke up beside him and popped his head up to listen,
she was talking so loud even he could make out everything she said.

"I don't care. I don't want to do it. Tell them I'm busy," he repeated
about to hang up but Zhang stopped him.

"Do it. And tell them you want double."

Simon rolled his eyes. "Are you serious?" Zhang squeezed his partially
erect member in reply.

"Who's that? Is that-" Ming exclaimed. "Oh my god, Simon! Where are
you? Are you in Xinyu?"

"F—k..." Simon ran a tired hand through his hair. "Yes, so you know
what we've been doing for the last three days..."

"Oh my god!" She repeated excitedly. "No wonder we couldn't reach you!" She laughed sounding incredulous. "Tell Zhang I said hello!"

Ming had been his assistant for the last three years, her role making her privy to the most intimate details of his private life, including his on again, off again, on again relationship with Zhang. A fan of BL herself, he had to endlessly chastise her to stay focused on the job and get herself a damn boyfriend to stay out of their romantic business. Having woken earlier last year just as the show's popularity skyrocketed, she was focused on supporting Simon and the studio to carry out his mission. She also knew how important it was for him to get Zhang back on board.

"Yeah, he heard you. Listen, if I do this, I want double and he's coming with me. He's long overdue for a facial and haircut and I look like shit so tell them to be ready for us both. In fact, from now on for all of my gigs, he's coming with me."

"Wait, what?!" Zhang exclaimed sitting up now fully awake. "I can't go with you."

"Why not? I'm not leaving you," Simon responded to him before he turned his attention back to his assistant.

"In fact, tell Elle Magazine to fly us first class not business class, and I want a suite. And we need extra security as well. I don't want anyone hounding us. Otherwise, I'm not working with them again."

"Aiii! Boss, you're trying to get me killed!" She wailed just before he hung up and tossed his phone to the side then rolled over onto Zhang. He stretched his naked and aching body against him and nuzzled his neck. Zhang was quiet.

"We better go shower and start moving. She's very efficient and will probably be texting me the details very soon," Simon growled kissing him on the mouth and ignoring the fact they both hadn't brushed their teeth in days.

"Do you think it's wise we're seen together now given all the shit that's been going on with me?"

Simon snorted and grinned that wolfish grin of his as he patted Zhang on the head. "Babe, now that we're both awake and we work as a team, we've got this."

CHAPTER NINE

Commander Zhang and the Mission to Fornax (aka Simon
and the slight mishap on Fornacis

The day started out pretty ordinary.

"Greetings everyone. I am Captain ZhangZHXO511. This is Lieutenant SimonGJXO1129. I will be your commanding officer for this little mission and Lieutenant is my second."

Zhang walked up and down the line, hands behind his back addressing the group of 24 scientists and 6 gunners waiting to board the massive transport ship. Zhang had been tasked to fly the Class B Science Explorer, a state of the art light craft newly commissioned by the Confederation that could easily transport 100 scientists and all their equipment.

Though a science explorer, she was equipped with huge defensive lasers capable of ripping crater size holes in a predator ship. Earlier, they'd joked about testing the lasers out somewhere but quickly realized there was no way they could do so without alerting the galactic confederation the lasers had been triggered. And since neither could come up with a reasonable explanation that wouldn't immediately call their competency as officers into question, they quickly scrapped that idea.

Every mission began the same way. With Zhang addressing the crew as they stood at attention usually in the ready room or shuttle bay while he sized them up individually, laid down a few ground rules and scared the shit out of them.

"I will get straight to the point. We all know there are alot of risks and dangers, some of which we can't anticipate as we have very little data about the shithole we will be heading to other than what we already shared on your smart pads that came from the Athena. So if you get injured on this mission, I'm not carrying your sorry ass back to the ship and neither is the Lieutenant. So be sure to buddy up with someone who can lift your carcass and make sure they don't get killed either if you want to return home." This last bit had the crew of scientists looking at each other with worried expressions. Simon watched from the sidelines and tried not to laugh.

"Just kidding. We are one big family here and we all help each other. Once we reach the drop point, we will set each unit down at their respective data collection points until all units are on the ground and in place. There will be 3 units of 8 with 2 armed escorts each for defensive purposes only should it become necessary. I trust you all know where you need to be. We anticipate taking no more than 3 solar rotations here to get this job done so look sharp."

The Commander came from a long line of captains and loved to fly. As a child he often accompanied his father and grandfather on numerous missions throughout the galaxy. His love of flying had him promoted to captain at an early age. His precision made him an expert in handling many different types of craft within the confederation. Since he'd agreed to take on the additional responsibility as commander, he'd flown over 400 missions and been made responsible for thousands of lives, mostly scientists and their gun crew.

That morning, Simon checked the vast amounts of gear and equipment being brought on board and did a visual inspection of the craft as part of his duties. The mission was typical, to gather data on soil composition, mineral resource availability, gather plant samples, and also plant and leave a few different types of greenery that had been grown on the Athena behind to determine whether the planet was suitable for future habitation. Once the data was gathered and analyzed, it could be uploaded immediately in flight into the vast database of information available to all civilizations of the confederation who might be in need of a new home.

As they reviewed the plan, it was determined that they were a few bodies short to accomplish all that was needed. He and Simon agreed to assist with the collection of minerals in the more mountainous regions and gather the necessary samples. They left at the appointed hour and headed for Lido, a planetoid in the constellation Fornax. As they made a pass over it, and the computer LiDAR scanned the terrain below for the database, they saw dark brown landscape with scant vegetation, no trees or water features to speak of, and tall, dark mountainous peaks. In short, it was a blank slate. After circling back around, he dropped off the crew and unloaded their equipment one by one as scheduled until all three units were safely on the ground.

He and Simon then flew off in the light craft, heading to the mountains a distance away to gather their mineral samples. As the terrain was rough, Zhang found it necessary to land at a distance requiring a 5 km or so trek to the base of the mountain.

Laden down with equipment they began walking. They laughed and joked as they hiked their way with their gear and then upon reaching the base of the nearest peak found a suitable spot to begin collecting. Simon used the core sampler and plunged it into the ground in a few places before retracting it and placing the samples in the specially designed case to protect them. Meanwhile Zhang studied the various gradations in the soil nearby for traces of iron, calcite and other minerals and punched the data into his computer on his sleeve. It was then they both saw a flash from behind them that pierced the otherwise still air.

"What the hell was that?" Zhang asked turning around to look. This was followed by another flash from the same direction. He looked down to find a token size hole in his suit just to the left of his abdomen where an ungodly heat was beginning to radiate outward. As he reached behind him, he found there was a hole there as well.

"Ouch!"

Whatever had pierced him had entered him from his back and had gone clear through him. They were under attack. He immediately yelled to Simon to find cover.

The expression on Simon's face was one of surprise but seeing the hole in Zhang's suit, he immediately pulled out the cauterizing wand he carried in his suit and sealed Zhang's wounds before sticking him in the stomach muscle with the regenerator syringe saving him from bleeding out and healing the wound as they ran.

"Who is it?" Simon asked breathless but before Zhang could answer much less hazard a guess, there was a loud crack followed by an ungodly explosion as a crater size hole tore open in the mountain ahead. By the time Zhang sent out the beacon on his suit to request back up, Simon had already taken the brunt of the concussive blast from his position in front of him which blew both of them into the air with such force, it knocked the wind clear from their lungs. Zhang landed hard on the ground stunned, his ears ringing. It was a moment before he was able to gather his wits and roll onto his side, his ribs broken. Whoever had been firing upon them had stopped.

He sat up with difficulty and looked around. Simon was no where to be found. His ears still ringing, he crawled to his feet and immediately sent out another beacon to the Athena and whomever was in the vicinity that could provide assistance. Then he hurried to check the computer embedded on the sleeve of his suit to locate Simon's whereabouts and tracked him to some distance away including his trajectory. Simon had been blown in an arc and down into a crater approximately 100 meters to his left. Zhang stared in shock.

Using another regenerator syringe, he stuck it into the area near his ribs with as much force as he could muster as he ran to the edge of the massive crater and peered down. He immediately spotted Simon's figure, his suit glistening against the backdrop of inky dark jagged rocks upon which he was hung up.

"Hold on, buddy!" He yelled not allowing himself to think, only on getting to his partner as soon as he could. He sent out a mayday into the array but heard nothing in reply. He carefully made his way down the rocky crevice to ensure he didn't pitch headfirst himself. If Simon was injured, he'd need the remaining two regeneration serum syringes Zhang carried on him until they could make it back to the ship's small med bay. Simon was wedged headfirst in the dirt and buried partially by fallen rocks and debris. From what he could already see he was missing his left foot and right forearm. This can't be good.

Stifling down the panic that was threatening to overwhelm him and instead allow his years of training to kick in, Zhang took a breath and began clearing away the rocks. He only managed with some difficulty to finally pull Simon free and turn him around. His heart dropped. Simon's face and head were a bloody mess. Both feet had been blown off and he was missing a few fingers on his left hand.

"No!!! F—k! Simon!" His whole body was a mess. Despite the extra resilience of their suits, it was pockmarked with holes and torn in a number of places, no match for the force of the blast that had jettisoned him into the jagged rocks. He cradled Simon in his arms in utter shock and pushed away his long blonde locks from his face now matted with blood. Simon's eyes were still open and staring blankly off into the distance. He reached down to close them.

"Simon!" He yelled, frantic and still in shock overwhelmed by the horror of seeing his partner's lifeless body in his arms.

From behind him he heard. "How's it look? Should I try to jump back in?"

Zhang nearly shot out of his space suit in shock. "What the —"

The amorphous form of his partner came to stand before him observing him as he held his body. Simon was in light body form.

"Are you trying to kill me?" Zhang screamed. "Aghhhh!!!!"

"Sorry…"

"What-the-hell- happened?" Zhang asked as Simon squatted before him to assess the damage to his body before looking him over as well.

"Are you ok?"

"Yes…I broke some ribs but took some regeneration serum…I don't think I have enough left here to heal you," Zhang mourned.

"No…you don't. But it's okay. The ship…somehow there was a mis-cue. It fired upon us."

"Wh- what? That was the ship? Are you sure?"

"Positive…there's no one near it. That was definitely an AI malfunction. Did you set off the beacon?"

"Yes…twice."

"Can you walk?"

"Yes…Just give me a minute…wait, the friggin' ship fired on us? What kind of bullshit is that?"

"It likely thought it was under attack and fired."

"Shouldn't that be a decision I make when I'm seated in the control seat?"

Simon chuckled. "You'd think. Maybe it's a new function. Didn't you read the manual before starting her up?"

"Of course, I read the manual!!! And there's nothing in the friggin' manual that says to fire on the crew responsible for flying her back home!" Zhang yelled expressing his frustration at the newly commissioned ship. "The damn thing killed you and nearly killed me!"

"It's not that easy. I'm right here. Come on, we need to get out of here. Are you sure you can walk?"

"Yes…" Zhang stood up and pulled Simon's lifeless body upright with a grunt. He was dead weight. "But your body…I think…it's…toast…."

"Can you get it back up the hill? I'm thinking we might be able to salvage it."

Zhang looked doubtful given the condition of his head and face alone, not to mention the missing limbs and digits. Still, there was no way he was leaving his partner's body to rot behind in a ditch. "I think so."

"Just levitate it."

Zhang was horrified. His best friend, partner and soul mate deserved far better than to be moved around like a piece of heavy machinery or equipment.

"I am not levitating your body, Simon…just give me a minute to catch my breath and I'll carry you," Zhang said with deep emotion.

Simon was quietly touched.

CHAPTER TEN
Zhang Has a Change of Heart

Zhang positioned himself and heaved Simon over his shoulders and navigated his way back over the boulders and rocks to slowly climb out of the crevice. Many moments later, he was back on solid ground, his lungs about to collapse with the exertion. He reminded himself to work out with the pulmonary enhancer more.

"How much do you weigh? It's like I'm carrying your whole family on my back!" Zhang wheezed, certain if he took another step he would pass out.

"Same as you give or take a gram. Save your breath, commander. You still have a ways to go." Simon pointed to the ship in the distance where they'd left her.

"Right," Zhang wheezed again. He tightened his grip around Simon's waist and took a step. They'd been in far worse situations. The last time they'd been fired upon by Ciakahrrs, Simon and another colleague had both gotten blown in half and he managed to carry them both back to the shuttle craft although it took him a few trips. Thank illuminations it hadn't been parked that far. Now he wrestled and dragged Simon along heading back to the gleaming white disc that was their ship which now sat silent right where they had left her. The rays of the setting sun danced over her hull and she sparkled like some crazy light show as if mocking them. He silently cursed the ship.

It would be dark again in a few moments making visibility difficult, so he stopped and engaged the lights on his space suit and attempted to do the same on Simon's but found they were all damaged.

"All I am saying is that the damn ship better not fire at us again," Zhang heaved and gasped as he struggled to stay on his feet and not drop Simon's body.

"It won't. The main computer system on the Athena will have registered the blast and investigated. It should be already reporting the malfunction and doing a diagnostic which should reflect on your personal server. They should be seeking your input right about now," Simon answered from beside him sounding unperturbed his mangled body was being dragged along by Zhang as he struggled to carry him back to the ship.

"Can you see any signal on my sleeve?" Zhang asked as he huffed and puffed his way back, Simon's arm draped across his shoulder, afraid that if he stopped to check he couldn't garner any strength to keep moving. The others would be wondering why they weren't back yet and were stranded without them. The star had already made its fourth rotation around the planetoid if he calculated correctly.

"Nothing yet," Simon said moving close to him.

Then Zhang thought of something else. "Can you detect any other malfunction? Can she still get us out of here and back to FornacisBeta?" Zhang adjusted Simon's body against his again to get a better grip, tempted to stop and rest.

"She should. Her weapons system has nothing to do with her flying capability. And you can also override it even if the two somehow get crossed and work in tandem. If the computer recognized the error I doubt the lasers will work again until they are manually reset."

"Well…let's…hope…we…don't…come…across…any…hostiles…..I've -I've…got to… stop…I need a minute," Zhang gasped. "You're so damn heavy!" Zhang wheezed and struggled to take in air. He didn't want to set Simon's body down for fear he wouldn't have the strength after his own injuries to lift him back up. Even though he could feel the regeneration serum working, it wasn't exactly instantaneous. It didn't help Simon's bloody corpse was slippery as hell and was still leaking making it difficult for Zhang to hold on to. He was covered in the viscous blue liquid, the scent like blueberries.

"Almost there."

"Liar!" Zhang yelled out. Simon laughed.

"I'm not. Come on, you have this. You've carried me before in basic training."

"You weren't dead back then, Lieutenant. Don't make me speak!" Zhang growled. Then, "Okay, maybe…maybe if I carried you over my shoulder-" Zhang figured if he could just take it one step at a time like always, and not think too far ahead or too much about it, he could do this.

"Can you get me up that high without squatting?"

"No…definitely not…not without…passing…passing…out!" Zhang gasped in fits and starts.

"Ok, well there's a rock over there. Maybe you can set me down upon it in order to get some leverage," Simon suggested helpfully.

"Where?" Zhang frowned swinging his head to look about from beneath the crook of Simon's good arm while still struggling for breath.

Simon pointed to a rock about 50 meters away.

"What? I'm not carrying you way over there when the ship is that way!" Zhang made a face as if Simon had lost it.

Simon shrugged. "Just a suggestion, Commander."

"Just-just let me....take a quick breather." Zhang huffed once again shifting Simon's carcass against him and adjusting his grip around his waist before starting up and slowly lunging forward.

Eight excruciating earth hours later they came to rest within 20 yards of the ship. Close enough for Zhang to actually believe they would make it. His lungs felt as if they were about to explode. He stumbled and dropped Simon at his feet and landed on top of him, completely drained of vigor. He couldn't even cry if he wanted to. Depleted, it was as if his system was struggling to function on nonexistent reserves from the prolonged exertion. He only hoped he didn't completely shut down and had enough left in him to fly the ship.

"I can't believe....I can't...we're....here." Zhang wheezed after a while righting himself onto his knees and dropping his head. His vision still threatening to go black. Meanwhile Simon who had disappeared to inspect the ship hours before now came over to inspect his body more carefully given that Zhang had finally managed to carry it back. He tsk'd.

"You okay, buddy?"

Zhang waved him off, still too winded to speak.

"Hmmm....Now that I'm thinking about it, maybe it would've just been better to have dumped it and buried it back there," Simon opined surveying the damage critically.

"Wh- Are you friggin' kidding me? I thought you wanted to try to salvage it?" Zhang screamed. "I wouldn't have carried it halfway across the friggin' planet had I known you were ok with me just chucking it!!" Zhang managed to continue in one fluid breath, eyes bulging. "Aghhh!" He flopped onto the ground and groaned.

"Well at first, I thought it might be worth salvaging but now that I'm really looking at it... it does look a little beat up. I may as well just get a new one. What do you think?"

It was never much of an issue as the Sirians like most advanced civilizations possessed the technology to regenerate a new physical form. This could even be done easily on the mothership. It was no longer even a matter of DNA as some developing species still relied upon, but simple chemical compounds put together just like baking a cake. All it took were a few simple instructions and Simon could have a new body, an exact replica if he so chose within a mere 10-12 earth minutes of laying in a med bay pod.

"You think? You're friggin' missing an arm and both feet and your face looks disgusting.   Half the back of your head's caved in," Zhang said pulling his partners head up by his matted hair for effect before letting it drop with a thud. He pushed at its shoulder in frustration before rolling into a fetal position, his back to it.

"Hmmm....well, while you're at it you should probably requisition yourself a new suit.   That one's covered in blood and has holes in it."

Zhang had the blue viscous fluid smeared everywhere on him due to standing beside Simon as he'd been hit by the blast, and from his valiant efforts to carry Simon's heavy carcass that great distance over his shoulder, on his back, in his arms, dragging him beside him...any which way he could until his strength gave out. He'd even tried kicking it a few times to get it to move.

"A new suit, huh?" He said crawling back to his feet as Simon's amorphous form before him wavered in the light emitted by Zhang's suit. Zhang stood there arms on his hips.

"Really Lieutenant? You know what? When you get your new damn body, I swear...I'm going to kick your fu -"

Just then the sound of a radio crackling broke through the air. "Commander? Lieutenant?   Are you there? Can you hear us?" It was Sondmi, the team leader of Unit 2.

"Copy that…" Zhang said and stood up straighter as he glared at Simon. "We just had a slight mishap…everybody ok?"

"Yes! We heard some chatter in the array but couldn't make it out. Thank illuminations you are both ok."

Both Zhang and Simon glanced down at the crumpled mess that was Simon's body and shrugged. "Yes…more or less. Let the others know as soon as we load up here we'll swing around and pick everyone up. Sorry for the delay." They disconnected. Zhang moved toward the ship's bay and the door silently retracted greeting him in that soft computer voice.

"Welcome back, Commander ZhangZHXO511. Systems check ready."

Zhang shook his head in disgust. "Thanks for firing on us, asshole!" He huffed getting a medical bag to stuff Simon's carcass into before going back to where Simon waited outside.

"Hey! I just thought of something. Wouldn't you look totally heroic carrying my dead body back to the Athena! Like they do in the western movies in the H-deck! That would make it totally worth it for you to have carried it all the way back here. Of course, you should look a bit more torn up about it rather than pissed off to really pull it off. Just sayin'…." Simon said excitedly as Zhang leaned over his carcass and prepared to place it into the bag. Zhang ignored him.

"Oh, and did you happen to bring back the mineral samples?" Simon added. They'd been in the process of collecting them when the mishap occurred.

Zhang began to laugh. It started out like a low rumble and then slowly worked its way up the commander's chest until it sounded absolutely frightening. "No! I didn't bring the friggin' mineral samples! In fact, I don't even know where the hell they are, Lieutenant! Do you? I was busy trying to carry your sorry -"

Sensing Zhang was moving out of alignment, his inner harmonium disturbed, Simon sent a wave of calming energy toward him silencing

81

him in his tracks. He calmly added, "It's ok, Commander. Let's just bring a couple of rocks from around the ship with us and say this is all we found."

Zhang zipped him into the body bag and dragged it up the ramp into the storage without another word. Never mind Simon was face down.

Simon took his seat at the navigation console up front and waited for Zhang to take his place beside him. The computer recognized his signature and immediately greeted him in that pleasant female voice.

"Welcome back, Lieutenant SimonGJXO1129."

"Hey, thanks for shooting at us. You almost killed us both," he chided doing a quick systems check before verifying the AI malfunction and confirming if it had already been reported in.

"I am sorry. I do not comprehend. Please repeat, Lieutenant."

Meanwhile Zhang went outside, picked up a bunch of rocks and pebbles off the ground before returning back inside and tossing them into the bag containing Simon's carcass.

By the time they picked everyone up and headed back, another solar rotation had passed. As the groups filtered in and took their seats it was hard to miss the captain's blood-soaked spacesuit and the Lieutenant's amorphous form in the navigation chair beside him. No one dared ask what happened.

Zhang and Simon exchanged glances and shrugged, knowing they painted quite the scene. "So...welcome back, everybody! How was the mission? Everybody got what we came for?"

The ship remained dead silent.

Commander Zhang flew them back home.

The confederation had no clue the lasers had ever been fired.

CHAPTER ELEVEN

Calling All Volunteers to Earth

The call came through the array across the multiverse reaching the 5th through 9th dimensional STO (Service to Others) frequency bands. SL-52 or Terra was ascending with Sol, her consort and needed assistance.

Her ascension was unprecedented in that it would also cause the ascension of every planet in that sector of the universe, all of it divinely guided.

Terra had started out as an experimental biosphere. Her true name was Gaia. Just about every advanced race had contributed to her creation and terraforming, providing plants, flora and fawna from various planets as well as animals and other life forms to inhabit her from far across the multiverse. She had been a place of great cooperation until other humans who were service to self beings intervened in the grand experiment and caused a terrible imbalance to occur there. Then others claimed her as their own and everything went sideways.

This led to great wars, pole shifts, and the destruction of her original land masses and mutations to the genetic sequencing of the developing human races there. These mutations were dramatic alterations of the original carefully planned human DNA causing subsequent generations of earth humans to be disconnected from Source and their brethren everywhere. As a result, most Terran humans were unaware the multiverse was teaming with life including their own ancestors to say nothing of the multitude of light beings and extra-Terran beings who had a hand in the earth project to begin with. It also paved the way for more parasitic races to come to earth and start colonizing the planet.

Because earth humans were also disconnected from their memories of who they are, from the earth that is their home, and their innumerable innate gifts, coupled with the interference of these service to self races, Earth became a place of survival of the fittest. Her resources stolen and exploited by the very human earth guardians under the influence of negative galactic races, many who lived deep underground or in the shadows or out in the open disguised as humans and cooperating with the various world governments. Over time, the vibration of earth dropped so low, Gaia, an advance conscious being herself, had no choice but to put out a call for help.

Zhang and Simon were being debriefed on Pleiades Star 7 when they both heard that call being broadcast, the message dropped into their consciousness like a song that just won't leave your head.

They'd just completed yet another successful mission, this time with a mixed crew of Leonid and Mantoid beings and positive Reptilians who brought with them three grays who basically served as canon fodder. He and Simon were the only humans on the team.

"We need to go," Simon suggested.

"Go where?" Zhang asked signing off on their report with flourish. His signature was comprised of nothing but a sloppy wiggly line. The gray droid tasked with the information gathering seemed to frown as he regarded the illegible mark, those bulbous eyes judging him. Zhang ignored it and turned to look at Simon.

"Terra Earth."

They had 8 solar rotations before their next assignment, a reconnaissance mission to gather intelligence about some illegal trafficking going on in the U11/Orion's belt. They'd planned to take it easy in the meantime. He had heard there was a new retreat and spa with an advanced meditation pod in Sector 9 created by the Arcturians, master healers in their own right, that he hoped to enjoy with his partner.

"Way over there?" Earth was in a remote sector of the galaxy and he'd heard she had been a planet in crisis for some time. "Sounds like work."

Simon snorted. "It's the greatest show on earth and the place to be. We can't miss it. It's been prophesized that the light there will transmute all contrast and Terran humans will lead multiple star systems in ascending an entire dimensional frequency. Gaia just needs a bit of help."

"You do realize it's a call for assistance and not for front row seats." Zhang frowned as they strode to their shuttle craft in their gleaming white spacesuits. Zhang gave his partner a side look and smirked. Simon looked great as usual in the form fitting suit. His slightly whitish blonde hair cut bluntly just past his shoulders. His pinkish red eyes were in sharp contrast to Zhang's own blue orbs and that of most of their people. Those beautiful iridescent eyes distinguished Simon as part Neubin, a race of highly advanced light beings known for their ability to anchor energies at the highest realms. Thus, his presence had a calming effect to say nothing of how beautiful he was. In all other respects they had similar builds, coloring and style of hair, pale features and wide almond eyes as did the rest of the population on their planet.

At 8-feet-tall and with muscular builds they cut an imposing figure although they both were dwarfed by a visiting colleague on their last mission, a reptilian who stood at near 15 feet and gave Zhang the willies.

"It will be a bit of both," Simon grinned. "Since when are you not up for the challenge? We've been on dangerous missions just about everywhere."

"Since you got us lost and then stuck in that ice cold tundra and we almost froze to death all because you forgot to bring the Gamma 3 device that would have informed us we were heading straight towards that frozen hell hole!" Zhang reminded. Simon pouted, his look apologetic.

"Jeez! You had one job, Neubin!" Zhang jabbed at him. In all seriousness it had been an extra complicated mission requiring them to extract lava core samples from deep within a newly birthed planet. Already a man short due to a last-minute reassignment, the galactic confederation higher ups nonetheless assured them they'd be fine alone. How hard could it be to retrieve a few samples of lava core?

Of course, they failed to mention the lava core was in Altarian territory. Shortly after leaving they were fired upon and then relentlessly pursued by highly agile Altarian light craft. Their shuttle craft was heavily damaged necessitating their evacuation and with their navigation shot to hell they veered way off course and got lost. In the end not only did they lose the core samples they'd carefully extracted when they had to escape in the uber-cramped two-man pod as they fled for their lives, Simon left the Gamma 3 Detector device under his seat. To make up for it he insisted on doing the calculations by hand (he was horrible at calculations) which only exacerbated their predicament. They survived only by eating snow and ice.

Zhang refused to talk to him for the 96 years they were lost together even though they were forced to sleep skin to skin the whole time to stay alive when their protective suits failed. As they lived thousands of years, the 96 years he refused to talk to Simon was really only the equivalent of about four and a half earth days. Still, he made his point by giving him the cold shoulder, no pun intended.

"You're still mad about that? It was an honest mistake given I was busy trying to provide defensive cover at the same time sending them unconditional love while you figured out how to work the escape pod release in the first place." Simon shot back still giving him that pout.

"I've never had to escape before so how was I to know it was a simple "press and release" system?" He countered. He knew no one else on Sirius XO51129 who had that same disarming look as Simon which was why it was so hard to resist or stay mad at him for any length of time. They both grinned at each other.

The new suits not only looked good but thus far also functioned well ensuring their protection from the changing conditions on the various planets and more importantly provide the consistent atmosphere necessary to sustain their physical bodies. It took care of their basic needs as well as more advanced chemical and biological bodily functions, both monitoring and adjusting their physical, and emotional states as necessary. After their mishap on Lido in Fornax, they'd also made the suits laser and blast proof. In short, the high vibrational suits courtesy of the engineering team were a welcome upgrade considering the previous itineration of protective gear always malfunctioned, and then had been damaged to hell during the skirmish with the Altarians, to say nothing of the confederation's own misfiring laser defense system.

Although members of the Science and Exploration away team, and occasionally providing logistics and strategy support, it wasn't unusual to encounter resistance on their missions or come under attack. Thus, they were provided with high tech defensive equipment all the same. The operative word being defensive though they could be lethal. As beings in service to others, unlike those who provided contrast like the Altarians, who were resonating yet at the lower frequencies despite their technological prowess, Sirians like he and Simon served the Light and were officers of the galactic confederation. Thus, they were tasked with spreading light and peaceful awareness through sending the energy of unconditional love, the force behind all things. Source Light.

Their people had evolved away from the lower frequencies including the use of violence millions upon millions of years ago. But their cooperation with the confederation meant they encountered many different beings in their work including those whose vibrations were below the cut. And when there was an occasional slip even amongst them, someone was always there to help restore them back into balance.

"It sounds like fun. Besides everybody whose anybody is going to help. It's all hands-on deck." Leave it to Simon whose always optimistic, yet pragmatic outlook made a shit show like their last assignment which almost got them both killed, sound like fun, not to mention an Earth mission.

"How about we hit that retreat in Sector 9 the Arcturians have going on and plug into the meditation pod?" He suggested instead.

"Meditation pod? That sounds a bit lame. Why can we not just plug into the mind waves of Athala on the H-Deck and tune into the high frequencies available to us right on the mothership? We should reach her in a few moments." The mind waves of Athala were basically a user-friendly AI program, one of many endless experiences available on the hologram deck or H-Deck for short on the mothership Athena.

Despite its sheer genius, there was usually a long queue to use the H-Deck given the experiences one could create were endless and extremely realistic thus it was a favorite escape for officers, crew and visiting dignitaries alike. Zhang really didn't feel like queuing up just to meditate. To him the H-Deck was best used for more vivid experiences like paintball, playing earth basketball or even golf, which he excelled at and enjoyed.

"Really? Somehow, I knew you'd say that. I just want to relax at the retreat, maybe get a massage, lay by the infinity pool and tune out. I hear the meditation pod is incredible! I've been dying to try it out and focus on strengthening my qi."

Simon looked at him with great pity, those pink orbs gazing into his soul. "Alright, I understand. I see that you need real rest. How about I submit both our names for candidacy for the earth mission and also accompany you to Sector 9."

Zhang was too tired to argue and took his place at the control panel in their shuttle craft. "Yeah, whatever."

Famous last words.

CHAPTER TWELVE

The Retreat and the Near Screw up in Betelgeuse

"I can't believe they charged us for the use of the facilities. I thought the Arcturians were the boon of compassion and healing in this sector of the galaxy," Zhang complained as he fired up their craft to return back to the mothership.

"Didn't you read the brochure? It said it was a love donation for upkeep." Simon shrugged looking fully refreshed and grinning, his pinkish red orbs shining with mirth.

"Donation? Aren't they seventh dimensional beings? Who still uses currency anyway?"

"Apparently the Arcturians," Simon volunteered still grinning. Thankfully they were able to use the replicator on their shuttle craft to create the necessary tokens and get in. Otherwise, the trip there would have been a total wash. He had to admit he did feel great.

Aside from that minor hiccup, the spa facilities were top notch. The spa and retreat consisted of eight oblong shaped buildings set on 6 hectares of beautifully manicured grounds situated high on a bluff. Thus, it gave off the impression of being exclusive yet spacious while still having a cozy feel to it. The female half Mantis/half human therapist who gave him a massage was drop dead gorgeous with those wraparound eyes and in addition to working out the kinks in his 8-foot-tall body, she also put him into a relaxing state with her hypnotic singing voice and use of crystals.

Afterwards, he visited the famous meditation pod where he promptly fell unconscious (dead asleep). Meanwhile Simon got a facial and then relaxed by the pool to watch the sunset and sunrise at its unique 4 hour intervals while chatting with other retreat guests.

Before leaving they were provided with green and white layered protein drinks to nourish their bodies that tasted slightly sweet and immediately made them feel invigorated. The drinks consisted of specially made ingredients, the glass topped with a beautiful, rare orange flower found only in the Arcturus star system. Zhang also noticed a fizzy sensation in his brain after tanking his drink in one go and that suddenly his thoughts seemed clearer. He reminded himself to use the replicator to make more of it later on.

"Where to commander?" Simon asked in a chipper mood.

"Well, we're not due back for another 7 solar rotations before that U11 mission. How about we head over to the belt in advance to check out Betelgeuse next door? We can easily meet the rest of the crew at the rallying point from there."

Simon readily agreed. They'd both been told that a segment of Betelgeuse in Orion was a free zone with just about every vice available in the galaxy at their disposal. There was a little bit of everything from exotic skin, gambling, virtual gaming, shopping for rare and questionable artifacts, to medicinal and mind-altering plant substances and drinks to be experienced first-hand. It was a veritable carnival in their book and as long as they watched their backs since they would be rubbing elbows with lower vibing service-to-self beings, there was no harm in indulging a little bit.

The neon-esque signs pointing to U11 could be seen from quite a distance away in space. It took them less than several moments to arrive from their position using the particle bend drive and find parking. The place was teeming with all sorts of life forms from just about every sector of the galaxy including non-Terran humans and resembled a huge shopping district with bars, eateries, gambling dens, pharmacies and gaming and virtual establishments several stories high as far as the eye could see. The place had a vibe of excitement.

Standing at the edge of the district, they both laughed, their excitement building as they took it all in. Orion was a place of experiences with a reputation for living up to its name. It was also a place of refuge on account of its free zone status, and attracted all kinds of elements, including fugitives. As long as they watched out for each other and kept their noses relatively clean, they had nothing much to worry about.

They easily located the information station after walking down the main drag a short ways. Being trained as they were in all sorts of missions, they both naturally sought to familiarize themselves with the layout and places they wanted to check out, possible entries and exit points.

As they waited their turn to access an information droid, Simon was approached by a female Alnitakan, the bluish horn in the center of her massive forehead indicating she was in heat. She was dwarfed by their height, no more than 4.5 feet tall, had grayish blue skin that hung in folds and thin layers around her that gave the skin on her pear-shaped body a wrinkled appearance. Her usual 3 cloved feet were encased in black heels. She otherwise wore no clothes.

"Hey handsome! How about a free ride on my horn," she said in a sing-songy voice.

Zhang snorted beside Simon.

"That's very kind of you but perhaps another time for me. I'm here to try some mind-altering liquids. But my friend here may be interested," Simon grinned pointing to Zhang who gave him a look.

"Tell you what, I can let you both take turns riding since you come together," she said sashaying between them to take both their arms in hers.

"What's your name?" Zhang asked, staring down at the hook shaped horn glinting on her massive forehead and wincing. He couldn't imagine anyone riding on anything shaped like that and surviving the ordeal. Still, not wanting to insult another conscious being he decided to engage her while waiting for the droid.

"My name's Lekran. What are your names?"

"I'm Simon and he's Zhang."

"First time here?"

"Yes." They both answered in unison, Simon grinning.

"Well, you are in luck! The bar I work at just around the corner is offering free drinks for newcomers."

"Mind altering drinks?" Simon piped up, excited.

"You bet! Ha! You boys aren't from around here, are you? Are you Pleiadeans?"

"No—"

"Yes—"

They answered in unison. She laughed and pulled them along. "Come on, it doesn't matter. Everyone is welcome here except the dregs from the confederation. They are always trying to shut the place down." They exchanged a look with each other as she led them around the bend. Simon shrugged and laughed. "Well, we wouldn't want those confederation dregs to do anything like that!"

As soon as they rounded the corner, they were in front of a huge 3 story establishment with a large blue neon sign that blazed "Cheap Skin" in script Zhang recognized as from a small moon orbiting Bellatrix in Orion. The blazing blue light made Lekran's horn seem even more ominous. It was then they could see the implant pulsing in the tip of her horn. Zhang couldn't immediately tell what it was for but suspected it was some sort of tracking or tagging device.

They both hesitated for a split second, brows furrowed until they saw the impossibly long wraparound bar with more blue neon lights inside behind which were hundreds of colorful bottles lined up in rows on high shelves.

Mind altering liquids!

They stepped inside grinning like idiots.

A gray being with a huge cranium and spindly arms and legs wearing an unwelcoming expression approached from their left in a threatening manner as if to stop them from going further but Lekran quickly intervened.

"They're good! They're with me!" She smiled sweetly at the bouncer who let off and only eyed them warily as she led them toward the huge bar. As they approached seats were made available to them.

"What's with your friend over there?" Zhang nodded back toward the spindly gray bouncer as they settled in and she waved at the bartender - a humanoid looking mole in a tuxedo.

"I thought all were welcome here," he followed up observing Simon as he spoke. Simon had extraordinary gifts of intuition that alerted them of any impending danger but he seemed to be more interested in studying the bartender out of curiosity rather than alarm, so Zhang relaxed a bit. He could also detect discordant energy, another gift as a Neubin hybrid and provide calming energies if needed.

The mole people were a hybrid project of the beings on Polaris, Earth's current North Star, who were famous for their outrageous half human/half animal creations. They had made quite the name for themselves, (the Polarians not the mole beings), as the Gods of ancient Egypt. He'd met the jackal headed "God" Anubis once on the mothership Athena in passing and in Zhang's opinion he was arrogant as hell. He had to admit he was possessed of powerful innate abilities as well as technologies. His staff alone was a formidably curious tool though most of the time Zhang only saw him use it as a walking stick or to poke people in his way. Zhang couldn't help wondering now why a Polarian creation like this guy would end up peddling drinks on Betelgeuse dressed in a tuxedo.

"We've had some trouble with the confederation hitting up this place and sending spies.   So, Zander's a bit sensitive."

Just then the bartender came over and wiped the counter before them. "What can I get you two?" Zhang could see from the way his little brown nose rapidly moved he was sniffing them out.

Simon immediately leaned forward and pointed to a red bottle on a high shelf. "What's that?" Despite appearing to not be engaged, Zhang knew Simon was tuned into their conversation. He had a number of other gifts, one of which was remote listening, and an ability to pick up and tune into multiple conversations and sounds at once making him

95

excellent at communications and data gathering. And because he had such a calm and friendly disposition he blended in well and no one would be the wiser he was constantly listening in.

The bartender smiled, baring his little teeth at Simon who leaned back slightly. "That? We call that Dragon Fire. Just a little bit of that stuff will make you forget your name!"

"Yeah? We'll have that then!" Simon said gleefully speaking for them both. Zhang shook his head and laughed as the bartender went to retrieve the bottle and two shot glasses.

"What are you having?" Zhang asked turning to Lekran who stood between them carefully observing them although she only smiled flirtatiously.

"Me? I'm on duty so nothing for me," she answered. "Are you boys together?" She asked looking from one to the other curiously.

"You could say that. We grew up together," Zhang responded careful not to reveal too much. The last thing they wanted was to reveal their identities and that they were officers of the confederation to boot given they wouldn't be welcome otherwise. He saw no harm in indulging in a little mind-altering fun while waiting for their next mission to begin. After all there was no admonition in the confederation to visiting the place, he was certain. Besides they'd both worked pretty hard these last ten or so missions and deserved a break. Why not indulge a bit?

He scanned the crowd. In the sea of beings crammed in the joint while he did spot a few other humans milling around he couldn't immediately tell their origin. The rest were a conglomeration of reptiles, hybrids like mole guy, grays, Ebens, amphibians and other exotic races like Lekran of the male, female and androgynous persuasion. The place was hopping with an upbeat party atmosphere. There was even a bit of rhythmic drumming and string music being played with a few people dancing in a corner.

Lekran smiled, her tiny round eyes sparkling at Zhang's half-efforted answer. He could instantly tell by looking at her that she was tamping her true self down, putting on an air of seductive coyness to bring customers in and keep them engaged when she really probably hated every asshole that walked in the joint, including them.

He also ventured her pimp was somewhere watching them closely ready to kick the crap out of them should they get out of hand with her. His eyes went to her horn again and he shuddered. She'd have no problem with them tonight.

"Why is the confederation so interested in this place?" Zhang asked still impassively observing their surroundings. "It looks like just about every other establishment here." He noted there was a lift bay to the right of the bar beside which were a replica of ancient looking wooden stairs that led to the second and likely third levels. The place had no windows at least none that he could see on the first level. Patrons with apparently female workers were walking up and down the stairs, arm in arm. He saw no immediate sign anything was amiss.

She shrugged. "The word is they are looking for trafficked beings, I suppose. Apparently, there's a huge market for earth humans across the galaxy, and a number are thought to make their way here." Lekran shrugged looking indifferent.

Trafficked humans? Was that what their upcoming mission was about? He must have misread the report as he had thought they were hunting black market minerals which were a valuable commodity in some sectors with beings coming from the farthest reaches of the galaxy to procure them.

"Just humans?" Zhang pressed. He had heard trafficking and human slavery was a bit of a problem in times past but had thought the confederation had that under wraps. He recalled an operation from less than a generation ago that successfully rescued enslaved humans who were taken to a mothership for healing before repatriation back to earth. But that was long before their assignment to the confederation.

"As far as I know," she said. Something about the way she responded gave Zhang pause. Before he could suss her out further the bartender placed their shot glasses before them on the bar.

"Bottoms up!"

Simon raised his glass in toast. Zhang reached for his glass with a grin, eager to try the mind-numbing substance when a blinding flash from behind lit the place up followed by loud screams and a familiar crackling sound near the door that made the hairs on his arms stand up. They both recognized it as a Hamaker Laser Weapon set to stun used by the confederation. Another such blast when slightly altered could be lethal. He grabbed Lekran to shield her as he and Simon hit the floor.

Simon still had his shot glass in hand. Ducking his head, he took a quick sip and grimaced. Zhang shook his head and looked behind them to see Gunner, Alpha6 and eight reptilians from the confederation, weapons at the ready, looking sharp in their tight-fitting white suits entering the place, the same white suits he and Simon also happened to be wearing.

Zhang groaned. Everyone from the door to the bar was crouched down like them, head bowed. "Keep your head down, kid," he said to Lekran who was frowning up at him as if calling him out.

"Hey, I never said we were not from the confederation," Zhang said in their defense with a sheepish look.

"Everyone stay down and don't move!" One of the reptilian commandos growled raising the hair even on Zhang's arms. Given the enormous size of the reptilians that dwarfed everybody in the place, not to mention their fierce look, no one was foolish enough to disobey. Gunner immediately spotted him crouched down and made a strange face before he made a beeline straight for them.

"Commander! Lieutenant! What are you two doing here?" Gunner was a Pleiadean human and built roughly like them. Even their blonde hair and blue eyes had people mistaking the two races for the other. The truth of the matter was that they were related as humans went, having common origins in the Lyran star system before the Orion wars. The

Sirians however were a far older race and had several frequency bands over them, thus were considered the parents of the Pleiadeans and the grandparents to earth humans.

Zhang sighed and glanced at Simon who had the good sense to finish the drink in his shot glass before standing up. "Reconnaissance?"

Seeing his glass was still untouched on the bar, Simon, looking serious, pushed it over to him slowly muttering, "To our careers."

Zhang followed his partner's lead and downed the glass ignoring the liquid heat that raged like molten fire down his throat and into his belly. He was vaguely aware of Lekran peeking up at him, a look of suspicion and shock on her face.

Zhang grabbed her arm pulling her to her feet and led the way out of the bar. This was the beginning and ending of their very short adventure to Betelgeuse and how they rescued a trafficked Alnitakan named Lekran.

The bartender lied. Not only did they not forget their names, they realized soon after that the drink was nothing more than a concoction of dihydrogen oxide and capsaicin ($C_{18}H_{27}NO_3$). In short, it was chili water. This indeed saved them and lent credence to their mutually concocted story that they had gotten intel about other trafficked skin workers besides earth humans and decided to check it out in advance of the U11 mission.

Little did they know that since Simon had signed them up as candidates for the earth mission, they automatically had gotten bumped from the U11 mission to begin with and had been replaced by Gunner and Alpha6. The mission itself advanced by 7 solar rotations. Neither he nor Simon had bothered to check the mission roster for updates when it was broadcast. As Zhang had been dead asleep in the meditation pod and Simon was lounging at the pool and yabbering with other guests watching the sunrise and sunsets at the retreat in Arcturus, both had missed the transmission.

"Well done! Both of you! Apparently that Alnitakan worker had been enslaved for some time before you boys rescued her. She'd been forcibly taken from her home and sent there to work. Your quick thinking enabled us to identify her as a being at risk given we had only been scheduled to rescue the earth humans."

Zhang and Simon stood there at attention, staring straight ahead and wisely said nothing as their commanding officer Captain Olin Alpha1 went on. "Given your foresight, initiative and incredible bravery going in alone as you had, I've submitted my recommendations to the Earth Everlight committee to consider both of you with our highest commendations. Congratulations boys! You are going to Earth!"

Simon secretly clapped inside while Zhang quietly swore.

CHAPTER THIRTEEN

Earth Incarnation Sucks - WhereIn we Become Earth Humans

Zhang looked around confused.

What the —

Just moments before he had been standing in a short line beneath a flashing red sign that said "Now Boarding-Priority Seating" while talking to a guy from Rigel who was also heading to Earth. The next moment he was naked, upside down, covered in some horrible smelling muck and being smacked hard on the ass. Worse, he was in a miniature, wrinkled human body. He yelled out in protest and found that he could only muster a pitiful high pitch wail that grated on his own ears.

Just what the hell was happening here?

Mencius, his Master Guide, was standing beside a man wearing a green physician's outfit who still had him by the feet - - the bastard who hit him.

Mencius was looking his tiny, wrinkled body over with a rather pleased expression. He was dressed in a dark purple and black gown that glimmered in the harsh lighting of the tiny spartan room, the walls white-washed, an odd chemical smell to the air. His jet-black shoulder length hair was slightly wavy and adorned with what looked like an inverted gold crown that dipped to a "V" at his forehead. He looked younger than Zhang remembered seeing him and had a princely bearing.

"I dressed up for the occasion," Mencius explained without moving his lips. Zhang frowned at him.

"What is this bullshit?" Zhang screamed but rather than his own usually melodic voice, he only heard that loud grating wail in his ears, startling him. He found he couldn't really control his arms or legs and his head seemed to weigh a ton.

Had he come in paralyzed?

Everything seemed slow and heavy in his strange form. Tamping down the panic, he recalled the 3 months of intensive training for the mission he'd undergone with his partner and the extra class on the Earth birthing process they both signed up for. *So this was it? I'm in?*

He snorted. No matter how many times he studied it back at the briefings, it didn't compare at all to what he was experiencing. He glanced over at Mencius and gave him a look that said as much. Someone needed to update that birthing class manual.

"Remember Earth is third density. So, you have to allow some time to acclimate to your new physical form. Believe me when I tell you that's the least of your worries here," Mencius said telepathically and moved closer to him. He began to speak in earnest, his voice now soothing. Zhang leaned in to listen, the guide's familiar voice providing him a measure of calm. He yawned.

"Do your best to resist the forgetting process. That's the most important thing. It happens once the conditioning begins at around age 4 or 5."

"Four or five. Got it!"

"Your partner will be arriving in approximately 18 earth months. You should be able to recognize him quite easily once you meet in 28.5 earth years. Everything is set up according to plan."

Zhang nodded already switching to mission mode.

Mencius continued, "After meeting your partner things will escalate quite quickly and get a little hairy but you are both fully prepared not to mention capable for this mission. Stick with the plan we discussed, reveal the corruption and take down the Artists Association and government here and all will be well. We will be standing by observing you from the higher planes."

"Got it! Wait, what? The government, too? That wasn't in the plan, was it? If that's the case, we might need some extra time here."

"Expose one and the other will follow. Don't forget now. Things work a bit differently here as Earth is a free will planet. That means your guides can't intercede unless you ask except for dire emergencies. This will all change once the veil drops even further."

"Yeah, so you said." He bemoaned aloud. Once again it came out as a grating wail.

"Good luck! By the way you are so adorable like this!" Mencius smiled before he vanished. Zhang felt the absence of his immense presence immediately followed by a cold chill. Thankfully he was quickly swaddled in a blanket by a nurse who handed him off to a woman— his "mother" who lay reclined in a medical bed. She looked like hell. Her short jet-black hair was matted and plastered to her forehead with sweat and her skin was flush like she'd run for miles. Her humble white be-speckled cotton garb hung messily off her right shoulder, though she was possessed of a kind smile and narrow, dainty Asian features.

He wondered about this then remembered only moments earlier he'd been violently pulled out of her belly. He shuddered. He reminded himself to be kind to her throughout his earth years. Earth life was indeed as brutal as they warned.

She looked very happy despite having just given birth to him. His heart warmed seeing her. When he looked in her eyes, he instantly recognized the chief information officer from the Athena. She had always been exceedingly helpful to him preparing for all of his galactic missions and ensuring everything was in good working order before chiding him to take good care of himself. Whenever he returned and checked all his equipment back in, she was there to warmly welcome him. In that form, she was a 1.5-meter-tall gray with large almond shaped eyes that wrapped practically around her head. He'd been told she'd been reassigned to another unit shortly after the return of their last mission to retrieve the lava cores. It must have been to incarnate on earth as his mother.

"Dina! How are you? I'd wondered where the hell you went off to!" He greeted her happily with a wail but rather than answer him she grabbed ahold of his bundled form and promptly stuffed a pale round teet into his gaping mouth, instantly silencing him. The shock of it all was quickly replaced as a warm milky nectar flooded his mouth. It was like mana from the heavens making him think of nothing else but floating on clouds and the beautiful sunsets on Sirius XO51129.

He sighed and settled in against her warm bosom and happily suckled away. It appeared this earth mission business was going to be a breeze after all.

Meanwhile Simon watched it all on the big 40' x 40' screen from the comfort of the Round Room on the mothership Athena parked 8.5 light years away. He was laughing his head off and exchanging high fives together with about 400 others who were supporting the mission or who just came by to watch Commander Zhang incarnate as a 3D human. From the sounds of laughter around him, everyone was having a good time of it. The females in the group all oohed and aww'd as he made his slimy appearance out of the birth canal. Despite being covered in birth muck, Simon had to agree he was a cutie.

"He really is adorable, isn't he?" Simon said to no one in particular then stuffed a handful of cherry nuts into his mouth. He had ordered a whole bowl full of them from the cafeteria just for the occasion and rushed to get front row seats to watch his partner in action. He now stared proudly at the mega screen marveling at the odd noises coming out of Zhang's little mouth although he could hear his thoughts as clear as day. As could they all. Zhang's bewilderment and every thought was being broadcast telepathically through the 5th through 9th dimensional bands in the communication array. For all they knew everyone in Sectors 9 through 20 was getting an earful.

Apparently, Zhang had forgotten he'd be flying into the tiny human body after being ejected off the incarnation belt, the shocked look on his little face and the vile expletives that came out of his mouth were absolutely priceless. Simon pressed the panel before him and took a quick screen shot before saving it to his L-382 smart pad. He reminded himself to show it to Zhang when he got back to the mothership, certain he'd get a kick out of it.

When Mencius made his appearance, everybody clapped in reverence, even commenting how great he looked and how well he cleaned up. They all agreed how lucky it was to have a master guide, which was common protocol, especially one so experienced, attend to the birth. Seeing a familiar face went a long way to comforting a newly incarnated human from the initial shock. Except in Zhang's case. He looked pissed.

"That was something, wasn't it?" Bradoc4 said from the seat beside him. He was an accomplished medical officer and tactician and also a Sirian human scheduled to make the jump to earth in a few short earth months. Unlike Simon and Zhang, he was heading to Cameroon on the African continent to provide future medical support. The three of them had all grown up together on Sirius XO51129 and had joined the galactic confederation and been assigned to the Athena around the same time.

"He sure didn't seem to see that coming." They both laughed until they had tears in their eyes. Simon's heart swelled. There was no one in the galaxy quite like his soul mate, he was certain. Zhang had a way of looking at things that made him suitable for earth life. He was certainly much more grounded and philosophical about things, seeing directly through an issue and asserting his opinion in a way that was both humorous and honest. He was an old soul and wise despite his posturing, his highest incarnation being at the 8th dimensional band where he was an Ascended Master like Mencius. Despite his sometimes-cranky nature, Simon could sense the depth of all of his incarnations in his 7th dimensional Sirian form, which was currently crammed in a stasis pod in the med bay as would he be in a few earth months for the duration of their earth mission.

When one incarnated elsewhere a small part of the vastness that was one's soul or spirit of all one's incarnations were encapsulated in their new incarnation. Sometimes they chose to transition out of their current form and just incarnate elsewhere in another body or form. Other times like the now moment, they packed their bodies in cold storage and stuffed them in an unused warehouse of sorts while the new incarnation was on its journey. He and Zhang once stumbled upon a few ancient stasis pods while scrounging around on the mothership for scraps to barter. The beings in them looked partially dried up due to a pod malfunction. Others were crammed two or three to a pod. It was the stuff of nightmares.

The medical officer who would be overseeing their physical forms while he and Zhang were incarnated on earth assured them this would not happen to them given the advance in technologies. Still, they found it a bit strange and honestly, a little disrespectful to the beings involved and voiced their concern.

Seeing their dismay, the medical officer stridently reassured them the damage was just cosmetic and nothing a little saline water and nitrogen salts couldn't easily repair. They had their doubts, nonetheless. The last thing they needed was to return and their beautiful muscular bodies were shriveled up like corpses. Zhang would really kill Simon then for pushing the mission.

Simon was confident that Zhang was fully capable of completing the mission with top honors and thus there was little to worry about. All one's memories and abilities from each of one's incarnations across the planes could be accessed as needed across all incarnations. And now that he was a 3D earth human, all Zhang had to do was not forget who he really was.

By age 5, Zhang forgot 99.99%.

What he didn't forget and which Mencius reminded him every day of his earth incarnation that was indelibly inscribed in his heart was this: Your job Zhang is to demonstrate through your earthly experience what it means to be human and still rise above the occasion. This is your role as an Ascended Master.

CHAPTER FOURTEEN

Simon's Origins

His home planet was a deep red and gaseous. Whenever one walked upon the surface of the perfect sphere, it was as if the planet rotated beneath one's feet much like in a dream. The illusion was created by the winds that blew close to the surface and stirred up the tiny sediments there. The color and make up from a distance and on approach to Neubin, a 9th ascending to the 10th frequency band planet, was like that of the Ring Nebula. To a physical being, the planet seemed deserted of sentient life but in fact was the home of millions of light beings living in beautiful cities of light both on the surface and in beautiful underground crystal caverns. The days and nights were one, the sky always painted an orange reddish hue due to its high nitrogen content. Their oceans in contrast were a brilliant aquamarine in color, as it was rife with oxygen. All knew it as the piercing color of the eyes of the Archangels who were their parents and grandparents who birthed Neubin together with the Time Lords, beings who made all physical matter possible, including planets.

Neubin's sands were a fine pink— the color and floaty texture of earth-made cotton candy. The planet itself was relatively small, no more than 700 miles in diameter, just slightly bigger than Ceres near earth's sun, her surface flat with very few land features, trees or plants. But those that grew were of intense greens, blues and browns, massive in height and girth, providing tremendous amounts of shade and oxygen although as light beings it was more for aesthetics than necessity.

Everything else envisioned was a product of one's will to call it into existence. Created by thought alone. Much like a hologram, beaches, parks and mountain scenes, flowers, 'shopping' malls and holographic theaters were all called into existence by the mind and heart space alone.

During their last collective ascension millions of light years past, the beings of light on Neubin had reached the 9th dimensional frequency band. All were of one mind although each also retained their separate consciousness. Thus, when one experienced ecstasy, it was experienced by all. If one were to experience sadness, all would experience it collectively. At these higher dimensions, the ability to permanently sustain a high vibration was innate. Thus, even if it were possible for one to drop in vibration the experience would be fleeting as to not exist at all, likened to a scientist on earth impassively studying some such phenomena and then setting it aside to study something else.

The entire planet could be moved at will with just a thought and no one would be the wiser. Its current coordinates were just outside the M7 Open Cluster in the Constellation Scorpius.

Simon's true form was that of light. While they could assume a physical form, more like a wispy humanoid shape, very few on Neubin chose to do so. They often assisted earth Terrans and beings of other evolving civilizations by remaining close to them at all times, protecting their bodies and energy fields from harmful vibrations. Those who could see interdimensionally would see them as amorphous or wispy light or even as "angels" when they took on a slightly denser physical form.

As with all sparks of Source, the desire to experience and create and thus evolve was innate. Each experience added to the collective whole that was Source, the goal being to experience and create while eventually returning back to Source. The farther one moved from the Light the greater the risk of forgetting one's true origin is Source Light and they are beings in service to others, beings of unconditional love.

As part of the drive to experience and create, it wasn't uncommon to have numerous incarnations on different planes. Thus, as a 9th dimensional being ascending to the 10th, he chose to have a part of his consciousness incarnate in the physical in the 7th dimension. As he had always thought the Sirian human form beautiful, he didn't hesitate to choose it.

Both he and Zhang had been conceived on Sirius XO51129 under the sign of Hegen and the auspicious new moon a little over a thousand earth years prior. Thus, it was no coincidence they were soul mates and best of friends. Simon's mother, a true Sirian human had met his father, a Neubin light being on a mission and decided to become a union to host his creation.

Zhang's parents on the other hand were both Sirian humans. Both Simon's mother and Zhang's parents were of the Science and Exploration clan or family thus it was only natural that children conceived by intention to join the clan would also be part of the Science and Exploration clan. Even then as fully conscious beings the decision to create another life form to join the clan was a collective one. The prospective incoming soul was asked why they wished to join the clan and assuming their answers were satisfactory, they were welcomed once all clan members were also in full agreement. Thus, ensuring a warm, collective welcome and upbringing by all.

As fully conscious beings from the time they were born and raised in the collective they knew they were soul mates the moment they laid eyes on each other. It was a soul level thing. They had been two years old and in class when their names were called. ZhangZHXO511. SimonGJXO1129. From that moment on they were inseparable and did everything together, even challenge their elders and accepting the loving consequences afterwards.

Neubins love to be of service as it is their nature. They work collectively to influence the beings they protect in ways that preserve their life force. On earth they are known as the seraphim although some earth religions have confused them with other beings.

Many Neubins were currently on assignment on earth to assist with planetary ascension and serving as angelic guides to earth humans. Thus, even those who chose not to directly participate through an earth incarnation or as guides were on motherships or on Neubin observing and having a front row seat to the greatest show in this sector of the multiverse.

Their close proximity also enabled those who had incarnated on earth to benefit from the extremely high frequencies the planet was transmitting in collaboration with many other planets, motherships, and beings both light and physical. All who offered energetic support to raise the frequencies of Earth Terrans and aide Earth in her upward movement in frequency.

"You were born a star." His father once told him as apparently all Neubin parents told their kids. *Created with the same force and energy that creates the entire cosmos. Thus, the energy that creates worlds flows through you. All are sparks of light. Nothing is ever miscreated.* Simon's heart and soul had swam with that lofty knowledge shaping his consciousness and defining his very being.

But as he sat across from his temporary partner, an Adharan named Bonti who looked pretty much like a fat green toad, he wondered if his father had just been pulling his leg. Simon kept his eyes averted and instead focused on the boots encasing his feet.

"So, I told my wife, listen…if you want to create more tadpoles, go ahead. What do I care? Leave me out of it. She's already birthed about a million of those little buggers since we met at the Orion way station, ha ha ha—"

"Uh-huh." Simon nodded. This guy hadn't stopped talking since they first introduced themselves to each other in the shuttle bay of the Athena. Boy did he miss Zhang. Had they been on assignment together Zhang would be going over all of the details with him instead of yabbering on about his wife's reproductive capabilities. Zhang would be also flying the light craft and he'd be right next to him providing navigation and technical support. He wondered now how Zhang was doing and if he had made the right choice in encouraging him to participate in the earth mission.

At any rate he would be making the jump himself in a few earth months' time and they'd be together again. He told himself for the umpteenth time he needn't ever worry about his partner. Not only was Zhang capable, he was determined. And stubborn as hell. That alone had to be worth something even on a planet in crisis like Earth. And once he made the jump himself, he'd be able to look after him from the ground. He also knew the guides had things in hand and were guiding Zhang along. Still, he couldn't help but worry.

"We are making the approach to Z145. It's a bit bumpy so hang on tight." The captain droned over the speaker system. Everyone on this six-man crew was new to him. It had been awhile since he'd worked with strangers like this but they were all from the science and exploration teams of their respective planets save the pilot and his Reptilian navigator/warrior named Zeeter so it was expected to be just another routine mission. In and out in less than a single rotation's time. He'd only accepted the assignment so he wouldn't be glued to his smart pad observing Zhang's every belch and diaper change out of worry for him and instead could keep his mind occupied.

He checked and double checked his space suit and helmet. The tiny planet 18 light years from where the Athena was parked was directly on the other side of the Earth in a sector of the galaxy earthlings had yet to explore. He sighed. *Earth again.* He needed to stop worrying.

"Are you married, Simon? My sister-in-law is single and still looking. Beats me why as she's quite the looker. I think it would be interesting if someone like yourself hooked up with her. Wouldn't it be something if her tadpoles had those pinkish red eyes of yours. Ha! Ha! Ha! Ha! Hell, that would be pretty shitty, wouldn't it! Man, I don't even know how you even see out of those things!"

Simon rolled his eyes and braced himself for landing. His father had definitely been pulling his leg.

As soon as the ship touched down Simon was out of his seat, unbuckling his harness and grabbing his gear. After Zeeter checked the perimeter Simon was the next one off of the ship, pushing ahead while Bonti struggled to unbuckle his harness.

"Hey! A little help here, partner? I think this thing's stuck on a fold or something—"

Simon ignored him. According to his smart pad readings there was no sentient life present on the planet but his innate senses told him differently. As he tuned in he could feel them acutely. He turned toward the direction of a small bluff ahead to listen more fully and closed his eyes to better tune in.

"Boy this place stinks! What the hell is this called? I tell ya' the last time I was in such a shithole was in Bellatrix—"

"Keep it zipped, Bonti!" The captain admonished saving Simon the trouble. Then, "XO1129 keep your partner in line! Everyone be on the alert."

Simon sighed and nodded at Bonti to follow as he retracted his helmet into his suit.

"Sir my readings say there is no sentient life here so it should be a smooth mission," First Officer JZ11, a biologic organic robot said. Simon begged to differ, but he kept silent for now, as he detected no danger or threat other than from the toad next to him whom he was now babysitting and was certain would talk him to death.

Instead, he focused on observing his surroundings. Everything was the color of tawny brown. It was dusty and barren, with few observable land features except small dune-like hills and the bluff ahead. It was night here until Z145's sun climbed over its horizon. From their vantage point they could see an orange and green planet in the near distance - a beautiful giant sphere.

The ground beneath their feet was hard and packed tight like dirt. He could detect the faint smell of nitrogen and phosphorus in the air confirming the first officers reading. Suddenly he felt eyes on him and turned to see Zeeter the 15-foot-tall Reptilian grinning down at him, his ominous fangs bared. When he saw Simon looking back at him, he took that as an invitation and leered down in Simon's face. Slightly alarmed, Simon pulled back. The stench rolling off of him was like uric acid and sulfur. Simon hadn't noticed it before, as like everyone else Zeeter was fully packed up and encased in a spacesuit with his helmet on. But now, with his helmet retracted, they were breathing the same air. The smell almost caused Simon to pass out. He settled with gagging, completely setting aside propriety. Zeeter didn't seem to notice.

"It was pretty something seeing that partner of yours coming out of that birth canal, huh." Still choking on Zeeter's noxious fumes, yet only detecting humor from him Simon stayed silent wondering if he should put his helmet back on just to breath. He hadn't realized Zeeter had been there watching the show, too, but then again, it had been standing room only. He wondered when Zhang had gotten so popular.

"I wonder what that was like." Zeeter continued as they walked abreast heading north to the target collection area. Simon tried to walk a bit faster to stay upwind, but Zeeter's strides were enormous. He actually slowed down to keep pace with Simon. Simon cursed his luck.

"Maybe try it out at the holodeck," he offered while breathing sparingly.

"Heck no! That's disgusting!" Zeeter huffed out looking horrified by the very suggestion before he stormed off. Simon stared after him wondering what that was all about. Then he remembered reptilians were born from eggs that hatched naturally. Despite all their technological advancements they still relied on eggs to house and carry their fetuses to term which he found curious. He'd been told by a science officer the reptilians believed the process sacred. As more and more reptilians had come to the Light over the last millennia, it was not so unusual to encounter them as before. Simon knew them to be quite intelligent and excellent warriors but other than that he hadn't really interacted much with them. He decided to try to expand his horizons a bit and connect more with Zeeter when the chance to stand upwind of him arose.

"Hey, wait up, pretty boy!" Bonti huffed from a few paces behind him.

Simon picked up his pace but Bonti caught up anyway until they were side by side. Bonti was struggling to carry his pack. Simon sighed and grabbed it from him, hoisting it over his broad shoulders. Unlike his own gear which consisted of specimen-gathering equipment and a clean shirt, he heard crinkling and crunching in Bonti's bag now slung across his shoulder.

"Hey, be careful with that. That's my emergency food supply in case we get stuck in this shithole. That happened to me and my other partner out in Sector 18 once and I nearly starved to death! May his soul Rest in Peace!"

Simon gave him a sideways glance.

"Hahahaha! Naw I'm just messing with ya', pretty boy! He's living it up somewhere near Darius, I heard."

Simon sighed, truly missing his partner all the more.

CHAPTER FIFTEEN

Wherein Things Actually Get Going on Earth Again...

"What is that?"

"Your pendant. Mencius gave it to Nada who gave it to me to give to you when you woke up," Simon said handing him the small pendant he'd tucked into his shoulder bag as they headed for the shower in Zhang's apartment in Xinyu. The bluish white stone was from their Sirian home planet and had the appearance of cloud and sky swirled together. It was a beautiful stone in an intricate platinum housing which dangled from its platinum chain.

Zhang stared at it curiously.

"Let me put it on you," Simon said taking it back to drape around Zhang's neck.

"How did Mencius get it here to Nada?" Zhang asked allowing him to put it on him and patiently waited while Simon, with those big hands of his, fumbled with it.

"Teleportation, I suppose. I didn't ask."

Zhang looked down and studied the stone pendant and was instantly reminded of his mother and father on Sirius. He looked up in shock at Simon, confusion marring his face. How did he remember that? Before he realized it, he felt himself getting drowsy.

"Hey-" he began and then he was under.   The stone pendant was the XO511 family stone.   It identified Zhang's family's connection with each other. He was suddenly feeling a deeply familiar feeling of unconditional love enveloping him and he sobbed out. He then heard the familiar voice of his Sirian parents.   He could feel their energies. They were speaking to him telepathically as one collective voice. He tuned in and was instantly teleported to his home where he was seated before them in their comfortable living space.

Everything was spartan white yet evoked such warmth and love it enveloped his whole being. There was a warm glow of light around his parents auras as they stared back at him and although at first the image was a bit blurry, it began to get clearer as he focused his attention more fully. The Sirian sun was blazing in the east lighting up the entire room. How was this even possible? He could see all of this even though he was on earth.

"Our son. You look well." His father was a massive pale looking human with short white blonde hair and strong handsome features. His mother was also massive but sat a head shorter than his father. Her white blonde hair done up like something out of a sci-fi flick, with ringlets to her side and a bun on top. Their eyes were exceedingly kind like nothing he had ever seen before on earth.

"Hello Father. Hello Mother. I am well." Then, "I- I miss you."

"It has been awhile but we have been following your progress since you left for your assignment on the Athena. Your twin flame told us you had since incarnated to earth and he is now there." Instantly Simon's image came to mind together with the vision of Simon in his present earth incarnation communicating through the array with them in a meditative state.

"I am sorry to worry you both and for not reaching out sooner…things got a bit complicated after our last couple of missions and then we had to prepare for this one."

"Rest assured our son is fully capable and will bring the Light of Sirius to the earth plane with certainty exactly as your forefathers and mothers did."

"And so shall it be. Please do not worry for me. Simon is here to assist and doing well."

"All is in divine right order."

"I exist in the Light because we all exist in the Light." They recited together bowing their heads in reverence to one another before closing. He marveled at how easy the words flowed from his heart as they spoke their parting salutation.

When Zhang opened his eyes next, he was in the shower, under the steaming spray, completely naked and drenched as Simon gripped his hip and shoulder from behind and shamelessly thrust inside of him.

"Holy shit! You're not gonna' believe —" Zhang said excitedly only to get a mouthful of water. "Wait, what are you doing? Was that even real?"

"Yes, it was real and I'm taking care of us," Simon said already a little breathless.

"That was real? Those were my parents?"

"Uh huh." Simon panted picking up the pace.

"What??? Could they see us?"

"No...don't think so."

"Well, couldn't you have at least waited 'til I was done?" Zhang protested bracing his hands against the pristine marble shower wall to avoid smacking into it as Simon thrust harder.

"No, we have a plane to catch," Simon answered now panting noisily and nuzzling his opposite ear. Apparently, he had been going at it for a few moments already as his breath was irregular and starting to come in gasps. Zhang looked down and saw that he was fully engorged himself and groaned.

"I had a hard on the whole time I was talking to them?"

As if reminded, Simon reached around to firmly take him in hand. "Pretty much," he answered. "It was so hot!" He moaned and then cried out as he began to climax, his hips pistoning faster behind him.

"You jerk!" Zhang protested but as Simon began to spurt inside him, suddenly his own balls clenched upward, and he dropped a hand to Simon's massive paw around his member and together they jerked him off until he was shouting his own climax and his life erupted from him and splattered against the wall before him. Finally, out of breath, he would have collapsed had Simon not held him up. Before he had regained his composure Simon turned him around to face him and then kissed him thoroughly. When he pulled back, he grinned.

"So how are Reese and Maya, anyway?" He asked. "Are they well?"

Zhang frowned and punched him in the shoulder before reaching for the soap.

"Ow!" Simon laughed. "Ha! Ha! Ha!"

"Like I said, you're a jerk!"

They quickly dressed and Zhang packed an overnight bag as Simon went about collecting and tossing his dirty clothes and bedsheets in a pile by the washer. Then he used Zhang's phone, marveling that his passcode was still his birthday, and texted Zhang's housekeeper to come on by. Within the half hour they were heading to the airport as Simon navigated the streets in his pristine black SUV complete with new car smell.

"Is this new? Didn't you have a BMW?"

"Mmm. Courtesy of a recent endorsement with Jaguar." Simon shrugged glancing out the side mirror and changing lanes before gunning it. Some guys had all the luck.

"What time's the flight?"

"2:30p. Are you hungry? We can pick something up along the way."

"Yeah, I am. Famished."

Three minutes later Simon pulled up in the McDonalds drive thru and turned to him. "What do you want."

Having never indulged in greasy fast food before he regarded him in shock. "Seriously?"

"It's just to fill your stomach until we can eat something more substantial."

"I don't know. What do they have here that won't give me diarrhea?"

"Hello! Welcome to McDonalds. Can I interest you in a cheeseburger Happy Meal or chicken McNuggets?" The speaker beside them blared.

"Try the Happy Meal." Simon grinned then turned to the speaker. "Yes! Both sound wonderful with plain water, no gas, please."

"What type of sauce with your chicken McNuggets?"

Simon turned to Zhang and they both grinned at each other before he answered.

"Oh, I don't know. Pick your favorite! Hee! Hee! Hee!" Simon laughed before he slipped on a mask and tossed one to Zhang.

Two minutes later, masks discarded, they were back on the road and gunning for the freeway sharing the tiny order of french fries from Zhang's Happy Meal and commenting how addictive they were while trying not to spill any on the floor and between the seats. They then polished off their individual meals. Simon made quick work dodging traffic as they raced through the downtown area of skyscrapers, banks and shopping centers heading to the airport.

After valet parking the SUV, they made their way anonymously to the airport lounge, digital boarding passes on their phones. Neither had bags to check so they spent time checking their emails and accounts and Simon texted Ming they were on their way as they waited for their flight.

One good thing about wearing the face masks was that it gave them an extra layer of anonymity. Throw on a baseball hat and they had a perfect disguise. Since no one expected them to be traveling together they appeared like two casually dressed students in a vast sea of people. Zhang resisted the urge to hold his hand, feeling vulnerable and still worried they'd be spotted and all hell would break lose and they'd have to make a run for it. He glanced around nervously trying to blend in. But Simon took it all in stride and smiled calmly through his mask at him.

"Don't worry. Everything's fine." When they heard their seat section called, they headed toward the jetway and boarded without incident. The first-class section was hardly full and the seats next to them empty. As soon as they sat down the flight attendant offered them drinks and a snack without appearing to recognize either of them. As they settled in and the flight took off, they held hands and rested against each other. There was something to be said about misdirecting the public. Zhang's caustic posts ensured most of the rabid fans and circus media would never ping them as being together. With that in mind Zhang relaxed further and closed his eyes to rest.

"Oh my god! Oh my god! I can't believe you got to him and you two are here! Welcome back, Zhang!" Ming greeted them at the airport in Beijing and quickly shuttled them to an awaiting black van. Immediately Simon went into boss mode.

"Where are we staying and what's our schedule like?"

"At the Westin Beijing. In a suite, first class all the way. I got one for Zhang but I figured you two wanted to be together so I'm taking his for myself. Elle is taking care of both of you and want Zhang in the shoot, too. Hair and makeup are tomorrow at 8am, the shoot is from 9:30 to about 3p."

"Where?"

"What? I'm scheduled too?" Zhang leaned forward to look at Ming who was in the front seat.

"Calm down, baby. It'll be fine. It's time you got back in. Where?"

"Studio Eleven so it's a closed set. All the security has been handled."

Simon nodded.

"Uh, that's all well and good but CAPA hasn't reinstated my name yet."

"You're being licensed under a studio in Korea as a Korean super model under the pseudo name Model X."

"Huh? So, I'm Korean now?"

Simon looked up from his phone at him and grinned, "I think it's hot. I always wanted to date a Korean super model."

Zhang frowned at him. "So, what difference does my fake name and fake nationality matter if it's still my face?" He wondered whose dumb idea that was. The reach of CAPA wasn't anything to joke about. He was just one of a string of performing artists over the years whose lives had been turned upside down and were cancelled by them. Sometimes for something as nonpayment of taxes, and in his case taking a stupid selfie.

"It's all being handled by Elle's overseas office so it's out of our hands," Ming interjected turning around in her seat to comment.

Simon was tempted to ask what she brought in that clumpy plastic bag crammed between her feet so she'd quit staring so hard at his lover.

"They were pretty excited to know you'd be coming. They assured me everything will be taken care of. Apparently, they worked with Park Min Bo after he was blacklisted and jump- started his career practically overnight in Korea and Japan."

"Who?"

"He Lian."

"He Lian is now known as Park Min Bo?" Zhang asked exasperated.

He Lian was a 32-year-old model slash actor who got embroiled in numerous scandals four years prior. The "crimes" against him included tax evasion, failure to timely register for mandatory Communist Youth service activities and allegations of assaulting a netizen who stalked him relentlessly. Even after he paid the back taxes, registered and did extra community service and cleared his name with the courts, he was still branded as a traitor to the country. His case had dragged on for many years, his career grinding to a dead halt, until his name practically faded from everyone's lips.

"He's known as Supermodel Park Min Bo formerly known as the model He Lian. He's even more famous now," Ming said quickly retrieving her phone to show him a picture of the Korean slash formerly Chinese Model slash Actor on some photo shoot.

"Hey! I thought I was on your wallpaper!" Simon protested reaching for her phone but she wisely kept it out of his reach. "What a crappy assistant!"

"You were my wallpaper until you ignored all my texts." She eyed him resentfully. "What a crappy client."

"Boss, not client." Simon corrected.

"So, I have to change my name and identity?" Zhang interjected ignoring their childish exchange.

"Just for the shoot. Like I said it's just to get over the hurdles," Simon pointed out. "If anyone will be held responsible it's Elle and they are more than happy to take the risk. If they don't use the shots here they will just use them overseas. You already have a presence in Europe and the rest of Asia with them anyway. That's still intact. You might be cancelled in China but you're still alive and well in other countries. Nobody with any brain gives a shit about CAPA overseas."

Zhang looked doubtful, having had the doors slammed one by one in his face over these long months. He was still subject to CAPA and its net as a Chinese citizen.

Simon meanwhile tapped away on his phone: Rally Point 2 - Accomplished. Detailed report to follow. Lt. SimonGJXO1129. (Never mind the check in came 3 days late given he and Zhang were busy making up for lost time).

The message was instantly broadcast to the Athena where enthusiastic cheers resounded all around. This immediately set off a wave of celebrations on account of Simon having successfully turned things around against all odds and the duo's glowing success.

"COMMANDER, LIEUTENANT! CONGRATULATIONS TO YOU BOTH!" Came the reply which blipped on his screen.

"Stop worrying. Smile!" Simon then said turning to take a picture of him. Zhang made a face.

"Hee! Hee! Hee!"

"What are you doing?"

"Posting it on your IG account."

"What?"

"Don't worry. I'm not in it. It's time you stepped out more anyway. We'll take a few more while you're getting your hair done as selfies. People need to know you're still alive and well and not sitting around sulking."

"I wasn't sulking," Zhang said dryly. "How are you able to post on my account anyway?"

"Because you're still using our birthdays as your password."

"Oh, that's so sweet!" Ming piped up from the front seat batting her eyelashes at Zhang.

Zhang smiled embarrassed while Simon just ignored her. "It'll take a few weeks before the Elle shots come in so no one will be the wiser in the meantime. That'll give us some time to strategize more. By the way I reported in that we accomplished Rally Point 2. The Athena sends her congratulations."

Zhang looked surprised but nodded his acknowledgement. He was still walking the line between completely accepting this new reality and thinking it was all just some dream. He supposed it would take time for the veil to fully lift and he'd be totally convinced this was all part of another galactic mission.

"Ming, did you bring water?" Simon asked now looking at her testily. As people who made their living on their appearance, he and Zhang needed to stay hydrated. Thus, drinking water was a must. Never mind they spent the past three days steadily draining each other of bodily fluids and probably had all but two bottles of water between them the whole time. The truth was he had been watching her fan-girling all this time and right now he just needed her to focus on anything other than his man.

"Water? Yes! Here!" She said reaching into the bag at her feet to pull free two 16 oz cans of peach flavored water. "I also brought snacks," she said hurriedly reaching into the bag.

"Good girl! That's why you are the provisions officer on the New Jerusalem!" He grinned at her taking both cans and opening one for Zhang then handing it to him before popping one open for himself.

Zhang stared at her strangely before he drank. "For real?"

She only grinned back. "I am actually a strategy officer on the K12Jinway, a class B ship orbiting earth at the moment."

Zhang only stared back at her incredulous. Was everyone fully awake but him? Still exhausted from the entire ordeal and being thrust into a new paradigm practically overnight he drained his can and lay his head back to rest and closed his eyes with a sigh. He guessed they really did have it all in hand.

"So how was the drive to Xinyu? You did end up driving, didn't you?" Ming asked Simon who took the empty can from Zhang's hand to set it aside.

"Exhausting. I was worried the whole time he'd kick me out and call the police," Simon answered. "That's why I still look stressed." Simon pointed at his own face with a pitiful look.

"I almost did," Zhang muttered without opening his eyes.

"Lucky he was even home," Ming opined, sticking her nose where it didn't even belong while staring in complete adoration at Zhang's serene face in repose. Simon snorted. He couldn't really blame her. They often joked about who was more in love with Zhang, him or her.

It wasn't the first time he'd caught her fan-girling his man, even letting him know whenever Zhang posted anew on IG. She thought it was hilarious that Zhang was totally pissed at him and teased him relentlessly about it until he threatened to fire her. Sometimes it seemed she forgot she agreed to come to earth to work for him.

"I had a key anyway." Simon smirked at her.

"You never gave it back?" Ming jabbed looking shocked.

"Uhh, when are we arriving at the hotel?" He rolled his eyes changing the subject.

"With this traffic, another forty-five minutes easily," she answered.

"How is the company switchover coming along? Why haven't I seen any documents yet?"

"That takes time and the law firm is handling it. They will send them over and have you e-sign it."

"E-sign? Will I even know what I am looking at? I don't recall playing a lawyer yet in any tv drama," Simon said sounding all business like.

Zhang opened an eye lazily and peeked over at him. "What are you talking about?"

Simon explained the business consulting team he hired recommended the 4-person studio he'd been operating under the current name be disbanded and operations be handled instead under Shanghai JunZhe Culture Media Co., Ltd., a company he formed back in 2019. Over the last year with the increase in his popularity and studio business, the income he'd generated had increased substantially. This meant he had additional tax obligations and filing requirements that were better met under the new company. He'd carefully vetted the new team and gotten the all clear from Mencius and the rest of the guidance team overseeing the mission ensuring there would be no hitches. All was in divine order.

He'd also made provisions for Zhang as well ensuring that when they finally saw all of this through, they could quietly enjoy their lives together. Zhang stared at him thoughtfully. Simon really did have his back.

When Mencius received word of Simon's Rally Point 2 check-in, he cried.

CHAPTER SIXTEEN

Why Mencius Cried - Meeting with Lord Michael at the Water Cooler

The ship was all abuzz. Word had it a very special visitor had dropped by and was now on board shooting the breeze in the break room. The captain had been alerted and was on his way to make his greetings along with half the Athena who had come to gawk. Mencius knew if he didn't hurry there'd likely be a long queue to speak with their distinguished visitor and his boss.

"Greetings, my lord!"

"Mencius!" Lord Michael was dressed as a buff Greek soldier, complete with armored chest and shoulder plates, and a fashionably short armored skirt, his sculpted legs encased in sandals that strapped up his calves, his muscular arms encased in golden vambraces that gleamed. He chose to appear this time with long golden curls that rolled over his scalp, cascading downward to just barely graze his shoulders, his piercing eyes of the deepest aquamarine hue.

Those hourglass shaped pupils gazed deep into your soul and made you feel you were talking directly to Source Creator and not just an Archangel closest to that point of Light. To say he was handsome was a damn understatement. Wherever he went he had the entire galaxy fawning over him. Half the Athena was crammed into the break room to get a glimpse of his magnificent presence. He held his helmet under one arm while the other arm was slung over the water cooler, leg crook'd, looking as relaxed as he could be as he spoke to a short fat white guy straight out of a Steven Spielberg movie. Mencius could see it was Lady Master Ma'at in another one of her crappy disguises. Never mind the warrior prince was busy wielding calls nonstop from all sectors of the galaxy for assistance with finding parking spaces, to exorcising demons (mostly reptilians in disguise) and other favors. Mencius had to push his way through the crowd that seemed too intimidated to even get close to him other than to gawk.

"You look good, Mencius. How goes it with your charges on earth?" Lord Michael turned to Mencius after an inexorably long time of ignoring him as he waited for Lady Master Ma'at to skedaddle. He decided to ignore the sarcasm.

"Uh, yeah...about that...." Mencius didn't dare avert his eyes. He was about to launch into his prepared speech, how given for the past several thousand years he'd had absolutely no luck calling any of the beings assigned to him back to their higher states of consciousness, and that despite his best efforts, giving the poor working conditions, long hours, unhelpful staff, and dismal pay, perhaps it was time he just throw in the towel, accept a demotion and re-enroll in ascended master training all over again. Three times was a charm.

But first he thought to get him up to speed knowing how busy he was being "God's Right Hand" and all. And it was Mencius' job to report on behalf of the Athena. More importantly, it had been Lord Michael's suggestion to send in Simon and his partner Zhang to do the job in the first place.

It was hoped sending in the pair would position them both close enough to some of the worst offenders in the business in China. For if the two could successfully bring their light to bear and blow the door wide open on the corrupt systems in play in their chosen industry, it would have a ripple effect in unmasking and toppling all the other corrupt institutions.

The effect would be the mass awakening of potentially billions of people on earth, more light and Gaia would have the ability to ascend. It would also avoid the mass earth changes and catastrophes Gaia had as a failsafe to shake off the offending humans like fleas on a dog to solve her own problem. But that wasn't going so well.

"Not so good...we're having a bit of trouble uh...with Zhang and Simon."

"*The Dynamic Duo*? I have my money on those two and even voted in the poll!" Michael exclaimed.

Mencius waited for him to finish.

"Well, there's been a slight hiccup."

Lord Michael leaned in and did a mind meld pressing his cranium to Mencius' that had Mencius' eyes rolling about and fluttering around in his head. In the few seconds it took for Lord Michael to glean the gist of it, Mencius almost fainted.

What Mencius had wanted to say before Lord Michael almost made his head explode was: "Listen Michael, everyone knows the incarnates to earth have been having a tough time of it with this problem yet the Angelics and galactics have been sitting on it for quite some time even making me look bad. As I said before, sending more galactics down to help and making me their master guide would only complicate the problem. Hell, had it not been for that Siddhartha Buddha guy (whose philosophizing and talent for soliloquy and ability to walk fast saved him from being killed outright by his own soul mate Devadatta who made the jump with him and promptly forgot the mission); Yeshua, that darling from Sector 15, who had quite a messy time of it towards the end (but still managed to be loved by many and even had a book written about him); and, a few other nameless stars, my reputation would be toast!

"And yeah, a few of your angelic buddies finally agreed to incarnate given the little grays finally figured out how to cram those ultra-high dimensional light bodies of theirs into a densely vibrating human baby without mother and kid exploding and making a mess of things, but honestly, Mike, if you ask me it's a case of 'too little too late'."

"And well, while I know everyone had their hopes on Simon and Zhang to turn things around, figuring they could just complete their missions and rescue my golden boys, the Jefoks wreaking havoc in China while they are at it, but there's a slight hiccup. Zhang ain't waking up and he's starting to drag his partner down, too. I mean like big time. He's writing letters, doing videos, singing songs, taking to SM. It's a god damn mess."

"I thought they shut his accounts down."

"Yeah, well he weaseled his way back onto IG."

"Smart!" Lord Michael smiled in approval. "Have they accomplished the first rally point target?" Lord Michael asked when Mencius' eyes finally stopped rolling and came back to center although he was still having trouble focusing.

"Rally Point 1 isn't the problem. That was like watching newlyweds on their honeymoon. It's Rally Point 2 that isn't working out."

Mencius knew if they failed to make either Rally Points, he could kiss his ass and reputation goodbye. Fed up like an employee with nothing more to lose, he was about to let fly a few choice words and tell his big boss where to stick it when a broadcast over the Athena's loud speakers was made:

Rally Point 2 - Accomplished. Detailed Report to Follow. Lt. SimonGJXO1129.

The ship and break room went up in cheers.

Mencius cried.

Lord Michael leaned in with a knowing grin. "You were saying?"

CHAPTER SEVENTEEN

Zhang and Simon Plan their Incarnations

When they both finally sat down in the Round Room to plot out their soul plans for the upcoming incarnation, they were late, their usually pristine Officer uniforms slightly disheveled. They'd been practicing their Pleiadean Cultivation skills which had since become quite the favorite pastime for them and simply lost track of themselves. Never mind they were Sirians.

Mencius was already waiting together with Zhughe, an auxiliary guide who was a master at karmic charts. Appearing as he had in his last earth incarnation, he was thin, with short gray hair and kind features and dressed in a dull gray robe. Zhughe was a candidate for Ascended Masterhood assigned to help on their case. While he apparently had had many exemplary lives on earth, he didn't quite have the required number of merits to ascend on account of a minor glitch resulting in an accounting error and lost paperwork. He was now stuck earning extra merits to fast-track his ascension.

Both were glad to see Mencius had someone as skilled at his side. Mencius ignored their lack of decorum and was ready to get down to business, his pale face austere as it was a reminder he'd been young and handsome once and full of zest for life much like them. Now he just looked a bit tired of herding rogue incarnates as rumor had it a few of his charges had been recycling on earth for eons with little signs of waking up. This naturally was a real headache and point of contention for him.

Simon had wondered aloud earlier if Zhang was sure he wanted to pick Mencius as their Master Guide on account of said rumors. But Zhang said Mencius had come highly recommended by a friend of a friend of a friend he'd met once in a bar at Z28-11 in Sector 12 who said he was good at what he did. He'd then heard the story of how Mencius single-handedly appeared during a time of great upheaval on earth and taught that human nature is righteous and humane. Thus, a state or governing body with righteous and humane policies would by its very nature flourish. When this occurred, citizens, under such magnanimous leadership were then free to take care of their elders, their wives, brothers, and children, and be educated with rites and naturally become better citizens. As it sounded quite reasonable to hear Zhang tell it, Simon then readily agreed.

"Seeing neither of you have any karmic debts to expiate on account of neither of you ever having been to earth, you only need be mindful of accumulating karma once there. You will have to clear it up at some point if you do either with another earth incarnation in 5D if you choose as it looks like that option will be made available for this purpose or add it to your karmic chart elsewhere." Zhughe disclaimed.

"How do we do that?" Simon asked for clarification.

"What? Accumulate or expiate?"

"Both."

"No harm to yourself or others in either thought, word or action. As long as you live in alignment you should be fine. Remember earth humans are there to learn the interconnectedness of everything in the universe including themselves and acceptance by means of unconditional love. You're there to help teach them by example," Zhughe continued. "If you do accumulate karma then you expiate it through learning the lesson. It's a process of reversal."

Knowing something of karmic charts himself Zhang shrugged as they decided on the final details of their intersecting soul plans. "How hard can this be? We go in, spend the equivalent of 3 of our days there and we're out!" Zhang exclaimed grinning.

Mencius smiled at his enthusiasm. He was counting on these two knuckleheads to successfully complete the mission in order to redeem his own slightly tarnished reputation. Many…well most…almost all of his charges were still mired in their human dramas on earth, the region he'd once called home when he was still in human form. Thus, if the duo completed their missions, it would ensure his charges could finally transcend their human lives of suffering, awaken and peacefully transition off world to a state of healing before returning to their home planets. But if the two failed and got stuck themselves….

He especially worried about those from Jefok who had been trapped in the reincarnation cycle on earth and then unable to ascend for what was going on now the equivalent of several thousand earth years. The four had been cycling back in an endless karmic loop and getting more and more embroiled even causing tremendous suffering for others. Thankfully the Athena had made special provisions to safeguard their physical bodies in stasis since their consciousnesses had incarnated into human bodies to assist earth all that long ago.

After pleading this special case on behalf of the Jefoks, he'd been personally assured by Lord Michael, the Archangel to whom he and all other Ascended Master Guides reported to, that if the two made it at least to Rally Point 2, he'd personally intervene and ensure the Jefoks made it back home to Epsilon Indi immediately. Thus, there was a lot riding on their shoulders.   They'd have to face justice on earth though for their crimes against humanity. But they would be embraced and undergo divine healing after they transitioned or were taken off world.

"So basically, we get born to earth mothers-" Zhang recited staring at the holographic images displayed before them which Mencius and Zhughe controlled using their smart pads, rotating and clicking through the images of their "future" lives on earth in rapid succession.

"As twins?" Simon asked.

"No, we scrubbed that idea because then it would seem too cliche when
we and everyone else discover we're soul mates."

"Oh, that's right. You jump first-" Simon nodded recalling that detail.

"Correct. And my mother will be? Did we decide on that yet?" Zhang
asked.

"That's a variable but we have several excellent candidates in mind,"
Zhughe said.

"Got it! So, I have a fairly normal life, working middle class family,
mother divorces father, remarries, yadah, yadah, yadah, I get through
school, attend Shanghai Theatre Academy, start acting in some dramas,
make variety show appearances, start writing songs and
performing...so this last bit is done all at the same time?"

"Pretty much. Don't worry as it'll all come naturally to you," Mencius
reassured.

"Good! I take a lonely —"

"It's called a selfie- "

"Selfie, sorry.   And that starts the ball rolling."

"Essentially yes but it will be a few years before that goes into play,"
Zhughe clarified.

"Good! Then he and I meet on the set of a new soap opera a few years
later -"

"I think it's just a drama series," Simon interjected. "Our meeting up
then will be Rally Point 1."

"Ok, and we just have fun, enjoy ourselves for a couple of years during
filming and afterwards, make appearances, get our names out there, do

a couple of endorsements, connect with our fans, and all that...then what's Rally Point 2 again?"

"When you two meet back up again. There will be a brief period of separation while Simon takes care of some things for the mission. This will take place after the scandal and you go dark. All country sponsored social media accounts go offline and you're banned from the limelight for a bit," Zhughe reminded. "After that happens Simon will swing back around after completing his half of the mission and connect back with you. It's during this period especially   you must be mindful not to unnecessarily create any karma. It's usually when under extreme stress this occurs for earth humans," he followed up.

"Roger that! And about how long before I hear from him?"

"If all goes well, just about the equivalent of three maybe four earth weeks. Remember wait to hear from him."

Both he and Simon made eye contact and nodded. "Sounds reasonable."

They then went over Simon's plan. "Simon you will be born in the same country but in Chengdu and also have a rather ordinary early life. Father falls sick, mother becomes an entrepreneur to hold the fort, you study drama in high school and slowly you make your transition into the industry." With a few taps on his smart pad Zhughe changed up the hologram to Simon's life plan. An image of Simon as an earth male child around age five popped up.

"Wait, is that what he'll look like as a kid?" Zhang asked observing an adorable, Asian and slightly Caucasian looking kid. "How come his ears don't stick out like mine?"

"I think your ears are adorable," Simon beamed at him. "I'm sure you will be even more beautiful once you grow into them. That's a thing there I heard. Besides you'll have a fabulous jawline! Now that right there is pretty special!" Simon said.

"You're right. You're right." Zhang nodded as the two exchanged meaningful looks seemingly forgetting Mencius and Zhughe were still in the room.

The duo was giving Mencius a real headache. He waited for them to finish before he continued, refraining from rolling his eyes.

"Simon, there is a chance we might postpone your entrance to university to have you handle another quick assignment," Mencius said. "There are some Hyadeans from the original Lyra system already in Beijing on a separate mission that could use your 9th frequency band angelic energies to anchor more light there. You can later choose to attend either Nanjing or Donghua University when you're finished with them and still be on the path to intersect with Zhang's scheduled timeline. We'll leave that up to you as there's room to make some adjustments."

"Sure! Happy to help!" Simon beamed. It wasn't unusual for him to lend his angelic energies where needed working in tandem with or on behalf of even higher angels as he was one of the few on the Athena who had an incarnation moving from 9th to 10th that had time on his hands when he and his partner weren't busy mucking around the galaxy.

Zhang smiled at him proudly, over the moon to have been blessed with an angelic for his soul mate.

"Alright," Mencius interrupted seeing them about to get lost in the other's gaze again. "There will be plenty of time for that later. We will have a few more briefings, fine tune the plan and then get your final agreements in order before you make the jump."

"Sounds good! Let's go get lunch!" Simon jumped up and clapped his hands.

"Wait a second, don't we have class?"

They both grinned at each other.

Mencius rolled his eyes and left the room. Zhughe quickly followed.

CHAPTER EIGHTEEN

Whereas Sex Cultivation is Practiced with some Fun Loving Pleiadeans

As part of their training for the upcoming earth mission, Zhang and Simon eagerly awaited the start of the class even turning up early to get a front row seat in the Round Room. Added to the class syllabus at the last minute was a three-day workshop on sex cultivation put on by a group of visiting Pleiadeans, apparently masters of the art of sensual and sexuality as a means of spiritual cultivation. Zhang didn't know what nonsense this was, but he applauded the Pleiadeans for taking the initiative on it, making it a thing and taking it to a whole 'nother level.

To the Pleiadeans, sex was spiritually sacred as well as a means to transfer information carried via one's energy from one soul to the next. Simon thought this interesting as it mirrored the Sirian's thoughts on the energetic exchange all were capable of once tapped into another vibrationally. This enabled one to access another's thoughts, feelings, and just about everything else, making them an open book. Physical touching therefore wasn't necessary as all were energetically connected by the thread of life on the vast network and web that always exists. But he was open to hearing them out and seeing what they had to say because the pictures on the e-brochure looked quite interesting.

They'd heard of the practice of sex and sensuality although the Sirians had since evolved in the last few hundred thousand earth years in the reproduction arena, instead opting to use technology to produce offspring rather than risk harm to the mother. This upgrade thus eliminated the need for sexual contact. The Pleiadeans however viewed the practice of sex as a means of spiritual connection and having assisted in the seeding of earth humans felt it important that anyone incarnating be schooled in its art form as apparently there was plenty of sex still happening on Gaia.

The e-brochure had been titillating to say the least and they'd heard the master sex education teacher would be in residence, the beautiful Lady Master Thala. Nonsense or no, both he and Simon couldn't wait to get a peek of her in action as there was speculation that she would be doing firsthand demonstrations of this unusual spiritual practice butt naked.

Simon and Zhang couldn't wait. They had studied the images on their smart pads and were thus somewhat familiar with the sexual acts of humans but were eager to get the live demonstration and practical experience. Apparently, they weren't the only ones. The room was packed. Zhang was certain not all of them had been chosen for the mission to incarnate on earth either.

The three Pleiadean females there with their male colleagues were as stunning as they were beautiful. With their platinum blonde hair, voluptuous forms encased in their uniforms and demure looks, they were about as tall as the average Sirian woman standing at 7 feet. Although similar in appearance to Sirians, they were nonetheless very different in culture, philosophy and lifestyle although both civilizations served the Light.

And then there was Lady Master Thala. If ever there was someone of the female persuasion that could be called Lady Master and a goddess, Zhang was sure it was her. Unlike her female colleagues, her blonde hair actually had very light brown threads in it making it look like streaks that matched the slightly tawny color of her skin. The faintly brownish tinge made her look more exotic than her colleagues, even her large almond shaped eyes were a bit rounder about the edges. Her long hair was also a tad more wavy than the other three as it bounced down her shoulders and waterfalled down her back. Perhaps she was a hybrid like Simon of sorts.   Whatever the case Zhang found himself getting even more excited in anticipation of doing a couple of practice rounds with her when the time came. The way she kept eyeing and smiling at him only cemented this thought.

He sat up a bit taller in his chair dressed in his white and black officer uniform and grinned back. Meanwhile her colleague seemed to have an eye for Simon who had also dressed up for the occasion in his officer's uniform but with the added Neubin designation of his family crest. The Pleiadean males meanwhile seemed focused on some of the female soon-to-incarnate candidates seated around them and were having much the same impression on them. For the females seemed to be smiling more than usual. The temperature in the room rising just by the exchanged glances and suggestive looks alone. Zhang was practically buzzing in his seat and was pretty sure Simon was doing the same next to him.

The lights in the round room were dimmed as a 5D hologram popped up in the center of the room. It was a true to form naked human male and female body practically in their faces.   Simon's eyes were glued to the figures as the image rotated slowly so everyone could get a good look.

They looked quite similar to their own bodies but daintier and more fragile rather than muscular proportioned and wore their hairstyles different. Even so they were quite beautiful to look at. The images morphed from white to brown to tawny, to olive colored, and the various earth skin hues and features were represented. Each race from Asian to African to Native American and the whole gambit in between, including mixed race humans were shown to represent the various ethnicities their group would incarnate as. Zhang and Simon took notes while mentally musing on how amazing it would be to try sexual cultivation with a female of each race while on earth if they had enough time.

"As you are aware, we Pleiadeans are masters of sensuality and sexual cultivation. We have discovered that during the act of sexual contact between bonded and loving partners, the light coded filaments of the partners become entwined with one another. Thus, when one becomes sexualized the chemicals in the body begin their dance, the whole body lining up in one direction." Lady Master Thala began. "When both parties are lined up, their energies align. This is even more so the case as both parties move toward sexual climax."

Both Simon and Zhang tapped away on their smart pads taking prodigious notes.

Across the room one of the male Pleiadeans began to speak, his voice deep and resounding. Aside from his slightly more narrow and grey blue eyes, he looked like a Sirian male, they were so similarly built. "Your body turns into a magnet and when partners achieve a heightened state of sexual arousal, the result is an electromagnetic pulling and a balance between partners. When you get really attuned in this way, physical contact becomes unnecessary to experience this. You can create this web of love between you and your partner and it's through this force field that your inner body rises and can go into other worlds and states of existence."

While he spoke, the holographic images before them which were as detailed as a high-definition movie began to move into more alluring and suggestive positions starting with a simple exchange of lip pressure earth humans called a kiss. The act itself seemed quite technical, a mixture of slight head movements, proper angling, timing, followed by exacting pressure of lips. Zhang felt his pulse begin to thud. The simple kiss seemed to progress to something else entirely as the figures' lips parted and then their tongues began to gnash. As the figures were realistic the bodies of the subjects displayed were also showing signs of physical reaction, becoming more flush as their limbs began to move about with some urgency.

In addition to the images of the two parties on screen, there were other data, graphs, waves and charts visible apparently plotting and charting the physical, emotional and presumably spiritual reactions they spoke of.

Lady Master Thala resumed her narration. "We wish you to understand that in addition to the physical pleasure entailed in sexual acts between two individuals, sex allows the parties to hold energy between them. This energy enables you to transport yourself elsewhere. All of the body's chakras fire up. You experience exchanges of energy between all your chakras and those of your partner as represented and demonstrated here by the color wheels." She strode about the front of the room occasionally making eye contact with Zhang and his partner.

"And when you really learn to lift the energies from the genitalia up the chakras, you really can increase the flow substantially. The sexual energy in the body is one's life force thus it must be honored." The Lady Master intoned. "Likewise, you inherit the blueprint of every person with whom you have sex. When two bodies come together in sexual union, they become bonded energetically. There is a merging of each other's auric field." The holographic image of both parties became enveloped in a translucent column of light.

"Are there any questions thus far?"

"Yes. Are the limb movements necessary to complete the kissing procedure or are they exemplary?" Someone wisely asked. Zhang turned around but didn't recognize the being.

"You will find that they are quite natural once the kiss continues, and the partners wish to progress further. The physical act itself produces both a chemical and physical reaction in the body. You can see this from the formulas and color sequencing representing those complex biological responses in the holographic display."

Both Zhang and Simon nodded and continued to type away into their smart pads not wishing to miss a single step lest they fail in this important aspect of their earth missions.

"Don't worry about taking notes now as you will be practicing in a few minutes. For now just focus on observing and taking in as much details as you can," Thala said in her low seductive voice.

"And is the act of sexual pleasure solely for reproductive purposes on earth at this time? I heard in some cultures sex outside of reproducing was otherwise taboo." Someone in the front row asked sounding confused.

"That might be the case but that is very rare, and we were told none of you will be incarnating in such a society. Thus far, sex is both for the purpose of inducing pleasure and of course is still relied upon in this developing society to reproduce. It also carries intense spiritual and energetic properties of exchange as well which is the crux of the lesson here."

As the questions progressed and became more complex, Zhang was starting to worry he wasn't getting everything. As he met Thala's eyes a slight sensation of angst came over him. What if he didn't make the cut? He'd hate to let her or himself down by bungling the lesson during practice.

They watched several more titillating moments of kissing coupled with increased arousal on the part of both holographic parties. As they were just observers, as curiously exciting as the act was to watch, they were still just passive observers much like scientists. Thus, the complex physical and emotional responses and heightened arousal they were witnessing seemed unrelated to the act itself.

"So, are you saying all of these responses will occur naturally? It's not something we will need to conjure up to successfully complete these physical acts?" The guy in the back asked. Zhang knew he had the mind of a science rat with no practical experience on other matters outside the lab. He needed to get out more, Zhang scoffed.

"Correct. But let's go ahead and demonstrate firsthand as this will eliminate much confusion and give you an idea of how it feels and the body's natural response," Thala announced. He and Simon grinned like foxes at each other, each having an eye on a Pleiadean female instructor to partner with for the demonstration.

"So, if there are no more questions, go ahead and turn to your partner beside you with whom you will be incarnating as soul mates and practice kissing for the next few now moments," she continued.

Wait, what??!! Zhang and Simon exchanged looks of utter confusion. Perhaps they had misheard. But from the sound of movement all around them the other students were already positioning into place. Simon frowned and looked down at his notes. He hadn't recalled the demonstration involving two male subjects engaged in the act, his face registering his acute bewilderment. Zhang wasn't so polite and raised his hand.

"Excuse me but are you suggesting that the Lieutenant and I re-enact the kissing demonstration with…each other?"

"Are you two not going in together as soul mates?" Thala checked the smart pad she'd been carrying around to control the presentation. "Let's see…."

"We are." Simon piped up just as vested in hearing her meaning, a frown of concern marring his face. They'd been close since they'd both been children, doing everything together including attending school, joining the academy, going on dangerous missions together. There was nothing they didn't know about the other that any of those activities entailed. What they weren't familiar with was that part of each's other physical anatomy other than admiring how similar they looked in size and build and occasionally complimenting each other on their appearance in their spiffy space suits. This was uncharted territory and quite frankly one that never crossed either of their minds before.

"Yes… you indeed are soul mates. So, what's the problem?" Thala asked looking genuinely confused. The three of them stared at each other until finally they realized she wasn't about to change her mind or the exercise up just for them.

Zhang wracked his brain. He supposed there were no particular taboos involved for Sirians that he could recall as long as it was done out of unconditional love. And they were soul mates. Still, it was uncharted territory. Simon sighed, shrugged his shoulders, and wiggled his index finger at him beckoning him over, "Alright…come here."

Zhang cleared his throat and slowly and awkwardly leaned in, his eyes wide open.

"This is so unfair," he heard Simon complain as their lips moved closer and lightly grazed one another's. The immediate feeling was quite strange, and they both pulled back and looked at each other.

Thala who hadn't moved from her spot before them coaxed them to try again. "Try it again and this time one of you take the lead and tilt your head just as in the demonstration. In most of the cultures on earth since it's the males who usually take the lead, you can both take turns."

The awkward lip contact had them both insisting they take the lead and tilting their heads to the same side resulting in their faces and cheeks clashing and neither giving way to the other.

"Commander. Lieutenant. This isn't a competition. Why don't you take turns," Thala instructed. Being competitive by nature, neither capitulated to the other until finally Simon grabbed him by the hair and held Zhang's head in place as he angled his head in the opposite direction.

"Ow!" Zhang complained as Simon chuckled at his own ingenuity of outsmarting him, the result being both their lips being slightly parted just as they made full contact. The result was electric causing a jolt of energy to shoot from their crowns down their chakras, shocking both their senses. In the next instance, eager to repeat the unusual sensation, they both mashed their mouths together in a battle of teeth and tongue as the hedonistic sensations rapidly escalated. It wasn't long before they were panting and breathing hard against the others' mouth and their hands, which had heretofore been idle, began to roam over the other without the least hint of inhibition.

When they finally pulled back to catch their breath, they noticed the

147

room had gone oddly quiet and everyone was staring at them. Zhang cleared his throat as Simon casually wiped his mouth and they both glanced around questioningly. The room suddenly erupted in applause followed by exclamations of "That was amazing!", "We should do it like that!" And "Commander and Lieutenant can you demonstrate that again?"

Thala was beaming proudly at them. "I have a feeling you two will be naturals at this."

Thus, the two took every moment to practice that entire afternoon and into the evening, regardless of who was around…while in the cafeteria, lounging in the officer's quarters, while queuing up for the H-Deck, and finally again for a few minutes before retiring to their separate quarters. They were determined to excel on the mission and complete the assignment with accolades.

They both anxiously awaited Lesson 2.

CHAPTER NINETEEN

The Bell Ringing Incident on Earth's Moon

Captain Olin Alpha1 looked beside himself, the corner of his lip curled in a scowl, a deep frown cutting into his forehead. He had even cleared out all of the control room's crew save a gray and Mantis to dress down the two decorated officers. He stood as he was known to, ramrod straight, hands behind his back gazing upon the two with fiercely critical eyes like he was seriously considering whether to boot the two off his ship.

Zhang and Simon stood practically shoulder to shoulder, their gear dropped haphazardly at their feet as they stood at attention and averted their eyes.

They were so, so dead.

Zhang stared straight ahead, stressed, sweat pouring down his back from his exertions of trying not to scream.

Just breath, Zhang. He told himself. So your entire ace flying and piloting career is toast, not to mention demotions will likely be handed down, but no need to panic.

It's ok. Just relax. We've got this. Besides he doesn't look that upset, right? He heard Simon telepathically and felt him waving over some of that fairy dust-like angelic energy at him. He wanted to stomp on his toes and tell him to quit it.

The captain turned back to the large screen where the whole sordid scene was being replayed on the bridge including every last bit of commentary as it happened.

Earlier they had headed to the earth's moon, an ancient galactic-made satellite occupied by a few industrious humans working with some not so honest ETs known as the Eben, Reptilians and other service-to-self beings. The confederation had asked the duo to do a quick fly over for reconnaissance and monitoring purposes.

They had already been collecting soil samples on Mars and had been on their way back to the Athena when the request to deviate course came in. As the once thriving red giant had suffered a nuclear catastrophe, its core and surface had yet to recover from the damage millions of years later and the confederation was following its progress.

The new instructions were simple. Scan for any unusual gamma ray readings on the earth's moon as the confederation had intercepted chatter the satellite's occupants were using banned technology below ground.

"Anything?" Zhang asked as he did their first fly over, careful to avoid detection as the satellite's occupants were known to be a little hot headed and trigger happy.

Simon studied the smart pad and shook his head. "Nothing. Maybe we should do an on the ground reading to be sure." Simon suggested.

"Good idea," Zhang said reporting in then visually scanning the area for a suitable place to land.

They selected a spot just below a ridge where Earth humans had successfully landed some years before before being chased away by the enterprising occupants. Someone had taken the little flag they had planted in the dirt in celebration of their accomplishment and tossed it aside. It was still laying there. Zhang made a mental note to upright it again.

"Stay here and monitor for trouble," Zhang said unstrapping himself from his seat and grabbing the portable scanning unit on his way out.

"Copy that," Simon said switching programs on his smart pad as Zhang exited the craft using the rear door.

"How is it looking?" Zhang asked doing a visual inspection from outside the shuttle craft and seeing nothing on the ridge ahead nor in the vicinity of the ship.

"Deserted as can be," Simon responded. "There is no one around for thousands of omega klicks."

They'd heard that the confederation had been busy cleaning house lately in anticipation of the earth's ascension. The units responsible for patrolling the area were mostly Pleiadean defense forces. If they needed support Zhang knew he could always reach out to them.

"Ok, well I'm going to just gather some readings from a couple of spots. Keep an eye out will 'ya," Zhang said starting to hike away from the craft.

"Got it."

Simon observed Zhang as he strode off just ahead in his line of vision before double checking his readings and confirming they were alone. After Zhang had been gone awhile but still well within his view, Simon unbuckled his harness and slid into the control seat.

"Since no one's here, I want to take her for a spin across the ridge," Simon said.

Occasionally Zhang would let him take the helm although he was always in the seat next to him.

"Are you crazy?" Zhang chuckled down on a bent knee, scanner in hand.

"Come on…there's absolutely no one around."

"That's not what I'm worried about." Zhang continued. "Do you think that's a good idea, buddy?" Zhang asked although he wasn't really too worried as Simon had an affinity for flying.

"I've got this in hand! How hard can it be? I'm an angel, remember. Angels can fly!" Simon laughed already lifting off the ground. Zhang shook his head as Simon did a pass over him then headed for the ridge line. He skimmed along the jagged region for a time before jettisoning back toward Zhang's general direction. Then he did a rapid 90 degree turn passing to Zhang's right and buzzing him as Zhang righted the little flag.

"Ha! Ha! Very funny, Lieutenant. I'm about done here so just land the damn thing," Zhang said bending down on his knee to get one last reading. Simon did another pass this time in a zigzag pattern. Then in a whimsical swinging motion he moved over head from left to right before zipping by him again and disappearing in the distance. A second later he was back before he shot upwards and disappeared once again. He appeared a moment later near the ridge line before he abruptly stopped and reversed his trajectory and came back to hover before him with a wave and pointed to his ear. [You Are - Got7]

Zhang watched him. Simon then raised up the craft a little and hovered. Then he did a swaying motion swinging past Zhang's left before swinging all the way over to his right as he began to sing first in his left ear and then his right in alternating fashion. Zhang laughed.

He watched as Simon then zipped around him in the little spaceship in tight circles all the while singing and alternating in Zhang's left then right ear and behind him. Zhang turned and followed him, their eyes locked, grinning from ear to ear. The combined effect was to heighten the sensation of Simon buzzing around his head as he serenaded him. Zhang laughed again, deeply amused and began dancing around as Simon continued to sing and maneuver the ship in whimsical fashion over his head for several enjoyable moments. He had to admit it was damn clever.

"There's so much we can do with this craft than just shuttle people around and gather dirt samples!" Simon laughed watching him. "We can be entertaining whole civilizations like this in 8D!" He declared gesturing with his arms.

"That's pretty good, Lieutenant," Zhang said watching and grinning. "I hope you remember how to land."

"Got it!"

"Whoa! Watch your front end! It's dropping!" Zhang warned observing as he made his approach.

"I'm accessing your thoughts on the landing protocol from Mars, and it seems -"

"What? No, not that one, dude!" Zhang yelled in a panic as the ship suddenly lurched and banked hard before slamming into the dusty ground with a loud bang. Had he been any higher in the air, the craft would have surely flipped over with Simon in it. The impact reverberated loudly like a gong forcing Zhang to cover his ears and turn away from the impact blast.

"What the - Are you alright?" Zhang yelled as Simon got out all casual like.

"Yeah, fine. What the hell is all that noise?" Simon yelled back as the two inspected the damage. The reverberations could be heard as well as felt beneath their feet.

"Probably the satellite," Zhang said. "Are you sure you're alright?" Zhang asked as the they stood side by side.

"Uh yeah, but that looks a little bent." Simon pointed to the left landing strut. "Though the rest of the ship doesn't look too bad," Simon followed up. Zhang gave him a look. Beneath their feet they could still feel the powerful reverberations from the impact resounding upwards through their bodies giving them a slight headache.

"Uh, you think? What the hell happened?"

"Nothing, I was just accessing your memories to get the landing protocol, but it was like your brain short circuited or something." Simon frowned.

"Never mind. Come on we better get the hell out of here. This noise is going to alert them we're here," Zhang said.

Zhang lifted the craft into hover mode so they could stand beneath it and inspect the damage further. While the hull was intact, the entire left landing strut had broken off and was embedded in the dirt.

It took them awhile to dig it out of the ground by hand. When they'd succeeded, they found it was too heavy even for the both of them to lift on their own so they levitated it and guided it into the cargo bay at the back of the ship. They then high-tailed it out of there to avoid detection. It was definitely no small matter for a confederation ship to crash on earth's moon. They had some explaining to do.

"I'm sorry for breaking the ship, Commander," Simon said telepathically with genuine remorse throwing in a pout for good measure.

"We better get our stories straight if we plan to keep this detail." Zhang responded in kind.

"I'll just tell them the truth." Simon continued the silent communiqué.

"That might not be a good idea for either of us." Zhang looked over at him.

"You know I can't lie."

"I'm responsible no matter what so you don't have to say anything."

They went back and forth in this manner until they were safely back at the shuttle bay. When the craft came to a halt, she sat at an odd 45-degree angle. No sooner did they touch down when Captain Alpha1 called them to the bridge.   The two unbuckled from their seats and prepared to disembark.

"The strut's in the back," Zhang called over his shoulder and gestured with his thumb to the bay crew of little grays and Sirian humans before grabbing the rest of their gear and heading to the bridge.

"Just let me do all the talking, ok?" Zhang said telepathically as they rode the sleek elevator to the control deck level and made their way down the corridor to where Captain Alpha1 waited. Meanwhile Zhang's heart was pounding in his ears with yet no clue what he was going to say.

"No way! And have you sink us both?" Simon protested.

Zhang threw him a look. "You were the one that crashed the damn thing!"

"It was a simple mistake." Simon shot back.

The door to the bridge slid open to reveal the captain's stiff back as he reviewed the footage on the large screen before him. The video was projected from the shuttle craft's interior as well as exterior front cameras. The sinking feeling in Zhang's gut went to a whole new level of low. The cameras caught everything in ultra-high definition, from Simon at the controls singing with such passion, at times his eyes closed, to Zhang down below laughing and grinning back at him in obvious amusement and then dancing around like a happy fool for several moments as Simon buzzed around him in tight circles. *What the f—k?*

"You two must think I run some kind of circus here." The captain didn't even look at them.

"No sir! It was an honest...error of judgment," Zhang said measuring his words carefully. What could he say when the evidence was being replayed for those on the bridge to see. Simon may as well have just handed him his ass in a sling.

"So, commander you're telling me you lost control of the craft that you are responsible for as a decorated officer of this confederation and a member of the Athena's crew," Captain Alpha1 grilled him.

"Ummm, not so much he lost control, but I took it from him," Simon corrected and added, "Sir!" Then cleared his throat nervously.

Zhang thought back as the whole sordid scene replayed in slo mo in his head. He didn't even need to look at the footage on the screen. He prayed the captain had not reviewed any prior footage, in particular his haphazard landing and near miss on their approach to Mars. They were dead if that was the case. If the captain thought the moon footage was bad.... Zhang could kiss his flying career goodbye. They'd both be demoted to cleaning or cafeteria duty for sure. For his thoughts, as Simon had alluded to, had become unstable and chaotic on account of the very man who stood beside him being equally dressed down by the captain.

The gray to their left had turned in his seat, his hand hovering over the console in a threatening manner as he waited for the captain's word. Zhang could feel the little bastard's large black eyes boring into him, ready to hand him his head.

They were so screwed.

The captain nodded toward the gray. Zhang swore the little turd smirked at him with that slit of a mouth.

The video footage that immediately appeared on the screen appeared at first glance to be standard bearer as they flew towards Mars without a hitch.

Zhang was at the controls of the Science Explorer X1161. His calm voice could be heard as he checked and rechecked the ship's data per protocol as they made their approach. Simon sat in the seat beside him as usual, confirming his findings as he checked the navigation details on the smart pad in his hand.

Earlier the two had exchanged easy banter as they discussed aloud the details of their upcoming earth mission, the interesting classes they were taking in preparation for the mission and their hopes that they would be ready for their incarnations. In particular they wondered whether they had sufficiently grasped the Pleiadean cultivation skills they had learned and whether more practice was needed.

Zhang's heart pounded wildly and he had to take several deep breaths to avoid passing out as they both knew what was coming next.

Simon was then seen unbuckling his safety harness and climbing onto Zhang's lap to face him, grinning. Zhang could be heard initially protesting that he couldn't see much with Simon blocking his view, much less properly land the ship. This was followed by laughter from both of them before Simon leaned forward in an open-mouthed kiss. Zhang met his mouth with his own and the two passionately kissed and giggled and murmured to each other before kissing again as they hurdled through the asteroid belt toward the giant red planet.

Simon could be heard questioning where else his lips could go to make the commander smile in like fashion. To which Zhang replied he had an idea.

Moments later as they were making their approach, still quite preoccupied, a warning sounded in the cockpit and the ship banked hard to avoid a passing asteroid. This was followed by even more laughter as Zhang barely paid the warning any mind and threw the ship on autopilot before the two went back to entertaining themselves. The ship landed safely moments later. It took them awhile to notice.

Both he and Simon turned three shades darker, neither daring to speak much less look at each other.

Both knew no amount of explanation could clear their names. They...were...done...for.

The captain slowly turned to look at them both. The look on his face one of utter exasperation best described by three words: *'Really, you guys?'*

Both Zhang and Simon lowered their eyes, unable to bear the captain's condemnation.

The captain sighed aloud, then nodded to the gray who sat there eyeing them the whole time, it's castigating gaze drilling into them accusingly. Turning its small body slightly it ran a long spindly finger in an excruciatingly slow pattern on the console, its eyes glued to Zhang in clear judgment.

The words "VIDEO X1161: 281932|x-2: PERMANENT DELETE SEQUENCE PROTOCOL INITIATED" flashed on the big screen just as the monitor with the damning evidence went blank.

The captain turned back to them.

"You boys are dismissed," he said under his breath before he went back to his duties.

Zhang and Simon grabbed their gear and practically ran out the door.

Neither looked back.

CHAPTER TWENTY

Wherein there is Pleiadean Sex Cultivation and Bonding at The Westin the Night Before the Elle Photoshoot

As soon as they shut the door on Ming who was trying to fill Simon in on more boring business nonsense, they were in each other's arms.

"Did you just get even more handsome since we last did this?" Zhang chuckled mashing his mouth against Simon's in a voracious kiss.

"I was just about to say the same thing," Simon quipped back. He'd been dying to try something new with Zhang but wanted to be sure his partner was ready and adjusting well enough. After all it had been only a few days since things had turned around after months of hellish and relentless struggle. He reminded himself to tell Ming to order room service after they were done so Zhang could eat a bit more before it got too late. [Got7 Miracle]

Things rapidly escalated and soon they were naked and coupling on the dais at the foot of the king size bed. Zhang was mounted and seated on Simon's lap as they kissed deeply, their limbs tangled and akimbo. Zhang lifted and sank up and down slowly, his breath heavy as he savored the pleasurable intrusion at the base of his spine. Simon threw his head back and moved against him in tandem, using his large hand on Zhang's shoulder to deepen his upward thrusts, while his other hand braced against the back of the dais for leverage. They hissed and moaned in unison, taking their time and savoring the sweet and slow rhythm of their lovemaking.

He gazed at Zhang who had his eyes closed and head thrown back and thought how beautiful his partner was and how natural it felt for them to couple like this. Occasionally, unable to resist that long, pale throat and adam's apple, he'd lash out his tongue and drag it slowly up and down the protrusion then work his way down and along his collarbone while also palming his root. He wanted to do this simple thing for him, to allow him to forget for just a little while the troubles that had plagued him all these long months. Even though he was awake, and they had powerful backup they still had a bit longer to go.

Getting Zhang used to being back working in the industry if even in a limited way would go a long way to rebuilding his confidence. It pained him to see the hesitation in his eyes where there had been nothing but enthusiasm, boundless determination and raw grit before. He knew with time and more exposure as well as direct contact with their support team and the ship, Zhang would come around and be back to his unified and multidimensional self.

Zhang was moaning more urgently and Simon coaxed him to lift up his legs and carried him over to the bed. Zhang didn't protest nor open his eyes as Simon carefully maneuvered them without dislodging. He laid Zhang on the bed and hunkered over him and continued moving his hips thrusting long and slow as he began to breath more rapidly, tensing beneath him. Zhang's hands held him in place by the hips, digging into his sides as he dipped his head to thoroughly kiss him, doing a slow perusal of his mouth as the noises from Zhang's throat became more urgent. His skin was flush indicating he was very close. Only then did Simon extract himself slowly, shimmying down his body and stopping to kiss his stomach and thigh.

Zhang's eyes flew open in protest, "Don't stop-" he moaned hoarsely reaching for Simon.

"Shhh," Simon coaxed bending his head down to take Zhang's root into his mouth swallowing him down to the balls. Zhang hissed at this and entangled his hands in Simon's hair, capitulating. His hips jackknifed slamming his root into the back of Simon's throat. Simon retreated slightly to keep from asphyxiating and squeezed Zhang's member then slid his lips upward to slurp at the bulbous head. After swirling his tongue to gather the juices oozing there, he swallowed him again and took his sac in hand and gave it a gentle squeeze. The soft groans Zhang made were now long and protracted, his entire body flexing and tensing, signaling he was about to lose it.

At that moment Simon pressed the area at Zhang's perineum, the small area between his nether region and his balls anticipating with excitement the effect it would have. Dislodging his root from his throat, Simon burst out in gleeful laughter as Zhang shot off the bed, his whole body lifting upward like a stiff board, his eyes squeezed tight moments earlier, now wide and unfocused, his mouth slackened as a protracted guttural sound escaped him in unbounded ecstasy. He'd been dying to surprise him with it and use the move on him after learning about it while using the H-Deck shortly after Zhang incarnated. He accessed the auxiliary library and perused several advanced programs and sexual manuals produced by the Pleiadeans and "practiced" with his partner in the simulated reality.

From what he had witnessed, the unusual and intensely pleasurable little trick, caused an orgasm while stifling the ejaculation thus holding the life force inside the body. One's orgasm changed into a multi-dimensional, full bodied, cosmic experience. The look on Zhang's face was almost priceless and zen-like. After he came down and he somewhat quieted as Simon held him, Zhang gaped at him.

"Where the hell did you learn that?" From the way his body was still flush and jumping about, Simon guessed he had thoroughly enjoyed himself.

"Hee! Hee! Hee! The H-Deck. Was it good?"

Zhang laughed. "Good? That was incredible!" He gasped then rewarded Simon with a soul stealing kiss before offering himself up and promptly returning the favor.

Later as Zhang lay fast asleep in his arms in the hotel suite Ming had managed to conjure up, Simon's mind wandered to the night before Zhang made the jump to earth. They had spent it gazing at the inky black night and myriad stars that sparkled from the observation deck of the Athena. After a time, the captain advised they would be jumping through a worm hole to enter the fringes of the Milky Way where they would be treated to a most spectacular view of earth from up close. As they did not wish their presence to be detected yet by earth humans as that would come in short order, the captain would get them as close to the Naara jump point (what the earth humans called Venus) as they could.

Simon would have been lying if he didn't say he felt a bit sad his partner was heading out before him on the mission and also a bit worried. Neither of them had ever dropped so low in density before without protective gear and certainly not into such a dense, sluggish and harsh environment as 3D earth. The more horror stories that reached his ears, the more concerned he grew. But they'd been reassured the little grays tasked with handling the birthing and consciousness insertion process were well trained in their duties, the matter so routine for them they could do it in their sleep.

They would be constantly monitoring, adjusting and tweaking the entire process as necessary to ensure there were no glitches. Once he incarnated, Mencius would appear in light body form and immediately go over the details again and any last-minute reminders with Zhang. From there the rest of Zhang's numerous guides, angels and teachers who made up his support team would oversee his journey. He consoled himself that he would be joining him in short order where he would be able to protect him both energetically as well as physically, relying on his 9th dimensional abilities and angelic roots to remain in constant contact with the array and their myriad support team.

He wanted to make their final evening together on the Athena special. So, he reserved the entire observation deck on Level 40 for the occasion for just the two of them. He borrowed a couple of those overstuffed cushions from the officer's lounge to make sure they'd be comfortable and after a light meal of green protein drinks as recommended for all intended incarnates, he and Zhang lay on their backs, hands beneath their heads, and stared out at the stars as the captain initiated the ship's move.

The displacement momentarily caused the seemingly infinite number of specks of light in view to blur, and a rushing sensation to befall them as a translucent light wave filled the room. Moments later the giant ship reached her target destination and was maneuvered into place. They both reveled in the tingly and heady sensations in the aftermath as their bodies adjusted to the almost instant transfer. They lay side by side, their arms and legs touching and marveled at the simple beauty before them as the beautiful blue gem that was Gaia came into view. They ended up falling asleep while holding hands not long after.

They were awakened by the bio-alarm and the announcement for the day's first group of incarnates to prepare to meet in the med bay for consciousness transmission.

Simon had walked him to the medical bay where Zhang and approximately a few thousand other Sirians scheduled for incarnation in the 1:00 am to 1:01am slot had gathered. From there their consciousness would be extracted and transmitted to the Naara relay station nearby in preparation for their human births. When Zhang's number was called, Simon helped his partner into his stasis pod, made sure he was comfortable before kissing him on the cheek and closing the lid over him. Zhang seemed calm and unconcerned as usual, likely doing a mental review of the assignment at hand and ticking off boxes as was his habit before every mission.

A few moments later when all pods were ready, a series of soft tones then sounded throughout the med bay indicating that all systems were go. The technicians responsible for their operation and safekeeping began the extraction procedure. Simon waved at him and Zhang smiled back at him one last time before closing his eyes and appearing to fall asleep. Simon knew his seemingly lifeless body was actually still very much functioning although devoid of his consciousness. That was now awaiting transfer into his new form. The sensation for Zhang and the others awaiting incarnation on earth was like being at a transport station waiting to board a ship.

Afterward, Simon made his way to the cafeteria to grab breakfast, ordered a bowl of cherry nuts and headed to the Round Room to secure himself a prime seat to watch the show- - Zhang's incarnation on earth.

As Simon reminisced, Zhang who lay snuggled against him, startled in his sleep. He was having a nightmare. Simon brushed his hand gently across Zhang's crown then watched him settle back down in peaceful slumber. He then scanned the darkened and vacuous space for any sign of discordant energies but detected none. Zhang was likely just worried about the next day's shoot.

Simon marveled at how quickly things had turned around for them. It seemed to him just moments before he had seen his partner safely into his stasis pod and was waving goodbye.   From his perspective he knew it was in large part due to the tireless efforts of the guides whose help they had enlisted before they incarnated and who were on standby at the ready while they were on their earthly mission. The complex system of the still as yet unseen realms for most humans, he and Zhang had firsthand knowledge of. With any luck, this would be available for all of humanity to see...well, most of humanity from what he'd been told as a lot for whom the shock of rapid change was too much invariably would choose to leave.

Yawning himself, Simon squeezed his partner's hand in reassurance before falling asleep.

They had a big day ahead of them.

The alarm on Simon's cellphone went off at six. This was followed immediately by a call from Ming to ensure he was awake and the shrill ring of the phone for a wakeup call from the front desk she'd set up just to annoy him. Still, they dawdled in bed, their hands roaming about beneath the covers seeking out the other's morning wood as they stretched and exchanged curse words at the early hour. Targets acquired, Simon made a move first, ducking his head under the blankets and disappearing. Moments later Zhang was moaning softly above him, eyes closed, legs sprawled open, his root lodged deep in Simon's throat. Simon didn't disappoint and within minutes had him thrashing around like a rag doll, fingers knotted in Simon's mussy hair, moaning loudly before enthusiastically flooding Simon's windpipe with his seed. Not quite satisfied Simon crawled up Zhang's body, kissed him thoroughly offering up a taste of his own essence before taking his place between Zhang's legs to have his way with him once more, seeking his own release. Zhang came again. Hard. No surprise there.

"I love my smell all over you. Just like before when we first met and started doing it, don't shower. Let's see how long you can go without people noticing," Simon mused nuzzling Zhang's neck and leaving a very visible mark there. Zhang had to agree. He loved Simon's seed all over him. When Simon was done, he pulled back to study his handiwork.

Despite Simon's plea, they hurriedly showered, inspecting and moaning prodigiously about their double eyelids and puffy cheeks, aching muscles and sore assholes before meeting Ming downstairs at 7am. (To say nothing of the swollen lips and obvious marks of passion on the other's necks.)

"Think anyone will notice?" Zhang asked rubbing at the still tender spot where Simon had maw'd him as if that alone would conceal it.

"Nah," Simon shook his head in all seriousness. "Who the hell would notice such a small mark as that? It's no bigger than a mosquito bite."

CHAPTER TWENTY-ONE

Wider Baby, Smile!

"Jesus! You two look like shit!" Ming hissed as soon as she saw them emerge from the elevator. Leave it to Ming to express her unsolicited opinion as she passed out coffees from the lobby Starbucks and dialed up the car. "Did you guys have a buffet going on up there that I missed? What is wrong with you two?" She cried gesturing at their necks.

"Don't be gross, Ming." Simon rolled his eyes.

Meanwhile Zhang's hand flew to his throat again. "What? Is it that obvious?"

"Uh, yeah!" Ming snorted leading them out to the port cochere. Simon made a face and shook his head at Zhang to contradict her, knowing they could both show up looking like homeless people and the stylists and makeup artists attending to them would turn it around for them. Thank goodness they had others managing their appearance with such diligence. All had to sign non-disclosure agreements so no matter what they saw, they had to keep quiet at the risk of never working in the industry again. Zhang didn't even bother to comb his hair stuffing his head instead in a baseball cap. Simon noticed he was walking with some difficulty and snickered although he wasn't doing much better.

By nine thirty, hair and makeup done, they were ushered from their chairs into the studio looking like supermodels once again where a big fuss was made over their joint appearance and the photographer immediately went to work. They quickly fell into routine, Simon posing like the boss model he was given his long years as the Little Prince of Advertising. Zhang meanwhile stood around, albeit a bit stiffly, looking very much like just a regular guy in the business of melting hearts with his natural good looks and boyish smile.

Upon hearing the photographer's command for "more sexy" and "come on, really give it to me, baby!" Zhang would merely angle his head slightly and offer up a wave without the slightest clue what the lecherous bastard was asking of him. They took a slight break to stuff themselves on bagels, cream cheese and orange juice at 10:30a before they endured another bout of touch ups to their hair and makeup and quickly changed outfits, their garments coordinated with just enough similarities to avoid clashing. This was followed by more touch ups to their hair and makeup which they quietly endured.

Zhang enjoyed watching his partner in action, so methodical and exacting in his work. He marveled how Simon could so radically transform his look with just a slight change of his expression and a little hair gel. He was truly masterful at all this modeling business needing very little instruction to get the exact look they were aiming for. And he was beautiful. Looking so extraordinarily sexy and sophisticated in every shot. He on the other hand didn't see what the big deal was about his own looks. He was just a regular joe in his book. Sure, he cleaned up well and looked good in expensive or casual clothes, but Simon was different.

Zhang's heart squeezed watching him and he wondered how the hell he even survived being away from his partner so long. Even from where he stood off to the side waiting for his turn he could see Simon radiated a powerful angelic aura, his light so bright it was blinding even to him. Not to mention all the female staff who were standing around ogling his partner who apparently was oblivious to the attention. He made everything, life even, look so damn easy.

"Wait! Ugh! I need a bathroom break! That coffee's about to run right through me!" Simon suddenly yelled, instantly shattering the image of perfection and princely elegance as he sprinted for the toilet. The abrupt interruption left his female admirers in a tizzy of giggles anxiously awaiting his return, not at all caring Simon had just publicly announced he had to take a dump. Zhang debated whether to follow him, the coffee not quite doing its magic for him yet, but he was called in to take Simon's place.

After loading more film, the photographer began working him in earnest amidst shouting even more nonsensical commands. Zhang glanced at the giant utilitarian clock on the wall dead ahead and mourned.

11:15 am.

It was going to be a very long day.

Simon came back minutes later and watched as Zhang finished up, smiling that goofy smile at him. Ming meanwhile ignored them both and instead chatted away on her phone to the side seeming to be giving instructions to someone. Wardrobe, makeup and hair wizards swarmed around Simon like flies as they effortlessly put him back together. Zhang had to laugh and shake his head.

"That's it! Yes, sarcasm and humor! Great look!" The guy snapping away with the camera yelled, pleased. Zhang ignored him and scratched his back and side.

Zhang's eyes naturally kept going over to his partner and seeking him out eliciting admonition from the photographer to "uh, look this way!" But he couldn't help it and kept doing it as Simon giggled at him watching him back. Finally giving up, the photographer asked Simon to join Zhang under the lights. This began a series of mostly tasteful collaboration, poses that had one laying amidst styrofoam rocks as if on a beach (Simon- as Simon draped on rocks or just about on anything else with that long elegant physique was always eye candy), while the other reclined against his chest or lap suggestively, intertwining their arms while gazing over the other's shoulder, or sharing the same faraway look. Zhang reveled in the close contact with his partner, secure in his presence. While he wasn't usually so jittery and feeling vulnerable as he was used to working on his own in the business, today was different. Simon picked up on it and smiled that knowing smile that said, "Don't worry. You've got this."

"You're so beautiful, Zhang," Simon whispered in his ear when their heads were positioned closely, they were practically knocking against each other. "Makes me want to eat you." Simon grinned mischievously as the camera clicked away.

Somehow the comment made him flush and grow warm all over. Simon knew which buttons to push for sure. The photographer came over to reposition Simon's foot and left arm.   When he moved Simon's knee and pushed it open a tad, Zhang felt a sting of jealousy overcome him. Seeing the subtle change in his expression, Simon cleared his throat, looked dead at the offender and said, "Just tell me what you wish to do. Don't touch me, please, or him." After which he smiled back at Zhang as if nothing had happened.

Zhang almost laughed. Simon meant business. And while he appeared a delicate flower or a bit dizzy at times, he obviously had everything under control. He also knew his boundaries and silently applauded him.

The next several commands by the photographer, who now wisely kept his distance from them both, had Zhang's crotch tightening.

"Let's kick things up a notch. How about Simon you sit up here with your knees slightly apart and lean forward a bit. Excellent! Let's try it with the left leg extended just slightly to elongate the look. Yes! Perfect! Now, hand up to the chin in a sort of contemplative look, draw it out a little, that's it! Eyes straight ahead. Now Zhang, get between his knees. Uh, no face the other way. That's it. Head slightly angled back so that you're looking up at him as if resting your head on his thigh....Lean back a little and hold—"

The camera whirled in a dizzying series of rapid clicks to capture them. "Simon drop your head and lean over just a bit and really look at him. Closer! Yes! Now right arm relaxed on your right knee for an easy lean.

"That's it! Perfect! Don't move Zhang!"

Simon tilted his head of his own volition perfecting the look and gazed down at him with a look so seductive Zhang felt smoke coming out of his ears. *Holy shit!* It was the smoldering look of Wen Kexing, the Ghost Valley Chief in full on hot pursuit all over again. Zhang stared at his lips and swallowed hard as he was instantly transported back to the days on the rundown set, a series of mostly ugly green screens, small props, crowded and steaming hot, dusty rooms and notoriously soaking wet ground. Yet they had been in total heaven, ensconced in their own world once they realized they had such explosive chemistry and the director yelled "Action!"

They were a devilish pair, clearly made for one another as anyone with working eyes could see. These were times when all else ceased to exist, and it was just the two of them pushed closely together, left to their own devices. They'd collaborated on each scene rehearsing it over and over until every nuance, action sequence, every emotion was captured on film, and their love story was told with perfection. And that chemistry wasn't just reserved for on screen.

Back then the long hours of filming, normally especially draining made all the more excruciating when one's opposite lead and costar was a fluke, were sheer bliss with Simon. Zhang recalled feeling melancholy as the day wound down and it was time to go back to his RV to rest, yet wanting nothing more than to follow his costar around like a puppy dog.

In the beginning he shyly bid his costar good night, before taking out his body's frustrations in the tiny, cramped shower of his camper with just his hand, all the while envisioning Simon's massive paws on him. Part unspoken lust, part growing infatuation with his male colleague, the result was the very real burden of carrying around wood under layers upon layers of costume they were forced to wear for hours on end. That part of his journey had been exhausting and lonely.

Until the day Simon pressed up against him during a scene and discovered his secret. Zhang had been horrified, after all they were just acting, working professionals tasked with crafting someone else's story for the big screen. Zhang couldn't even meet his eyes. But the look on Simon's face in the aftermath of the discovery was priceless. And telling. Simon promptly forget all his lines. *Bless the bastard.*

Being a quick study, Simon made up for it as soon as the director yelled "Action!" again. Enthusiastically encircling both arms around his waist, he shamelessly pressed his face against him, Zhang's root against his cheek and lower jaw so that every word and line spoken of his long soliloquy vibrated against it. The sensation raised the hair on Zhang's arms and neck. Zhang knew then that the feelings were mutual.

Afterwards, it was as if a wall between them that neither knew was there, dropped. They became bold and even shameless. He couldn't stop touching him. Any excuse to get closer. To connect with that electric energy that was Simon. He became a drug he couldn't do without.

At the end of the day's work, rather than go back to his own trailer, which had been parked next to Simon's, to rehearse his lines or wind down for the day, he'd find his way to noodle in to his colleague's caravan, sometimes boldly following in behind him as if he lived there, with unspoken expectations. There they would discreetly sate the tension between them that had been building over the long hours of filming before promptly falling asleep only to do it all again the next night.

To say others began to notice was an understatement. They relied heavily upon the thousands of staff members attending to them or on the set to be discreet. Because he and Simon could hardly say they were. They could barely contain themselves stopping short of outing themselves but for the director's incessant admonitions to "control yourselves!"

"And let's call that a wrap and take a 45-minute break!" Elle's studio director yelled breaking Zhang's revelry. "Good job, boys!"

Zhang's armpits were soaking wet. He'd been staring so deeply at

Simon's lips he hadn't realized he was perspiring with the exertion.

Modeling was hard work. No wonder Simon was in such great shape.

"Yea! Let's eat! I'm starving," Simon burst standing up and pulling Zhang with him. Ming was immediately at Simon's side and rattling off more studio business. Simon only half listened as he and Zhang headed to check out the buffet that had been prepared for them and the staff in a side room. They each took two bottles of water and sat off to the side to feast as Ming joined them.

Just then Zhang's phone buzzed. It was a text message from his lawyers' office. His petition against slander filed against a particularly rabid media personnel had been accepted. A court date would be set and his presence may or may not be necessary. He showed Simon the text.

"Report that to Mencius but I think we should definitely go."

"How?"

Simon gestured for his phone. Zhang promptly handed it over.

Simon went into the settings function, went into the AI mode and began tapping a series of numbers and letters from memory before turning the phone to Zhang so his reflection appeared in the screen. A second later an unfamiliar American sounding voice blared loudly on the little speaker.

"Proxy 2122104UNSAX41 set up complete. Facial recognition established. Welcome Commander ZhangZHXO511." Zhang's eyes nearly popped out of his head before he quickly looked about to see who was looking. Simon laughed, sucking in his breath and intoning in that weird way only Simon could. "Funny, isn't it?"

"What the hell did you do with my phone?" Zhang stared at the screen which had gone dark again in shock. A second later Mencius appeared on video. Simon quickly tossed the phone back to Zhang and waved both hands motioning to indicate he wasn't around to talk.

"Ah, Commander! It's good to see you!" Mencius beamed. Bewildered, Zhang stared down at the strange Chinese looking Gandalf-esque man with long, wavy graying hair, beautifully manicured eyebrows and smooth pale skin. There was a luminescent glow all around him. Zhang swore he was looking at God. Until Mencius moved his head slightly and Zhang saw the glow was merely from some overhead lights and there were other people passing behind him, trays of food in hand, some even slowing to wave in greeting when they saw his face, "Hey, Commander!"

What the —

"Let me put this up on the big screen so everyone can see," 'Gandalf' said fiddling on his end before Zhang could protest. His mind struggled to understand what exactly was going on while a vague but growing niggling he also completely understood it all ate at him. As odd as he looked to Zhang, the guy looked familiar...*I know him!* He sucked in a deep breath as his mind struggled to make the leap. He rubbed a hand over his eyes and frowned at the screen which suddenly went blank.

Mencius accidentally hung up.

"What's going on?" Simon asked. While Zhang was having a *kafkaesque* moment, Simon was wolfing down his food. "Did he hang himself up again?"

"I- I think so."

Simon took the phone back from him.

"Are you sure we should even be talking to this guy?" Zhang asked, still reeling.

"He's our master guide. He's alright. A bit strange but...." Just then the phone made a melodic series of tones Zhang had never heard before. Simon swiped right and handed it back to him. Zhang stared blankly at the screen and immediately could tell by the cheering sounds in the background he was up on said 'big screen' although he pretty much still had just a headshot of Mencius filing his view.

"There, sir. He's back!" A subordinate's voice could be heard in the background. Apparently, Mencius had asked for help.

"Hello...." Zhang cleared his throat and plastered an awkward smile on his face. Simon chuckled from his seat across from him.

"Things going well, I trust? Glad to see you back online. The captain gives his regards and has ok'd this to be broadcast throughout the mothership."

Simon began cracking up at this making that strange intonation Zhang was certain only his partner was capable of.

"Is that the Lieutenant?" Mencius asked. "Good, I have a message for him too. We will be downloading a new assignment for him in a short while."

Simon got serious. "Mmmn," he said stuffing rice into his mouth. "Tell him about the court thing," he said around a mouthful of meat and veggies gesturing with his chopsticks.

"Uh...the court accepted my petition against Xi Li and Simon wants us to go together when it's decided."

"Good idea. Though it's not just your petition, Commander Zhang. It has the backing of all of the Angels, Guides, Masters, and beings of Light as do you. You are not alone and have nothing to fear. It's not just Simon who has your back. You walk in the Light."

Zhang was stunned. How the hell did this guy pick up on what he'd been so stressed out and feeling so alone about and with just a few short words of encouragement lift it off of him? He wanted to ask if his attorneys were also part of that team.

Mencius leaned in and smiled. "That's why I'm your master guide, son."

Zhang felt tears pooling in his eyes. Immediately there was a chorus of "awwwww" heard in the background and he quickly swiped the tears away.

Then, "And no, those clowns were picked by that damn Li character who sometimes has cotton in his ears. But we can still work with them for now. Just use your internal guidance system to continually assess their motives. You'll be fine."

Zhang nodded, quickly learning his thoughts could also be read. Thinking on what he and Simon had been doing since Simon blew back in his life, he wondered in alarm what else they could hear and had heard. Mencius didn't reply. Instead, he said, "Rest assured we will be providing you more insight and guidance as the day for the hearing draws near. In the interim, hold the course. You're doing wonderful! By the way, your hair looks great like that!" Mencius said before the screen went dark again.

Zhang stared at it for some time before Simon reached over and slowly took it out of his hand and pushed his bowl of food at him. "Babe, you better eat a little something. We're not done yet and you need your strength."

Need his strength was right. Zhang didn't know how much more he could take as the shoot seemed to go long past the promised 3 o'clock hour. Finally, at 5:11p sharp, the Director called it a day to loud cheers all around and congratulations for a job well done.

"Let's go eat!" Simon the foodie immediately piped up and grinned at him. Zhang barely had any energy to change out of his wardrobe and slip his baseball cap back on, yet Simon looked like he was ready for another 8 hours of work, smiling and joking around. Even Ming looked like she was having trouble keeping up with him.

"There's a new hot pot place I heard about that I want to check out and maybe do a vlog on," Simon said already researching on his phone. Zhang was about to protest.

"Found it! Come on, babe. Let's go get drunk!"

Zhang immediately perked up thinking that was the best idea ever.

CHAPTER TWENTY-TWO

Simon and Zhang Do Domestic

By weeks end with the long hours they spent roughhousing and sating themselves on the couch, the floor, in the bedroom, in the shower, and even on the kitchen counter back at Zhang's apartment, even Simon was dragging his ass.

"What the hell? Didn't those Pleiadeans say sex was supposed to revitalize you? How come I feel so drained?" Simon complained still slung over Zhang's back, naked and slick with sweat after doing "it" yet again.

"Maybe we can just Google it," Zhang said from somewhere beneath him, his ass so raw he swore he was starting to crap blood. He had a vague feeling their sexual knowledge and growing prowess wasn't as innate as much as it had been "taught" to them though he couldn't remember anything close to it from high school or college. Certainly not the kind of man on man sensual action they proved they were capable of again and again.

Simon groaned and rolled off of him with some effort. "Maybe they lied." He grumbled before they both heard a terse female voice in their heads.

"We didn't say to do it five times a day! Everything in moderation." She was using the 5th through 9th density array to broadcast just to them.

Zhang popped his head up just as Simon laughed. "Did you hear that?"

"Next time put that in your manuals!" Simon huffed before answering. Thala had since left the array. "That's the array. She jumped in to respond to us."

"Who?"

"Lady Master Thala. She's the Pleiadean goddess you had your eye on on the ship before you realized that your loving partner and soulmate was a damn good kisser himself and you promptly forgot all about her." Simon winked. Zhang had a glazed look in his eyes. Simon rubbed his shoulder. "Don't worry. It'll come back to you. Come on, let's go shower."

"So did we only practice kissing on the ship, or did we do anything else?" Zhang ventured to ask as they sat down to dinner later. Simon had cooked some fried noodles with veggies and chicken proving his talents also lay outside the sack.

"What do you think?" Simon teased serving him a bowl and sitting across from him. "What is that saying? Oh yes, practice makes perfect! Hee! Hee!" He beamed proudly.

Zhang snorted and shook his head. "And so, this is a thing on the ship too?" He asked gesturing between them with his chopsticks.

"Up until the Pleiadeans showed up, no."

"What happened?" Zhang asked seeking to jog his own memory. He knew what he felt for Simon was real. His heart and soul told him he was madly in love with him. That they were meant to be. But he was still trying to wrap his brain around the fact they were a thing elsewhere, soul mates who traveled around the galaxy as commander and lieutenant, much less he and Simon were 8-foot-tall Sirians laying in cold storage while they carved out this earth mission. He also wondered why his memories were not coming back to him as quickly as Simon's had.

Simon had wondered the same thing, too, and had asked for assistance in the array. Lady Master Thala replied and suggested he try the "trick" to jog Zhang's memories faster. Zhang could also try deep meditation. Simon opted to use the "trick" and to do it as often as they coupled, which was pretty often.

"We signed up for their Master Class on Sensual and Sexual Cultivation. We sat in the front row and took a hell of a lot of notes," Simon said scarfing down his food and chasing it down with a bottle of water.

"Is that why we're so good at it?" Zhang chuckled digging in as well. "This is really good by the way. Thank you."

"You're welcome. After doing a bit of lecturing and demonstrating using a hologram of two people kissing during the first class, we got the idea in our heads that these hot Pleiadean females would be our practice partners."

Zhang burst out laughing. "Don't tell me they said, 'now turn to your partner beside you and start practicing'."

"Exactly! So, we did! We got high marks too!" They grinned like fools at each other.

"So did we actually do "it" on the ship?"

"No…actually we didn't. We attended all three days of the presentation and learned mostly about the spiritual energy transfer and how we can reach states of consciousness that are beyond simple sexual pleasure."

"Sounds boring….so if we didn't learn how to do it during the class, how did you know what to do?" Zhang remembered their first night in the caravan. Simon had been an animal. It was all Zhang could do to keep up. Well, before their little mishap. But after that, before he knew it they were giving each other blow jobs, sticking tongues up butts and he was being expertly taken up the ass and he reciprocating with Simon. He never looked back. On any given night it was a toss-up who topped who, although usually Zhang was too lazy to do anything but just lie there leaving Simon to do the heavy lifting. Thank god he didn't mind. Everything he knew he could thank Simon for. The guy was a monster and the friggin' Master of Sex.

Simon grinned at him.

"Don't tell me the holodeck."

"Ha! Ha! Ha! Ha! Ha! Ha!" Simon burst out laughing. Zhang couldn't help but join in as Simon's laugh was so infectious.

"You are such a goofball! So, was I your partner in the holodeck, too?" Zhang felt his heart squeeze. He'd be devastated if Simon didn't say yes to this. But he also knew Simon would not lie to him.

"Of course! Artificial Intelligence is amazing!" Simon grinned broadly. Zhang let out the breath he'd been holding.

"So, when we go back...after all this is done, will we remember what we did here or are we just going back to Commander and Lieutenant? Can we even do this up there?"

"We can do whatever we want, babe. As long as it's done out of unconditional love, everything is in divine right order." Then, "Do you want to remember and do this on the ship?" Simon got very serious suddenly. Given Simon had all his memories of their lives up there, Zhang knew the matter was to be taken with the utmost gravity and consideration. Simon's intense gaze only underscored the matter and it made Zhang's heart thud. He swallowed hard before he allowed himself to answer, the weight of Simon's words hanging on his heart.

"What kind of dumb ass sort of question is that?!" Zhang snorted. "F—k yeah, we're remembering and doing it! Every friggin' chance we can get!"

Simon burst out laughing as Zhang joined in.

"That's right!" Simon said, the serious look in his eyes giving way to the joy in his heart as he stared back at his beautiful soul mate. They were in effect twin souls. "We'll have to requisition for a bigger room we can share," Simon said already thinking ahead.

"Wait, we don't have apartments up there? I thought you said it's a mothership?" Zhang pfft'd.

Simon thought this funny and began guffawing again. "We're just a couple of single guys up there. Even the captain doesn't have a full apartment."

"Well maybe this Mencius guy can put in a good word for us," Zhang said smiling at his mate. He was starting to look forward to knowing more about this other life his soul mate spoke of so readily. They spent the remainder of the evening with Zhang asking questions and Simon answering them. Like did they have gay marriage up there? What did they usually do for fun? Could he bring his guitar? Did they play video games and golf? Did they eat Chinese hot pot? Where did they go to high school? How did they learn to fly a spaceship? Why was Simon only a lieutenant and he was a commander? How much did they get paid? All of which Simon answered patiently and in good humor.

Seeing neither of them seemed to be any good at restraining themselves, for the next three days they agreed to keep their hands off of each other temporarily to avoid getting into situations where they would just end up fucking before they had fully recuperated. They spent the time instead playing video games on the couch, catching up on watching reruns of *The Untamed* interspersed with Zhang commenting often about how hot that *Lan Zhan* guy was. Simon on the other hand thought the sexier one was the darker of the two with those flowing black robes, black flute and black smoke he gave off. They argued about whether to watch whole episodes of *Word of Honor* or *Better Call Saul* on Netflix which Simon bootlegged using advanced encryption codes he stole out of the Athena's vast computer database. (Mencius knew about that and promptly warned him about creating karma for such trifling things while on earth to which Simon replied such a trifling thing shouldn't even be considered karma producing.   Mencius didn't reply.)

Their refraining from sexual cultivation lasted less than 16 hours and 13 earth minutes. Even then they thought they did pretty good.

Over the next couple of weeks, they ventured out more, going shopping in the outdoor mall and walking in the nearby park holding hands and taking selfies. No one seemed to bother with them much less recognize them although to be safe they wore masks and baseball hats and stayed away from crowds. Simon couldn't remember when he'd been so at ease. Zhang too seemed to relax into their routine.

It was then that Simon's phone buzzed. Expecting to see a message from Ming bugging him about when he planned to get back to the studio, instead he saw a message from Mencius. He had received instructions for his next assignment.

It wasn't so much that this mission was top secret, but because the team felt Zhang needed to stay on track with his own mission, they decided not to clue him in until later. This way he could focus fully on the upcoming hearing and exposing the corruption he was facing. This was after all a mission that needed to be tackled from multiple angles. So, after two more days of bumming around, Simon left his car for Zhang to use and flew back to Shanghai promising to return as soon as he could.

They kissed deeply in the car in the passenger loading zone at the airport, Zhang in the driver's seat, clinging to him tightly.

"I promise I'll be back as soon as I can. It shouldn't be too long. Let me know when you hear about the court hearing and if I can get away sooner, I'll come back for it and you right away. Then we can drive back to Shanghai together and it'll be your turn to stay with me."

Only then did Zhang have all his assurances and Simon felt comfortable leaving him behind.

Zhang cried on the ride all the way home.

CHAPTER TWENTY-THREE

Zhang Loses it...Again

Zhang felt something was off when he couldn't reach Simon and then
when he failed to check in that night before he went to bed. It'd already
been a month since he'd seen him last, and he was barely holding it
together without him. He'd heard from his lawyers that the hearing set
for the last week of the month that he'd been anxiously preparing for
had been postponed and a new date would be scheduled shortly. Had
he'd known that in advance he would've followed Simon to Shanghai.
Instead, he'd been stuck waiting and running to appointments to prep
his testimony and strategize with his legal team.

While staying together, he and Simon had easily fallen into a routine
that was unlike anything they'd ever had before. It wasn't just the
incredible sex every night when he'd been there. Simon had also insisted
on cooking and cleaning and keeping house (not that he was a slob)
although he had to admit the house did look and smell far better when
Simon tended to it. He began to believe this was their new life together.
But then Simon got called away again for work and had to go back to
Shanghai. He would have gone with him had it not been for the
scheduled meetings and hearing preparations at the lawyers office. He
knew it was important that he stay focused on it but still he missed

Simon so much. It was a constant dull ache he carried in his breast.

They took to speaking several times a day, he looking forward to hearing his voice and seeing what he was up to just like before. Only then did that heavy feeling leave him. Since he couldn't access his Weibo and WeChat accounts, Simon made sure to post on IG for him, sending coded messages only he and the most astute fans could pick up on. So, it was unusual when he didn't hear from him after a time.

They'd spoken just after 2pm as Zhang was leaving the gym downstairs. Simon had said he was heading to a meeting with Chairman Luo to discuss a joint Studio HK GJ Studio collaboration for a new product endorsement. Chairman Luo was a big wig. To Zhang it was a huge opportunity for Simon if he could snag it. But he didn't really have any firsthand knowledge of the guy having never worked with him himself. He'd just heard rumors. But as the evening and night dragged on, he began to feel uneasy. He called him again. When that didn't work, he texted him. His phone remained silent.

He went to bed thinking Simon was likely just tired, fighting the awful feeling he'd experienced before just before things went south for him. It started as a nagging feeling that he couldn't shake and then became an unbearable, ugly heaviness culminating in the belief that he'd been abandoned by Simon and that only recently went away when they reunited. To be safe he kept the phone by his bed in case Simon was able to call. When he still hadn't heard from him by the next morning, he panicked and called Ming.

It went straight to voice mail. Knowing she was always with Simon, this caused him to go even more into a panic. He fumbled with his phone settings to call Mencius. He hadn't yet had the hang of using the AI feature and also had no clue of how to tap into the array. He'd been meaning to ask Simon but had forgotten. Now as he searched thru the phone settings he couldn't find any trace of the AI function nor that it ever even existed.

He decided to just text Simon.

CrazyZhang1: How'd the meeting go? Is he as big a douche as they say? I'm sure you totally nailed it.

StudMuffinGJ: .....

CrazyZhang1: Babe, everything ok? I was looking forward to hearing your voice tonight before going to bed. 😟 call me when you can. Miss you miss you 😘

StudMuffinGJ: .....

CrazyZhang1: Hey babe, are you ok? Call me. Miss you.

StudMuffinGJ: .....

CrazyZhang1: Hey! Been missing you something awful. It sucks using my hand. How could you abandon me to this fate? 😣

StudMuffinGJ: .....

CrazyZhang1: Wow you must really be busy. I thought you'd call by now. 🫤 . Is everything alright?

StudMuffinGJ: .....

CrazyZhang1: Is this about me leaving the toilet seat up? Because if it is, I promise to leave it down when you come back. Ok just thought I'd put it out there. Missing you big time!! 💀

StudMuffinGJ: …..

CrazyZhang1: Ok, you're starting to scare me. What's going on? I can't even reach Ming. Dude, call me back, please.

StudMuffinGJ: …..

CrazyZhang1: 🖕 Not cool, dude! Not cool! 😡

StudMuffinGJ: …..

CrazyZhang1: Whatever it is, babe we can work it out. You know I love you so so much. I miss everything about us. I am going nuts here without you. 💀 🍙 🍙

StudMuffinGJ: …..

CrazyZhang1: Why aren't you calling me? What's going on with us? I thought everything was going well but obviously I missed something. 🐻 😡 😳

StudMuffinGJ: …..

CrazyZhang1: Are you cheating on me? If you are, you're dead! Haven't even heard from you in days. If you cheating call me tonight. 😡 😳

CrazyZhang1: *aren't cheating

StudMuffinGJ: …..

CrazyZhang1: Simon! You f—en jerk! 😡 😡 😡 Who is he? Some freak you met in Shanghai? You make me sick! 🤢 🤢

StudMuffinGJ: …..

CrazyZhang1: Die, motherf@#!r! Die!! 😡 ☠️ 💀

StudMuffinGJ: …..

CrazyZhang1: You know you're dead to me right?! RIP asshole! Good riddance!! 😡 ☠️ 💀

StudMuffinGJ: …..

CrazyZhang1: I'm sorry, babe. I didn't mean all that. I just miss you so so much.   Please call me. 😞 😢 🙇

StudMuffinGJ: …..

CrazyZhang1: On second thought, you know what, asshole? I did mean it!! I mean it times 10!!! WE ARE OFFICIALLY DONE!!! 😡 😡 😡 GOOD By

CrazyZhang1: *BEE

CrazyZhang1: *BYI

CrazyZhang1: *ByE!!!

StudMuffinGJ: .....

By the third day with still no word from either Simon or Ming, Zhang was ready to jump out his 12-story window. Every insecurity that he had ever experienced on account of his on again, off again, on again relationship with the love of his life and soul mate was expressed in the numerous unanswered texts not to mention the 59 or so voicemails he left on Simon's phone just in case he didn't get his texts.

Every way he tried to make sense of any of it he found himself smothered in feelings of deep anxiety, helplessness and worst of all the knowledge he'd been abandoned again. Was it possible that Simon had only messed with his head as he'd originally led himself to believe? That the whole friggin' 9 1/2 weeks of sheer bliss and head spinning adventures they'd been on before he went back to Shanghai was all just a god damn sham? What else could it be? Unless he was lying in a ditch somewhere? They'd both suffered a lot of negative attention including having to deal with unbalanced stalkers in the aftermath of their meteoric rise to fame. Maybe something had happened?!

He thought of going to the police. Of filing a missing person's report. But wouldn't Ming or his parents already have done that? After all Ming would never leave Simon's side for very long. Certainly if he really was missing, she'd be the first to know. And she knew he was important enough to Simon to be one of the first ones she'd let know, right? Unless...it...was... all...a god...damn mind f—k all over again.... He spent that week in bed bawling his eyes out. Too heartbroken to eat or

190

sleep and hiding under his blanket, his phone under his pillow.

He found himself retreating into that deep dark pit again of no return. He swore this time he would kill him. No explanations would ever soften his heart up to him again. He'd never be stupid enough to fall for the asshole like he had allowed himself to do. He needed to take his message to IG, the only SM platform that he could access. He needed to let the world know what a friggin' loser the Little Prince of Advertising, China's tv darling, the fake and truly evil actor & idol Simon truly was. And to have been burned by him not once, but twice — *Aghhh!!!!*

Meanwhile Simon was busy, neck deep in a battle for the Light.

CHAPTER TWENTY-FOUR

Simon Undertakes His New Mission

Chairman Luo "The Chairman". Billionaire movie maker and industry mover and shaker Luo Gu Xian. A big, imposing (ok fat) man who liked to throw his weight around and liked pretty boys even more. While widely known to favor young and tender skin, everyone in the know knew he was a predator, choosing his prey among the hopefuls and aspiring artists. But thus far no one dared come forward to openly accuse him for fear of being blacklisted.

As the Chairman had a long reach, with contacts that were decades old and the list of co- conspirators a mile long in just about every industry, taking him down had to be carefully orchestrated if they were going to finally succeed. Prior attempts had not been successful, resulting at most with lessor accusations against him for things like failure to file for a business license or building permit or to pay the interest on a loan or some other bullshit that always seemed to vanish after the payment of a fine or slight reprimand. In short, he was a slippery weasel.

That's where Simon came in. Peddling his pretty ass to ensnare the fat bastard and finally take him down. His assignment was to get an audience with him for the purpose of blowing everything wide open. It was well known the entertainment industry was full of sexual predators, some like Chairman Luo operating in the open and protected by their friends.

He learned long ago of the underbelly of the business having firsthand experience what it meant to be sexually harassed and vulnerable, particularly as a struggling young artist. Expecting to attend an audition or relying upon promises by an agent, he'd find himself before an audience of lecherous old men that included influential politicians, producers, and other big industry names. Back then he relied on his lack of sophistication to politely decline and hurriedly remove himself from the situation. He swore he'd never become that desperate. But a lot of his colleagues, both men and women had. He didn't blame or judge them, but he himself could never compromise.

Even back then, fresh faced and hopeful, he only appeared as if he had no one but his dreams to back him. But in actuality, he was biding his time and learning to navigate the slippery slope that was the performance arts industry. What he saw only informed him. Early on he realized the need to create his own agency and studio starting with just a few fellow students. Since then, he had steadily built a name for himself. He had occasion to bump up against them every now and then but not everyone in the business was filthy. He worked on establishing his studio's connections with them until he was practically on level footing with many of them. Enough to be noticed. Enough to be taken seriously.

He cared less when others scoffed and called him the Little Prince of Advertising for his reliance on modeling gigs. Instead, he laughed his way to the bank, knowing that all he needed to do was steadily work on boosting his popularity and image and remain firmly in control of it while taking care of his obligations and helping his parents through an honest living. He wasn't just a pretty face in the industry who sometimes acted awkward or sang off key. He saw those attributes, while vaguely amusing, to be a powerful tool of disarmament.

In a society like theirs which valued status, good looks, money and most importantly power, he knew a healthy balance of all of that coupled with a firm sense of self-humility would have him standing a head taller than all of them. None of it was an act. It was just who he was. He said what he meant, and he always meant what he said. Thus, Simon who had a penchant for looking good in front of the camera as well as having a somewhat goofy personality was a seasoned veteran, astute businessman and a force to be reckoned with.

And now, Simon endured the scrutinizing gaze of Chairman Luo's number two man as they sat across from each other in the sleek white limousine. Ray Lin was purportedly a Hong Kong businessman slash movie producer slash actor of questionable background.

To Simon he looked straight up gangsta' with his heavily cratered face, shifty eyes, slicked back thick, black hair and gray Armani suit. He sat opposite of Simon ogling him rather suggestively as they navigated the narrow hilly streets leading up to the chairman's Northern Hunan estate. While the guy's constant beady eyes on him even sliding down to his crotch on occasion were unnerving, Simon knew the gangster henchman wouldn't dare lay a hand on the goods reserved strictly for the big boss. And if all went according to plan, Simon would be served up to the Chairman in just under the hour. Things would really get interesting then.

So, Simon allowed himself to be ogled shamelessly as it wouldn't be the first time and as a model, he was used to people looking and touching though he'd never let it cross the line. He even went so far as to toy with him, knocking his knees open slightly, a finger suggestively in his own mouth as he gazed out the window, head slightly tilted in that faraway look. The other hand pointed suggestively at his own crotch.

He and Ming had taken pains to make sure he looked absolutely stunning this evening, picking out a red Givenchy shirt, gold lamay jacket and black pants. He couldn't look any flashier if he tried. His hair and makeup had been done to perfection, down to the Tom Ford #16 shade of red lipstick slathered on his lips. If he had to say so himself, he looked pretty damn handsome. Too bad it wasn't for his baby but to rope in a disgusting perv and predator whose time had finally come.

He knew the operation had taken months to plan and he'd been called in just at the tail end of it. His colleagues had worked tirelessly to set things in motion, some as victims, others as business colleagues, household staff, and security personnel all to ensure that in the end,

Chairman Luo would be taken offline and sent for healing. The more they could clear away the lower vibing energies and bring peace to the hearts of the masses, the faster Gaia could ascend. That required taking offline those who insisted on keeping the status quo at the expense of the hardworking people.

The plan Mencius shared with him was for Simon to get an exclusive invitation to meet with the chairman at his estate in Northern Hunan away from prying eyes. As the chairman was only in residence there a few times out of the year, it was imperative he get in when he did. This gave the team he'd be working with time to set things up without anyone suspecting anything.

He'd been told that the limo driver, some of the security detail outside, a maid and house manager inside were all colleagues of the light, undercover for years working for the chairman or the household in an effort to gather information and evidence they could present to the proper officials. They just needed one big scandal to tie it all together. That's where Simon came in. A face well enough known to be easily recognized should a scandal befall him, yet fresh enough to appear as if he were still looking to climb the upwardly mobile ladder with assistance from the likes of Chairman Luo.

One of his many abilities was clearing away large amounts of low vibrational energy. It was why he had been approached with the earth mission by Lord Michael before he even discussed coming to earth with Zhang while they'd been on Pleiades Star 7. And it was also why he was so adamant in convincing Zhang to come to earth with him.

If he could get close to the chairman in his earth form, he would be able to bring the higher vibrational energies to bear, anchoring the energies and putting the Chairman on notice. For this giving his ranking, all Simon had to literally do was show up as a fully awake being. As the chairman was a sexual predator and rapist, it was a dangerous assignment. Zhang meanwhile would work on taking down those responsible at CAPA linked to the Chinese government and follow the money trail. While Simon risked his ass, Zhang would risk his career.

Originally the plan was for another colleague to be a victim who would gain exposure by bringing the Chairman's deeds to the public. Her highest incarnation was at the 6th level. But she ended up capitulating under the intense pressure and the mission was scrubbed. She was now working at Subway and receiving therapy on the weekends. Knowing how easy it was to get sideways on a mission especially when one wasn't yet awake and only believed themselves a 3D human, he couldn't blame her.

He'd experienced firsthand the frustration seeing his own partner deeply suffering under similar circumstances. It was by sheer willpower and a little bit of angelic magic he was able to even get close enough to Zhang to help him lift out of that dark fog he'd been in.

As an ascended master in his highest incarnation, Zhang himself was no lightweight.   Even though he temporarily succumbed to the forgetting and later to lower discordant energies, he had deeply influenced so many people with his deep thinking and sunlike presence it was no joke. He was able to foster supporters even before the hairier part of his mission began. Even while in the dumps, he managed to turn many detractors into his fans. That was the hallmark of a Master and distinguished him from the rest of the masses, some of whom had suffered under similar circumstances and completely wiped out never to be heard about again.

"Looks like we're here," Gangster Ray said with a smirk, eyeing him as Simon lazily looked back at him. He gave a doe-eyed smile and nodded. The limousine door opened, and he was ushered out to a large, beautiful stone masonry building in the Italianate style. The place looked more suited for Tuscany than deep in Hunan territory.

As expected, several of the household staff were on hand to greet him. Not knowing who was who he gazed at them one by one as he made his way up the short stone stairway toward the huge wooden front doors.

There were twelve men doing security in the yard that he could see. All looked as formidable and as serious as Hong Kong Ray. Only one paid him any mind nodding at him as he passed. Simon scanned his energy and felt his heart was good. The others not so much. He nodded back, his long legs leading him further along.

There were two females and two males at the top of the stairs. Around them he could see their clear auras. Of the females, a woman in her 30s was dressed in a black and white maid's outfit. The other aunty was perhaps in her 50s and dressed in a long black robe and apron. Simon guessed they were the head maid and house manager. They bowed deeply to him as did the two men who stood opposite them dressed in household laborer attire, perhaps a butler and footman.

"Greetings, my Lord," he heard them say telepathically. They said nothing aloud only averting their eyes humbly. Humbled himself by the gesture, Simon greeted them back, a hand over his heart chakra. "Thank you for your diligent service," he replied also telepathically.

He gleaned from their energies they had already been alerted in advance by Lord Michael to expect him and although he wasn't on par with the Archangel, he was an awake angelic being in his highest incarnation and anchoring those frequencies nevertheless, one of only several thousand such beings in China although more were jumping in here and elsewhere. He took a deep breath and tuned in to what was going on inside even before he was led through the doors.

The energy inside was heavy, but not horribly so. Perhaps there was hope yet for the chairman. The lingering low frequency energies were nothing a good room clearing wouldn't take care of. He did so with a flick of his hand.

He smelled the faint smell of cigars, and something else…sage perhaps and then noted the incense burner by the door. As it's smoke was vaporous, it was multidimensional and thus had the power to clear. But a home of this size needed more than a few wisps of smoke especially if evil was done here often as he knew took place in the chairman's study. By evil, that meant low vibrational acts against oneself or others.

CHAPTER TWENTY-FIVE
Chairman Luo Makes a Poor Choice

The foyer of the chairman's Italianate mansion was vacuous and decorated sparsely but exquisitely with expensive looking porcelain vases that stood waist high as well as china, some he recognized from the Ming Dynasty and thus quite valuable. It made the entry to the Chairman's home seem much more like a museum than a residence. It also meant the Chairman was loaded and indeed well-connected to have such priceless artifacts just lying around.

Dead ahead was a huge marble stairway that cut to the left and right leading to the upper floors and a long balustrade behind which there stood a large sofa looking table. Upon the table sat a monstrous vase of freshly cut flowers. Simon loved flowers and could smell their lingering fragrance from where he stood.

He was ushered to a room through a door to the left of the staircase, the Chairman's study. Indeed, as he approached, he felt the energies acutely. As ordinary as it appeared, this place was the scene of countless torments as victims were chased and overpowered and forcibly taken. A part of what they lost remained here like nightmarish memories for the chairman and all his guests and future victims to soak up. Ugh. It was also where many careers were born, if the chairman liked you enough.

He heard music playing from inside, as if on an old gramophone, a symphony though whether it was Bach or Beethoven he couldn't say. At least the man had good taste. As he entered the room on the heels of one of the two men who'd welcomed him, he much expected there to be a group of old men, all waiting for the entertainment, *him*, to show up. But the room was devoid of anyone but furniture on this eve. "The chairman will be with you shortly, Mr. Simon. His daughter has just arrived, and he is tending to her and will be here afterwards. May I offer you tea or anything else?"

"No…I am fine," he said and waved his hand. The man bowed deeply, bathing in the fairy dust-like energy Simon brought with him and smiled gratefully. If all went well this colleague's assignment was up and he could return to the ship or go elsewhere to assist Gaia. Same for the other Light workers at the residence. The others would likely see jail time or worse. That wasn't his department. Rather than take a seat he moved around the room. The energy here was heavier than outside, much more so by the large wooden desk to the right and the area around the two overstuffed red leather chairs nearby. It made his skin crawl.

Behind the desk lining the wall was a floor to ceiling wooden bookshelf filled with classics and what appeared many first additions. There were also glass cases with what looked like more early period artifacts better suited in a museum than someone's private collection. He went about studying them as he waited for Chairman Luo. A chipped cup of unknown origin and a flat utensil beside it of matching material caught his eye.

Beneath that on a lower shelf there was a glass plate and bowl and ancient tea set tastefully arranged. In another large case nearer the two leather chairs were two wooden statues- about a foot in size each - one of a gentle looking female bodhisattva and the other a scary reptilian-looking creature. Simon laughed inside thinking how the reptiles just couldn't catch a break, not even on earth. He also thought the pair oddly out of place. There was dark energy on both statues that left a heavy atmosphere around it.

As he sussed them out further, he recognized they had been used in a ritual calling on some fallen energies fairly recently. They also carried

199

the energy of fear and helplessness of many who fell victim in this very room. Thus, the wooden pieces somehow acted both as a sponge and a battery to keep the energies intact. He paid this no mind for the time being and only projected the information back into the array.

"Duly noted, brother. Be well." Came Lord Michael's ethereal sounding reply. Simon had expected Mencius but was glad his reinforcement was tuned in as well.

He moved to the two oversized red leather chairs that were near a window and went toward them to peer outside. Darkness had long since fallen obscuring his view of the little courtyard there somewhat but not entirely. Upon a concrete patio was an outdoor seating area. He could make out some patio furniture and a small table and three white cast iron chairs. Beyond that was a heavily landscaped little garden in the middle of which sat a fountain. Past that were lots of mature trees. An otherwise pleasant place to contemplate the day.

He heard footsteps resounding behind him coming closer as they moved across the marble floor. They were hurried in their pace, excited even and Simon instantly could tell they bore the weight of a man of ample size and girth who was used to getting his way, even if he had to take it by force.

Game on. He made sure his clothes were in order and double-checked that his lipstick hadn't smudged using his reflection in the glass. He took a deep breath and centered himself.

"Ah, Simon...my most esteemed guest! Finally, we meet!" A robust voice sounding of middle age spoke, greeting him. It was showtime. Plastering a smile on his face, Simon turned and prepared to engage the chairman.

Simon instantly recognized him and took pause. He did however look much younger than he should have likely on account of the dark energies he had collaborated with. Long ago when Simon was still in high school, a visiting teacher from a performing arts school took an interest in him. She had been recruiting students for a local production and told him she thought his height and looks were suited for show biz.

The theater where she had asked him to go to was on the campus of the school and he recalled walking through the main hallway and looking at all the pictures that graced both walls. The largest picture was that of a 50-something year old man who had short cropped dark hair, expressive though narrow eyes, a calculating smile and sharp teeth. Simon thought he looked much like a reptile back then with no good intentions. The nameplate below the photo simply stated Luo Gu Xian, Founder.

Roots humble, the school nevertheless had seen countless aspiring artists through her doors, many who made a name for themselves, and still more who felt they owed homage to the school's founder for their success. Perhaps even for life. As Simon had gotten his start there with that teacher who cast him in the local production, he figured a man like Chairman Luo would think he owed him something, too. He'd been a boy then, but already recognized at some point the people who believed they helped him would eventually come back to collect. While his teacher had since died, this man, the chairman seemed to grow in stature until he became as influential as any politician. And just as wanting. It was time to make payment.

Simon crossed the room with his arm outstretched, a warm smile gracing his face. "It's a pleasure to meet you, Mr. Chairman." He saw the surprise register on the chairman's face as soon as he gazed upon Simon's own, followed by a very pleased expression. He was familiar with that look along with the one that followed. *Desire!* He gripped Simon's hand tightly and pulled him to him so that their shoulders touched in a half hug. It was then that Simon disdainfully noted the chairman wore no underwear beneath the long Nehru like gown and worse, he was sporting wood.

Simon held his gaze, pretending not to notice. The chairman held his hand almost reverentially as they stood eye to eye. The chairman was a big man, at least 250 lbs. Simon was 6'1", 158 lbs soaking wet. Despite their difference in weight and build, Simon knew how to handle himself. He noted how the chairman fondled his hand, rubbing his thumb along the back of his palm twice before letting it go. Simon immediately tapped into his energy.

He was gazing into the eyes of a predator. But the man was also conflicted. On the one hand he had strong desires, desires that he hoped to sate tonight with Simon whether Simon was willing or not. But on the other he was familiar enough with Simon's energy and wished to revel in it. In this way, he recognized Simon's soul on some level. To converse with him, chatting him up and being around him made him feel good. Simon knew he had that effect on people, too. He waited for the chairman to offer him a seat and sat across from him on one of the two offending red leather chairs. Their knees were practically touching.

This gift, this energy he held wasn't something he could turn on or off at will so he used it to his advantage. He decided to engage him straightaway. "I know who you are, and I have been sent here to pass along a message. Yes?"

The chairman started, his eyes going wide. Simon knew what he was thinking. 'Some young upstart telling me he had a message to relay? Ha!' Simon ignored the chairman's mind chatter.

"That lest you stop in your perverse ways and return to the light, we will have no choice but to detain you and transport you off world where you will be held accountable for your crimes against innocent souls and made to accept healing." He thought about how odd that statement would have sounded had he been talking to an ordinary human. But Chairman Luo was no ordinary human. He was Jefok8731.

Long ago Jefok8731 had come to earth. Much like he and Zhang, he had been guided by an Ascended Master named Mencius and a team of other spiritual beings. He had come to earth, incarnating as a human to experience the beauty that was earth, further develop his spirit through taking on earthly lessons, and to aid the upwardly evolving humans through service and unconditional love. His arrival coincided with the era of the Mayans.

A gifted engineer he soon caught the attention of the ruling Maya and was put to work designing with their stone masons a grand pyramid temple to honor the gods, Jefok's own ancestors who once before visited and lived among them. But it had been generations since the Jefoks came in their original forms instead choosing to incarnate as humans. As a human his relationship flourished with the ruling Maya and the common people. It was when the humans began to resort to blood sacrifice as a means to contact and commune with their "Gods", the Jefoks, things went sideways.

When he spoke out, advising the ruling Maya that to destroy life in order to commune with the gods was an abomination, he was horribly tortured and imprisoned then sacrificed. Unable to accept this fate, he grew resentful in spirit and then was trapped in the reincarnation cycle. Despite the guides best efforts to help him understand during the short window before another incarnation on the reincarnation belt began, that one's life is a direct result of the choices one made prior to incarnation, and that as odd as it sounds, especially to one trapped in suffering, that they chose that path, as well as had the ability to transform it through love, he ignored them.

Every time he reincarnated thereafter, he became further entrenched in the human drama believing it was the only reality there was, instead of realizing he was there on a mission to do good.

Thus, Jefok8731 in subsequent incarnations became further lost in darkness every time he encountered suffering or was "victimized". The sad part was, forgetting his original mission to help the humans and that he was a being of the Light, he was stuck on earth creating karma even after the reincarnation net was dismantled, this time preying on young artists for sexual gratification.

Whether he remembered his original incarnation from thousands of years ago much less his last, Simon was doubtful. Still, he came to give him an ultimatum, to help him see the error of his ways and return home safely to his body that was yet rotting away in the Athena's warehouse.

Jefok8731 wasn't impressed. Simon guessed he was still fast asleep. In the next instant the chairman launched himself at Simon grabbing for his throat. Had he not anticipated this, the chairman would have successfully pinned him to the chair whether to kill him or have his way with him. Simon wasn't about to find out which.

As the chairman's fingers clamped around his throat, being quick Simon dodged and took advantage of the chairman's bulkier weight and lower center of gravity to knock him sideways. The chairman went down hard grabbing for Simon's jacket in the process, tearing his beautiful red Givenchy shirt at the collar and ripping off his entire right jacket sleeve.

Simon stumbled backward and fell against the glass cabinet unleashing a wave of dark energy as the glass shattered. He quickly grabbed both wooden statues and sent a blast of angelic energy through them before promptly bringing them both down on the sides of the chairman's head like two clubs, knocking him out cold. Everything suddenly went dead quiet. Blood trickled down the side of Simon's head from a minor wound at his temple. He must've been cut by a stray piece of flying glass. He reached into his pocket for a handkerchief to dab at the wound.

He stood there in the aftermath admiring his handiwork and surveying the scene. *Well, that was easy.* Catching his breath, his clothing torn and in disarray, his jacket sleeve still in the offending clutches of the chairman, he glanced down to see the obvious and embarrassing bulge at the unconscious man's crotch and tsked.

So, this was Jefok8731. It was hard to reconcile that a being sent to earth to do such good could fall so low and end up on the floor of his own home unconscious and sporting a woody.

He took out his phone and captured a full-bodied pic of the sordid scene, his glittering torn golden sleeve in the chairman's hand and sent it to Ming. Then he waited as the sound of harried feet from outside the spacious study entered and the chairman's security detail came in to detain him. Had it not been for his colleague in the security detail he would probably have been knocked around pretty badly straightaway.

Not taking any chances, he sent out a wave of light to surround them all and instantly brought a measure of calm to the space. The police were called and 20 minutes later, Simon was taken away.

CHAPTER TWENTY-SIX

Wherein They Forget to Tell Zhang

"I'm in!"

A week after Simon walked into the "trap" set by Chairman Luo, Simon reported in. He was a little woozy from the lack of food as they had yet to feed him but a few pieces of fruit and a bottle of water since he'd been detained. Despite Simon being the victim, the Chairman to save face immediately had Simon arrested when he came to and pressed charges.

Regardless of the sensationalism of the whole ordeal, the media had been a little slow to catch on, on account they were in a remote area of Hunan where Chairman Luo's estate was and the local newspaper was only open on Monday, Wednesday, and Friday, and the whole sordid incident took place over the weekend. The video of him being escorted away captured only by the sweet older aunty that had greeted him at the door via her cellphone.

"Great! How are you holding up?"

"Fine. Just glad to get this part over with."

"Well, we're starting to see some local chatter about the assault and your arrest. The larger networks should start to pick it up right about now." Zhughe, the karmic whiz, conferred. He was taking over from Mencius who had gotten some work done in the med bay. Things hadn't gone as expected and he had been in his quarters resting ever since going on five earth days now. Everyone wished him well. "Your legal team of Emerthers from the Athena are already in play. Expect to hear from them any minute now."

It had been a full week since he'd last contacted Zhang. Thinking he might be worried for him, he thought to ask.

"Great. Somebody did tell Zhang about all this, right? Ming mentioned someone would since I've been on the assignment." This last comment was met with dead silence. "Someone did tell Zhang, right?" He repeated. Then, "Please tell me someone told Zhang I've been on assignment," Simon said a little louder. When Zhughe only coughed nervously Simon lost it and screamed, "No one told Zhang I've been on assignment?! Are you guys trying to get me killed?!"

"Didn't you call him?" Zhughe offered.

"What? No! They take your cell phone and all your stuff when you're arrested here, Zhughe. Jeez I can't believe no one told him. Where the hell is Mencius? The last thing he told me when we spoke a week ago was that he'd be sure to cue him in. Why isn't Mencius here talking with us now?" Simon felt his blood pressure at near boil. Zhang in the dark was most definitely not a good thing, especially given their history and his having to deal with what any sane person would've thought was his abandonment.

"He's been recuperating after getting some facial and dental work done. Let me check with him now."

"Don't bother. What about the array? I don't sense Zhang in it...." Simon was using the array now as he sat on the lone bench in his 8x10 jail cell. To outside appearances it looked like he was just sitting there staring at his white, hideous jail-issued shoes rather than arguing with Zhughe the master guide in training.

"Uh apparently he hasn't been in it since it was accessed by Lady Master Thala some time ago," Zhughe reported apologetically. "Are you certain he is even aware how to get in?"

"No…shit…he might not…. What about the Proxy? Can you reach him using the AI proxy on his cellphone?" Simon said trying to stifle down the panic that was about to take his whole mind of reason off-line. My god this was the worst oversight after he'd painstakingly reassured his partner and got him back on the mission. He reminded himself to give Mencius and Zhughe a critically honest review when this was all over. Two stars tops. One star if they didn't fix this immediately. Hearing this last bit Zhughe quickly apologized.

"I will definitely make it up to you both."

"Have Ming reach out to him, too. I can't believe you guys let that slip. Shit he must be flipping out of his friggin' mind!"

"Let me try them both now…."

Meanwhile Zhang had spent hours working on the video to post on IG. He selected a simple t-shirt and gym shorts for his wardrobe and sat down before the camera (his phone) which he carefully angled (propping it up against some books and a used coffee cup). After looking himself over, using the video setting, he decided to change his clothes, first into a collared shirt, and then into a long sleeve Henley.

Settling on the original t-shirt and shorts casual combo, he ran his hands through his hair a few times before hunting for some mousse to get rid of the flat, lifeless look. Finally satisfied with his appearance, he went to work on his message.

He recorded it once with a mind to tell the bastard off once and for all and ensure that Simon would get it. The message was simple. *Drop dead motherf—r!* Of course, to get around SM etiquette and the language restrictions imposed by IG and common decency, he used other choice words to ensure he wouldn't get sued while still adequately expressing his outrage and disdain.

After that he began the task of carefully editing out the "umms" and

"ahhs" and occasional crying and sobbing he broke into which took another couple of hours until finally he had it looking perfect. If Simon didn't see it his fans most certainly would and Zhang knew Simon's fans would broadcast it on YouTube, IG, and onto platforms he currently couldn't access including Weibo and WeChat. Simon wouldn't be able to miss it then.

Exhausted but relieved to get everything off his chest and his message out to the ethers, he took one last step to save the file, Airdropping from his iPhone9 onto his computer.   Just as he was about to press send and upload his masterpiece on IG, the internet went down.

"Motherf—r!!!!"

Right about the same time Simon was freaking out in the array and screaming at Zhughe, Zhang was being guided by an urgent voice in his head to turn on the television. His mind in complete disarray, he obeyed. Right now, he knew that if he didn't distract himself from thoughts of that asshole Simon, he would literally die. He had nothing more to lose anyway. Seeing the Wi-Fi was still down, the only thing that worked was basic cable. He flipped to the news.

"Coming next! The actor known as "Simon" arrested!"

Zhang gaped at the screen then promptly burst out laughing. "What? No friggin' way!" Simon arrested? "Now this I gotta' see!"

He couldn't even imagine those pale thin wrists in handcuffs much less that statuesque frame of his in an orange jumpsuit. He scrambled to turn up the volume and sat glued to the screen as the commentator described the whole ugly event. "What did you do now?"

"Star 121 News has confirmed Idol and Actor Simon known by many as the darling of advertising, and star of the hit series *Word of Honor* was arrested one week ago for assaulting influential movie producer and Chairman Luo Gu Xian at his estate in Northern Hunan province. Apparently, the actor in a drunken rage assaulted the chairman after being told he did not get the lead role in a highly anticipated romance drama set to star Chairman Luo's own daughter Luo Min Ho."

Then he saw the footage of Simon captured by some woman's shaky cellphone video as he was being led away and guided into an awaiting police car. Simon's clothes were torn and in complete disarray, his right sleeve missing, his head down. There was a rivulet of blood oozing down the side of his head. Zhang's blood ran cold.   This was bad. Not only did Simon never walk with his head down, ever, as it just wasn't his way, he was bleeding! Something horrible had happened. Zhang knew then whatever story they had spun, none of it was true. Not only did he know for a fact Simon would never star in a tv drama with Luo Min Ho on account of her horrible acting and penchant for throwing temper tantrums on the set, but he also hated doing romantic dramas. The last one he did he practically outed himself as he jokingly complained during interviews about his female costar's bad breath and poor brushing habits every chance he could get. Nor would he be so stupid to get drunk before someone like Chairman Luo.

As the footage of Simon being led to the police car played again and again, and the news reporter continued, Zhang grew sick.

"Filming was to begin later on this month but may now be postponed due to this frightening incident. We wish the best for Chairman Luo." Zhang sat back in shock, the huge weight on his chest that represented his abandonment suddenly morphed into something far worse. His baby had been assaulted and was being set up big time. He ran to the sink and threw up.

Knowing now why Simon hadn't picked up or answered any of his texts, he immediately dialed Ming.

When Simon finally got his phone back and the rest of his belongings including his black shoulder bag, wallet and lipstick from the jailer, he found he had 62 voicemail messages, 59 of them from Zhang, and as many text messages, some with nothing more than angry or skeleton emojis. Scrolling through them he shook his head. From outward appearances alone it looked like Zhang had a tough time of it.

He immediately dialed his number. The bastard didn't pick up. Sighing, he gazed at Ming.

Although it was a bit of a crush to get through the crowd that had gathered outside the police station and get into the van as they left the jail, he hardly noticed. The only difference between the usual crowds that boxed him in when he was on the move and the folks who waited in the cold out front of the station was that these were mostly press. A few fans who had come out in support waved and shouted his name, expressing their love and belief in his innocence.   He waved in heartfelt acknowledgment and gave them the LLD sign he and Zhang had pushed.

"How did he sound when you talked to him?" Simon asked as soon as the van door closed shut. He desired fresh clothes as the torn red shirt and single sleeved lamay jacket and black pants ensemble he started the mission with which he was still wearing did appear a bit worn for the wear. Ming conveniently forgot to bring him a change of clothes. She did, however, bring a hat and mask which he now donned and tossed him a bottle of water. The black van she'd commissioned sped them away from the Central Hunan police station and jail where he'd been kept for the last 7 days while he waited for the story to gain traction and his legal team to step in.

"He sounded…pissed…at you, not me," she clarified. "Oh yes, and he was fine with my not picking up. You, not so much," she said smugly.

"You, my dear, need your own man." He shot back dialing Zhang's number again.

Unlike the frenetic text messages, (he could only imagine the voice mails and decided to listen to those later with Zhang beside him just for laughs), Zhang calmly answered the phone.

"Oh hey, babe. Everything ok?"

Simon rolled his eyes. "Are you ok?"

"Yeah, why wouldn't I be?" Zhang countered sounding unperturbed, puzzled he would even ask.

Simon stared at the open text message screen and recited word for word the two that had caught his eye:

"Die, motherf@#!r! Die!!!" 😡 💀 ☠️ "You're dead to me! RIP asshole! Good riddance!! 😡 💀 ☠️?"

"Oh uh…yeah that…about that…" Zhang said sheepishly. "I got a little stressed." He confessed. Simon snorted. "A little?"

"Well, I didn't know where you were and what happened to you, babe. You know how crazy I sometimes get? I didn't mean any of it." Zhang quickly explained.

"Oh, is it babe now? Not motherf—r or asshole? And what do you mean sometimes?"

"What can I say? I don't do well under stress. It makes my eyes puffy and my cheeks look fat. But I am better now. Where are you? I saw the tv footage and you were bleeding."

"On my way to stop for clothes," Simon hit the back of Ming's chair to make sure she was listening, before continuing, "then getting on a plane for Shanghai. It was nothing. Just a tiny cut. I'll explain more later. Where are you?"

"In your apartment on your bed in your bathrobe drinking a bottle of water and staying hydrated while watching you leave the jail and being hounded by the press. That must feel weird. Not that I know anything about that," Zhang joked. "That cut's not going to leave a horrible scar, is it? If it will I'll have to reevaluate this relationship. You know I like my men perfect."

Simon snorted. "Your men? Jerk."

"Why are you going to buy clothes now? Didn't Ming know you were being released today and bring you any?"

"As a matter of fact, she didn't bring me clothes. I'm firing her as soon as we get to Shanghai," Simon droned eyeing her with malice. Ming only stuck her tongue out at him and then gave instructions to the driver to stop at a local convenience store for her to jump out.

"Hmmm. Bathrobe did you say? Does that mean you're naked underneath?" Simon asked breathing out and now gazing out the window as they sped through downtown.

"Why don't you come find out, asshole." Zhang laughed then hung up.

Simon grinned and shook his head. Two hours later they were in the air, on their way to Shanghai, Simon's ruined shirt, pants and jacket in a plastic bag at his feet. He was now dressed in a cheap, yellow convenience store t-shirt with a smiley face and rainbow on the front and an ill-fitting pair of light blue jogging trunks.

He was definitely firing Ming's ass.

CHAPTER TWENTY-SEVEN

Simon's Earth Journey Begins...Simon Incarnates Like a Boss

After emerging from his mother's womb, as serene and zen-like as the Buddha, Simon received a standing ovation.

Much like with Zhang's first moments on earth, it was witnessed by his colleagues, a standing room only crowd packed shoulder to shoulder like sardines in the Athena's Round Room. Even the captain was on hand to witness the legendary event.

One could even describe his entrance as beautiful as it was godlike, those peach blossom eyes opening as if on cue only to gaze back at the big screen that captured it all before a smile graced his precious little lips. His aura, an angelic glow of ethereal and rainbow light, was tangible and surrounded him like a halo. Even the attending doctor took notice. So this was what it was like when an angel incarnated on earth.

At that moment, some of the female spectators in the room let out a piercing scream, a primal cry born of some unspoken and as yet indescribable need, giving the males in the room a firsthand demonstration of what it meant to 'fan girl'.

It was priceless. A moment to be etched in the minds of all who witnessed it, a thing sure to be discussed for generations to come. Some even likened it to the birth of earth's holiest of holies, the Christ Yeshua who happened to be observing and was heard commenting in the back.

"Hmmm. Impressive...."

Simon himself watched it on the big screen and thought he looked pretty good, too. As a fully conscious multidimensional being this was a thing.

What no one knew was that he meticulously rehearsed in the H-Deck as often as he could up until the last minute, almost missing the consciousness transfer roll call. It was well worth the sacrifice. Though the accommodations in his mom's birth canal were indeed a bit cramped for the split second (okay it was more like four earth hours) as he squeezed his way through for real, it was a bit like being all bound up, arms and legs made immobile as one wiggled their way out of a tunnel. All told, he wanted to demonstrate the process wasn't half as bad as his partner had made it out to be.

From the reception he received from his shipmates watching he did pretty well. His female colleagues even squealing out their appreciation. He reminded himself to thank them personally on his return, for it served as confirmation he had done something right. Even Mencius who appeared beside him on cue was speechless, a tear sliding out of the corner of his left eye.

From the moment he arrived on earth, Simon hit the ground running. His mission however, required little of him for the first 5 years or so other than to be a filial only child, and get accustomed to life in the notoriously sluggish and dense 3D. And because his parents were loving and ordinary, he had an easy enough time at it. On account of his boyish angelic looks, people treated him well, and friends were plentiful. He had little to no complaints and was otherwise quiet and courteous.

Still, despite his best efforts to blend in, he stood out, his reactions to life a bit unusual. Like the time in grade level 3 when he'd been happily playing with a classmate during recess and another student snatched the toy car out of his hand before grabbing the other from the hand of

215

his friend. Simon just jumped up and went to play with something else. He'd been getting bored anyway and saw no harm in letting others play. His friend however hit the other child, starting a fistfight that ended with one of them with a bloody nose, the other with a black eye and both in detention.

Simon couldn't understand how things had gotten so far over something so small. It was these rather unusual responses from Simon that began to attract the attention of others who thought him a bit strange. To compensate he grew more introverted to avoid being seen as too different and revealing himself unnecessarily.

He busied himself with his studies but not enough to stand out, easily made friends taking a liking to computer video games which were popular and checked in every now and then into the array.

When he was fifteen, he was introduced to acting when a visiting teacher from a performing arts school felt he had a knack for it and suggested he look into it on account of his looks. Simon was glad he and Zhang had decided on their star quality appearances during the soul planning process. Things were on course.

Despite his efforts to appear like any normal teenager, he grew accustomed to those who would insist on treating him differently. Not everyone who encountered him understood who he was. Thus, occasionally there would be some who tried to bully him on account of his awkwardness or reserved personality. This always backfired, though, leading to their experiencing some unfortunate circumstance or event, what Simon called *The Boomerang Effect*.

The boomerang effect was what occurred whenever someone attempted to slight or act against him from a place of low vibration. Being of a very high resonating vibration himself he had the ability to assist people in clearing karma quickly. Thus, as the laws of cause and effect apply even in the 3D, the offenders would ultimately experience an immediate, most often unpleasant effect which in reality was a lesson they called upon themselves, hence the boomerang. This of course was all on account of the energies he carried, who he was, and the beings of Light he channeled.

To prevent anyone from being unnecessarily blindsided by this quirky ability of his, he did his best to head things off at the pass, speaking up for himself, setting clear boundaries and making them known to others. He grew more blunt and direct, his actions intentional, demonstrating he was always in control. This made him stand out even more so he decided not to stress on it. The effect was not appearing to be bothered by anything, instead it seemed he floated through life with ease.

A byproduct of this being opportunities constantly knocked at his door. People would see his fortune and grow resentful or petty without realizing it was theirs for the asking, too. But he long recognized people on earth suffered unnecessarily and often caused others to do the same out of frustration and jealousy. Still, he could only do so much to help them.

Knowing his earth mission, he stayed focused and let nothing bother him too much.

After high school he took the preliminary exams for Nanjing University of the Arts. This was part of his soul plan putting him on a path to meet his partner. After he received word of the several Hyadeans requesting angelic energetic assistance, he decided to head to Beijing under the guise of studying and honing his acting and performing skills more.

The Hyadeans, he soon learned, were a bunch of jerks. He'd been warned they were clique-ish and liked to stay to themselves on account of their history during the destruction of their home world in Lyra. In short, they didn't trust anyone but themselves, nor did they enjoy mixing least of all with a Sirian Neubin soul like him.

The Hyadeans were a colony of refugees from the Ahel human race who fled to the Hyades star cluster after their home world was devastated by some pesky service-to-self Reptilians from the Ciakahrr Empire. As Lyra was a beautifully diverse star system still talked about in the now moment, and the Ciakahrrs had been attacking them for some time, the Ahel humans and other Lyrans left aboard four massive ships taking just about everything they could of their world that wasn't nailed down to start fresh elsewhere, much like Noah's ark. These four motherships went in different directions, thus although racially the same as their fun-loving cousins, the Pleiadeans, and a mix of some of the other Lyran colonies, they much preferred to stick to themselves.

Their tendency toward staying together and trusting no one made his job to assist them challenging. Collectively the idea was using his energy to clear the way for them to infiltrate the growing number of performing arts associations gaining influence in China's post-civil strife world. These fraternities had become more powerful and mafia-like in their evolvement with a penchant of allowing some into their inner circle while excluding most others.

Given they didn't trust even him, the Hyadeans who had incarnated as Chinese drama and choreography instructors decided instead to bully him. They worked him hard spending more time criticizing him for his lack of focus and coordination and his even worse singing skills than taking advantage of the high-vibing energies he offered to springboard them forward on the mission.

What Simon knew and the Hyadeans should have known and helped spread the message was that the energy that creates worlds flows through every being. This knowledge in those in the higher dimensions and realms, even those who are in service to self, enables a being to manifest and accomplish amazing, seemingly magical things. Even world building. But through a series of setbacks and genetic manipulation by some enterprising hybrids known as the Annunaki to earth humans, earth humans became disconnected from this truth and from each other.

Thus, 3D earth humans have forgotten this innate power and that the Light flows through their veins. The result is controlled chaos, low self-esteem, physical, emotional and even spiritual violence against each other and other races.

After getting nowhere with the Hyadeans (who were still asleep) despite trying he instead focused on honing his craft as a performing artist under their tutelage. He then returned to Shanghai and enrolled in Donghua University's Performimg Arts department. While just a little bit disheartened by his experience with beings who should have known better, he nonetheless was happy to be on track to reuniting with Zhang.

Mencius later reported that the mission to Beijing had indeed been successful as the offending Hyadeans had since been promoted to positions of influence within the performing arts arena as planned on account of the boost of angelic energy he provided. Their ill treatment of Simon was not however without consequences on account of said boomerang effect. But Mencius assured him that it wasn't his to worry about. So, he didn't.

Meanwhile, with that knowledge under his belt, Simon worked harder, involved himself heavily in community service projects lending his angelic energies wherever he could, and living by example as he awaited with increased excitement and anticipation meeting up with Zhang.

CHAPTER TWENTY-EIGHT

Rally   Pointn 1-Wherein the Two First Meet

"The sea was restless that day, my friend!" Simon cracked up as Seinfeld played on the tv screen of his tiny apartment as he got dressed. He had a 1pm audition for *Word of Honor* as a lead but knew with certainty he would nab it on account of that was how he and Zhang would finally meet.

He took his time getting dressed, opting for casual (baseball cap, freshly washed t-shirt and jeans and a pair of high-top sneakers), then drove across town to the hotel in Shanghai where the auditions were set to take place. When he got there, the place was packed with people already waiting in long queues. He found the line for the audition for the Wen Kexing role and checked in. Then he joined the few hundreds of others sitting around in the large waiting room.

When it was his turn, he walked in, script in hand and introduced himself. Producer and Director Ma both smiled at him before Producer Ma chose two scenes for him - a Wen Kexing drinking scene and a melancholy scene after Long Que's death. He was quite familiar with both having thoroughly studied the script as well as found the web novel online which he read twice. By the time evening rolled around, he was told the part was his.

Production was to start immediately. To introduce the cast and crew a dinner was held at the hotel in one of the ballrooms. Up to that point he had yet to meet Zhang. He'd been told that Zhang had a private audition on account of his veteran actor status, as he pretty much already made a name for himself. Busy himself he hadn't really taken the time to see any of Zhang's other work but did look him up on SM.

When their eyes met at the dinner table, it caused Simon to stumble a little. Zhang stared back blankly at him, his reaction devoid of any of the enthusiasm Simon was certain to see at their first earthly meeting. Rather than a bear hug, high fives, laughter and 'jeez what took you so long?', Zhang seemed almost aloof and cold. Even after they were made to introduce themselves, Zhang seemed distant.

To Simon it was as if he were just doing his duty, working the crowd, a seasoned actor who was used to showing up and ready to start work. Undeterred, Simon tried to engage him hoping to jog his memory but quickly noticed while Zhang seemed lively with just about everyone else, he was almost lifeless and disinterested in him. Simon felt the slight acutely and thereafter excused himself to go to the bathroom. To distract himself he checked in.

"Rally Point 1 - Accomplished. Detailed report to follow. Lt. SimonGJXO1129."

"Congratulations Lieutenant! You both are well on your way!" He received a text reply almost instantaneously making him wonder if Mencius had it on auto reply.

Likely asleep, Mencius obviously hadn't seen their first meeting. To say it was awkward was an understatement. He sent another text to Mencius before he went straight to the array to express his concern. Mencius sounding very much as if he had just gotten up, voice groggy, reminded him Zhang was likely still asleep and just to give it some time. Simon asked for a bit of help to smooth things along before they disconnected.

When he emerged from the bathroom, Producer Ma called him over." Hey! You two exchange Wechat and Weibo info yet?"

"No...not yet."

"Well, what are you waiting for? Go break the ice." She'd obviously noted their odd chemistry, too.

Impressed at the speed at which Mencius worked, he immediately sought Zhang out.   Zhang was deep in conversation with the beautiful actress who had been cast as Liu Qian Qiao.

"Hey, Teacher Ma says we should exchange WeChat and Weibo info," Simon said zeroing in on Zhang and admiring his beautiful jawline.

Zhang frowned at him in obvious irritation. Realizing his mistake, Simon profusely apologized to them both.

"Can't you see she and I are in the middle of something?" Zhang barbed not moving to take out his phone. Seeing only his soul mate before him, Simon only smiled his love back at him. Zhang frowned back at him, seemingly puzzled he didn't get a reaction from Simon. He capitulated and pulled his phone from his pocket and quickly exchanged information before resuming his conversation with their female costar. Seeing they weren't getting anywhere, Simon left early that evening. He received a download from Mencius confirming Zhang was not yet awake and to take his time.

On schedule, a week of intense martial arts, weapons and costume training began straightaway. As their roles required plenty of close bodily contact given the nature of the script, training also required them to practice body mechanics together. This last bit gave Simon the excuse to finally touch his soul mate under the guise of practicing which he had been dying to do.

When filming started, however, Simon still struggled to connect with Zhang. Despite dropping into a routine quite quickly of rising early followed by extra-long hours of filming, he also couldn't get deep enough into character. Not one to give up, he carefully memorized the script and practiced religiously with the prop he had been given - a fan which Wen Kexing welded both as a weapon and for aesthetics.

Taking notice of his partner's diligence and that he'd even memorized Zhang's lines, Zhang was impressed. As the veteran of the two, he offered up pointers whenever he could sensing Simon was still having trouble finding Wen Kexing.

"Should we rehearse this again?" Simon asked feeling the gap between them despite his best efforts and struggling to assume the ambitious role he agreed to play.

"Yes, but how about we take it from the scene before because it'll flow better. But remember Wen Kexing is a damn chatterbox so he's not shy like you at all," Zhang offered.

Simon thought the comment odd. Although he was a bit of an introvert, he certainly wasn't shy. He felt the gap between them widen. Back on the ship, he and Zhang knew everything about each other. It was why they got along so well. But here they were like total strangers. Disheartened, it was yet another unexpected setback.

But he had other issues. The character Wen Kexing was nothing like him. In fact, he'd never played anyone so complex. While he was a bit quiet and kept to himself most of the time, Wen Kexing was aggressive, outgoing and thick skinned. He was also hell bent on bedding Zhou Zishu, another complex character with an interesting backstory and the one he recognized as his soul mate.

After calling it a wrap for the night, Simon went back to his caravan, his home on the studio grounds for the next several months. He searched for his copy of the web novel and studied it again. As he lay in bed afterwards meditating wondering how a guy like Wen Kexing would handle the situation between he and Zhang, it suddenly came to him.

Wen Kexing was playing a role himself. On the one hand he was the Ghost Valley Chief hell bent on revenge. But on the other, wasn't he really just the boyishly handsome, fun loving sex cultivator waiting for his soulmate to wake up? He shot up in bed, light bulbs going off in his head.

He became Wen Kexing overnight.

A few weeks later, Simon bed his soul mate.

"F—k, Simon! You're so damn hot!" Zhang hissed trying to speak and kiss him at the same time. He was so damn horny he was practically shaking.

Zhang had no clue how he went from admiring the guy's improved acting skills to making out with him in his caravan.

"Yeah? If you think that's hot, wait til we really get started!" Simon murmured back against his mouth. Zhang was about to flip his lid. Everything was telling him to put a stop to it. ZHANG!!! STOP!!! You're not into guys!!! But he couldn't help himself and allowed Simon to pull his shirt over his head as they navigated their way around the tiny caravan.

"Yeah, done this before?" He asked, surprising himself. One minute he was watching Simon struggling to find his character, the next Zhang was following him around like a dog in heat. The script itself had been pretty risqué to begin with, but still. It all started with that intense stare. It was so friggin' sexy and had him feeling and thinking things a straight dude shouldn't. By all accounts Simon wasn't gay, either. But Zhang had always been of the mind to try new things. And Simon kissed him first. Plus, he was damn good looking. So, he decided to just go for it. He pulled Simon's own sweaty tee shirt off his body and attacked the dude's nipple.

"I know a thing or two," Simon laughed back.

"Show me!" Zhang challenged, not the least bit concerned he had no damn clue what to do with a guy or if there was even much difference other than who put what where and how exactly. But at the moment, Simon's mouth was working its way down his throat and the underside of his jaw. The result was so sensual and so awesomely hot, Zhang's eyes rolled back in his head.

CHAPTER TWENTY-NINE
Rally Point 1, Phase 2

Zhang didn't even notice the uber satisfied grin plastered on his costar's face as Simon melded their mouths together and picked him up and carried him toward the twin size bed in the back of his caravan. Wrapping both legs around Simon's thin waist, Zhang shamelessly clung to him.

Simon gently laid Zhang onto the bed, and lowered himself on top of him, unwilling to relinquish his mouth. His movements were unhurried, as were his kisses as he set about exploring every tooth and crevice of Zhang's mouth, his left hand doing a slow caress down the full length of Zhang's body. His eyes were closed, head cocked to the side as he deepened the kiss.

It was sexy as hell.

Zhang found himself reciprocating, although his movements were far more erratic, wanting to touch him everywhere, his pubes on fire as he felt Simon's hard root pressed up against his own. Simon ground his hips down in a slow mash of their roots. Zhang jerked his hips up to meet Simon's, seeking to intensify the sensation. His hands, however, unlike Simon's which were slow and measured, continued their frantic perusal and were all over the place, up and down Simon's back, his sides, his butt, grabbing his head, all the while he wondered if what he

was doing was ok and if he was even doing it right. He wanted to touch the endless smooth and long planes of Simon's perfectly sculpted body everywhere. He couldn't recall ever being this excited before with any girl. But now, he felt like he was lifting out of his own body, about to lose total control, every nerve and fiber alive yet misfiring.

He groaned as Simon moved a hand over his bare chest to play with his nipples plucking at them, one at a time, alternating between pinching them between the back of his forefinger and middle finger and using his thumb and forefinger before steadily moving further downward in a slow caress across Zhang's belly, the tips of his fingers touching his root. Zhang groaned low and deep with the simple contact. Encouraged, Simon grasped his entire root firmly in his palm and gave it a hard squeeze before he began to rub Zhang in earnest with the full length of his warm palm through his pants.

Simon used every inch of that monstrous hand to his advantage, rubbing and caressing and gripping Zhang's root in his fist, only a thin layer of material separating him from his end goal.

Meanwhile Zhang was flipping out as that mouth worked sweet magic at his own, his lips pressed against Simon's in an open-mouthed kiss, Simon's tongue swirling against his teeth, his tongue, his lips in calculated yet unhurried fashion.

"Dude, I'm gonna shoot if you so much as —" Zhang rasped against his mouth his hips jackknifing against the torturous ministrations of Simon's hand. He recognized immediately just how out of his depths he was but there was no way he was going to back out or ask Simon to stop.

If Simon heard him, he didn't let on, only deepening the kiss, making sweet love to his mouth in painstaking fashion, his palm now stroking the outline of Zhang's burgeoning root in firm upward strokes through his shorts. The guy was obviously a friggin' master at hand jobs and an expert kisser even though he'd yet to even reach into his shorts and take him in hand. Zhang felt his whole body undulating, his senses in disarray as Simon masterfully moved him steadily towards climax. The

227

guy was insanely good!

He groaned low, his breath coming in deeper as Simon worked him into a frenzy. If Simon so much as touched his root with his bare hand, Zhang knew he was done for.

"Si- Simon - - I -I think - oh f--k - I think I'm gonna - I -"

"Hmmm?" Simon murmured against his mouth, turning his head in the opposite direction to kiss him even more thoroughly, still taking his time, licking and sucking Zhang's lips, his tongue, suckling his mouth as Zhang's body tensed and flexed beneath him in rapid fashion, his breaths coming now in gasps. He couldn't hold on. The vibration alone of Simon's expert mouth against his own as he hummed was enough to send Zhang over the edge. He clenched and unclenched his legs hoping to stave it off grabbing Simon's head and whimpering against his lips.

Taking that as his cue, Simon casually reached into Zhang's shorts to grasp him firmly in his large warm paw. Zhang's eyes rolled into his head, and he cried out, his hips shooting upward, forcing his root to slide up into Simon's palm as he arched his back and moaned. He was coming. Through lowered lids he saw Simon move in a flash, ducking his head and curling himself around Zhang's waist as he wrenched his shorts down his hips. Zhang was instantly bathed in hot, wet heat. *Holy Mother of God!* He saw stars as his climax ripped through him into Simon's mouth.

Zhang went apeshit, blindly clinging to his head, his legs scissoring and jackknifing in convulsive fashion as he wailed and thrashed about and his orgasm violently exploded from him. He felt Simon reach up to cover his mouth with his hand to stifle his cries while the other arm wrapped firmly around his waist and pinned Zhang against him as if afraid he'd get away. He swallowed Zhang all the way down to the balls as Zhang's root spasmed wildly down the back of his throat. Zhang had no clue where he was as Simon continued to swallow his seed until he was sucked dry.

"Oh my god—!" Zhang heard himself groan in the aftermath against

Simon's fingers at his lips, his eyes rolling into the back of his head. He ceased to exist on the earth plane, lost in ecstasy as Simon hummed around his member and rolled his tongue around it a few times with a satisfied expression before lifting his head to grin at him.

Zhang stared dumbfounded. "Holy shit, dude! That was the best orgasm I've ever had," Zhang said breathlessly, covered with sweat, his shorts halfway down his thighs, his root still fully erect. Simon licked his lips, then swiped his tongue across the head of Zhang's member to ensure he didn't miss a single drop of his juices, as he took the compliment in stride. Zhang groaned. That was the hottest damn thing he had ever seen! But he had no time to bask in his mind-blowing climax as Simon flipped him over and began kissing a slow trail down his sweaty back.

"I know some other tricks you might like," he murmured dragging his tongue along Zhang's spine before sliding it across his ass cheek and biting him for effect. Zhang yelped.

"Yeah? L-like w-what?" Zhang stammered.

Simon sat up, slipped out of his shorts before he lay on top of him, his root pressed up against the base of Zhang's spine.

"Are you going to let me?" He breathed sexily in Zhang's ear.

"You know I uh, I've never done this before-"

"Neither have I," Simon confessed licking around his ear and nibbling at his neck. Zhang's whole body twitched beneath him.

How the hell could that be? The guy was a friggin' genius at it.

"But I'm pretty sure I have an idea of what goes where." Simon raised his hips slightly before bringing it down again as if to demonstrate, his root bumping up against the sensitive spot at the base of Zhang's spine and the crack of his ass. Zhang dropped his head and squeezed his eyes closed as a low moan escaped his lips. Simon would kill him yet. Simon meanwhile took his time, nipping at his shoulders, licking and kissing at his neck while Zhang came to a decision. Zhang couldn't think straight (haha!), instead he unconsciously spread his legs and raised his hips to encourage the contact.

"Is that a yes?" Simon whispered then kissed him again.

"Y-y-"

Simon made his move and went for it, grabbing the base of his root and pushing the tip of his member in. Zhang hollered and spread his legs further as Simon barreled his way in.

Zhang hollered some more and Simon immediately stopped.

"What are you doing? You can't stop!" Zhang panted out turning his head, a hand firmly on the back of Simon's thigh.

"It's not going in-"

"Oh, it's going in! I can feel it."

"Maybe we need some oil-"

"What? From where?"

"Up there! There's some on the counter-"

Zhang looked up and saw where he was pointing. "What? Sesame Seed Cooking Oil? Can we use that?"

"Yeah, I think it's ok." Simon said reaching for it. But they found he was a few inches short. So, with Zhang refusing to let him dislodge, the two shimmied their way closer until Simon grabbed the bottle.

"Got it?"

"Yeah."

Zhang laughed as Simon snapped the top open. "It's brand new."

"How much shall we use?"

"Maybe about a tablespoon. If we need more -" Simon said lifting his hips just enough to angle the bottle and allow the oil to drip liberally onto his member and down the crack of Zhang's ass.

They giggled and then Simon set the bottle aside. "Ready?"

"F- -k yeah!"

Simon repositioned a little and pushed his way in. Zhang's cry gave way to a protracted groan as Simon breached muscle and slowly slid home.

"Oh, my gawd-"

"That feels so damn good!"

"Oh yeah, baby-"

"Does that feel hot?"

"Yeah, real hot-"

"No, I mean it really feels kinda' hot, like —"

No one noticed that the bottle of oil they'd just opened and used didn't just say "Sesame Seed Oil" but rather "Sichuan Chili Sesame Seed Oil".

The two were heard screaming bloody murder and cursing in the little caravan parked in the grassy area at the edge of the studio followed by the distinct sound of grown men sobbing as Simon leapt off Zhang's back, his root on fire. Zhang fared no better, eyes wide, tears gushing down his cheeks, the feeling as if a red-hot poker was stuffed up his ass overwhelming.

Needless to say, they received immediate medical care, swearing the entire medical staff to secrecy.

Zhang didn't speak to his costar for three days.

On the fourth day, they reconciled and tried it again this time using the tube of personal oil another sympathetic costar, who shall remain nameless, brought from home and left on Simon's doorstep in a brown paper bag.

In the aftermath of their successful coupling, they lay there staring in each other's eyes and grinning like two idiots. Zhang knew then he was in love and found his soul mate.

Meanwhile Simon, sweaty and breathless from the exertion, reported in via the array: Rally Point 1, Phase 2 - Accomplished. Detailed report to follow. Lt. SimonGJXO1129.

The report was three days late.

Mencius rolled his eyes.

There was no 'Phase 2'.

Nevertheless, Lady Master Thala and the Pleiadeans who previously had a good laugh, now cheered.

CHAPTER THIRTY

Zhang Finally Remembers and Kicks CAPA Ass (Zhang and His Magic Button)

Upon the suggestion of Lady Master Thala, the duo tried Sensual and Sexual Cultivation as a means to jog Zhang's memory. It took them 3 days, but it worked.

After 3 days of pressing Zhang's "magic spot" practically nonstop on the advice of Lady Master Thala to jog his multidimensional memories, Zhang finally woke up for real.

"I remember!" Zhang cried out as he shot upward with a yelp almost flipping off the bed for the umpteenth time. He was completely drenched in sweat and naked as the day he was born.

Just moments before both he and Simon were heard to complain, "Are you sure it's even working? We've been pressing it for days!"

To which Thala yelled into the array in complete and utter exasperation "Hit it, again!"

Simon had reached out into the array for help on getting Zhang to remember earlier in the now moment. She hadn't realized they were actually in the very act of trying to regain his memory. Since sexual cultivation was meant to help humans reach higher states of consciousness, she was certain it would help Zhang reach deep into his and recollect everything.

So, Simon hit it again this time using his tongue and all the pressure he could muster. Then Zhang as if on cue went cosmic with a shout and protracted moan that had Simon climaxing as well.

In the aftermath, Zhang felt like he was about to drop dead and rolled off his partner's face. Simon popped his head up and cheered. Since trying the new position, Zhang had actually remembered at around the 18-minute mark but was having too good a time of it with his jewels on Simon's head to say anything. Thala left the array in disgust. Not because he used his tongue or because Zhang's jewels had been hanging on Simon's forehead for the last hour and a half, or even that she heard them both climaxing, but because the two had been bugging her nonstop for help for the last few thousand now moments (roughly about the last hour and a half) followed by childish banter and commentary equivalent in irritating fashion to the proverbial, "Are we there yet?"

The jerks.

She had been so close to throwing in the towel on account of those two, even contemplating relinquishing her esteemed Lady Master title. She'd heard Mencius had been close to losing it with them, as well. Now she understood why. When they connected back to the array to thank her, breathless and satiated, she didn't pick up.

As a multidimensional being, the first thing Zhang remembered was that he was a commander assigned to the spaceship Athena. He also remembered the myriad missions he and Simon and various crew members under his command had been on and successfully accomplished due to his leadership and decisive action on the Athena. He also remembered why he had come to earth.

The first thing Commander Zhang did was fire his legal team (after he and Simon finished their memory inducing 'button pressing' cultivation exercises). It went something like this:

Zhang: "I think I'm going to fire my lawyers."

Simon: "Yeah, they're kinda' lame. Slow, too."

Zhang: "That's sorta' what I was thinking. But maybe I should give them more time?"

Simon: "Ten months with no results is a lot of time…just sayin'.…"

Zhang: "You think? Yeah, you're right. I'll give them another week."

Simon: "Do it now."

Zhang: "Good idea!"

As he'd been asleep since age 5, (26 years), it was still a tad bit slow in coming for him.

The new team of Xu Dewitt and Chang recommended by Lady Master Nada hit the ground running filing petitions to substitute counsel immediately. Since being made a scapegoat, one thing Zhang never could fathom was how it happened. One minute he was enjoying a rising tide of fame and myriad opportunities including brand endorsements, the next he was a pariah and all his sponsors had cut him loose; his SM and online accounts were cancelled, and he became history all because of a photo from 2018 that had been taken innocently and without malice. Zhang's new legal team set out to find out why and more importantly who was behind it all.

In effect by bringing on a fresh, new legal team, Zhang let the dogs loose.

They first set out to untangle the web and closely scrutinize the obvious culprit who blacklisted him in the first place without legal redress - the China Association of Performing Arts or CAPA. Despite almost ten months under his prior legal team, he still hadn't gained much traction in clearing his name. He didn't doubt they were doing their best to navigate the slippery slope of politics and messy ties in sussing out the complex and intertwining story. They just weren't moving as fast as

Commander Zhang was used to moving.

Almost overnight after Xu Dewitt and Chang stepped in the reports and results started rolling in. Once his new team was in play, they filed a motion in court to stay the proceedings, delaying it until Simon's criminal matter could proceed further along.

This was a calculated move as this allowed his legal team to rely on discovery from Simon's criminal matter gleaned against the Chairman to sniff out and follow the money trail in Zhang's case and use the momentum to push his own investigation forward. Discovery was a legal procedure that gave both sides equal opportunity to review evidence the other party had collected to support their case. This was to prevent sneaky tactics like hiding evidence or even blindsiding, a common trope in high stake cases such as this.

While the government sought to control the moral fiber of the Chinese people by heavily scrutinizing its role models, Zhang's team suspected something else was going on: money was changing hands. Lots of it. It wasn't long before they discovered the motivation had always been more financial than blind rhetoric to guide the 'moral upliftment' of the Chinese people. His team was hell bent on following that money trail.

They hit paydirt. Chairman Luo the billionaire had a lot of friends and a dirty reputation much like Jeffrey Epstein with his black book in the US. Thus, just reviewing the Chairman's contacts gave Zhang's team a plethora of information and names, most of who were associated with CAPA and had voted to blacklist Zhang. Thus, it just became a matter of sorting out who was who. There were a few other notable names in the book as well, including current government officials.

The second thing Commander Zhang did was turn the heat up on CAPA. It was really the lawyers' idea, but he wholeheartedly supported it. People should never suffer on account of someone else's greed. He did this by directing his legal team to file injunctions against CAPA to cease the illegal blacklisting of his name. He then ordered them to file lawsuits against CAPA as well as the various government agencies associated with them, halting the illegal seizure of assets, illegal interference with commercial contracts due to the wrongful termination and revocation of Zhang's more than 25 company endorsements. Most importantly, he sought pecuniary damages, as well as filed a suit against the Ministry of Culture and Tourism, ordering their immediate cessation of the unlawful blacklisting as well.

CAPA, while a voluntary association of management companies and members of the entertainment industry, nonetheless answered to the Ministry of Culture and Tourism, thus many of its members were heavy hitters in the industry and collectively welded a lot of unchecked power. It naturally had a tendency to overstep its authority on the basis of its widespread industry influence and clout. And Zhang felt it important to slam them hard for their purposeful transgressions. So, he did.

Not to be outdone, Simon's legal team of Emerthers also filed an injunction against CAPA, the Ministry of Culture and Tourism, ordering the immediate cessation of the unlawful blacklisting and illegal seizure of Simon's assets. They then filed a separate petition with the International Court of Justice and the International Criminal Court to have Chairman Luo answer to crimes against him as a sexual predator, trafficker in flesh, and for crimes against humanity.

The ICJ and ICC had been responsible for taking down the likes of the Vatican's most notorious child traffickers and rapists with more on the way. While both the ICJ and ICC were not yet recognized by some countries, they were recognized by China and thus any verdict they issued had the full force and effect of the law.

This was followed by the firms' US and Japan teams filing suits against Chairman Luo for defamation, interference with contracts for the many endorsements of Simon that were on the line as a result of the criminal accusations (as they'd all seen the video and Simon clearly looked as if he'd been attacked.) This coupled with the almost 100lb difference in size between Simon and the chairman, only proved Simon had been the victim. This was followed by a long list of other alleged crimes and civil irregularities by the chairman, his agents and assigns.

All told more than a hundred different legal complaints (lawsuits), injunctions, cross complaints, petitions, answers, and motions were filed within a short period of time.

The court hearing Zhang's original defamation case had no choice but to *sua sponte* continue the case a second and then a third time to review and sort everything out. (A legal procedure that in essence meant "on the court's own motion"). Meanwhile, this gave time for Zhang's team to uncover the links between Chairman Luo, the Ministry of Culture and Tourism, CAPA and a wide network of other players.

Once the net was cast, it was no longer just corruption the legal teams and the public became interested in, but the link to crimes of a sexual nature suffered not just by Simon but a long list of other victims who came forward encouraged by both cases. The media went nuts.

With solid people at his back, and Simon by his side, he did what he came to earth to do in the first place.

Commander Zhang soared.

CHAPTER THIRTY-ONE

Commander Zhang is in Da' House

With his newfound mojo, his lawyers suggested he address the media and public. They needed to hear from him while the courts mulled over the complaints and petitions. They decided to do so immediately in the parking lot of the main courthouse in Xinyu City where a stage had been set up for this purpose.

Commander Zhang dressed in a pair of dark pants, crème colored white t-shirt and a light-colored suit jacket, an ensemble Simon helped him pick out, cleared his throat, took a breath, and stepped up to the mic and prepared to address the masses. He hadn't really prepared anything beforehand. The night before at his apartment, he and Simon spoke with Mencius using the array who suggested he should just speak from his heart as Sirian Commander Zhang. So, he did.

The usual lighthearted mischievousness, a brightness that one saw when he gazed back at you or gazed at the camera, was now replaced by something else...a look many were not familiar with or used to seeing. His expression was serious, grave even as if what he was about to say carried weight, depth, and profound importance it warranted your complete and undivided attention. Because somehow, you knew your safety, your survival even, depended upon it.

Simon was familiar with that look. He'd seen it countless times during missions when the Commander took the helm, prepared to face unknown dangers and was well aware he held the lives of his comrades in his hands. He took every mission seriously yet brought in a touch of humor so as not to scare everyone. It was also the look that carried the wisdom, depth and more importantly the compassion of Zhang the Ascended Master. The Zhang that he revealed in his songs and writings bearing messages of such profound wisdom.

Commander Zhang's look as he gazed at the crowd of reporters and fans and curious onlookers who had gathered, was one that pierced your heart. It had the power to rally another who had perhaps fallen behind, was beaten down and defeated, or too exhausted to keep moving after a long and protracted fight. It was a look that had the strength to somehow carry everyone forward. His was the strength when yours ran out. His was the courage when yours fled. And when you could no longer walk or stand, or crawl even, he was there to support or even carry you on his back to ensure you made it back home, too. Simon was well familiar when the commander was in the house. And today, Commander Zhang was back and reporting for duty. It made even him stand up at attention.

"My friends....there comes a time when we are called to step onto a path....one filled with uncertainty...one we must sometimes walk alone, to face of our own accord....it may be a space or situation that may be unfamiliar, perhaps uncomfortable or scary even....a place perhaps we would never have in our right mind chosen had we knew what lay ahead...a path we may feel we have absolutely no control of."

"And that path is wrought with challenges and dangers we didn't even know could possibly exist which is overwhelming, impossible even...and all around you there is a darkness that you can't hope to see your way through. Well, many of you are aware that I've been there myself...." He paused and took another deep breath. A sigh even.

"When I felt the whole world was against me...that I had been forsaken...because of a mistake I made...one that I didn't know I had even made and would be heavily judged for....one that would rob me

240

of my career, my safety, my livelihood and threaten to also take my soul…"

He looked around at the crowd of reporters gathered before him. The crowd listening in was dead silent. Listening to every word Zhang was sharing knowing it was coming from a place so raw, so vulnerable, and yet shared with such force and humility one knew he was speaking directly to you. And so, you felt compelled to listen…to hear every word.

"Some may say I'm still on that path…that I deserve it even. I would be lying to say I wasn't afraid…that I wasn't totally unprepared. The fact is I was pretty naive going into all of this thinking people would understand I meant no harm or disrespect. Yet, as I found myself heading further along on this seemingly endless road, there were times, so, so many times when I, Crazy Zhang, who never feared anything and believed we should try everything at least once while we still can….I doubted even myself…that I would make it and be able to see it through the end….because no matter how hard I looked, no matter which way I turned, I couldn't see the light. It was so damn dark and I felt completely alone…."

Some of the reporters in attendance looked down, as if what he said rang true for them, too. Others quietly dabbed at their eyes or reflected back on their roles in the drama he faced as they stared at the small monitors on their camera screens.

"I believe the reason I doubted my own ability was because like many of you, I have witnessed so many others on the very same path struggle, suffer terribly, and who became so overwhelmed by that suffering that they lost their way…some even took their lives just to get that suffering to end." He paused for a long while as he seemed to recall and replay in his mind what he and others had experienced.

"There was a time I believed that that was the outcome that was also in store for me…that I would be defeated and lost forever." Commander Zhang took a breath before he continued, his words and their tone measured.

241

"Well, I am here to tell you, that the outcome...the outcome is uncertain only for those who don't believe. Because you bring the light to the table. No, you know what, I take that back, you ARE the LIGHT. So no matter how obscure or endless the darkness may seem at times, the path so rocky and filled with obstacles and difficulties....no matter what anyone throws at you, or says to you, or how they may bully you into believing something else, YOU are LIGHT....and that means, you hold the key....the solution....you are the solution and the one you have been waiting for."

"And know because you are Light, you can create whatever outcome you choose for yourself. And you can light the way for others who are still mired or lost in the darkness and unaware that they are Light too. Because where there is Light, darkness is gone. Having no place to go, nowhere to run, and nothing to do but hide like cowards."

"And I wish to tell you that your Light is so incredibly bright and strong....so beautiful and amazing that nothing can hold a candle to it....But I also wish to say that even the worst offenders are Light, too. They, just like me at first, didn't remember. And like a bully who goes looking for a fight, to take advantage of another who they believe is smaller, weaker or less worthy, or has something they wish for themselves, when you stand up and shine your Light, you can even light the way for them. To help them reveal their Light as well."

"So...find your Light, your genius, your spirit. It's what makes you, you. It's the reason you are here. Why we all are here. To light the way for each other, not to beat each other down. We are here to help each other remember."

"Believe that you are light. Because I know it, your guides know it, Source knows it...that Light is you." He cleared his throat. "So, I hope you can join me and the rest of your brothers and sisters who are here to be of service like you. We have a lot of work yet to accomplish as there are many here who won't believe these words and will try to fight us. But I am here to tell you that we will never give up on them or you. Because we are all One. And this world...as much as we think it isn't, is actually powered by unconditional love. And once we understand this…once we recognize this, everything here changes. All the darkness, all the hatred, the gossip, the backbiting, the cyber bullying…the corruption and the greed…that is coming to an end. Gaia is ascending and we are here to make sure it happens. You will want to join me… join us…."

The Commander paused, seemed to think for a moment before he politely thanked everyone and calmly walked away from the podium and off the stage to where his legal team, Simon and Ming stood watching and listening. The crowd stunned by the unconventional but oddly encouraging speech were still silent. Suddenly they broke from their revelry and began shouting out questions. Meanwhile, Commander Zhang gazed upon his partner who met his eyes and nodded solemnly at him before walking side by side with him to the awaiting black van.

When they were settled in beside one another with Ming up front, Simon turned to him, a look of utmost respect and reverence in his eyes that was accompanied by a hint of a smile. "Welcome back, Commander."

On the ship as everyone watched via the monitors while others listened in on the array, the captain stood on the bridge at attention, arms behind his back. His heart beating with emotion, the look in his eyes one of undisguised pride.

"Well done, Commander," he said into the array. "Well done."

He was then heard on the broadcast speaker to say:

"All systems go. I repeat, all systems go. Commander Zhang has given the signal. Prepare the ship for final take down of the fence and with it all corrupt institutions. Level 8 broadcast approved."

CHAPTER THIRTY-TWO

Wherein Heads Roll - The Government Created Scandal Involving CAPA

"This is a real shit show, isn't it?" Zhang mused as he tried to keep up with all the legal pleadings and filings being exchanged. He was glad the galactics with expertise in such earthly matters were now in charge.

"Get ready for more heads to roll," Shen Wu, his team's lead attorney smirked. Unlike his other lead attorney, it was clear Shen enjoyed a good fight and was prepared for one. The firm's track record evidenced they were in it to win. And Shen and his colleagues went in swinging. Hard...cleverly using the court of public opinion as much as the legal system to their advantage. Zhang left them to it.

Simon's team was equally effective in handling matters. Since Zhang's speech, people began to rally. Some took to social media, others to the streets in protest of everything from cyber bullying to corporate fraud and misfeasance, and most of all CAPA and government corruption. This spawned a series of investigations by public interest groups, re-evaluation of school and company policies and sexual impropriety at every level. Everything was questioned.

When Chairman Luo lawyered up, now on the defensive, Simon and Zhang knew they finally got him. He was the first to fall. They celebrated with hot pot and beers. Ming paid.

Ju Xinxi, the head of CAPA lawyered up next. The rest came in
succession like dominos just as Mencius had said. The next was the local
provincial governor of Xinyu who had been under investigation for
fraud and bribery.

All they needed to do was follow the money trail. But it also revealed a
larger, more insidious plot that had very little to do directly with Zhang
other than to target him at random. The government created scandal
aimed at targeting those artists and their fan base that had reached in
the hundreds of millions worldwide. While a ploy of the government at
one level, those responsible at CAPA for carrying out the scandal
against the artists were also heavily rewarded for their role. Their palms
greased.

All told, more than 25 billion RMB had changed hands at the expense of
performing artists and their careers since 2018 alone when the mandates
cracking down on role models came down. The artists had been
blacklisted by the players in exchange for lining their pockets. While
these schemes generated billions in Yuan in revenue, the artists were
targeted seemingly at random sometimes based on a simple unfounded
allegation. Depending upon their response, they would be boycotted, or
worse, or they would be exonerated. While Simon himself had been
targeted, his studio immediately filed a lawsuit for defamation which
quickly silenced his detractors. Still asleep, Zhang wasn't so lucky.

The revelation was staggering and caused an avalanche of backlash.
Confusion reigned and dominated social media. It created a snowball
effect until the real players and mysterious reason behind Zhang's
blacklisting was finally publicly revealed. Also uncovered was the
interconnectedness to other darker, more notorious crimes which began
to surface in rapid succession.

They had Chairman Luo and his black book to thank for that obtained
after an investigation launched into what occurred at his Hunan
Mansion involving Simon. The images of a bloodied and disheveled
Simon replayed over and over on SM and the media until it sunk deep

into the consciousness of every adult in the country, fueling outrage among mothers, fathers and the younger generations who saw themselves or their own children as potential victims of these high-level predators. That coupled with Zhang's speech also repeated and replayed served as a rally cry for the outraged masses who now firmly stood behind him.

Given the number of people waking up, Commander Zhang realized they needed to give the netizens another thing to focus on besides him. He handed them CAPA for starters. Simon handed them Chairman Luo. As expected, the media ate it all up. Both the traditional media outlets and SM were on fire. The headlines were all over the place.

"Government created scandal"

"Sexual Improprieties Abound"

"Chairman Luo facing Intense Scrutiny"

"Other victims Come Forward"

"CAPA Now Under Investigation"

"Idol 'Simon' Marries Female Costar, Divorces Practically Overnight"

"Tampa Bay Lightning Bolts Win the 2022 Stanley Cup!!! Not!"

"Weibo, WeChat, Douyin Sued by Disgraced Actor Zhang"

"Actor Zhang Reinstated"

"Government Found Complicit in Sexual Predatory Practices. Many Officials Resign!"

Despite the widespread coverage and the plethora of information uncovered during the investigations, there were still some misguided netizens and vengeful press who nonetheless found satisfaction in bashing them. They bashed Simon for his assault on the Chairman which was chalked up to his arrogance due to his rising popularity, his greed for desiring a bigger stake in the business, and of course his ill-fated association with a traitor like Zhang.

Zhang was bashed as a vengeful, jealous, do-gooder whose online and heartfelt writings and soliloquies as well as songs about Light and Love made him a romantic idealist and nothing more.

They had a good laugh at this and shortly thereafter the detractors suffered heavy retribution on account of the phenomena known as the 'Boomerang Effect' - when a low vibing being clashes with and attacks a high vibing being, transmuting the karma of the lower vibing being, otherwise known as "instant karma" or "cause and effect in action". They were promptly served lawsuits by others who'd been smeared by them.

To do their part in curbing the negative media and control the dialogue, neither Simon nor Zhang gave any further interviews. This was lauded and condoned by their legal teams who also kept hidden many of the things they uncovered while releasing info on others. But it drove the media rabid like a pack of wild dogs fighting for scraps. The result was a sort of controlled chaos leaving the social media and traditional media reporters with no choice but to follow the trail and behave or get nothing.

As the attention had shifted to CAPA, Chairman Luo and all their cronies, the media tore after them instead with a vengeance seeking answers and putting them on the defensive. Simon and Zhang meanwhile had nothing better to do than sit around and play video games, eat hot pot, 'wrestle', and watch from their newly crowned positions on the sidelines.

The next thing Zhang did was go after SM platforms Weibo, WeChat, Douyin, and others, and the media for their roles in vilifying the two performers, using China's own regulations against violating social etiquette and morays, online bullying and defamation of character to throw his punches. The result was opening the door even wider and going after them all at once. This was all Zhang's idea.

This put other online haters and negative press including China's official press, the People's Daily and their so-called morality monitoring judgment-based reporting and a slew of tabloids officially on notice. Some even went bankrupt after the court accepted the petitions and ordered they pay Zhang and Simon restitution. The two laughed all the way to the bank. Simon's studio donated most of it to charitable organizations as he was accustomed to doing while Zhang's recouped fees went to paying off his other attorneys (at a substantial discount as negotiated by Lady Master Nada) and paying down some of the other debt he had subsequently incurred as a result of the scandal.

With what was left he went out and bought a pair of engagement bands. They chose a CP fan's small custom jewelry company as a personal endorsement of her thoughtful work. She screamed and fan-girled hard even though they swore her to secrecy for the next sixteen months. She even gave them a discount.

To Zhang and Simon, it was interesting to watch how quickly the distraction created by these parasitic organizations and industry players of targeting artists quickly turned away from the two of them and hit the perpetrators back squarely in the ass. Zhang was even motivated to write a song about it.

They watched from Simon's apartment in Shanghai as Chairman Luo gave a scathing speech maligning his detractors, most of all, Simon who he claimed had orchestrated lies to entrap him. This speech was made as he was being led away in handcuffs to serve his time in jail.

"He looks good in duralumin and stainless steel, don't you think?" Simon mused as he drank down a can of flavored water with his face on it.

"A hell of a lot better than you." Zhang shot back removing his shirt. Simon grinned, set his can of water down on the table and did the same. Similar scathing speeches were made by Ju Xinxi, the head of CAPA and Xinyu's local provincial governor aimed at Zhang as they were also led away in matching duralumin and stainless steel bracelets from court.

Zhang moved to him in unhurried fashion, and before Simon could work his usual magic, Zhang latched onto a nipple and began suckling him there.

Simon threw his head back and laughed. "What are you doing? That's ticklish!"

Zhang, around a mouthful of man boob mumbled, "I always wanted to do that with a woman's boob."

Simon made a face of abject horror. "What? That's gross!" And pushed him away.

"Gross? You had your tongue up my - -"

Simon cut him off. "Dude! I was busy trying to help you remember."

Zhang grinned at him at this, "Thanks for reminding me."

Simon snickered and lead him into the bedroom. Before they even reached the bedroom door's threshold they were out of their clothes. They did what two dudes with a seemingly bottomless appetite for giving and receiving pleasure do. They made love.

Then they temporarily disappeared from public view. Mencius reported the second wave of government, banking, pharmaceutical, insurance, telecommunications, and other big name corporate corruption exposure was underway.

Exhausted, Zhang eagerly awaited his promised healing with Simon.

Fans spotted them boarding a plane to Hawaii together. This time setting off a media storm and speculation the two were heading to the US to get married. The pair couldn't care less.

CHAPTER THIRTY-THREE

Lady Master Ma'at and the Retreat in Honoka'a - Wherein They Meet the Lady Master and Follow Her Home

They found Lady Master Ma'at at the crystal shop in downtown Honoka'a. Despite worrying they would get lost they quickly realized they really couldn't miss it. Aside from the fact there was only one main road going in either direction, it was also the only such shop in the tiny town of whitewashed wooden buildings and high ceilings anywhere on the island.

They drove straight from the airport as soon as they retrieved Zhang's duffel bag and all 8 of Simon's suitcases full of his wardrobe, hair and facial products and 52 pairs of Zhang's favorite basketball shoes. They rented a huge black American Model SUV as it was the only size car everything could fit in. Seeing its monstrous size, Zhang insisted on driving and immediately got behind the wheel. It was clean and luxurious and had very low mileage on it and easily fit 10 people.

Zhang noted it was no more difficult to drive than a shuttle craft although the cars he inadvertently cut off and those lined up behind him as he drove 30 mph on the main drag begged to differ. He waved them around him as he got used to the SUV's feel.

They navigated the streets with relative ease thereafter as there was very little traffic unlike the streets of Beijing or Shanghai. After about a 45-

minute drive the GPS indicated they were approaching the town of Honoka'a where Mencius had told them they would find Lady Master Ma'at. She owned a crystal shop and was likely to be found there during the day if she was on the island. Simon had reached out to her in the array, and she welcomed them readily to visit when they were next in town. 30 seconds later they were in her face taking her up on her offer.

Honoka'a Crystals was sandwiched between a tea shop and a yoga studio. Despite the sleepy nature of the town the shop was busy. The inside of the shop was also whitewashed with a rustic patina and welcoming with an aura that naturally drew customers in. The large picture windows and glass door gave those walking by a clear view of the huge Amethyst geode tastefully displayed on a white table that greeted everyone upon entry.

Simon zeroed in on it, mesmerized by all that dazzling purple and violet crystal anchoring powerful healing energies. Zhang meanwhile walked past it to eye a large crystal skull in a nearby display case that was shaped like the head of a Jefok. He laughed and pointed it out to Simon.

Lady Master Ma'at stood behind the counter beside two other females. She had shoulder length dark wavy hair and reddish mocha skin, exotic mixed-race features and almond shaped dark brown eyes. At maybe 5'4 or 5"5, with a slim build, they towered over her. She had a welcoming dimpled smile and recognized them immediately, coming around the counter to greet them. Simon couldn't stop looking at her, the person who he had been speaking to in the array for all these months to garner energetic healing support for Zhang was finally standing before him like an old friend.

They both knew of her in her higher incarnation by reputation alone. While not an Archangel, Lady Master Ma'at was a being of Light and Ascended Master in her highest incarnation and a force to be reckoned with nonetheless. Revered on earth as a goddess during her time in Egypt, she was almost always depicted as winged much like an angel. Thus, her incarnation even then was associated with Light and she was much loved for her service to humanity. Neither had ever seen her in her Goddess form either, except in drawings gleaned from temple walls

251

on their smart pads.

To Simon standing before him in her earth form, she was both beautiful and loving. And though her face was not one he recognized, he felt her calming and healing energies acutely.

Meanwhile Zhang who'd heard so much about her from Simon stared openly and in curious awe. He had a feeling they had met before perhaps in another incarnation, but he couldn't put a finger on it. The thought was fleeting and disappeared soon after.

"Commander, Lieutenant! You made it! I finally get to see you here in the flesh!"

Simon melted like a goofy puppy and immediately shook her hand enthusiastically, smiling broadly, never mind he had reached the pinnacle of handsome and poised as a top male model. At the moment he simply gushed at her like he was meeting a celebrity and not the other way around. Zhang fared no better, staring back at her in wonder. He followed suit and shook her hand before they both found themselves ensconced in a warm, disarming embrace.

"Aunty, your store is so beautiful! Can you show us around and pick us out some stones?" Simon asked in English when they finally broke apart.

Zhang couldn't explain what he was feeling except that hug was like finally coming home for him. It humbled him and made him a little emotional and he dabbed a tear from the corner of his eye.

"Of course! Come let's start over here." She then led them to a tasteful display of books on 5D, consciousness raising, mudras vs madras, Goddess energy, crystals, healing plants, books on channeling, Buddhism, and one entitled "The Wild & Zany Galactic Adventures of Commander Zhang & Lieutenant Simon, Soul Mates Who Incarnate on Earth and Save the World" by Ariitzka. On the back sleeve was a picture of Lady Master Ma'at.

Before the book sat a little placard noting it was #1 on the NYT Best Seller List on Spirituality as well as Science Fiction. Before Simon could pick it up, she quickly drew their attention to the side wall where shelves of beautiful journals sat side by side with eye catching designed boxes of tarot and oracle cards.

All around the center of the store were displays of incense holders, candles, packets and boxes of incense, sage and palo santo, specially designed and curated jewelry, scarves, bags, and specialty teas. On the left side of the store there were small stones arranged neatly in bowls and on an impressive wall display. There they found both polished stones of various shapes and colors and hues as well as rough stones, all of it appealing.

Zhang stepped forward to look. Some reminded him of the color of the sky, others the color of the ground of planets he had walked on including Simon's home planet of Neubin. Others looked like candy or bubble gum. He grabbed a pink stone that caught his eye.

"That's Rhodonite. That's actually one I would have picked out for you Commander. This beautiful stone is one of love, forgiveness, compassion, and acceptance. It helps open your heart to love, helps heal the inner self and can detoxify the body. It's also a stone of compassion. It's associated therefore with the Heart Chakra," she said placing her palm on her chest.

Then she gazed at him soundly. Used to people staring at him as an actor and celebrity, he endured her gaze which was both warm and insightful. "You look well, Commander. You've had a difficult but successful journey and have taught so many of us what it means to be dignified and humble no matter what we may face. The captain was right about you and your record of exemplary service. I am so happy for your successes and that we could be here at this time together. I am deeply honored for your service and all you've done for Gaia and humanity. For all of us. We can never forget it in any lifetime," she said with deep emotion.

"It's time to fully heal now," she continued with a smile. She then turned to pick out a stone for Simon. Surprisingly he understood everything she said without issue but remembered as a multidimensional being he had no need for translators.

"And you, beautiful child, pure being, pure Light, his partner and protector in all lifetimes. I watched you being born and joined in the celebrations," she beamed at Simon.

"What celebrations? How'd you see him being born?" Zhang interrupted, puzzled. "Did I miss something?"

"You didn't tell him?" Lady Master Ma'at turned to Simon who shook his head.

"I didn't want him to think I was bragging," Simon said still shaking his head and looking as if the very thought would have Zhang in a small hissy fit.

Lady Master Ma'at laughed. "It was beautiful! You should tell him," she said nodding encouragingly.

"I received a standing ovation," Simon turned to Zhang and explained.

"What? Wait, did I get one too?" Admittedly, his recall and multidimensional consciousness were still not at 100%.

They both made a tentative face, which quickly turned into scrunched up looks of consternation as they shook their heads.

"No, baby." Simon recalled the uproarious laughter that filled the Round Room and cringed.

"Not even close!" Lady Master Ma'at followed up. "We did enjoy ourselves, though. And you were so adorable!"

Zhang's head was then filled with images of his birth side by side with images of Simon's. He could clearly be heard bitching and moaning, a look of surprise and then anger on his small, hideously red face that matched his hideously wrinkled slime covered body.

While Simon was equally plastered in slime, his birth was serene and quiet, a meditative quality to it even. Zhang thought he also heard soft music. When little, tiny human Simon opened his eyes and smiled it made even Zhang's heart stop. "Is that photoshopped?" Zhang asked. They laughed and shook their heads as they looked back at Zhang.

"Holy shit,babe! You are an angel!"

Simon only grinned at his partner, pleased. Zhang chuckled and squeezed Simon's hand, undisguised pride in his eyes as he gazed back at him.

"This is for you, Lieutenant," Lady Master Ma'at handed him a small pink stone with gray and white swirls, still chuckling.

"Call me Simon, aunty."

"Ok, beautiful angel Simon. This stone is Rhodochrosite. It's a healing and comfort giving stone, related to the Cancer Sun sign. It promotes smooth energy flow, emotional expressiveness, tolerance and self-love. Here." She handed him a little card with information and then gave one to Zhang. "There is also a transformative energy with this stone. Old emotional hurts surface to be forgiven and cleansed. It is also useful in meditation to help one focus on one's personal mission in life and it is said to enhance memory and intellectual power. Associated with the root, solar plexus and heart chakras," she continued. "It's a stone of unconditional love. I sense you are already a master of this. So, let's just let this be a reminder of your service on earth."

"Thank you." Simon grinned. "Do we just put it in our pockets?"

"Yes, you can meditate with it, keep it in your pocket or somewhere on a table or shelf. These stones all have their own consciousness and so are ready to serve based on your intent."

"Aunty, will you marry us? Is that a thing you can do?" Simon suddenly blurted albeit nervously, surprising Zhang.

"Of course! and I'm most happy and honored to marry you both. But where's my ring?" Lady Master Ma'at answered laughing. Then she frowned, "No wait, sorry. I'm already married." Simon found her brand of humor right up his alley and immediately burst out laughing. She was obviously kidding. Zhang, still jet-lagging, had reverted back to his 3D self and was having trouble processing English with his sometimes on again, sometimes off again multidimensional brain. So, he looked at Simon for translation.

"She said yes she will marry us but you have to sing and dance first."

"That sounded like a lot more words than that," Zhang frowned. They all burst into laughter.

"Yes, I would so love you to sing. You too, Simon. We will enjoy ourselves and heal, too. It will be lots of fun." Then, "To make your union official we need apply for a marriage license. Then we can do the ceremony wherever you two like. The beach, at a waterfall, at the tide pools or in the valley." They both nodded, excitedly.

Before leaving the store, she picked out a few more loose stones for them.

She also told them about the healing meditations she had prepared especially for them they could do once they settled in at her home which wasn't that far. Zhang found out after the Arcturus retreat, he wasn't really good at meditation though he liked the general idea of being able to relax and zone out. It usually made him fall asleep. Nevertheless, Zhang could not wait for the healing to begin. He only realized later that it already had with their meeting.

CHAPTER THIRTY-FOUR

The Boys Settle in for Some More 'Healing'

It was with much excitement that they pulled up to Lady Master Ma'at's home situated on a high bluff overlooking the ocean with an unobstructed view of the magnificent Hawaiian sunset. Zhang realized she had created this space for those called to meet her to regroup, heal and relax. He felt it as soon as his foot touched the ground as he got out of their rented SUV.   He felt a familiar blast of warm and welcoming energy shoot through him. He recognized it as love and light, and one that he had experienced after a particularly bad time all those months ago. While he hadn't understood it then, it had put him at ease.

They hadn't been able to talk on the ride up as they drove in separate cars. They instead followed behind her white jaguar SUV, Zhang tailing her so close he almost rear-ended her when she stopped to turn left. They drove up a windy and slightly hilly road then down a short dirt and gravel path that led right to her driveway. They pulled up to the back of a simple one-story stucco home. She opened the automatic garage door and pulled in and gestured for them to follow.

As soon as they jumped out and grabbed some of the luggage and followed her to the door, Zhang took the time to express his gratitude and the awe of meeting her.

"Did I say what an honor it is to meet you, Lady Master," Zhang said as they entered her home.

Lady Master Ma'at chuckled and gave him a mischievous smile then lead them further inside without answering.

"What's wrong with what I just said?" He whispered to Simon as they followed and she led them to a hallway toward the right. Simon only grinned at him.

"You can put your things here." She stood to the side of a large well-appointed room decorated in a Hawaiian theme and let them pass to enter. The large room had a king size bed with a beautiful blue and green quilt of ferns and plants, overstuffed pillows, a handsome koa wooden desk, and two matching bedside tables.

On the desk were a couple of tour books about the island, some chocolate macadamia nuts and four bottles of water. On the walls were pictures of the native flora and fauna that they'd seen everywhere in the lush surroundings as they drove from the airport. The room was tastefully and yet simply decorated with an extremely warm and inviting vibe. They set the bags down and openly admired the space.

"No crystals?" Simon asked.

"Some people find them too energized making it difficult to sleep. I keep them in the living room or my study on the opposite side of the house. But you're welcome to move them in here if they resonate with you. They can be a bit chatty. Especially the amethyst." She smirked then pointed out another bedroom further down the hall and the bathroom in between. "There's another bathroom on the other side of the house so you don't have to worry about us having to share. There's plenty of fresh towels in the hallway closet here."

"It is an honor to meet her, right? I mean, the Lady Master Ma'at? Come on!" Zhang continued in a low voice as she led them back to the main open area.

"Maybe she saw past your shallow bullshit and just realized you need way more healing," Simon joked.

"Didn't you say she sent me some energy and healing when I was vulnerable? Well, I'm still vulnerable. Because I can't believe we're here in the presence of a real angel!"

At this last bit Simon frowned and cocked an eyebrow. "Really? You're going to go there?"

"Well, you're like a half angel, right? How does that even work?" Zhang said looking at him seriously as they followed her out. "I mean I've never seen you with wings so how do I know you're not lying about being one? At least she's got wings in all the pictures," Zhang continued.

She quietly listened to them chattering amongst themselves in Chinese without interrupting allowing them to get more comfortable in their new surroundings. Much like Simon she could pick up on the subtle energies and could sense they were very happy and just teasing each other.

The home opened up to a large and bright open sitting area. The modern looking home had the dining room and kitchen area off to the front right side of the house. To the left was another hallway that presumably led to her office and bedroom. Against two of the walls were high bookshelves filled with books and crystals tastefully placed around on sofa tables and shelving as well as frames of beautiful local photography.

Before the third wall next to the hallway to the left was a large flatscreen tv before which sat a light gray pit couch with decorative pillows tossed about and a sleek black leather recliner with a pillow on it. A small coffee table with magazines and an eye-catching book on crystals sat before the couch together with a nice sized chunk of a purple amethyst stone.

"The remote's over there. There's Roku and it's also a smart tv with all the channels.   You can relax here and everywhere." She gestured. They both nodded happily.

Zhang could definitely get real comfortable here.

Simon grabbed his hand and intertwined their fingers. The living room itself faced a wall of sliding glass doors and windows that led out to a magnificent large pool around which sat several lounge chairs. Nearby was a table with four chairs tastefully arranged under a maroon canopy umbrella.

Behind the pool was a grassy area bordered on all sides by native plants of ginger, bird of paradise, ferns and small palms that obscured the view on the left and right sides of the property and gave off a subtle almost powdery aroma. The effect was the feeling of complete seclusion in a resort paradise with a kick ass view.

Zhang almost cried. *What the hell?* How can a place so amazing even exist and not ever have been in his consciousness? People live like this? This was no home but a retreat! Even the Arcturians couldn't hold a candle to this place!

"You know what the problem is, Lieutenant. We're never going to want to leave this place and go back to our shitty apartments. I think we should just tell her now we're moving in. You did say she was a US immigration attorney, right?" Simon grinned bck at him and nodded enthusiastically.

Obviously having long used up his star power with her, and after seeing his expression of awe, Lady Master Ma'at cocked an eyebrow at him. "Relax and give it a rest pretty boy." She joked. "This is your home away from home, too. Make yourselves comfortable."

"You think I'm pretty?" Zhang joked back pointing to his face.

Simon burst out laughing.

She nodded enthusiastically. "Stunning. Both of you...simply stunning." She shrugged.   When they were out in the yard by the pool admiring the view, Lady Master Ma'at bowed to them both deeply before gazing at them slowly, one after the other. "Let me say it's an honor to meet you here on earth, Commander Zhang and Lieutenant Simon. I am so happy we could be here together, and you decided to come. I've been following your progress and am so pleased to welcome you both here," she said.

They both hugged her, and they stood there for some time enveloped in her embrace and basking in all that strangely inviting energy that seemed to radiate from her and the ground upon which they stood.

"Why can we feel so much energy of unconditional love here and not other places?" Simon asked looking around curiously. It was like they were in some kind of holographic bubble. Not that elsewhere felt unusual. It was just that as soon as they stepped foot on the property, it was much like the feeling of coming home after a long, trying journey and receiving a warm loving embrace from a loved one.

"It's called the Aloha spirit. It's imbued here on this land, and deep into the earth." She answered gesturing. "It wasn't always like this in recent times. The family living here had been struggling for a long time. Some of that seeped into the ground and the aura here. But I cleared all of that away and anchored Light on all four corners of the property and in the center of the home when we fixed up the place."

"Who's we?" Zhang asked.

"My husband and I."

Lady Master Ma'at had an earthly husband? So, she wasn't kidding. They both exchanged looks of surprise.

"But aren't you-" Simon began.

"In this human incarnation, I live a fairly normal life," she laughed. "You'll meet him shortly. He likes to keep a low profile. Right now, he's on Oahu getting supplies and seeing to some minor repairs on my family's property there," she continued.

This got them wondering what her old man was like and who he could be in his other incarnation to even be aligned with her. Even they could see the force field of energy around her that shot deep into the ground as if she was tapped in with Gaia and shot upward above her head. To them it looked a bit like a beam of translucent and rainbow energy surrounding her as she moved about, almost unaware. Simon had never seen anything like it. She looked at them with a bit of mischievousness in her eyes.

"I grew up on Oahu with my brothers and sisters. The house he's doing the repairs to is currently being rented out by a mainland corporation for their employees who come to Hawaii to work on short assignments," she explained.

"So, you have brothers and sisters, too?" Zhang asked what they were both thinking. At this she laughed.

"I told you I live a fairly normal life here much like you two." Then she paused as she studied them. "Well, nothing like you two experience as celebrities. I can't even imagine that. I'm somewhat of an introvert, you see. I don't really like the limelight too much. I prefer just a small group of folks at a time. Otherwise, it messes with my energies and I have to take multiple baths...." They were intrigued by this.

"He's an introvert too. But he likes the limelight." Zhang pointed to Simon. "I still can't see what the big deal is or why people fuss over me. It's just work to me. A job," Zhang explained with a shrug to underscore his point.

"I don't mind it. I don't know if I like it. It's just a role we play, aunty," Simon said deferentially.

"Aunty, again?" She asked, then smiled. "Yes, I always imagined and actually heard you calling me that. This one though calls me 'sister'."

Zhang nodded. "Yes, I'm not rude like him."

She laughed, "Whatever makes you comfortable. I want you boys to be happy here and make this your home away from home. You are welcome to stay here as long as your schedule permits. We can do some healing, some meditation, talk story, as I have lots of questions for you both. And you can ask me whatever you wish. We teach and learn from each other. Take your time relaxing, by the pool or have a swim. This is your home here in Honoka'a. Whatever I have here to eat or drink or read or play with is yours."

"Thank you!" They both chirped in unison.

"When did you arrive from Shanghai?" She asked studying them. They were sure they looked like hell from the long plane ride and were in need of a bath and face masks. Thankfully they brought a bunch of Korean truffle masks. They heard in the array as they were preparing for the trip that Lady Master Ma'at also preferred them and brought extras.

"This afternoon just before we came to your crystal shop," Simon answered.

"Then I'll leave you both now to it to rest or whatever. I have to go back to the shop as I am meeting a friend who flew in from Oahu for an overnighter. I'll bring her by later. Help yourself to whatever is in the fridge or cupboard. If you need anything else there is a grocery and drug store up the road. There's a set of keys in your room for the front door and to your room. Be sure to take them with you if you go anywhere."

"One last thing, there is plenty of privacy here if you decide to swim or lay out naked to tan, so don't worry. Just warn me if I walk in on you, unawares unless you don't care as it's not a big deal to me. I won't intrude. I am glad you boys are safely here. The pleasure is all mine." With that Lady Master Ma'at left them to their own devices.

Simon decided to take a bath to clean himself of the airplane and travel stench. As he was washing his hair, Zhang came in to join him. It wasn't long before his hands began to roam all over Simon in amorous fashion.

"Really A'Zhang? Here in the Lady Master's house?"

Zhang pfft'd. "What? She said to make ourselves at home. Isn't this what we normally do at home?" Zhang reasoned.

Simon figured he did have a point. "I plan to swim naked, too so get used to it." Zhang added.

"You better not embarrass me," Simon warned. Zhang smiled and looked down and grabbed his own waterlogged root and gave it a squeeze. It was surprisingly inert. "How could I embarrass you when I walk around with this? Why would you even say that?"

"What if she comes back because she forgot something?" Simon asked rinsing the shampoo from his hair as Zhang continued to fondle him and now himself.

"Then she'd find two grown men in the shower." Zhang laughed. "What's the big deal? I'm sure it happens all the time," Zhang continued leaning into him to peruse his mouth. Simon hissed against his lips. "Did you at least lock the door?"

"What for? It's not like she will walk in even if she does come back. Besides, we probably already gave her and everyone else in the array an eyeful."

Simon laughed. "They aren't that interested."

"Exactly. And if she does happen to walk in, she knows we're together. That you're my partner and lover and that we have needs. She'll see me as the gentleman that I am taking care of my baby," Zhang reasoned slowly kissing him and running his tongue around his mouth in a way that made Simon go into quiet enjoyment mode.

"Well, if you say it like that, then how could I say no?" Simon smiled and reached for his member and fondled him back. It wasn't long before things progressed, and Simon grabbed the soap and began preparing Zhang.

"No, let me do you," Zhang breathed out lathering himself up then sticking a well lathered soapy finger up Simon's nether region before he could protest and relished the breathy croon of appreciation that followed.

They coupled and then after rinsing off, stumbled practically comatose to the bedroom where they promptly fell asleep, jet lag taking over and driving them both deep under.

CHAPTER THIRTY-FIVE
Zhang Can Meditate

When they awoke, they heard soft murmuring in the living room followed by peals of laughter and went out to investigate, Zhang dressed in just his basketball trunks. Simon, meanwhile, had the decency to throw on a teeshirt as well, and bring an extra one out for Zhang.

"Oh shit! Did we wake you?" Lady Master Ma'at cringed apologetically.

"No, we got hungry," Zhang answered honestly as his stomach growled.

"Go eat but first come meet Gabi. Ms. Gabi this is Simon and his partner Zhang. The *Dynamic Duo* I've been telling you about."

"Wow! You guys are very tall! Very glad to meet you in the flesh," the other woman said uncurling herself from where she sat on the couch to shake their hands.

"Pleasure is ours, sister." Zhang nodded warmly back as Gabi studied his face and grinned. "You do really have a beautiful jawline. Oh, my gawd! I can't believe you're here. She showed me some of your pictures. I told her your face couldn't be real. And Simon, wow! I can't believe it's you in the flesh. You and those modeling photos of yours are—wow." She gushed as they stood there grinning.

266

"Alright, Ms Gabi. I think you're starting to fan-girl a little too hard. They came here for some healing from all that," Lady Master Ma'at joked watching in good humor.

"She's shared so much about you, all of it fascinating. Are you both ok? They really put you two through the ringer. You're like real life superheroes," Gabi continued happily. She was short, 5'1" tops also with wavy brown hair and brown eyes, her skin fairer though tan, her features perhaps Native American or Hispanic in origin. She and Lady Master Ma'at had a synergy about them they could see by the way their energies morphed and moved around and through each other.

"It's nice to meet you, Ms. Gabi." Simon nodded with a welcoming smile.

"Don't mind us. Go help yourself in the kitchen. You can make instant noodles if you like as there's some chicken breasts you can cook up and beef, and some egg and veggies in the fridge."

The two readily obeyed. As Simon cooked Zhang checked his phone and a text message from Lawyer Shen that his Weibo and Wechat accounts as well as other previously downed accounts and sharing platforms had all been reinstated. But now that they were far away from the energies of that environment, he felt little inclination to check for updates much less post anything. He told Simon what Lawyer Shen had shared.

"Post a pic of me cooking for your ass," Simon huffed rapidly in Chinese. Zhang snorted.

"What? They have to know we're together," Simon said heating up a nonstick frying pan he found under the cupboard and getting organized with the other pots and the ingredients.

"Uh yeah. They saw us leaving for the airport. Already there's chatter we left for Hawaii.   They better leave us alone."

"They will. This place will reject discordant energies. You see how much she carries. Good luck even if anyone finds out about this place. They won't be able to even get in unless they resonate high enough." Simon said. Meanwhile Gabi and Lady Master Ma'at watched them from where they were curled up drinking tea on the pit couch.

"Look at how cute and domestic they look," Gabi smiled, pleased.

"They are beautiful, right?"

"Just dreamy," she sighed in response.

They both giggled and continued to watch them, peeking over the top of the couch. Lady Master Ma'at sneaked a pic and promptly sent it to Lady Master Marguerite to prove they were finally there in the flesh.

"I saw that!" Zhang drawled lazily pointing his phone over at her and taking a photo of his own.

Lady Master Ma'at curled her lip and took another pic for good measure.

Just then in the array they heard the announcement. Jefok8731, Jefok8124, and Jefok9214 had agreed to Lord Michael's terms and were being escorted off planet with the aid of the Andromedans. The Andromedans were currently on assignment in Afghanistan where they had two ships assisting some refugees from a recent earthquake. The announcement was followed by congratulations to the duo from all who heard the message.

"Looks like our guys caved!" Zhang said. The message continued. "Chairman Luo has suffered a heart attack and is currently resting in the infirmary of the Central Jail awaiting transfer."

"Congratulations, Commander and Lieutenant!" Lady Master Ma'at called out and clapped.

Zhang and Simon high-fived. "All in a day's work!" Zhang followed up like it had been a piece of cake.

"All in a day's work," Lady Master Ma'at echoed. "Great job!"

The next day at breakfast outside, waking up just after ten and then coupling before coming out to look for food they found Lady Master Ma'at and her friend Gabi already outside at the table near the pool. There was food spread out.

"Good morning! Hey! Did you two just do "it", again? Thala warned me about you two."

This sent Gabi into peals of bell-like laughter.

Simon turned beet red. Zhang grinned back at Simon. "Told ya' Thala would tell on us," he shrugged joining them at the table to eat.

"There's extra sheets in the closet if you need them. You'll have to do your own laundry in the garage as Malia only comes to clean once a week," Lady Master Ma'at said.

"We'll probably need those," Zhang said sitting down at the table. "A couple of sets at least. We've been perfecting some of the Pleiadean cultivation techniques." He followed up with a glint of mischief in his eyes.

"Thala said you guys have reached a level of mastery that is second to none."

"Practice makes perfect, sister." Zhang laughed and she joined in as Simon joined them and they feasted on hard boiled eggs, bacon, a locally produced meat called Portuguese sausage, fresh cut fruit, orange juice and tea.

"Here! Here! Speaking of mastery, Gabi here is a master healer. After eating, we'll have you guys relax by the pool and she and I will do some clearing and energy work on you to clear any hindrances that are in your way. Then we can go to the ocean to swim and really immerse ourselves in some healing energies," Lady Master Ma'at said.

"That sounds wonderful! Thank you!"

"Let's do it!"

After Ms. Gabi returned home to Oahu later that afternoon, they swam and splashed around in the pristine blue waters of the Pacific Ocean and played hard like little kids. They got sand everywhere as Zhang and Simon would later find out. They then lounged under some coconut trees and napped right on the sand. Afterwards, they returned home and decided to do a healing meditation.

"I have to warn you I don't do so well with the whole meditation thing but I'll try," Zhang cautioned. He didn't want Lady Master Ma'at overexerting herself on account of him. As it was, she was allowing them to stay in her home and was such a gracious and really fun host. It was as if they knew each other forever.

"He falls asleep," Simon explained "We missed an important assignment update on account of him falling asleep," he continued.

Not to be outdone Zhang immediately barbed back, "Oh yeah? What about you, chatterbox? Talking while the update came through. At least I was asleep. That meditation pod was like being in my own bed!"

"They were some very nice people from Epsilon in Auriga," Simon countered. "They came from such a long way! Thousands of light years!"

"Really? Wow those Arcturians must advertise pretty well if they heard about the retreat from way out there," Zhang seemed to think on this.

"Don't tell me you were sleeping when you got the assignment to earth," Lady Master Ma'at laughed finding the two in her charge pretty entertaining. They completed each other so well. Small wonder they were soul mates and chose to come to earth together.

"Naw, unfortunately we were wide awake for that," Zhang bemoaned.

"Awww, come on. It's not that bad," Simon pooh poohed Zhang's pessimism.

"Easy for you to say. I was skewered for what seemed like forever. And then you abandoned me, twice."

Simon sighed, "I didn't abandon you. Both times were for the mission. You just didn't remember the first time and the second time you had to focus on your own mission." Simon patiently explained as Zhang pouted at him for dramatic effect.

"You see, he gets like this," Simon tsked gesturing to his mate who grinned back at him and then blew him a kiss.

"Well, we can work on that, too. And if you fall asleep, don't worry about it. It just means your body needs rest," Lady Master Ma'at consoled.

"Really?" Zhang straightened in earnest. That would certainly make him feel better knowing there wasn't anything wrong with that part of his brain. It just meant he was tired and needed a little sleep.

"No. You're not trying hard enough," Lady Master Ma'at barbed back then winked.

Zhang curled his lip at her as Simon guffawed.

"Alright let's see how this goes." Zhang sighed.

"Ok, for this simple, no stress healing rain meditation let's lay on our backs and stare up at the sky with our heads in a circle so we make our own little star," she said. They arranged themselves accordingly and lay in the grass under the late afternoon sky, staring up at the clear blue canopy before them. Zhang thought he'd died and gone to heaven.

"Rest your hands comfortably beside you or on your stomach, whatever

271

feels right for you. Some people find laying their hands palms up makes them enter a deeper state of relaxation. Now that you're comfortable, when you're ready, gently close your eyes. Allow this to be a signal to your body and your mind that it's time to relax and allow healing to begin for you...now, breath in healing white light from 360 degrees around you, filling your entire body....and exhale, breathing out everything that does not serve you...allow it to just fall away. Breath in, inhaling healing white light into your head, your neck, shoulders...your back...even beneath your feet...then exhale releasing everything back to love and light. Take another deep breath in, breathing in all that healing light from all around you, filling your entire body....and exhale releasing everything that does not belong to you, other people's energies back to love and light. Back to love and light."

Zhang liked it already. He never thought much about deep breathing but doing so with a visual like that was really helpful. Thus far the meditation was turning out to be quite pleasant.

"Now for the next few deep breaths, I want you to envision any unwanted energies around or in your energy fields to leave you like dark spots of rain moving upward toward the sky. Like rain in reverse. Just envision this in your mind's eye being lifted out of you and being transmuted back to love and light effortlessly. Just see them lifting off and leaving you. Any and all feelings of discord, or hurt or worry, maybe even perhaps that you're not good enough or worthy. All are worthy. You are enough. See those lower vibrational thoughts and ideas lifting away and going home to love and light to be fully healed. And with it lets release any feelings of fear or abandonment, or loss we may hold or harbor or cling to. For we are all so, so loved. Always embraced."

While he knew Simon hadn't really abandoned him now that he understood it from that perspective, he still couldn't seem to shake the fear of it happening all over again. He knew it was dumb to think that way about something that didn't really happen the way he thought it did. Still, he was having trouble getting rid of that feeling of being lost or left behind. He just didn't know how to let go.

"Now see and feel those energies lifting off of you and leaving you, allow them to leave. If you don't know how to do this, just give yourself permission and your higher self will step in to assist, releasing it all back to love and light leaving your aura light and clear and clean."

Zhang's breath hitched. Give myself permission! What a radical idea! In the higher realities, that's how they were able to accomplish so much more than in the lower densities. How could he have forgotten that? By simply allowing and accepting and intending. He felt all the things he'd been holding onto lifting away. He didn't realize he had been holding onto so much crap but envisioned them leaving him in a reverse heavy downpour, flowing upward into the sky.

"Now let's envision coming out of Gaia upon whom you are resting comfortably and going up through your body, beautiful balls of light the color of magenta from her higher self. The color of a deep reddish pink. That's the color of unconditional love and healing. Just see these balls of unconditional love and healing in your mind's eye flowing through your back and your chest, your butt, your legs, your feet, your neck, don't forget your arms, hands, your shoulders and your head. See that beautiful healing color magenta and all the balls of light moving through you not missing a single cell, or atom as it flows through you with ease going upwards into the sky. Send a fresh wave of magenta healing balls of light up through you and this time really feel it moving through you with ease, helping to further clear your aura. Beautiful!"

Zhang easily saw his body and the pink lights flowing through him, in fact he could even feel it.

"Now let's see if we can get assistance for healing from Lord Michael who has tasked you with your earthly mission on behalf of your higher selves. Lord Michael, greetings! We ask you to lend us a hand with your electric blue light and ray of protection and see it flow through us resolving any remaining discordant energies that have up to now hindered the Commander and Lieutenant whose service we are deeply grateful for. Thank you."

"Envision with Lord Michael standing close to us, his electric blue fire moving through us, enveloping us and clearing away all remaining energies that do not serve us. See those energies easily floating away. Beautiful. And before we close let's envision ourselves now standing in a column of light holding hands together, supporting each other with our beautiful and loving energies. See this column of translucent rainbow and white light as it flows from Gaia up enveloping the three of us, as it moves upward through our bodies, out through the top of our heads, lifting us upwards a few feet off the ground. Feel yourself floating! Beautiful! Let's enjoy that feeling of weightlessness for a moment, allowing it to support our spirits, our souls, effortlessly."

Zhang suddenly felt tears come to his eyes although he wasn't feeling particularly emotional. He allowed them to flow out of the corners and roll down the sides of his face.

"Now let's come back to our beautiful earthly bodies, our auras now clear, our hearts and spirits connected to the healing vibrations of this land, to Gaia, to our brother Lord Michael and all the angels and beings of Light who guide and protect us and we send them love and healing as well. And finally, let's see any energetic cords or bindings fall away, completely clear of our auras." They took a few deep breaths to center themselves before Lady Master Ma'at called them back and they slowly sat up. Zhang was surprised all three of them were wiping tears from their eyes.

"Wow! That was phenomenal!"

"You didn't fall asleep! Zhang can meditate!"

"How come our tears are falling? I know I wasn't feeling sad or anything." Zhang asked.

"I have come to realize after experiencing it so often that the tears are confirmation we just had a real healing experience," Lady Master Ma'at explained.

Later on, they spent time talking about what they saw or felt, and whether they were able to connect with Lord Michael. All confirmed that he appeared in Lightbody form to them as light although he often appeared in physical form dressed as a Roman soldier replete with helmet. Afterwards, they relaxed by the pool and silently watched the sunset.

CHAPTER THIRTY-SIX

Zhang and Simon Learn About Ubuntu, Aloha, and Ho'oponopono

The next day piggybacking on Zhang's successful meditation and that both were feeling quite incredible, Lady Master Ma'at led them in another meditation. This time it was based on the principles of Ubuntu, an African term meaning "I am what I am because of who we all are," the beautiful concept of oneness and living in alignment as still practiced in some indigenous communities. Ubuntu Healing Meditation

The three sat Lotus style on the grass just after a light breakfast when she led them through the exercise which was accompanied by some meditation music. Upon her suggestion, they each included someone they knew as well as themselves into the center of the healing circle they created and envisioned their loved ones and themselves completely healed, completely free of all blockages and walls, and in perfect balance and alignment. They found this meditation deeply nurturing as well as transformative as they each wiped away even more tears.

Afterwards, they laid out by the pool, the Lady Master under the shade of her umbrella as they took in a little sun on the lounge chairs and shared in some lemonade with fresh cut strawberries. Lady Master Ma'at then shared more wisdom. "There's a beautiful concept here known as Ho'oponopono. It's taught among the Hawaiian teachers and wisdom keepers or kahuna. I found it's a powerful tool for healing the perceived wrongs of this 3D world. Maybe you can bring it back with you to China."

Zhang who had his eyes closed peeked over at her. "Ho what? I don't even know if I can pronounce that."

Lady Master laughed. "You are so mischievous, Commander. Now I know all those rumors are true."

Simon burst out laughing. "Ha! Ha! Ha! Ha! Ha! Ha!"

This got Zhang sitting up in his chair and looking over at her, "Wait, what? What rumors?"

Lady Master Ma'at cracked up even more. "They are all endearing and make you much loved by all," she said when she calmed down. "It's why your twin flame here loves you so much." She pointed to Simon.

Zhang calmed down and looked over at Simon who was nodding. "It's true."

Zhang grinned back at her and laid back down. "Ho puh- puh-"

"Ho- oh- po- noh- po-noh," she repeated slowly as they followed along. "It's summed up by the wisdom and understanding of moving back into righteous or divine balance as all are part of the larger collective. It's known here as a means of healing through forgiveness. And it's based on the understanding of Aloha' which means, 'I see the divine in you, and I see the divine in myself.'"

Simon turned to her. "Divine balance? Our ancestors taught the people here that many, many years ago, didn't they?"

"Yes…and they still speak of their ancestors from the Pleiades who came here to teach them. Most ancient cultures relay these stories…"

"Pleiades? Have they forgotten us Sirians?" Zhang chimed in.

"Well, the Pleiadeans were here in more recent memory. And now you are here bringing it all back into full circle and building off the work of your Pleiadean brothers and sisters to help the rest of humanity finally get it right."

"Full circle. I like that...only for some reason I don't have full recollection of it." He looked over at Simon with a mischievous grin.

Lady Master Ma'at laughed. "How about I share with you again rather than have you two unnecessarily exhaust yourselves." She continued, "I've heard the ritual of Ho'oponopono described as love in action. More importantly 'mana aloha' or unconditional love in action. Essentially by the use of four profound statements, you forgive yourself and others for having inflicted any sort of hurt, or for having failed to help when needed and right your universe."

They were listening intently now.

"I am sorry. Please forgive me. I love you. Thank you."

She let that sink in for a minute. The two looked at each other. Zhang said what they were both thinking.

"That's it?" He cocked an eyebrow for more effect.

"Yep....To the Hawaiian people familiar with the ceremony, these four simple sentences work like a sort of a mantra. Like all truths, they operate through time and space, through the unseen realms to your higher selves and back down here into the 3D."

"People say those same words all the time and it doesn't seem to have that effect," Simon astutely pointed out.

"Yeah, people say a lot of things. They even say how much they love us and yet they treat each other like crap and sometimes even us...it's bizarre." Zhang chimed in thinking about the fans he'd seen and the way they sometimes behaved especially on SM.

"That's because they are often conveyed without the understanding that we are all part of the same interconnecting web of life. Thus, what they put out returns, good or bad. And the words are not coming from a place of 'mana aloha' or unconditional love. It's something else. If the people here understood that what they put out is still a part of them and attached with the same force and effect they gave out, there would be far less acrimony and venom here." She continued. "And if everything stemmed from 'mana aloha', we wouldn't need to be here helping Gaia, either."

"Romantic love or puppy love isn't the same as unconditional love," Zhang said softly.

Simon shook his head. "No. Its love but at a lower frequency band. So it's easily subject to being corrupted or misused."

"Well, that's why I always say if it makes people happy to love us, then that's ok. But also remember to give that same love to your brothers, your sisters, and your parents," Zhang said.

"That's awesome teacher Zhang. What a way to help them navigate and go even higher! You truly are a master!"

"Yes, but I don't know if they listen because it seems to just keep happening," Zhang sighed.

"Well, we all evolve at different times so just keep sharing like you always do.   Eventually people will understand."

"So how does that mantra help put everything back in balance?" Zhang pressed.

"As a forgiveness ritual, Ho'oponopono is a means to forgive yourself for your role in any suffering caused by others and release it back to the ethers. This is you going back into divine balance or pono - righteous balance. The best way to do ho'oponopono where healing takes place all around is to do it with the person you think is at issue. It's been done in whole communities to bring everyone together."

They all reflected on this.

"The mantra is actually very deep and beautiful. It allows you to release the deepest hang-ups and karma and advance with freedom when done with the intention the ritual was meant to be done with. Imagine whole communities doing this."

"What does it mean again, sister?"

"I am sorry. Please forgive me. I love you. Thank you."

Then, "The profundity of it is that it stems from unconditional love and not just any old love and explains how from the Hawaiian perspective which is in alignment with the higher frequencies that unconditional love or 'mana aloha' is the energy behind all things. This is what Yeshua taught. Unconditional love as it was taught therefore is unconditional acceptance."

They mulled on this and what it would look like in action.

"So, the unconditional acceptance is not the 'f—k it, I'm not going to let that bother me anymore' attitude like some people misunderstand it to be." Zhang reflected out loud.

"Correct! That's not self-mastery. That's giving up on yourself. There's a huge difference."

"And have you used this with any effect?" Zhang asked.

"I have in order to heal some old wounds."

"Like what?" Zhang asked bluntly.

"Ok, I'll give one example. From the time I was little, I was always very trusting. Especially of family members even when I was repeatedly taken advantage of or manipulated. In this case by an older sister. You see, I was raised by parents who were of noble heart, deeply loving and truly wished to see us succeed."

"I love that! They were definitely of the Light," Simon grinned.

"Yes, and what they weren't blessed with in money, they made up for with unconditional love and right living. Neither were religious in any deep meaning of the word, but both lived based on a deep inner code or philosophy that's hard to put into words. My father especially was a deep thinker. There really aren't many like him around. Growing up the way I did, I thought this meant everyone viewed the world like they did. Certainly, the kids they raised."

"How many brothers and sisters do you have?" Simon asked curiously.

"In this earthly incarnation there are seven of us."

Zhang almost leapt out of his chair. "Seven? That's insane! How did your parents not go crazy?"

This had both Simon and Lady Master Ma'at laughing.

"I think it's cool!" Simon added.

"Well, I'm sure they sometimes thought they were losing it but times were different back then especially here in the West. People had lots of kids. Not so much now."

"You say they weren't rich, aunty?" Simon asked with a puzzled look. "How could they afford to feed so many kids and themselves?"

"Less luxuries and more focus on the basics - food, shelter, clothing. I imagine a whole lot of praying helped, too."

"So, one of your sisters caused problems?"

"Maybe not so much for my parents as they were too advanced for her machinations until they were much older and had to rely on her. But even then, they weren't impacted by it the way you'd think. But me...different story. I was often manipulated emotionally, financially and even physically by her because that's how she operated. Only thing, you never knew you were being manipulated until much later and then she would pretend she didn't know what you were talking about. There was always a price for everything she gave out, so nothing was done freely or out of love."

"Sounds like a snake in the grass," Zhang snickered. "But you know what I think? She's just contrast."

"But even contrast has to be checked so you don't cause an imbalance and harm to yourself or others," Simon chimed in.

"Exactly! Well, after years of enduring that, I just felt so much anger and resentment toward her. So doing the ritual like a meditation, I had to ask myself even as a child what was my role around all that. And you know what I realized?"

"What?"

"When you don't stand in your own power, others will step in to teach you. There are some who incarnate with us just for this purpose. It became more clear to me when I realized she wasn't targeting me. She manipulates and takes advantage of just about everyone she can. It's how she's programmed or hard-wired. Young, old, healthy, infirm, nice, mean, rich, poor, it didn't matter. She will take every advantage she can. But you still had to watch your back while learning these lessons. Therein lies the contrast."

They listened intently.

"If you want to right the balance, stand firmly in your power and understand your role in the world you occupy. That's the lesson. It doesn't mean you stop watching your back or the contrast disappears. You just are no longer victimized by it. Now that doesn't mean she is self- aware of why she is doing it and causing others to become un-situated. For all I know she may even feed off of the despair or take pleasure in others suffering but that has nothing to do with me. So that ritual frees yourself from the situation. It's really genius."

"So, once you recognize the problem you thank them for making you aware of it. And your expression of your gratitude is like a gift. Then you release it and move on?" Zhang asked.

"Correct. No need to make it an unending drama or punish the other person or yourself unnecessarily. This too is a way to exercise your own power, isn't it?" Lady Master Ma'at said.

She let them mull that over as she poured them fresh glasses of lemonade.

CHAPTER THIRTY-SEVEN

Zhang Speaks His Truth and Lady Master Ma'at's Not So Interesting Backstory

Zhang guzzled down his lemonade thoughtfully as Simon chomped on a strawberry.

"Yes...makes a lot of sense," Zhang said then sighed. "I can see where I was naive too in the way I handled a lot of things...it usually takes a lot to turn my world upside down although sometimes it might not seem like it. But I am really pretty calm normally....I think though, that also contributed to my not realizing what was happening." Zhang began, scrunching his forehead up in thought.

"From the very beginning of my career, without realizing it, I let other people handle everything for me. What Simon did, the way he set things up he took control immediately. I think...I have always just had a different approach to everything...."

"Yes, you are usually very calm, stable and philosophical in your approach to life." Simon added with seriousness. "Zhang is really a very kind soul."

"Yes, but I also see it maybe caused some problems when I was being like that...too diplomatic about things."

"Like sometimes you still have to take a stand."

"Yes. Like Simon got smeared a bit and he filed a lawsuit and they dovetailed. I thought the best approach based on the way I see the world was to offer my words as I always have…but instead they attacked me, you know?"

Both Simon and Lady Master Ma'at listened intently as he worked it all out.

"I can see where you can still be very calm and trusting and loving but also have to stand in your own power too because it's not all loving and balloons and cake and ice cream here," Zhang said thoughtfully. "There's lots of contrast."

"I love who you are, Zhang…" Simon said. He turned to Lady Master Ma'at. "He's actually a happy guy and yet capable of thinking about things deeper than anyone else I know when he wants to be serious."

"I've noticed that in your writings Zhang…in your songs. Also, in a lot of your interviews. You're definitely a very deep thinker. That's why you can be so calm in the face of great upheaval. You're very funny too and like to joke around but I think when you stand in your power, that's when it actually takes a lot to turn your world upside down," Lady Master Ma'at said.

"Mencius once shared with me and I am sure this is why you are the way you are, 'Your job is to demonstrate through your earthly experience what it means to be human and still rise above it. This is what it means to be an Ascended Master.'"

Zhang's eyes popped wide. Suddenly it all made sense. He'd always felt in his heart that no matter what happened in life, he could and would always rise above it. Overcome it. It was like an energy, a knowing that fueled him and burned bright in his heart. He could only liken it to sunshine. To light. It was a feeling he knew well as it was indelibly etched in his heart and soul, but one he couldn't really describe, except to another who also felt this way.   He felt tears burn at his eyes again.

"When did you notice everything start to turn around with all that stuff back home?" Lady Master Ma'at asked.

"Mmmm...when I just decided to stand up and not take it anymore...I mean I always felt like no matter what, I wasn't going to really crash and burn....I always had hope. I just didn't know when."

"So, you decided to take a stand?"

"Yes, I just decided enough was enough. It's hard to describe but the minute I came to that conclusion, I felt like it already shifted," Zhang confessed.

"He became like a different guy overnight," Simon nodded.

"It was when I decided to take my power back everything changed," Zhang nodded in agreement. "I mean I still joke around and give him and everybody a hard time, but..."

"Did you ever notice when you do some things, it doesn't require much from you. Like you've mastered it. For instance, like Zhang flying a light craft or Simon being blunt. You're just in control and it's like second nature for you. But with other things, you feel like you're being dragged around by the nose, and you have no clue what you're doing."

"Yeah, like an idiot." Simon laughed.

"Right! Standing in your power can make a big difference in the outcome. And if you see the parallels, you'll realize, hey, if I got that, then I can get this too. Its merely the flip of a switch. Turning on that self-awareness. I think it all flows from the same space. That same stream of consciousness. Even if you're still stumbling along, coming to that realization that you've got this has the power to change everything for you. Just like what happened in your case, Zhang."

"I know I felt very different afterwards. More in control."

"Because you were. And people even responded differently. You turned everything on its head. Suddenly people began opening their eyes and hearing the real you. Your genius. That's the light speaking. And it was amazing!" She grinned at him.

"Light in action." Simon nodded.

"Yep, and you let people see and experience that light!" Lady Master Ma'at concluded.

It was after this discussion the two decided to go for it and just get married already. They chose to have the private ceremony at the seaside retreat where they could watch the beautiful sunset together.

She readily agreed.

They chose a date. That evening they celebrated and sang karaoke together to their hearts content lasting long into the night.

It was a beautiful and memorable time. After things quieted down, Simon shyly asked her to tell them her story. How she became an Ascended Master. Zhang nodded beside him as he popped open another beer.

So, she began to share.

Lady Master Ma'at was a human from a small desert like planet that revolves around Polaris, earth's North Star. She stood 8-feet-tall, had copper color skin, jet black hair, and large almond shaped eyes. All the females of the race looked thusly and adorned themselves with distinctive coal black eyeshadow that accentuated their mysterious eyes, decorative beads intertwined in their hair and were considered quite beautiful by all those who knew them. The humans on their planet lived alongside their hybrid sisters and brothers, those known as the Gods and Goddesses of Egypt - Isis, Horus, Nut, Anubis, Thoth, Bastet and Sekhmet, among the most notable.

She was a scientist on her planet whose environment was similar to the

287

desert regions of earth. Thus, she came to earth with her brothers and sisters in order to teach the evolving humans such things as science, agriculture, water management, food production, cross pollination as well as how to live in harmony with the earth, with the animals and birds, and with each other. Moreover, she taught them of their connection to the stars and that they were all equally sparks of Source.

It was all done to help enhance their lives on earth and help them understand their true galactic heritage. During her tenure, with the help of the Lyran Lion beings, her brethren built pyramids all over the earth, in Egypt, Mexico, deep in the jungles of Central and South America, Europe, Asia, even deep into Africa and North America. These pyramids served as communication devices that mirrored those on her planet. The purpose was to continually monitor the humans on earth and communicate with their representatives who had been left behind, namely the pharoahs and tribal leaders.

Because of her upright character, she was known as the Goddess of truth, justice and harmony. The "42 Laws of Ma'at" are attributed directly to her wisdom and reputation and were left to humanity to serve as a guide after she and her brethren departed and returned home.

Unfortunately, not all who came here were of the mind to help humanity. Many took advantage of the humans, enslaved and used them, and even told them outright they were gods even though it wasn't true. This belief stuck and to this day beings like Ma'at and her brothers and sisters are still considered, although wrongly so, as gods and goddesses.

To assist the humans who had bought into these lies and connect them back to Source Light, she decided to reincarnate back on earth with some of her brethren. This time she came back as Amenhotep, Son of Ha'pu, beloved royal scribe of the great and wise Pharoah Amenhotep III, father of both Akhenaton and King Tutenkamun. All told she in that incarnation served over 80 years as the royal scribe in the 18th Dynasty of Egypt.

Of humble roots, she as Amenhotep, Son of Ha'pu climbed up the social ladder purely by distinguishing himself through hard work and service. She was later promoted to the esteemed office of "Scribe of Recruits," responsible for organizing the manpower of Egypt for the king.   From there she quickly was promoted to "Overseer of all the works of the King," responsible for the construction of the king's temples at Soleb and Karnak, and for the monumental statues of the Pharoah at Thebes.

During the time as the famed royal scribe, she spent her time providing Light-based counsel to the Pharaoh and worked to serve the kingdom. It was on account of this lifetime that she later became an Ascended Master. Seeing as when she walked the earth as Amenhotep, Son of Ha'pu she was a short, skinny, awkward little man with a strange haircut, she chose to retain her original 8-foot-tall form and associate that image with Ascended Masterhood. Thus, she became known thereafter as 'Ascended Master Ma'at'and 'Lady Master Ma'at'. In the textbooks, however, sadly she is still considered as Goddess Ma'at' which directly contradicts the teachings she and her brethren originally brought to the people.

Since then, she has had numerous incarnations on account of the reincarnation net, but never forgot her mission to help humanity or that she is of the Light. And in this final tenure, she is tasked with helping clear the earth and anchor Light energy on account she carries a lot of it, provide spiritual counseling and healing and comfort to the earth humans and galactics who visit her home and wherever she travels.

Like Simon and Zhang, she (known to them by her cosmic name, Ariitzka), was here on a mission with her soul mate Captain Olin Alpha1, as galactic traveling partners and adventurers to bring and anchor light on earth and help humanity and other galactics like the pair during their earth mission.

Even before she finished telling her story, both Simon and Zhang had already fallen fast asleep. Zhang thought he was meditating.

She left them outside and went to bed.

The mosquitoes ate them alive.

CHAPTER THIRTY-EIGHT

Whereas Lady Master Ma'at hosts Simon and Zhang at her Healing Retreat and Promptly Comes to Regret It   (aka Zhang and Simon overstay their welcome)

On the second evening of their stay what began as just a few songs sung between them to satisfy Lady Master Ma'at's long held desire to sing some of Zhang and Simon's hit songs together soon morphed into something else when Zhang figured out how to hook up the Apple Music app on his phone to the tv. This soon turned into a full-blown high-flying fun night when Lady Master Ma'at finally broke out the karaoke machine buried in her closet and served up some ice-cold beers.

Their voices could be heard echoing even as far as the main road.

Just after midnight the neighbors next door who came to complain about the noise ended up staying on account of the cosmically high vibe energies the trio had generated by their renditions of Level 42's 'Something About You', Queen's 'You're My Best Friend', George Michael's 'I Want your Sex' followed by Zhang's own incomparable song 'Light'.   And the fact Lady Master Ma'at offered them cold beers and promised they could sing next.

Simon got wasted and sang a heartfelt but drunken rendition of his paen song 'Sweet' to Zhang.

Zhang cried.

Meanwhile Lady Master Maat clapped and laughed her ass off. She thought it was the sweetest thing she had ever seen and heard. Everyone listening in on the array thought so, too.

The neighbors promptly left.

And then there was the time the pair experienced cosmic bliss.

On the 8th day Simon and Zhang were experiencing what could only be described as cosmic bliss at the retreat. They'd entered a world where no one else existed, where all space, time and matter ceased. There was only the now moment. One that stretched on for them into an eternity of now moments. Nothing else mattered. There was nothing and no one but the two of them. They were in a world of their own…

…making out again on Lady Master Ma'at's pit couch in her living room.

So, they didn't hear her when she came home, announced herself to avoid any embarrassing situations, like Zhang walking around naked on account of having nothing to wear while all of his clothes were being washed (Day 4 of the retreat) never mind by Day 2, he'd already completely made himself at home.

Nor did they notice when she announced she was making dinner that evening - a sumptuous meal of Hawaiian style rotisserie chicken, macaroni salad and rice, and freshly cut pineapple. Apparently, they also didn't notice when she announced dinner was ready and then upon receiving no reply began eating by herself. Nor did they notice when she began watching reruns of *Breaking Bad* on Netflix followed by Season 4 of *Stranger Things* on said pit couch right beside them. Or when she jumped on the phone to call her sister Lady Master Marguerite and catch up. Or even hours later when it was finally time for her to retire for the night.

They were still laying one atop the other, slowly perusing the other's mouth before gazing into each other's eyes and grinning in rather nauseating fashion.

She now understood why Mencius had warned everyone about the two.

"Dynamic Duo, my ass...," she was heard to sigh as she locked up the house, shut off the lights and promptly went to bed.

Two days later, following their cue, Lady Master Ma'at and Chris were home alone, enjoying the peace and quiet. They were laying one atop the other on the pit couch experiencing cosmic bliss. They exchanged slow deep kisses then stared into each other's eyes before grinning, oblivious to all else.

Until the door opened with a bang and Simon and Zhang noisily walked in carrying bags full of groceries, chattering like school kids. When they spotted the two on the couch they promptly yelled out in unison "Oh, gross!"

This prompted Chris without looking up to launch a pillow in their direction. The duo managed to duck while laughing. Seeing they weren't leaving, Lady Master Ma'at let fly another pillow. She had a dead aim. The two were guffawing so hard they never saw it coming. It hit them both squarely in the face. Grinning, Chris and Lady Master Ma'at then migrated outside as the pair watched, then promptly stripped naked and dove into their pool.

By months end Lady Master Ma'at was ready to bid her two newfound friends goodbye after a wonderful retreat of heartfelt laughter, tears, deepening friendships and profound healing.

The problem was Zhang and Simon weren't ready to leave.

In fact, they were just getting started.

Thankfully Mencius came to the rescue and called them back to China. There were more important updates and the two were needed to make statements to the press, thanking everyone for their support and closing out the ordeal so the people could finally begin to heal.

They promptly left Lady Master Ma'at's home after expressing their deepest gratitude for all the assistance and incredible energies and healing she had generously surrounded them with at the beautiful Hawaiian Honoka'a retreat. Simon and Zhang both cried like two little boys saying goodbye to their mother on their first day of school.

Lady Master Ma'at secretly rejoiced. She'd finally get her house and more importantly her sanity back.

Two weeks later -

Lady Master Ma'at pulled into the driveway of her home after closing the crystal shop in downtown Honoka'a for the night. She'd stopped for a little bit of groceries at Times Supermarket down the street anticipating cooking dinner for one since Chris was back on Oahu finishing the repairs to the Maunaleo House. As she pulled into the garage her headlights caught a familiar looking black SUV rental. It was parked in her spot. All the lights in the house were on and there was music playing inside.

It was then she heard the unmistakable sounds of Zhang doling out his extra emotional rendition of 'Unbreakable Love' on the karaoke machine inside, his voice reverberating loudly.

"What the hell?" She rolled her eyes. *Oh my gaawd... They're back...*

When she entered, Zhang was on his knees, as he'd been the 48 other times she'd witnessed him singing the same damn song, eyes moist as tears rolled down his cheeks, and he poured out his heart to Simon, his beloved.

Meanwhile, Simon, wearing a garland of fake flowers on the crown of his head, a plumeria lei he scored at the airport, an ugly blue and yellow aloha shirt from the ABC Store in Waikiki, and a pair of surf shop board trunks, laughed like a doofus and clapped with glee.

"Hi, aunty!"

"Hey, sis! We're back!"

Lady Master Ma'at reminded herself to ask them next time to return her keys.

CHAPTER THIRTY-NINE

And the Winner is....The Award Ceremony on the Athena Parked at the Galactic Way Station; Zhang Cries

Things were wrapping up quickly on earth. Simon and Zhang had just returned from a 4 month long whirlwind tour in Asia. Together they made appearances and visited fans in China, Taiwan, Japan, and Korea thanking them for their undying support all these many long months while they turned the corrupt institutions one-by-one out on their asses.

Once the greedy and self-serving movers and shakers began to be fully exposed in China, those in the United States and their cronies in the rest of the world had nowhere to run. They fell like dominoes. For the first time since the fall of Atlantis, the people, no longer enslaved by these overseers, were allowed to breathe their freedom. The corrupt leaders were taken off world for "healing".

This gave rise to the release of long-withheld medical cures and tens of thousands of technologies previously kept hidden from the people. Fossil fuel became a thing of the past and photon energy became the new thing. It also resulted in the massive redistribution of wealth, so everyone was just as wealthy as the next guy, and more importantly were able to enjoy cross border freedoms.

People no longer felt the need to migrate due to poverty, or strife, or chronic conditions of war caused by those previously in control and instead stayed home and worked on building up their communities, caring for the earth and their children, and the animals. Others were free to explore their true calling instead of slaving away at their crappy 9-5 jobs as they were previously destined for more than half their lives. There was a sudden explosion of artists and yoga masters.

Still others volunteered their time or traveled the world and visited exotic places, expanding their horizons without fear. Others chose to learn more about their true histories and galactic origins and even took rides around on spaceships courtesy of the Pleiadeans and Andromedans and a few other fun-loving races.

The earth's first 8D concert series was simultaneously performed over every major city across the planet. This stunning visual and auditory marvel was courtesy of the Jefoks' engineering skills working in conjunction with the Arcturians who were also ace pilots. People celebrated and danced in the streets.

A lot of others, exhausted from years of chaos and oppression chose to just sit around binge watching Netflix, or petting their cat or dog while wondering how the hell they could have been asleep for so damn long. Others, unable to take all the amazing changes chose to just leave and return back home to their planets and dimensions of origin. It was a fun and interesting time.

Meanwhile, Simon and Zhang, were once again enjoying themselves at the retreat in Honoka'a with Lady Master Ma'at. She and her husband Chris had since come to view the two as their younger brothers and got used to coming home to find them lying around the house or swimming naked in the pool.

It was in fact on this particular visit to Honoka'a that the two actually tied the knot as it had taken the county longer than normal to process their marriage license on account of "Covid- related" office closures. Although by then, Covid and marriage licenses were a distant memory.

That very day it was also announced that the two were in the final running for the prestigious galactic award for the *Most Beloved and Successful Earth Incarnation Team Voted Most Likely to Succeed.*

Meanwhile, for their contributions to humanity, their celebrity status reached new levels of insanity. Their faces were plastered everywhere in Asia, Europe and even the United States. The first billboard ever in the State of Hawaii featured the duo peddling ecofriendly sun block. Ironically, Lady Master Ma'at's own levels of insanity grew in proportion. Go figure. It was all she could do to keep herself and the duo in check and grounded. Chris went along for the ride. There had been rumblings the *Dynamic Duo* would be returning mid-earth incarnation back to the mothership, gracing everyone with their presence for the Award Ceremony on the Athena. Lady Master Ma'at agreed to help coordinate.

There had been over a hundred teams in the running, most no one had ever heard of, including soul mates Resha from Cygnus3 and Zygot18 from Andromeda who incarnated as Michelle and Barack Obama, Lionel-181 a Ciakahrr Reptilian from a star orbiting somewhere near Orion, and his life size organic robot named Lilly14 who incarnated as Donald and Melania Trump respectively, and WobashAS3 from Deneb who incarnated as both Johnny Depp and Amber Heard. Yoko Ono, Will Smith and wife Jada Pinkett-Smith and a few other earth notables who weren't nominated showed up as well. All were welcome.

Such an appearance by beings still incarnated on earth was unprecedented and took careful coordination with the Medical Bay Stasis Oversight Management team, the incarnation team at the Way Station at Venus, the nominees' and visitors own guidance team, and of course each of the respective beings themselves, all working in perfect harmony to make sure everything went smoothly and without a hitch.

It was going to be broadcast to all the other motherships of the huge Galactic Confederation in near earth orbit, at the Mars Relay station, and a few other places able to get reception. For those too far out to attend, the Athena's captain decided to record the event on the ship's computer database for viewing later.

As anticipated, at the appointed hour, Zhang and Simon made a guest appearance at the awards ceremony and took first place. No surprise there as unbeknownst to everyone prior to leaving for his earth mission, Simon bought up all the back links and pushed the votes in their favor using the array and Proxy system ensuring they'd leave their competitors in the dust.

Of course, he left this little detail out as he proudly stood next to and watched his man give his half of their award acceptance speech. Dressed in his officer's uniform, Commander Zhang cut an imposing and handsome figure to all in attendance.

Everyone knew despite any setbacks, mistakes, and the many struggles he endured while on earth, most of which had been witnessed by his guides, colleagues and crew, he was never one to put himself before any other, nor his ego before any mission. Despite sometimes being a little rough around the edges, a bit self-indulgent, mischievous as hell, as Commander Zhang, it never came at the expense of a mission, nor any of his crew. And that was why he was much loved and respected by the Athena.

"Most of all, I want to thank my partner and soul mate, Lt. SimonGJXO1129 for his tireless efforts to follow his soul agreement on earth, never giving up on me when I was at my worst. For believing in me no matter what I did or what hardships I threw in his way, and for setting the example despite all odds, of exactly what it means to be a person of the Light."

Zhang finally received his standing ovation.

Simon clapped and beamed proudly.

Mencius cried (again).

He was seated in the back of the huge hall where he had reserved four hundred tables to accommodate all of his no longer wayward charges, including Jefok8731, Jefok8124, Jefok9214 and Jefok4860, players in their own earth drama who finally woke the hell up and were receiving healing. Mencius pulled strings to get everyone a day pass from the Arcturian healing ward to attend the ceremony to give gratitude to the two men on stage who rescued them.

The fun loving Pleiadeans, Masters of Sensual and Sexual Cultivation in the entire multiverse, to whom the *Dynamic Duo* were deeply indebted for all eternity were in attendance, too, drunk off their asses.

Lady Master Thala had already asked the two to be adjunct professors in their upcoming 3-day workshop. Unbeknownst to Zhang, Simon readily accepted on both their behalf. They would be immediately reporting for duty upon the completion of their time on earth.

Lady Master Ma'at was hanging out with Lord Michael near the water cooler where they were watching the award ceremony on the 24" inch screen in the break room. She was recounting their wild karaoke night in Honoka'a and some of the duo's more interesting and off the wall antics to which Lord Michael grinned and proudly whooped out an "Atta boys!" while pumping his fist.

Lady Master Ma'at now understood exactly where those two learned their less than stellar behavior.

Meanwhile Simon and Zhang's still awesome, hot model slash actor slash singer slash spokesperson slash brand ambassador earth bodies, careers fully intact, were still on earth in deep meditation (actually Zhang was just asleep), at Lady Master Ma'at's spiritual retreat in Honoka'a on the Big Island of Hawaii, their consciousness temporarily stuffed back into their 8-foot tall Sirian bodies by the genius little grays so they could make their appearance.

No one paid attention as Will Smith, upset by his and Jada's non-existent nomination, boldly strode up to the stage and hit Zhang squarely in the face.

He later apologized and was taken for healing at the facility in Arcturus.

"Shall we head back?" Simon asked as they left the stage. The award prize, the equivalent of a hand-printed but frameable certificate from Office Depot and cafeteria scripts worth approximately $43 American dollars gathered in the office pool were stuffed in an old envelope in Zhang's hand. Zhang and Simon didn't even notice their names were misspelled on the certificate.

Nor did they notice as they smiled at each other that a video short of them entertaining themselves during their time on the moon was being replayed on the big screen for everyone's enjoyment. People watched in amusement as Simon serenaded Zhang while masterfully flying the spaceship around his head and Zhang danced happily below on the moon's surface.   Everyone got up and began to dance in celebration.

Lady Master Ma'at and Lord Michael thought it was the coolest thing ever. Captain Alpha1 and the little gray did a high-five.

Meanwhile the duo left the ceremony unawares.

"What's the rush? Come on, I want to show you something," Zhang said grabbing his hand and leading him to the lifts where they swiftly rode together to Level 15 where the couples quarters were. The hallway was deserted as most were still at the ceremony enjoying the off- world entertainment of singing, music, and comedy hour that followed the presentation of the awards.

Simon looked around curiously noting how much more spacious the hallway was and how much warmer the ambiance was there with green plants, decorative artwork tastefully placed and an occasional window.

"Jeez they spared no expense here. Where are we?"

"Couples quarters." Zhang grinned proudly.

"Really? How come all the single guys get jammed into the dorms? What are we doing here?"

Zhang led him to a door that opened when their energy signature was read.

"Welcome home Commander. Welcome home Lieutenant. How may I be of service?"

"Turn on ambient lighting and play some sweet music," Zhang said leading Simon into the space. Immediately the room was softly illuminated, and Simon's earthly voice could be heard singing "Sweet".

Simon's face lit up and he began laughing.

"Baby you know what I mean, I've been wanting you so keen-" Simon began crooning in his cute Asian accent as he looked around. The room was much larger than their individual dorm rooms by more than double, the hygiene room itself twice as large with a his and his sink, a huge tub and a separate hygiene stall with dual shower heads.

There was even a separate and handsomely appointed lounge and a formal dining area with seating for eight before which was a large window, double the size of their dorm room. On the table was a large arrangement of fresh blue and white flowers with a handwritten placard upon which the words *Congratulations to you both!* were written in script. Another hallway led off to the left.

"So, this place is ours?" Simon turned to face him as he grinned and looked about with glee.

"Yep. Captain approved and everything!" Zhang beamed. "A friend put in a good word and helped decorate."

Simon went around inspecting everything, running his hands along the walls to wake up the control panels conveniently placed throughout the unit, opening cabinets, checking the replicator, looking out the window.

"Come'ere." Zhang led him through the short hallway to the left of the main door that led into a large sleeping area with an extra-large bed. Balloons in red, gold and white floated about festively on long colorful ribbons.

301

"Whoa!" Simon exclaimed reaching for a balloon that floated past whimsically. "You even managed to get balloons here?" He laughed.

"I had a little help." Zhang shrugged. Upon the bed lay a single red rose on top of a small white box. Zhang grabbed the box and took Simon's hand to turn him so they faced each other. "Come."

He then got down on one knee before him and opened the box and pulled out a white platinum band intricately carved with flowers and swirls.

Simon grinned down at him and affectionately cupped his cheek. Zhang had done the exact same thing in Honoka'a after Simon complained he wasn't feeling romanced enough by him and wasn't going to marry him until Zhang got a clue.

Zhang took the hint and after doing a quick internet search and watching a bunch of YouTube videos on the creative ways to get the job done, including a disastrous hot air balloon ride, dressing up in a clown costume, proposing over dinner by dropping the engagement ring into a glass of champagne (which in that case the bride-to-be promptly chugged and swallowed), he decided to just ask Lady Master Ma'at for advice. She suggested he cut out the fluff and do it like a man: take a knee and just ask. Seeing it worked with great success on earth, he decided to do it again on the ship in their Sirian forms.

"Babe, we've been through thick and thin together and survived all sorts of craziness and perils all over the galaxy. You've always had my back, watched out for me, put up with me, laughed with me, even cried with me. You're my best friend, my partner, my soul mate, my twin flame, and whatever other labels they make up on earth to describe what you and I are lucky enough to have and experience. So…I want to make what we have official here, too, and ask you to marry me," Zhang said with a smile.

Simon stood there staring down at him, eyes bright and expectant.

Zhang gazed back and waited, still smiling himself, confident he would say yes just as he had done in Honoka'a. But moments ticked by with Simon just standing there staring down at him before a frown marred his handsome face.

"That's it? You're going to say it just like that? No tears?" Simon asked.

"Tears?"

"You cried when you proposed to me in Honoka'a," Simon reminded.

"Are you friggin' kidding me?"

"A-Zhang, this is a big deal for me. A very special occasion," Simon said bluntly, his right brow cocked.

Zhang sighed out and nodded, "Ok. Give me a second."

He lowered his head down for a moment. When he looked back up, his almond shaped gray blue Sirian eyes were filled with tears that soon trickled down his cheeks.

Simon instantly lit up. "Oh wow! Don't cry! Yes! Of course, I'll marry you!" He said pulling Zhang and his spontaneously manifested tears to his feet as he laughed happily. Zhang chuckled, swiped at his face with his sleeve and slipped the ring on Simon's left ring finger then dug into his pocket for his and gave it to Simon to slip onto his own hand. Then Zhang sealed their commitment with a slow, measured kiss. After a short while, Zhang pull back, and pressed their foreheads together as he gazed deeply into Simon's eyes. His look serious.

"I value you to the highest and cherish you always."

Simon grabbed ahold of Zhang's wrist and nodded. "I value you to the highest and cherish you always," he declared back with complete devotion. "I will do anything for you," he added solemnly.

Zhang smiled then pressed his mouth to Simon's again, this time gently sliding a hand around the back of his head and threading his fingers in

Simon's long locks. What followed was a detailed and slow perusal of Simon's mouth, fusing their lips together as he ran his hand slowly down Simon's side and back and drove Simon into a bubble of pleasure. Only then did he pull back to gaze at him.

"And I will do anything for you," Zhang declared back.

Simon smiled and leaned back in to meld his mouth again to Zhang's. He moaned out against his lips prompting Zhang to gently tilt Simon's head back to expose his long pale throat and adam's apple. Zhang slid his tongue along his jawline, before latching onto his throat and suckling and lapping the extra sensitive skin there until Simon was moaning more urgently.

Zhang then whispered in his ear, "I'm going to make you come so hard for making me cry on my wedding night," before he fused his lips to Simon's again as Simon chuckled against his mouth.

True to his threat, his hands began to roam more earnestly about until Simon was alternately squirming, giggling and moaning the heady sensation that started in his groin quickly spreading up and outwards until his entire pubes were aching with need.

"Shall we?" Zhang asked when Simon was sufficiently vibrating in his arms.

"Mmm hmmmm." Simon nodded an almost incoherent assent, his eyes glazed. They wasted no time stripping out of their spiffy officer uniforms and christening their new quarters, making quite the mess of it. In the aftermath, they lay there exhausted, neither willing to move. There was seed everywhere. They were both covered with it.

"I love you, Simon," Zhang murmured, heavy lidded as he angled his head to kiss him again.

"I love you, too," Simon murmured receiving his mouth and caressing his face.

"We should take a shower and get back to the med bay and our pods soon…the Lady Master is probably expecting us," Zhang muttered groggily, he and Simon having been at it for some time.

"Good idea," Simon seconded. Moments later, they both fell asleep, exhausted.

Meanwhile, Lady Master Ma'at checked her watch. The pair had been laying on the floor and meditating in the living room on yoga mats for going on four hours. It had to be a record. She thought of coaxing them back but saw the look of sheer bliss on their faces, their hands entwined, ring fingers adorned with the beautiful wedding bands they had brought with them and exchanged during their wedding ceremony in Honoka'a as the sun sat on the horizon observing the beautiful union.

Instead, she draped a light blanket over them and decided to give them more time to enjoy on the ship before calling them back into their earthly bodies. Then she bid the both of them good night.

Two hours later, the pair were back and awake. Groaning and moaning about their stiff and aching backs and joints as they struggled to sit up and regain their bearings. There were blue and white roses on the coffee table before them with a card congratulating them both on their award and Sirian nuptials as balloons in red, gold, and white floated overhead.

There was even a small chocolate groom's cake waiting for them.

"Wow! This is all for us?" Simon beamed looking around the now dimly lit living room in amazement as realization set in.

"Holy shit! Thank you, sis!" Zhang laughed surveying the decorations. "You're awesome!" He reminded himself to tell Lady Master Ma'at they had bought the little house next door and from now on, they would be full-time neighbors. They would be moving in immediately.

Meanwhile, Lady Master Ma'at was already back on the ship, Captain Olin Alpha1 at her side as they carefully tucked the still naked (and sticky) duo back into their stasis pods in the med bay. Afterwards, they

305

joined the after-party they were hosting in the captain's spacious suite. Lord Michael was the guest DJ.

On earth, she and Chris were fast asleep in their bedroom.

Zhang found the karaoke machine she had carefully hid in the garage and carried it back inside before punching in a few songs. Simon went to the kitchen to grab the cake knife and a few beers.

The party in Honoka'a was just getting started.

THE END.

CHAPTER FORTY

ALTERNATE ENDING: The Incredible Photo-Worthy Explosion at Volcano House on the Big Island of Hawaii

Zhang and Simon, with Zhang behind the wheel, had driven the 70 miles from Honoka'a to Hawaii Volcano National Park together with Lady Master Ma'at, her husband Chris, Lady Master Gabi and her husband Ryan, Lady Master Marguerite and her husband Bart and her daughter. Just moments before they'd all celebrated their luck at the excellent parking spot they'd nabbed so close to the Volcano House's viewing platform, right beside the handicap parking.

Much like old faithful in Yellowstone, Kilauea volcano had been spewing lava over a thousand meters high over the past few weeks, making for a spectacular show and perfect photo- op for their group. The next explosion was scheduled to take place in 3 1/2 minutes give or take a few seconds. After that there wouldn't be another glorious display of lava shooting into the sky for at least another three hours based on the accumulated pressure readings and data the scientists and volcanologists who were studying the phenomenon had gathered.

The smell of sulfur was thick in the air and but for the shifting Kona winds, would have been choking to those in the vicinity of several miles. Otherwise, it was a beautiful and glorious day with clear skies above, a most auspicious sign.

"Hey babe, am I parked ok or am I still on the line?" Zhang asked, car door open as he dangled out the side of the monstrous black SUV to check his positioning. Simon had gotten out knowing it would take a while and stood at the foot of the stairs 10 feet away leading up to the viewing platform at the summit.

"It's ok, love. It doesn't have to be perfect. It's not like you're parking the ExplorerX1161 (aka TheZhangXO511) in the shuttle bay," Simon called out encouragingly as he leaned against the railing and waited. He'd been coaxing Zhang to give it up for the last 10 minutes or so as he struggled to maneuver the large American vehicle into the parking space. Despite his cajoling, Zhang seemed hell bent on getting it just right.

Galactic Confederation officer's code and regulation required absolute adherence to accuracy and perfection when maneuvering a federation craft including parking on the mothership Athena which as an accomplished captain with many years of training Zhang had mastered. Now that he had gotten the hang of driving the large black SUV, he seemed to be unable to give up the meticulous habit he'd learned in space. Simon rolled his eyes as he waited.

Meanwhile Lady Master Ma'at was urging them to hurry up to the viewing platform so they could take a group photo together.

"Come on you two!" Lady Master Ma'at excitedly exclaimed. "You don't want to miss this!" She had timed their group photo at the top of the viewing station to a tee making sure they left early enough to drive the 90 minutes from the house and beat the crowds.

As Lady Master Ma'at checked her watch and nervously looked back at the parking lot, she and the others watched Zhang, still dangling out of the driver's seat, slowly reversing, and then driving forward as Simon watched and waited nearby. Just then another car, a 1992 Oldsmobile station wagon with original side panels pulled in next to Zhang in the large blue handicap stall. They appeared to be in a hurry.

The driver, a large elderly Hawaiian man, soon realized that with Zhang so close to the line, his passenger, an elderly Hawaiian woman was unable to open her door and get out of the car. He looked over at Zhang with irritation clearly written in his eyes.

"Are you friggin' kidding me?" He growled and started up the car again to move over. After racing from Kona side and getting lost, they finally made it to Volcano House with only minutes to spare. Zhang meanwhile was busy concentrating behind the wheel, his brow furrowed, as he slowly backed up yet again and then pulled forward while painstakingly turning his wheels ever so slightly.

When Simon met the Hawaiian man's eyes, he immediately recognized Zeeter from Unit ZR. He laughed. He'd been told that Zeeter was coming in as a walk-in after he'd been scrubbed from Plan B when Simon successfully woke Zhang up. He somehow managed to score a much sought-after spot anyway for an earth incarnation to experience the highly prophesied Great Shift. He had chosen the body of the large elderly man who was visiting the area with his wife to pay homage to the Goddess Pele and witness the spectacular lava show. The wife was none other than Gunner from Sector 5. In the backseat was a black Egyptian looking dog— Alpha6 from Polaris, fangs bared at Zhang. They were all there to meet up at the rally point.

"Hurry! Hurry! It's almost time!" Lady Master Ma'at called waving down at them before she scratched her head. *Seriously Zhang?*

Just then there was a loud rumble that shook the ground beneath everyone's feet followed by a deep and guttural groan. It was as if the very earth was awakening from a millennia long slumber, slowly stretching her limbs, her belly ready to birth new earth as she bellowed.

Then Gaia roared.

Meanwhile clueless, Zhang continued his painstaking efforts to maneuver the big black SUV and again slowly backed up. "I got this, babe!"

It was the last thing he said besides *"Holy shit!* Are you friggin' kidding me?" as the ground behind him suddenly gave way and the shiny black SUV with Zhang still dangling from the driver's seat rolled backward into the fiery abyss. As he looked over, he saw the old station wagon that had been parked next to him falling in tandem in slo mo. Both occupants of the station wagon were scowling and giving him the finger. Even the dog was snarling through the back window, face pressed against the glass.

Simon, watching it from where he stood, didn't have time to react or shake his head as the ground buckled then caved beneath his feet sending him hurdling after Zhang and the SUV.

"Right behind you, babe!" He was heard to yell before they disappeared into Gaia's belly.

Those on the viewing platform fared no better as in the same instant the rest of the parking lot, platform, Volcano House and the entire crater blew up with a deafening roar rocking the area and spewing lava and house-sized boulders thousands of feet into the air in a catastrophic explosion that was heard all the way at the Maunaleo House on Oahu.

Minutes later, a meteor-size boulder was seen hurdling in a spectacular display heading towards the Hamakua coast, a fiery trail in its wake as it streaked across the sky. The impact came moments later—a direct hit on the retreat in Honoka'a, completely demolishing it and sending the entire hillside plunging into the sea.

In the aftermath of the deafening explosion, there was nothing but silence.

Back on the ship, Zhang, Simon, Lady Master Ma'at and the rest of the crew in stasis were climbing out of their pods.

"Holy shit! That was wild! Ha! Ha! Ha!" Simon laughed. Meanwhile, Zhang, eyes bulging, was shaking his head. "Wild? Really Lieutenant? Plunging backward in that humongous black SUV wasn't exactly my idea of a good time!" His voice excited.

"I was right behind you. You looked so cool!" Simon guffawed.

"I was screaming the whole way down!" Zhang exclaimed.

"Ha! Ha! Ha! Yeah, you were! I wish I had my smart pad to take a photo!" Simon continued. "By the way, why are you and I naked?" A gray working in the med bay hurried to bring them robes.

"I can't believe we missed the photo op! Did Gaia blow early?" Lady Master Marguerite asked as she helped her daughter out of her pod.

"I think she did. It certainly seemed like it," Lady Master Gabi responded.

Meanwhile Bart and Ryan stood there laughing and hi-fiving each other as Gunner, Zeeter and Alpha6 shook their heads and also belly laughed so hard, tears streaked down their faces. "Dude! That was friggin' awesome!"

Zhang was still carrying on with Simon as he slipped on his robe, "You could've at least warned me we were going down!"

"I told you to hurry," Simon grinned at him as he checked that Zhang was in one piece. "But my baby kept insisting on making sure the car was parked perfectly within the lines...."

Zhang grinned back at him. "Yeah, I did do that, didn't I. And you did tell me to hurry, huh....Thanks, that was pretty damn awesome, Lieutenant. Everyone ok?"

Turning to Zhang, Gunner and Zeeter both slapped him on the shoulder. "That was one crazy ride, Commander," Zeeter laughed still leaking tears from his eyes, his 15-foot-tall Reptilian body towering over all of them. His specially made pod looked like the med bay crew had hastily glued two separate pods together and even then, it appeared about a foot short.

"Yeah, but it would've been a whole lot better if we got to see it from

311

the viewing platform. Thanks, Commander Zhang," Alpha6 joked. They had shared the same horrifying view as Zhang as they fell backwards into the abyss and into the piping hot lava.

Meanwhile Lady Master Ma'at making sure everyone was accounted for, awake and out of their stasis pods, made eye contact with the commander who nodded before she relayed to the captain through the array. "The commander and lieutenant and all support crew are back on board, safe and sound."

The captain's voice was instantly heard announcing on the broadcast speaker from the bridge of the mothership Athena:

"Rally Point 3- Accomplished. Detailed Report to Follow. Captain Olin Alpha1." Then "Great job team!"

The ship erupted in cheers.

The captain had only gone along for the ride and joined the earth adventure when his wife and consort Ariitzka (aka Lady Master Ma'at) insisted on going to support the *Dynamic Duo* to help them see the mission through. Thus, only less than 1% of his consciousness had been inserted into his 3D body so that he could continue to man the ship and her myriad operations without a hitch. For him the jolt back into his body and full consciousness was the equivalent of no more than a 3 second buzz.

All heroes had returned safely. Mission Everlight accomplished.

Gaia ascended.

THE END.

CHAPTER FORTY-ONE
EPILOGUE

Zhang and Simon agree to answer questions posed by earth humans as officers of the Galactic Confederation about the shift, ascension, angels and other topics. The session was broadcast on earth from the Round Room of the mothership. They were both dressed up in formal officer attire, Zhang with his captain insignia and Simon with his Lieutenant designation emblazoned on his chest as Captain Olin Alpha1 and Lord Michael proudly stood by.

Q: "What happens to those unable to wake up in time for the shift?"

Zhang: "They'll blow up and die."

Simon: "That's not what happens."

Zhang: "Yes, it is. That happened on Mars."

Simon: "Who says?"

Zhang grinning: "Gaia TV."

Simon shaking his head in exasperation: "That's not true."

Zhang: "Oh really? Look at what happened to us! We fell into a cataclysmic abyss. Backward, I might add. I wouldn't wish that on anyone."

Simon: "That scenario was planned in advance. Well, except you backing up in the SUV like you did. That part...hehe...that wasn't planned. Uh, maybe just let me answer this question for the audience."

Zhang: "Be my guest."

Simon: "This honestly depends on their life state at the time of the shift and if they had descended from a higher plane to incarnate on earth or were earth humans ascending upwards for the first time from the 3D planes. This determines where their next existence would be. As many of the 3D ascenders are still asleep, they would be taken to a holographic planet much like earth created by the Sirians and Andromedans to live out their incarnations.

"At first glance, those beings would believe they were yet on earth as they would experience the same low vibrations they encountered and perpetuated on earth with a helpful push by the masters behind the hologram to heal and raise their vibration. This is being done because 3D earth will cease to be in existence at some point due to Gaia's ascension to a 5D planet."

"Contrast this with ascending Earth, only those earth humans whose vibrations are equal to or higher than 5th density can tolerate the new energies and will ascend with her. Either way the transition will be smooth as it's all done by and orchestrated at the higher dimensions which we agree to prior to our incarnations."

Zhang: "That's what I said."

Simon: "That is so not what you said."

Zhang: (grins)

Simon: (grins back)

Zhang: "So who goes where again?"

Simon: "Those not ready to make the shift -"

Zhang: "You mean the low lifers-"

Simon: "Just those not ready for the higher energies. They are moved to the 3D Hologram of planet earth. Those ready to ascend with Gaia stay on Gaia and enjoy the higher energies and Light on the new earth until they decide to go elsewhere such as back to their home planets or their assigned mothership."

Zhang: "Speaking of motherships, I hear the Pleiadeans have parties every night. Maybe we should ask the captain to reassign us."

Simon nodding over with his head: "You know the captain is standing right there."

Captain Alpha1: "I heard that. Request denied."

Zhang grinning: "Just kidding, Captain. This is the best mothership in this sector of the galaxy."

Other mothership captains from the array: "We heard that!"

Zhang: "Uh, next question please."

Simon: "Hee! Hee! Hee!"

Q: "So are you saying that the surprisingly visceral ending with Commander Zhang and you and the others dropping tail first into boiling hot lava or blowing up into smithereens was actually planned by you in advance?"

Zhang: "What my partner Lieutenant Simon means to say is that there are a number of scenarios surrounding one's manner of death on earth, all of which we agree to prior to incarnation, and which are much loved by us. Nothing is truly an accident. It's all part of one's earth experience and mission. It just so happens some lives and endings are more 'exciting' than others. No disrespect was intended."

Simon: "Yes, all that you are is done in your name. When you understand you are Light, and all is in divine order, you have absolutely nothing to fear."

Q: "Is there still reincarnation on earth?"

Zhang: "Our team took that fence down ages ago. People just kept jumping back in line like at an amusement park using the same ticket to ride the same ride."

Simon: "What?"

Zhang: "You know, that net's been down for years. Folks keep coming back because they enjoy it there."

Simon clearing his throat: "….The reincarnation technology was dismantled around earth's year 2012."

Zhang: "That's what I said. That's exactly what I said."

Simon: "Let me finish…this allowed those who died on earth and transitioned to go elsewhere, no longer being trapped in the reincarnation cycle."

Zhang: "Some of them came back. I'm sure of it."

Simon shaking his head: "No one came back. They are all on their next incarnation elsewhere or are receiving healing with their brothers and sisters of the Light."

Zhang: "You mean like angels? Like yourself…never mind, forget I just said that. You're just half angel."

Simon giving Zhang a look.

Zhang: "See a real angel would never look at me like that. Michael would never look at me like that."

Simon gesturing for the next question.

Q: "If there is no more reincarnation, why are people still being born on earth?"

Zhang: "Allow me…"

Simon nodding to go ahead:

Zhang: "What people don't understand is that birthing space is still at a premium. The line is still very long. For instance, I waited a week to get a seat-"

Simon: "You didn't wait that long.   It was less than an earth minute."

Zhang: "It felt like a week…"

Simon: "Are you going to answer the question for real?"

Zhang grinning before assuming a more serious vein: "Yes…happy to….Uh, can you repeat the question."

Q: "If there is no more reincarnation, why are people still being born on earth? Why are we still at 11 billion people?"

Zhang: "Because of galactics and light beings like Simon and me jumping in and taking up the vacated spots. And unlike in years past, everybody who applies for a spot at incarnating on earth as a human has to bring something to the table to help with the ascension. Gone are the days of just taking up wasted space, if you know what I mean."

Q: "But what about Gunner, Alpha6 and…Zeeter, is it? We heard they just went in at the last minute."

Simon: "Uh, what he means to say is that souls coming in are bringing in all of their gifts and abilities to bear in order to aide earth's ascension.

Gunner, Alpha6 and Zeeter were there to support the team and make sure we returned safely."

Zhang leaning over to whisper in Simon's ear: "Beautifully said, Lieutenant. Although I think they just went ass first like I did."

Simon: "Hee! Hee! Hee!"

Thala from the array who agreed to help monitor the broadcast: "Knock it off, you two!"

Q: "Are birds real?"

Simon: "Excuse me?"

Q: "I read or heard it explained that birds were part of a holographic program to provide depth to the human experience. So, their flying south on a set schedule and all that is part of the program. They are just AI or a hologram and thus aren't real."

Zhang: "I saw a bumper sticker that said that once."

Simon: "Said what?"

Zhang: "Birds aren't real."

Simon: "They are real."

Zhang: "Yes, I have to agree. Otherwise, they wouldn't shit on your head and everywhere else."

Simon looking at Zhang who grins back: "…"

Simon: "Birds are fully conscious beings on earth as guardians. Thus, they communicate with all other animals, insects, the land, the trees, the wind, the oceans and rivers, the flowers, even with the earth humans who choose to listen. They, like you, are all part of the larger symbiosis. They like everything else were introduced into the great biosphere project that is earth by many galactic civilizations working together."

Q: "So the birds are real?"

Zhang: "Oh, they're real, sister. So, watch your head."

Q: "Many of the principles galactics have shared in their communications with humanity are reminiscent of those taught by sages like Lao Tze, Buddha and Jesus. So, are you Taoists or Buddhists or Christians?"

Simon: "We are none of those as those are merely labels earth humans use to distinguish one from another as there are so many seemingly competing views and beliefs systems that your people call religion. Your religions all hold the same kernel of truth wrapped in different packages and mixed with a lot of additional dogmas and practices which are meant as a tool for humans to absorb much like a mnemonic."

"Unfortunately included in that is a whole lot of superstition and control. On the other hand, were those universal truths to serve as a way of life then it moves away from religion and becomes a philosophy. You see evidence in that in the way true Daoists or Buddhists or Christians live. It's a way to navigate life without the dogma. Thus, it requires extreme flexibility few on your planet have been able to practice and uphold."

"The core teachings that Menos411 or Lao Tze, Siddhartha and Yeshua from Sector 15 taught are merely ways of living in universal balance which is what our civilizations have sought to do for many millions of years. Thus, we do not subscribe to labels or dogma or rules of control and have resolved much of the conflicts and inner and outer disharmony that earth and earth humans continue to struggle with. The basis of all is unconditional love. It is Light. It is Source. It is balance with the universal divine. I believe the Hawaiians call this *pono*. Righteous or divine right balance."

Zhang: "Wow, you're like an encyclopedia. I couldn't have said it better."

Simon smiling and gazing into Zhang's eyes: ...

Q: "Are angels able to be born in human bodies? Zhang said something about the bodies blowing up earlier which sounds rather frightening."

Zhang: "That sounds like I was misquoted. Because I would never say-"

Q: "You said, and I quote 'they weren't able to fit and they just blew up. Even the doctors blew up in some instances delivering them...it was a mess...a real mess.'"

Simon laughing: "I remember you saying that."

Zhang: "I am pretty sure I didn't. If I did, I was just joking."

Simon, nodding: "I think you were."

Zhang: "Finally we're on the same page."

Simon smiling and leaning in to intensely stare at Zhang with a gleam in his eyes: "We're always on the same page, Commander. You don't need to worry about that."

Zhang staring back and smiling: "..."

Thala from the array: "Control yourselves! Alright! Let's end the broadcast before they forget we're even here."

Q: "But they didn't answer the question."

Thala: "We'll post a more complete answer as soon as we cut."

Cut Broadcast.

Meanwhile, Captain Olin Alpha1 and Lord Michael were laughing so hard they had to be escorted from the room.

Posted answer from veteran Ascended Master Guide Glenn: "Those from the highest densities like Simon had to wait to be born to parents able to withstand their higher frequencies. Thus, the process up through the actual birth of a high frequency being is highly technical and involves close monitoring. The incoming energies are adjusted and either increased or decreased depending on the circumstance to ensure a successful incarnation into the physical. The technical aspects of the process are handled by organic robots affectionately known as "the grays" in conjunction with earth incarnation teams which consists of master and earth guides, angels, archangels, healers and other beings of Light to ensure the smoothest process possible. If they succeed, the high vibrational being would be born as an Earth human. If anything is amiss, then to avoid harm to the mother the process may be restarted at a later date with the same host mother or perhaps another mother who has agreed to take on this special task. The physical encasement of the fetus if not sustainable is usually miscarried in utero but this is happening much less so there is no need to worry. All is in divine order."

END EPILOGUE

CHAPTER FORTY-TWO

Extras #1 Scavenger Hunt in the Athena's Medical Warehouse

"Hey! Simon! Simon! Get over here and take a look at this! What the hell-"

Zhang stared down at the dusty glass plate beneath which there appeared to be a leftover costume from the last masquerade party. They'd been scrounging around in the 11000 square meter warehouse on the Athena for things to barter for the mission to Rigel. They'd heard Rigelians had a great appreciation for Sirian junk and were in luck as the Athena's warehouse was full of outdated technologies that had collected over the years likely intended for recycling and repurposing. They saw no harm in helping clear some of it out and taking what they could salvage.

They'd taken to bartering for everything during their missions with both advanced and developing races for spare parts, food, safe passage, navigation equipment and anything else they needed. Often the back of the shuttle craft looked more like a junk transport than a top-of-the-line Science and Exploration light craft commissioned by the Galactic Confederation.

"What'd you find?" Simon sauntered over carrying a box full of loose parts and knobs, a chipped early generation smart pad, a medical monitor missing a few critical components and a pair of space goggles. As they stood shoulder to shoulder, he stared down at what appeared to be a dried-up face with a faded greenish blue tinge almost pressed up against the glass. The skin- like material looked leathered and desiccated, its facial structure collapsing into the grotesque 15-inch head, the left side caved in distorting its features. It had a strange bony structure that went from the crown down in the middle of the mask and ended in two holes for nostrils at the chin.

"Eww! What is it?" In its present condition he couldn't hazard a guess of what it was supposed to be or what it was used for much less why it was under 10 feet of junk and why his partner was hell bent on retrieving it.

"Just some old costume. Come on! Help me get it out. This would be great at the next ball! If we can find two, we could go as twins!" Zhang laughed beginning to move away the collected bins and boxes and outdated medical machinery that littered the area and buried the casing it was in. Simon set the box he was carrying down to the side and jumped in to help him, encouraged by his partner's enthusiasm and humor.

"Twin what?"

"I don't know. Reptoids," Zhang joked.

"That's pretty rude. I'm sure the Reptoids would take issue with that."

They managed to clear away all the debris around it and drag it with some difficulty into a clearer area. The box was heavy. The costume was contained in an old white capsule about 7 feet in length that was wider at the top than the bottom. Simon stood back and cocked his head as Zhang bent over it and used his sleeve to clean the glass face a bit more.

"Uh...why does the box have an identifying number sequence on its side?" Simon asked pointing to a corner nearest the floor. Zhang stopped what he was doing and climbed over the box to stand beside him. Simon quickly punched the numbers into his smart pad. They certainly didn't want to take anything for scraps that could be traced.

"Uhhh, Zhang. That isn't a costume...apparently, it's what's left of Jefok8731 from Epsilon Indi."

They stared at each other dumbfounded before both looked down at the image on the pad and confirmed. The Jefok race was a peaceful one from the constellation Indus working with the confederation. They were known as engineering whizzes although neither had occasion to work alongside one yet. Apparently, they had uncovered an old stasis pod with ol' Jefok still in it. In the image on Simon's smart pad Jefok8731, while not particularly attractive in his book, looked much healthier in his service picture than the dried up remains before them. Zhang thought he was going to be sick.

"What the?" Zhang struggled to process it all. "Why would he be in the middle of this place under piles of garbage?!"

"Did they just forget about this guy or something?" Simon chimed in looking equally horrified. "We better call someone," Simon said beginning to pace.

"Wait! What are we going to tell them about why we're in here and how we found it? We better get our stories straight first," Zhang warned, his voice commanding in a self-preserving sort of way, his wheels already spinning.

"Good idea." While considering themselves good Samaritans not technically stealing, the practice of salvaging for scrap in the Athena's huge warehouse hadn't exactly been approved by the higher ups much less their immediate commanding officer. It was best to keep a low profile if they wished to avoid a reprimand and possible demotion and ruin their pristine service record.

"Sheesh poor guy...I'd be pissed if I came back to this."

"Hey look! There's another one!" Simon pointed and headed past the pod containing Jefok8731's rotting remains to where a corner of another pod peeked free. After some maneuvering they managed to clear away the junk around it and found the pod had been turned on its side. Too heavy to use brute force to turn it upright, Zhang instead used levitation. As he was a bit rusty it dropped heavily to the ground with a thud. They went to inspect it and were horrified to find it was occupied by not one but three partially shriveled up bodies similar looking to Jefok8731.

"Oh!!! Oh!!!! That's gross! Oh, my illuminations! What the—." Zhang ran and hopped about in disbelief while Simon stared bug-eyed at the abomination before them.

"Three to a pod? Really now??? That's just— oh— unbelievable!" Simon yelled to no one in particular and retrieved the serial numbers before plunking them into his smart pad.   They'd found Jefok8124, Jefok9214 and Jefok4860.

The two stared at each other for a time before either of them spoke, each thinking the same thing. "We can't really just leave them and pretend we didn't see anything, right? I mean…" Simon began, his sense of righteous morality warring with the feeling they also might be in hot water.

"Well yeah, we sorta' have to tell someone, right? Maybe someone's been looking for these guys or something.…" Zhang reasoned daring to look at the three Jefoks crammed three to a stasis pod without doing another freak out dance.

"Well…They look pretty…old?" Simon shrugged raising his eyebrows. "The damn things don't even look plugged into anything. Shouldn't they be closer to a wall plug or something? I mean why the heck are they here covered up under all this junk like this?" In truth the stasis pods, even those of the older generations that housed the Jefoks, used crystal energy to power them. Each unit housing its own perpetually generating crystal battery that ran forever.   Perhaps the quartz powering the pods had been removed and used for something else.

"I don't know...they obviously were put in here some time ago...." Zhang said shaking his head.

Simon tried looking up on his smart pad information on why they'd been in stasis in the first place, perhaps learning of the mission they were currently on, anything to give them a hint as to why they ended up abandoned and drying out in a warehouse, but nothing popped up.

Zhang sighed then made the executive decision. "We better call someone. I'd be damned if something like this happens when we need to be in stasis," he grumbled. "Come on," Zhang muttered heading for the door.

Simon, following suit, took one look back at the four desiccated stiffs and hurried after him.

CHAPTER FORTY-THREE
Extras #2 Mencius and his Beloved Jefoks- Plan B

Simon, having consulted with the higher ups, asked for assistance in the array and sought permission to take more drastic measures to wake Zhang up. Thus far, it was yet under review. A decision still hadn't been made. At the rate things were heading it seemed the guidance team of which he was a member was already contemplating moving to Plan B. Mencius was not a big fan.

They had already waited more than 8 months and still there was no sign that Zhang had woken up. In fact, it appeared he was getting even more deeply entangled in the earth drama, even beginning to accumulate karma. This seemed to be the story for 98.25% of all of Mencius' charges. To date, the only ones sent to earth that he had mentored who woke up were...Simon (who never was asleep), Siddhartha Buddha, Yeshua (aka Jesus #1 of 2), that Alexander guy although he'd gone a little nuts and was still receiving healing, and the Athena's captain whose tenure in Egypt as a Lyran lion being human hybrid (he was still a Lyran lion being) had gone pretty much without a hitch. He, too, never fell asleep. But other than that...his record of success was sorely lacking.

Perhaps he wasn't cut out for this line of work after all. His four golden boys, the Jefoks were still trapped on earth after thousands of earth years. As his very first earth incarnated galactics he'd been in charge of as a Master Guide, he swore that he would bring them back safely if it was the last thing he did.

He'd contemplated stepping down as an Ascended Master Guide for some time but couldn't do it as long as he had galactics in human form still recycling back to earth. But then something amazing happened. Gaia sent out a call. Apparently, she finally figured out there was a problem there.

He'd always thought her a bit stubborn as when he'd brought up the reincarnation problem to her and the rest of the team before, she'd immediately shut him down and said she could handle it. Well, she finally figured out the billions of karma-laden humans caught in a downward spiral were also dragging her ass down too and asked the angelics and anyone else who could hear for help. Then another wonderful thing happened.

The technology team of the Galactic Confederation, led by Jefok engineers finally figured out how to dismantle the reincarnation net the service-to-self bastards had operating on the earth's moon.

The Jefok beings had first gone down to earth at a time when earth's civilizations were still recovering, retooling after tumultuous change brought on by the Annunakis. That was when the galactics had been more involved in helping the humans rebuild. The Jefoks had gone to the area now known as Mexico and Central America to help and share wisdoms and technology with the developing humans. They lived in peaceful coexistence for a long time.

But something had gone horribly wrong. The Jefoks decided to return home to their planet. They left 25 members of their race to remain to continue to help the humans. The plan was to return for them but that opportunity never came. Influenced by dark interdimensional beings and reptilians who had been living underground and manipulating the earth's atmosphere, weather patterns and the minds of humans, the Mayans killed the remaining 25 Jefoks and began that weird practice of human sacrifice to call back the other Jefoks, their "Gods" who had been kind to them and they believed were responsible for the good weather and abundance before they left.

The team responsible for the Jefoks was headed by the Angel Gabriel
who suggested perhaps some members from their race incarnate as
humans to try to find out what was going on and to convince the
humans of their erroneous ways. At the time Mencius had just
graduated from ascended master school. This was his assignment.
Jefok8731, Jefok8124, Jefok9214 and Jefok4860 bravely volunteered to
jump together. Even now Mencius remembered how the four of them,
rosy cheeked and full of optimism, swore to complete their missions.
But within one or two human lifetimes, things went south.

Jefok8731 was sacrificed by the Mayans. Jefok9214 and Jefok8124 began
an unlikely alliance with the reptilians to lure humans down into their
underground dens in exchange for power. Jefok4860 was the only one
who stayed the course, swearing with Mencius' help to save his
comrades. But within the next 3 human lifetimes, after becoming
enslaved by the Romans and worked to death, he became endlessly
trapped in the reincarnation cycle himself. He was now the President of
China Bank, responsible for laundering vast amounts of capital out of
the country for illicit purposes. Jefok9214 was now the head of CAPA.
Jefok8124 was now the corrupt provincial governor of Zhang's
hometown whose palms were heavily greased to ensure his cooperation
during Zhang's blacklisting and take down.

Plan B was the multi-leveled backup scheme that would involve taking
Zhang's IG account offline, then removing him permanently from the
business, transferring Simon to another mission altogether and
introducing three new players.

These new players were there not to assist Zhang in remembering as
they felt only his soul mate was truly capable of that, but to transition
Zhang back into public life but as a drama teacher at an obscure high
school out of the public eye. They felt there he could heal from the
trauma of the scandal and still eke out a living as a Chinese citizen. His
benefactor and the school's principal would be none other than Gunner
from Sector 5.

Gunner's incarnation into a human body would occur via a soul transfer. After a few years of this, Gunner, Zhang and Simon would be recalled back to the Athena where Zhang would receive more healing before being cleared back for duty as an officer on the Athena.

Meanwhile two of the other new players, Alpha6 from Polaris and Zeeter from Unit ZR who were not soul mates but who had closely worked together on several missions providing tactical defense to the Science and Exploration Teams would come in as the hot, up and coming performing artists of a popular boy band via a soul exchange. This would take place after an accident causing two of the band's members to have near death experiences which was part of their soul agreements.

It was not an ideal set up but would allow the new team to try to get close to the offenders without having to go through the birth process and take them out the old fashion way since time was of the essence. It was primarily a rescue mission for Zhang and a tactical mission for Alpha6 and Zeeter. Although the Jefoks would be recalled for healing as Alpha6 and Zeeter would take them out, it would leave CAPA and other big players to continue their corrupt practices. The confederation would be left to focus on other areas of society to fight the corruption. In short it was a plan that required huge compromises and create some karma for Alpha6 and Zeeter. Naturally, Mencius wasn't a big fan.

He needed Zhang to wake up. Without him the plan to rescue the Jefoks and humanity remained in jeopardy.

Simon needed to go in now. He took matters into his hands and gave Simon the go ahead.

CHAPTER FORTY-FOUR

Extras #3 Backstory to the Bell Ringing Incident on Earth's Moon

Simon's stunt actually somehow caused a serious malfunction to the ship's computer system. As soon as Zhang fired up the ship, it unexpectedly lifted off the ground then jettisoned off the moon at full speed. Backwards.

The pair were heard screaming at the top of their lungs in the array in a full-blown panic leaving everyone wondering just what the two were up to now.

When they sufficiently calmed down Simon quickly did an assessment and realized not only was the ship's computer system down but the rear cameras were also offline. They were flying blind, backwards.

"What the —" Zhang huffed as he quickly threw the ship into autopilot to allow the AI to take over. But the computer remained unresponsive and eerily silent.

"Well, that's not good. Let's try to reboot the whole system. Hopefully we can restart it again, as well. We can't be free floating through space or it will take us ages to get home." Zhang moaned not mentioning the obvious.

"Good idea," Simon said unbuckling his harness to access the AI system in the rear of the ship. Unlike in earth sci fi movies that required two crew members to flip a switch or turn a key at the same time, the system reboot in this case was the equivalent of opening a little panel just behind the cabin seats and running the pad of one's index finger in a circular motion a few times. The whimsical motion made Simon laugh before he called out to his partner.

"Anything?" Simon asked then moved to look out the small rear window. Thankfully there wasn't anything in their immediate path to cause alarm. Yet at the rate they were moving through space and with ships jumping in and out of portals the closer they got to the Athena, things would look different in short order.

"No. Ridiculous!" Zhang complained as he futilely kept flipping switches and pressing buttons. Left with no choice, he was forced to employ tactical maneuvers to regain control of the ship that he'd only vaguely heard about from his father and grandfather. Meanwhile they continued hurdling backward.

Simon returned to his seat.

"Well, this is a bit embarrassing. Although it wouldn't be the first time we flew in by the seat of our pants. That is assuming you are able to land her on the Athena like this." Simon opined sounding pretty nonchalant about it all now despite it being him who damaged the ship in the first place.

"Let's hope so," Zhang said not sounding very confident. But the idea of crashing into the Athena and burning on impact, (that is if the captain didn't decide to take proactive measures to blow them out of the sky first), kept him from giving up on trying.

"We can always ask them to use the magnetic field net," Simon suggested.

"Field net? Hell, if we're going to be captured and brought into the shuttle bay like a couple of fish by a dumb field net. You know how embarrassing that would look?"

"Ok, how about the teleport?"

Zhang made a face. "Too desperate. Besides, remember what happened to that poor guy from Cepheus. I heard he came back with his arms and legs all mismatched and backward, I might add. He was the talk of the break room for a while."

"Really?" Simon tried to imagine his left and right arms and legs switched and backwards and frowned.

"Yeah, I guess his body parts got messed up in the transfer. Dumb grays."

"Wait…That sounds like a made up story or something they tell to keep misbehaving children in line."

Zhang grinned at him.

"Ha! Ha! Ha! You almost got me." Simon guffawed.

"I'll just try to stick the landing."

"That would certainly be best. You know how cool you'd look doing that?"

"I know, right? The both of us! Our popularity would soar!"

"How hard can it be?"

Zhang pfft'd. "A piece of cake. Let's do this! Are our coordinates still accurate and matching up?"

"So far. But does anything even work besides the reverse thrusts and hyperdrive?" Simon asked watching Zhang continuing to try to get the ship to respond.

"Nope."

"Huh...well, since the forward, left and right thrusts don't work we have to approach with a fair degree of accuracy going in backward to make the shuttle bay," Simon shrugged.

"I'll just manually shut off the photon boosters a few clicks before approach. That way we'll just float right on in."

"Ha! Ha! Ha! Like clouds! I like that!"

"I'll just need you to guide me in by looking out the rear window. With any luck we'll avoid slamming into the Athena and wrecking the ship. If that happens, we won't have jobs to go back to even if we do survive."

"Mmmn."

"In the meantime, we better report this in."

"Hey, since you're going to call it in you might want to request access to an alternate landing dock. Preferably one with rear doors. You know, in case we come in too hot," Simon suggested.

"Sounds reasonable. That way if we come in too fast, we'll just jettison out the back. Wouldn't that be funny." Zhang chuckled then sobered up quickly.

"Of course, that'll be up to the captain," Zhang added. They'd be hard pressed to explain to Flight Control their situation without the captain being alerted. Special clearance was needed to land in an alternate shuttle bay for a mothership as busy as the Athena. As her bays were usually crammed full of space craft of all shapes and sizes, including those of visiting dignitaries, it required not only calling all captains on board to clear their crafts out of the bay, halting all incoming and outgoing traffic, but also special permission to open both bay doors for a stunt like that. On any given rotation, that would mean involving nearly 300 captains and shuttle bay crew.

Although the Athena had countermeasures to lock onto the ship magnetically, even its deployment required notifying the Captain. He supposed it was better than risking damage to the mothership and crashing the shuttlecraft in case he overshot it.

"Here goes." He sighed. "This is Commander ZhangZHXO511 in command of the Explorer X1161." Zhang radioed into the shuttle bay's array where navigation of all outgoing and incoming traffic was handled for the mothership.

"State your situation." Came the robotic sounding reply.

"We're coming in hot and need assistance in landing. Our craft is completely offline and stuck in hyperdrive."

"Yes…we heard your cries earlier."

The duo exchanged looks. "Hey, we weren't crying. We just had a little bit of a scare." Zhang protested.

"Yes, we were just caught off guard is all." Simon nodded enthusiastically from his seat beside him.

"We will deploy the net and shoot a quantum beam into her booster. If you like we can teleport you both out-"

"That won't be necessary. We'll stay with the ship." Zhang replied quickly as Simon gestured, axing that suggestion outright. No need to humiliate themselves further.

Thus, as they approached, the Athena shot a quantum beam out that surrounded the ship, in effect slowing her approach and bringing her back on trajectory and our two heroes in safely. None of the ships had to be moved to clear out the bay. (Simon's coordinates were way off by over an earth mile anyway ensuring they would have missed the entire mothership by a huge margin).

As they endured being hauled in like two fish, Simon looked over at his

335

partner.

"I'm sorry for breaking the ship, Commander," Simon said telepathically reading his thoughts and sensing Zhang's angst. His words held genuine remorse and he threw in a pout for good measure.

"We better get our stories straight if we plan to keep this detail." Zhang responded in kind.

"I'll just tell them the truth." Simon continued the silent communiqué.

"That might not be a good idea for either of us." Zhang looked over at him.

"You know I can't lie." …

CHAPTER FORTY-FIVE

Extras #4 Answers to Questions Zhang Posed to Simon about Life on the Ship

Do they really have gay marriage up there?

All things are permitted if done out of unconditional love and acceptance. We do not have unions as created on earth rooted in civil ceremonies or religious based dogma. Rather if two souls wish to be bonded in such a way it is a decision they make together. There is no need to make it official as on earth through the church or other means as their intention is enough.

What do they usually do for fun?

The interests of the ship's crew are varied. We have a number of activities much like earth as well as opportunities for recreation. If one wishes to walk in nature or exercise or play golf as in Commander Zhang's case, there are facilities including a bio-dome where there are numerous parks, as well as the H-Deck or Holodeck. These facilities are free to use and for the use of any and all who wish to enjoy them.

Could people bring their favorite items such as Zhang bringing his guitar or his hundreds of pairs of shoes?

Of course. The use of the replicator is also available which will replicate the exact item on the ship. But you will find on the ship such attachments to material possessions are not as highly regarded as they have been encouraged on earth.

Do they play video games and golf on the ship?

These are also available but unlike earth, video games are housed and available via a central database that can be accessed in one's quarters or the H-deck. The games and other programs can also be accessed in the various lounges. It is uncommon on the ship to use the smart pads for this purpose. Golf and other recreational activities you term sports can be done in the H-Deck.

Do they eat Chinese hot pot on the mothership?

While not a dish that is commonly eaten as with all dishes they can be replicated so that those who wish to experience them are free to do so.

Where did they go to high school?

There are schools here although the grade system as like you have on earth does not exist. Children and younger members learn by ability and collective schooling so there is no need for that type of separation.

How did they learn to fly a spaceship?

In Commander Zhang's case it was by hands on learning. This knowledge is also innate as we have technology that is tactile and thus the maneuvering of the ship is by intent. If we wish to go from point A to Point B simply thinking of the ship at Point B by the being who controls it is sufficient to accomplish its movement.   For ships that are not of this class there are simulation decks to accomplish this. In my case, it was by accessing Commander Zhang's memories, which is not...uh...standard protocol.

Why is Simon only a lieutenant and Zhang a commander?

All are equally capable. Thus, this is usually determined by merit. Commander Zhang received his commendation on account of his bravery in prior missions. During these missions he demonstrated courage, valor, the willingness to put the safety of others before himself and the ability to make good decisions under pressure. He also comes from a long line of officers in his family and is highly regarded.

How much do they get paid?

We are not paid in currency. One's performance warrants merits and commendations. But at the end of the day, even these represent increased responsibility and not necessarily just for the sake of giving accolades. For instance, one who is made captain of a ship or commander necessarily has more responsibilities not only to maintain the ship but for the safety of the crew and guests on board. The medals or pins or stripes he or she has on their suit or insignia are thus a reminder of their increased levels of responsibility and their duty to others.

CHAPTER FORTY-SIX

Extras #5 Galactic Confederation Mission and the H-Deck

Zhang gazed back at Simon with that heavy lidded look. Simon recognized it instantly. Zhang was horny again.

"Ha! Ha! Ha!" Simon laughed only too happy to help him out. He grabbed his hand.

"Come on. I know just the place to go."

Zhang's heart thudded as he followed glibly, anticipating another roll around the sack. The onset of the amorous feeling was sudden and so strong it took him by surprise. Thank illuminations they weren't in the middle of an assignment where it would have been highly inconvenient. Simon still hadn't figured out how to bypass the cameras in the cockpit and crew cabin in the shuttle craft after the last "mishap".

Simon meanwhile seemed to take their newfound intimacy on the ship in stride. Now was no different, leading Zhang by the hand and taking charge like a boss. Zhang felt the heat intensify and his suit suddenly felt uncomfortably tight at his crotch. He reminded himself to talk with the engineering department to requisition suits to better accommodate them, preferably one with an extra pocket up front.

"Hi Commander! Hi Lieutenant!" They heard repeatedly as they made their way along the pristine white walkway toward the elevator banks from the dining hall where they had enjoyed an early meal.

Zhang fully expected them to abscond back to their quarters as they had no more assignments for the next two rotations. But Simon instead led him to the H-deck where there was already a queue waiting including some families with small children all dressed as if they were going to an earth birthday party. They dropped hands and Simon walked him straight to the front of the line.

Since the award ceremony and earth's successful ascension, they'd been treated like celebrities on the ship, garnering attention not only from the usual female cadre as in times past but from their male colleagues as well as even the little ones. All viewed them as heroes who saved earth. They didn't know what the big deal was given it wasn't like it had just been the two of them down there all that time helping the earth humans.   Lady Master Ma'at helped a small bit, too.

This time was no different as those waiting in line recognized them and offered up rousing smiles and warm hellos in greeting.

"Hello everyone! How are you?" Simon said cheerfully as Zhang stood beside him wondering what he was about.

"Sorry folks. We have critical Confederation business that requires last-minute training in the holodeck. This might take awhile but you are all welcome to wait. It does mean however we need to jump the line."

Just then the door swung open and two male colleagues strode out laughing heartily as if they had thoroughly enjoyed their experience. With a wave at those in line, Simon led Zhang in.

"Captain's orders." Zhang added with a decisive nod before he hurried in after him and shut the door.

The room was fairly large and threadbare. Its white walls pristine and seamless. It was a blank slate for the myriad experiences to be had depending upon one's selection. There were larger rooms available for much larger experiences on other floors, but this was the room the duo had utilized the most whether it was to play golf, basketball, take dancing lessons, practice parking, and whatever else the two could cook up.

"What critical Confederation business are we on? I thought we were going to...you know...." Zhang said looking confused and sorely disappointed. Had he missed a memo or something?

Simon just chuckled and began punching in a few buttons as Zhang sidled up to him and looked over his shoulder. The muted lights suddenly turned bright as daylight filtered in and the pair found themselves on a beach complete with palm trees swaying with a slight breeze, crystal clear waves gently rolling on the shore and tawny sand beneath their feet. They were now uncomfortably way overdressed as the "sun" beamed down on them.

Zhang instantly lit up and began to strip. "Dude! You're a genius!" Then he recalled all the children still in line.

"I can't believe we jumped the line like that. All those families had kids with them. They were probably going to a birthday party."

"They love us. Did you see the way those kids looked at us? Like we're heroes or something." Simon shrugged.

"Huh...I only saw tears."

"Probably tears of joy having seen us up close and personal." Simon laughed and followed Zhang's lead in stripping out of his spacesuit.

The ground beneath their feet was instantly transformed into sand as they tossed their boots and spacesuits aside to enjoy the ambience now completely naked. Zhang looked around in amazement immediately recognizing the beach they had swum at in Honoka'a. Simon held his hand out to Zhang who took it and they walked into the water hand in hand.

The instant their bare feet touched the water, Zhang yelped at its realistic coolness.

"It'll warm up once we get used to it." Simon said diving in like a pro.

Zhang followed suit recalling their time on earth. His amorous needs forgotten for the time being as they laughed and splashed around again like kids and chased each other in the waves before Simon disappeared below. Zhang ran his hand across his face and looked around only to see Simon swimming beneath the surface and coming up between his legs to lift him up on his shoulders out of the water. Zhang laughed, lost his balance and went crashing back into the water before he resurfaced sputtering and laughing hysterically. He tried to do the same thing but Simon twisted and maneuvered like a fish escaping his attempts before he pulled Zhang by the arm out of the water and slipped his arms around him.

They bumped up against each other, chests and limbs slippery as Simon leaned in slowly to press his lips against Zhang's. Zhang sighed, lips parted as Simon angled his head and deepened the kiss occasionally swiping his tongue against Zhang's before exploring the rest of his mouth, even taking his time to slowly count his teeth.

Zhang gripped Simon by the legs and urged him to encircle his waist then carried him out of the water onto the pristine and tawny colored sand. He gently laid Simon on his back beneath the shade of a palm tree without dislodging, their mouths in a passionate and heart thumping exchange as Zhang hovered over him, one arm supporting him in the sand, the other hand cradling Simon's head as their tongues and lips sparred.

It was yet unclear who was seducing who as Simon suddenly flipped Zhang onto his back and draped himself over him, their mouths still joined as their breath became even more labored and shallow. There was both wet and dry sand everywhere, but they were oblivious as their hands roamed with increased passion over the others muscular torsos, sliding down along their sides, gripping and squeezing butts, as if discovering each plane and dip of muscle for the first time.

Zhang reached for Simon's root first angling his hand between them until he grasped warm and stiff flesh. Simon laughed as Zhang, with his sandpaper-like grip, began squeezing and pulling at him with vigor as Simon dutifully filled out in his hand. He could feel Simon begin to tense as Zhang's own root slapped up against his belly. Just as Simon was about to reach for him to reciprocate, Zhang pushed him off and back onto the sand. He then straddled him to sit back on his upper thighs. He then grasped both of their roots in his massive palm and began to rub them together. The sensation covered with sand as they were was interesting.

Zhang laughed as even more sand from his chest and shoulders rained down on Simon with his every movement. Simon meanwhile laid back, hands beneath his head, a smile plastered on his face as he thoroughly enjoyed the pointed service. The smile soon turned to abject pleasure as Zhang increased the pressure, the friction of their two massive roots against the other a mind numbingly pleasurable distraction. Soon they were both moaning loudly and twitching about as Zhang worked them steadily toward climax, their roots generously leaking fluids.

Just before they reached climax, Simon knocked Zhang onto the sand beside him and reversed his position so their roots were in each other's faces. They wasted no time opening their mouths to swallow the other's root into their throats as they groaned and hummed and whined around their prizes. Both were incoherent as their ground shaking orgasms exploded through them and their throats were flooded with their essence. They clung to each other for dear life choking and gasping as the other's hips pistoned with their exertions, alternatively lodging and dislodging in their throats until they were spent. Afterwards they lay there gasping and laughing and alternately spitting out granules of sand and wiping the tears from their eyes and cheeks. They fell asleep soon after, lulled by the sounds of the rolling waves on the pristine sandy shore.

When they woke up an indeterminate amount of time later, they sat up and stretched. Zhang's eyes dipped down to Simon's root which was miraculously still slapped up against his belly. He grinned and reached for it. His own root was fast working its way into similar position. Simon grinned back and then suddenly took off toward the water. Zhang raced after him and dived in behind him.

With the sun still high up in the sky, the palm trees swaying in the gentle breeze, the occasional sound of a seabird flying overhead punctuated by the waves breaking ashore, the pair once again cavorted and played to their hearts content. Now completely devoid of the annoying granules of sand, and wet and slick all over, Zhang took the initiative to urge Simon to lift his legs around his waist as he had before. As soon as Simon was in position, arms wrapped around his shoulders, his mouth crushed to Zhang's, Zhang slipped inside him with ease.

Simon groaned low and deep against his mouth, his eyes squeezing shut. Bending his knees slightly Zhang began to rhythmically slip in and out of him. Simon found by rising slightly in tandem without relinquishing his mouth he could deepen the thrusts and intensify the pleasurable intrusion.

Thus, Simon and Zhang monopolized the H-Deck for the equivalent of 12 earth shaking hours while those in the cue patiently waited wondering what incredible training the decorated Captain and Lieutenant were enduring on behalf of the Galactic Confederation. Their curiosity was only magnified as the quiet was occasionally punctuated by muted grunts, protracted groans and moans followed by periodic throaty shouts. They even heard a bit of wailing.

By the time the pair suited up again, reset the program to a blank slate and left looking beat as usual, the line to use the H-Deck wrapped around the building. The people waiting could only stare back in awe and reverence. The little boy who'd been standing with his family and were next in line when the duo showed up had tears in his eyes as he waved at the brave officers, his expression one of pride at their dedicated service, a silent vow to be just like them plastered on that little face.

Sometime during their foray, Captain Olin Alpha1 and Ariitzka (Lady Master Ma'at) had also joined the H-Deck queue. They planned to enjoy a romantic moonlit dinner and were both dressed up for the occasion. When the pair passed by, the captain cleared his throat, raised a questioning eyebrow at them and called out, "Critical confederation business?"

The pair quickly saluted the captain, greeted the Lady Master who gave them a knowing grin, before they beat a hasty retreat.

ABOUT THE AUTHOR

I am VEGASTARCHILD584.   The sun resides in my heart.
This is a tremendous gift given the challenges of living in the 3D
for most people.   This book was so damn fun to write and was
written with the intention of encouraging you, the two galactic
heroes upon whom the book is based and their myriad fans who
appreciate their contributions to the world. I also wrote it to share
the knowledge and wisdoms that have come through me as a
spiritual channel.   Thus, this book is written out of the utmost
respect and deepest love for all who will feel called upon to read
it. I hope in some way this fun, zany, wild sci-fi, steamy soul
mate romance, partly channeled, partly real-life drama, and
creative flow helps to encourage you to step into your power and
fulfill your own earthly mission.

See you at the Galactic Way Station!   Touch the Light! ❤

Pre-Order now www.vegastarchild584.com
(Avail 10/22/2023)!
Book 2: The Wild & Zany Galactic Adventures of Commander
Zhang & Lieutenant Simon, Soul Mates who Incarnate on Earth
& Save the World ~ The Missing Chapters The Starseed
Series)

Other books by this author (as A.E. Kendall) and available on
her website include:

Alain & the Duke, A Clash at Sea Series Novella
The Quartermaster & the Marquis' Son: Clash at Sea Series
Book 1

Into the Maelstrom, Book 2 of the Clash at Sea Series (Release
pending 2023)

Sign up for my newsletter for GIVEAWAYS, EBOOK FREEBIES, NEWS & MORE!
https://www.vegastarchild584.com

SM LINKS:

IG: https://www.instagram.com/vegastarchild584/
Facebook: https://www.facebook.com/AuthorVegastarchild584/
Twitter: https://twitter.com/vegastarchild52

Made in the USA
Middletown, DE
10 September 2023

37738002R00195